TOWERS OF BRIERLEY

TOWERS OF BRIERLEY

A NOVEL

ANITA STANSFIELD

Covenant Communications, Inc.

Cover painting by Wendy L. Davis
Cover and interior celtic knotwork by Cari Buziak

Cover design copyrighted 2000 by Covenant Communications, Inc.

Published by Covenant Communications, Inc.
American Fork, Utah

Printed in the United States of America
First Printing: August 2000

07 06 05 04 03 02 01 00   10 9 8 7 6 5 4 3 2 1

ISBN 1-57734-680-7

Library of Congress Cataloging-in-Publication Data

Stansfield, Anita, 1961-
    Towers of Brierley / Anita Stansfield.
        p.   cm.
    ISBN 1-57734-680-7
    1. Scotland--Fiction. I. Title
PS3569.T33354 T69 2000
813'.54--dc21   00-043052
                                                CIP

To my son, John

For your sensitive spirit
and your huge heart.
May you always trust your feelings,
and stand strong as a voice of all
you believe in.

pROLOGUE

Scotland—1798

Gavin waited quietly behind a massive tree at the edge of the trail. The rough bark felt familiar beneath his hands. He'd climbed this tree countless times for the singular purpose of spying on those who rode this frequented path through the forest. Hearing the familiar tread of the Earl's stallion, Gavin took a deep breath and stepped into the pathway. The horse reared back at the quick pull on the reins and trotted around quickly to gain its footing. The Earl's intense eyes danced with fury as they raked over Gavin in question.

"What is the meaning of this, lad?" he boomed, and Gavin felt briefly afraid. James MacBrier, the fifth Earl of Brierley, was a man of near legend in Gavin's narrow realm.

Quickly he swallowed and said, "My mother has sent me. She pleads that you come to her, my lord."

The Earl's eyes narrowed, but he didn't immediately disregard the request as Gavin had feared. "Why doesn't your mother come herself?" he asked with a voice both strong and terse.

"She is ill . . . dying, in truth."

"And what is the purpose of this request?" he persisted. Gavin's palms were sweating inside his pockets.

"I know not, my lord, only that she sent me to find you." There was a brief moment of silence as the Earl apparently contemplated this. Gavin took the opportunity to add the words of poetry his mother had rehearsed to him. "She said to tell you that . . . love can be found with the touch of a hand."

A startling change overtook the Earl's expression, and Gavin was certain the man uttered his mother's name, though it was more a silent movement of his lips. With little hesitation, the Earl held out his hand toward Gavin. "Get on, lad," he ordered sternly. "Take me to her."

Gavin felt a strange rush of elation shiver across his back as he found himself galloping through the dense forest with the Earl of Brierley. His mind raced with a thousand questions. While his mother lay dying, he wondered where he would go. What would he do? All of Jinny Baird's numerous efforts to find a place for her son outside the prison-like tower where they lived had proved futile. Someone was holding a threatening hand over them. Gavin didn't know why, but he clearly understood that his every effort to find work and keep it had been thwarted by unexplainable threats to his employers. His entire sixteen years had been spent in the tower with his mother, while he was expected to believe that such a life was normal.

But Gavin had observed more than his mother—or that dreadful woman who kept her stone-like watch over them—had ever realized. The knowledge of their banishment was deeply etched into his mind, and he had never ceased to puzzle over the reasons. He was now apparently expected to go out into the world and make it on his own, but the proffered free agency was a farce. They offered freedom, yet they blocked him at every turn. And would they continue to care for him after his mother was gone? He seriously doubted it.

Gavin couldn't see the Earl's face, but he sensed his surprise at being guided along a series of barely detectable paths through the trees, leading to the outside door of the northeast tower of Brierley House. The situation of the house was unique; it was built so tightly against the edge of the forest that this particular tower gave the illusion of being an independent structure, its stone walls running into trees too thick to move through. But in truth, the tower was a secluded part of the huge structure that comprised a world completely foreign to Gavin. And now it was evident that this part of the Earl's world was something he'd been unaware of. Gavin dismounted and tethered the horse while the Earl lowered himself to the ground, throwing the boy a questioning glance that pierced him through.

Without a word, the Earl followed Gavin through the door. He paused briefly to let his eyes adjust to the dim light, then took a few moments to absorb the meager surroundings of the makeshift, stone-walled common room. He looked to Gavin in question, and despite his youth, Gavin met the Earl eye to eye.

"This way, my lord," Gavin said and moved through a door to the right, where he found his mother almost sitting up in bed.

"The Earl is here, Mother," he said. Her eyes shifted to the man standing like one of the stones of Brierley House in the outline of the doorway. A heavy silence, fraught with question and pain, hung in the air. Without taking her eyes from the Earl, Jinny finally murmured, "Leave us alone please, Gavin."

Gavin brushed past the Earl, who closed the door gently—but not before Gavin distinctly heard his mother say, "Hello, James."

Fighting to breathe normally, Gavin could not resist putting his ear to the door in an effort to find out what kind of bond existed between his mother—a servant girl—and the Earl of Brierley. It was easy to hear what the Earl said, as his voice boomed with strength. But Jinny's whispered words were only heard in spurts. Impulsively, Gavin eased outside and moved to the half-open window of his mother's bedroom. There he could hear everything.

The Earl rambled on with questions that Gavin's mother evaded. "Listen to me, Jinny," he finally insisted. "I nearly went mad with worry when I thought you'd gone away. Now I come to find that you've been right here beneath my own roof all these years, and you expect me to be calm? I want to know why!"

"The reasons don't matter," she whispered.

"They matter to me!" he shouted.

"Please, James," Jinny's voice turned hoarse. "They promised to care for us if I kept our existence here from your knowledge. I had nowhere to go . . . no choice."

"I could have helped you," the Earl said, resentment edging his voice.

"It's in the past," she said, as if putting it away was the only possible thing to do. "There is no point in this. I have little strength . . . little time left. You must hear me out. It is for Gavin that I fear. Every effort he makes to find work and support himself has been thwarted."

"Why?" he demanded. "There must be a reason."

"I suspect it has to do with the rumors."

"What rumors?" the Earl asked in a tone that betrayed a bitterness for his ignorance. Gavin knew exactly how he felt.

"That he is your son, of course," Jinny answered.

The words ignited Gavin's glimmer of curiosity into an intense thundering in his chest. He'd spent his life keenly aware that he had only his mother's name; but in that, too, he had remained ignorant of any explanation. He knew the Earl had sat beside the bed when he heard the familiar creak of the only chair in his mother's room.

"If only he were," the Earl whispered gruffly.

"I tried to raise him to be like you, if that's any consolation."

"A bit, perhaps," he said tersely. Then he paused before adding, "Where did these rumors start?"

"I'm certain your attention to me didn't go unnoticed."

"My attention to you was never even remotely inappropriate," the Earl growled.

"Nevertheless, it didn't go unnoticed."

"By my wife, you mean." His voice was strained and bitter.

"And others," she said.

"Is that why you are here?" he asked pointedly.

"Your wife believes that Gavin is your son."

"But it's not true," the Earl said with a finality that filled Gavin with a mixture of emotions. He had no desire to be heir to Brierley, or any such preposterous thing. He only wanted to imagine that such a man as James MacBrier was his father! Although he couldn't imagine such a man ever taking advantage of a woman and leaving her to raise an illegitimate child.

"Of course it's not true," Jinny reassured him. "But anyone would believe that with a wife like yours, you would not hesitate to have an affair. No one believes our relationship was platonic. Still, I . . ." Jinny's words faded as she started to cough. Gavin had to fight to keep from jumping through the window to attend to her. Each time it happened, he feared she would never catch her breath again. A discreet glance told him the Earl was at her bedside, holding her in a tender embrace. She soon gained control of her breath enough to go on.

"James," she said with desperation, as if she feared her remaining words were few, "you must help me. The past doesn't matter. You and I both know who his father is, but I'm asking you, pleading with you, to help me find a means for him to be cared for—at least until he has a chance to finish growing up, as any boy should."

She coughed again and the Earl muttered gently, "I will, Jinny. I will! I would give him Brierley if it were in my power."

"I'm not certain he would want it," she said in a raspy voice. This brought no response, and she added, "There is too much hatred and deceit within its walls."

By the continued silence, Gavin wondered if this was a revelation to the Earl. Obviously Jinny's presence here was.

"I will care for him," the Earl finally said.

"But you must be careful. Don't cause trouble over it, I beg you. His life has already been difficult enough. All I ask is the means for him to leave here and make a fresh start for himself."

"I understand," he said tersely, which made Gavin wonder how much of Jinny's request the Earl would honor. His anger and bitterness were apparent, which left Gavin feeling an unspoken kinship with him.

"You must go now," Jinny insisted. "They must not find you here."

The Earl's agreement made Gavin wonder if this powerful man was somehow a prisoner in his own home—just as they were.

"I will return in the morning," he promised. "Don't you worry about a thing, my dear. I will see that Gavin does well."

"Thank you, James," she whispered, relief evident in her voice.

When Gavin heard only silence, he hurried inside to meet the Earl. They both entered the common room at the same moment. Their eyes met with an apparent tenderness that felt too elusive for either to voice. "How much time does she have left?" the Earl questioned.

"Little . . . if any," Gavin replied quietly. He wished his voice had displayed a little less emotion. He would like the Earl to think he possessed a degree of courage. But the thought faded behind a sudden desire to take advantage of this moment and find out all he could.

"So, you're not my father," Gavin stated.

The Earl looked briefly taken aback, then he smiled slightly. "Eavesdropping?"

"It's difficult not to when my entire life has been filled with so many unanswered questions."

"I understand," he replied, then gave a deep sigh and motioned toward the door. Gavin was walking casually beside the Earl through the trees before he continued. "No," he said, "you are not my son, though I could wish my son had half the dignity and integrity that you obviously possess."

"But you know who my father is?"

"A livery boy," the Earl stated. "He was a nice-looking lad. Had a passing fancy for your mother and took unfair advantage of her when she was feeling . . . vulnerable, I suppose. In truth, although she wouldn't admit to it, I believe he had his way with her very much against her will." He paused and cleared his throat. Gavin understood clearly what he was talking about. "I felt responsible for your mother in a way. We were . . . very good friends. When your father found out your mother was pregnant, he left Brierley in great haste, with no intention of making it right. Until now, I had believed that your mother also left before the baby was born. But that's a whole different story, lad; one that I intend to get to the bottom of." He remained silent as they turned back to where the horse was tethered. As no more questions were posed to him, the Earl mounted to leave.

"As I told your mother," he said, "I will return in the morning. See to her now. I'm certain she needs you."

Gavin did as he was told, sitting by his mother's bedside until very late, contemplating all he had discovered this day. At least most of the things his mother would never talk about made sense now. And with the Earl's help, perhaps the rest would fall into place. It didn't matter what the Earl might give him; the mutual respect they had spoken with made him beam inside, giving him a degree of hope that something existed for him beyond the shadow of his mother's death.

Deep in the night, Gavin was awakened by James MacBrier. He sat up abruptly, and the sheet fell around his waist. By the light of a lantern, he saw the Earl's eyes come to rest on Gavin's right shoulder. The dark, purplish birthmark was difficult to ignore. Gavin quickly reached for a shirt and pulled it on. The Earl seemed momentarily dazed, while Gavin wondered why his return had come hours sooner than promised.

"My lord?" Gavin said, startling the Earl from deep thought. His eyes shifted to delve into Gavin's, and an eerie tension descended between them. Gavin wanted to ask if something was wrong, but the Earl's gaze held him silent. With a tenderness that belied his brusque manner, he lifted a hand and set trembling fingers against Gavin's face. The boy felt fire from the Earl's touch, and the silence became unnerving.

"Is something wrong?" Gavin finally found the voice to say.

The Earl pulled back as if the contact had burned him. "Aye, lad," he whispered, "something is terribly wrong."

Gavin waited for him to explain, but the Earl only shook his head and moved his gaze again to Gavin's right shoulder. Though it was covered now, the Earl's eyes seemed to pierce through the fabric, absorbing the mark all over again.

"Something compelled me to bring this to you now," the Earl said, as if the happenings of the past moments had not occurred. He pressed an ornately carved wooden box into Gavin's hands. "Here is more than you will ever need, if you manage it wisely. Also enclosed is a map to guide you to a little house I inherited that no one else living has knowledge of. It was used in generations past to keep a mistress. I have gone there alone on occasion for solace, but it stands empty. I'm giving it to you."

Gavin couldn't find words to respond, but the Earl went on before he had the chance. "Now, this is important, lad." He slid a jeweled ring from his finger and pressed it into Gavin's hand. "This ring is one of two keys to a family safe that holds a treasure only you could appreciate. If others know you have this, they would kill to possess it. Guard it well, and be certain the safe is only opened in your presence." Gavin could only nod. "Live a good life, lad, and be wary. Perhaps our paths will cross again." The Earl took him firmly by the shoulders and looked him in the eye. "I may check up on you, son."

"Thank you," was all Gavin had time to utter before the Earl rushed into Jinny's room. He spoke too quietly for Gavin to hear, and remained only a few minutes. Then he was gone in haste.

Gavin hurried into his mother's room and knelt by her side.

"He has done as I asked?" she whispered feebly.

"Aye, Mother."

She smiled and sighed, then drifted into an uneasy sleep. Just before dawn, Jinny Baird died. Gavin was still sitting by her side when she took her last breath. He felt nothing but a painful shock as he tried to sort everything out and admit to himself that she was gone. Reaching for her hand to hold it one last time, he found a piece of paper crumpled there. The parchment was yellowed and the writing faded. Gavin moved toward the lamp in order to read the words scribbled there.

> *Love can be found with the touch of a hand,*
> *A glance that tells me you understand.*
> *Though loving you now is my greatest wish,*
> *Love can be found in the absence of flesh.*
> *Love left as now, in its perfect state,*
> *Will keep it safe through this life's wait.*
> *But one day, my love, in another time,*
> *The love will be answered with reason and rhyme.*
> *James MacBrier*

In the box, Gavin found everything that was promised and more. There were jewels beyond description, gold coins and paper notes, along with a map to the house and a key to its door. All of this was wrapped in a torn piece of tartan. MacBrier tartan.

He closed the box up tight and hid it, then he slid the Earl's ring onto the third finger of his right hand, exactly as the Earl had worn it. Attempting to swallow his emotion, Gavin went to tell Robbie that his mother had died, wiping at the tears with his shirt sleeve.

Robbie was the only ally—until now—that Jinny and Gavin had ever had in their secluded life together. He was one of the few servants of Brierley with a knowledge of their existence in the tower, and he had seen to their needs with kindness and assurance.

Gavin found Robbie sleeping in his usual place in a room above the carriage house, adjacent to the stable. He came to the tower and stayed with Gavin until some commotion took him away briefly. Robbie returned to report that the Earl of Brierley had been murdered in his sleep, a jeweled dagger planted in his chest.

Gavin felt the shock of losing his mother intensify. He'd hardly known the Earl, but the kinship he'd felt was undeniable. And somehow he knew the timing of his death was no coincidence.

With Robbie's assistance, Gavin buried his mother in the forest the following day. He placed the crumpled poem in the box with his treasures, somehow certain that the waiting was over for his mother and James MacBrier.

With a mixture of regret and hope, Gavin packed what little he owned and locked up the tower rooms tightly. He bid farewell to Robbie, then set out on foot to follow the Earl's map.

Chapter One
The Bad Man

Ten Years Later

Anya Ross awoke in the tiny attic room of Brierley and cursed the sun streaking over the floorboards, illuminating her torn, discarded scullery uniform. Together they seemed to taunt her in chorus. She only had to stir slightly to know for certain it was true. Every muscle in her body ached, reminding her that Cedric MacBrier had taken all she had left. She had fought with every ounce of strength she possessed, but it hadn't been enough. He had won. And her life was over.

Since the Earl's death, each MacBrier in turn had torn her down, toyed with her, and tormented her so thoroughly that she was certain it couldn't possibly get any worse. But now it was. What kind of foolishness had possessed her to think that Cedric, the present Earl of Brierley, actually had a romantic interest in her? It had all been a long string of lies, a game he'd been playing, no doubt urged on by his mother, with the sole purpose of tearing her down a little further. Well, this time they had won. What did she possibly have to live for now?

With effort, Anya swung her legs over the narrow bed and reached for the tattered uniform, if only to prove to herself how barbaric Cedric's advances had been. Callously she rolled the clothes together, threw them into the little fireplace, and knelt to light a match to them. They smoldered slowly away while Anya felt hot tears pushing into her eyes. Defiantly she choked them back. Groping for what little pride she had left, Anya took up one of the two uniforms she had left and put it on.

"I hate you, Cedric," she said aloud while tying the starched apron around her waist. "To the devil with you!" Shoving her hair up beneath the tight scarf she wore to protect it from the dirt and ashes, she splashed water on her face and headed down the endless string of stairs to a side door of Brierley.

The beauty of the morning seemed to mock her hateful shame. She attempted to ignore the brilliant hues of the sunrise and the shimmering dew where she blazed a trail across the lawn, circling around the house and into the forest, where the northeast tower rose steeply out of the closely rooted trees.

From a distance the four towers of Brierley looked identical, standing like great sentries at each corner of the house. But to a person standing at the base of each one, they seemed worlds apart. Anya pressed carefully through the trees, yearning for solace and peace, longing to feel as far away as possible from the wretched reality of her life.

Finally reaching the base of the northeast tower, she craned her head backward but couldn't see the top. The massive edifice called Brierley, set among the Scottish countryside as if it had grown there, had always seemed like a castle to Anya. Coming here as a child, she had been certain it was. In the days before the Earl's death, life had seemed one grand fairy tale. But the loss of her great-uncle had brought reality harshly home, and life had been little more than a nightmare since.

As she had done many times before, Anya walked the short circumference of the tower wall, then back again, before it pressed into trees so thick in both directions that it was impossible to go farther. And there in the center was the door, forever locked tight. Anya wondered what was hidden here in this tower, so perfectly tucked away from the very house it supported with its rising stone walls.

It was habit to press against the door, as if it might one day magically open, though Anya knew from experience that it would not. But bitter thoughts of Cedric MacBrier briefly fled as the door seemed to answer her plea, and the long-unused hinges creaked eerily at her touch. She held her breath and pushed the door hesitantly open, both afraid and intrigued by what she might find.

As a widening shaft of light spread over the stone floor, then filled with Anya's shadow, she wondered briefly if the rumors were true.

Oh, she'd heard them all—how the Earl's illegitimate son was born here and raised by his mother, banished from the rest of Brierley . . . and the world. But Anya quickly dismissed the thought. She could not comprehend the Earl she remembered ever fathering an illegitimate child. And if he had, he would not have sentenced him to such a life. James MacBrier had been too good a man for that.

Anya realized her heart was pounding as she stood in what appeared to have been used as a common room. The furnishings were sparse and eerily covered with dust and cobwebs. Nothing appeared to have been touched by human hands for many years, yet a presence seemed to fill the room. The feeling persisted as she investigated two small bedrooms and found a door, tightly locked, that apparently went deeper into the tower. Pondering over her discoveries, Anya wondered why this tower was open now, when it hadn't been for years.

That feeling washed over her again, as if she weren't alone. But Anya quickly brushed it aside as thoughts of Cedric flooded back into her reverie, and she felt tears welling up again. Fumbling through the dim light, she sank heavily onto a creaking chair in the north bedroom. There she cried helplessly, completely consumed with bitterness toward Cedric, nearly wishing she were dead.

Hearing a subtle noise, Anya lifted her eyes to see a man shadowed in the doorway. Startled, she jumped to her feet, crying out, "So help me, Cedric, if you ever lay another hand on me, I'll kill you. I swear, I'll kill you!"

The stunned silence that came in response made her realize this wasn't Cedric. A little gasp escaped her lips. She rushed toward the door, aware only of the dark plaid thrown over his shoulder that briefly caught the light.

"Wait," he called, his voice deep and rich. Strong arms encircled Anya's waist, bringing her abruptly to a halt. She could only think of Cedric's possessiveness the previous night, full of some warped, victorious contempt, and fear beat wildly in her chest.

"Don't hurt me," she cried, turning in his arms to meet deep brown eyes as the morning light glanced off his face. His features were strong and firm, unlike Cedric's, and his brows were as dark as his hair, thick and full of gentle waves. Anya felt briefly dazed, wondering where she had seen those eyes before.

He released his grip immediately, as if her reaction had somehow hurt his feelings. Anya fled for the door, but a formless urge compelled her to pause and turn back. His eyes were kind, his smile apologetic. She wondered why a warmth seemed to linger where he had touched her.

Gavin watched this girl closely, wondering what she was doing here. But concentrating on his purpose, he grabbed the opportunity before it was gone. "You're a scullery maid," he said, noting the coarse uniform.

"Yes," was all Anya could say, hating the way his words tore at her open wounds.

Gavin heard the bitterness, but continued his pursuit. "At Brierley?"

"Of course," she retorted, and the bitterness deepened.

"I understand Lady MacBrier is planning a social. Could you tell me when it will be?"

Anya wondered briefly over his motives. Why was he here? What did he want? And most of all, who was he? Then she realized she didn't care. She had far worse things to be concerned over.

Gavin could nearly feel her mind racing in the moments of silence that followed. He almost expected her to break down and cry again. He nearly wished she would. Something about seeing her emotion had touched him, something beyond finding her in the chair where he'd been sitting when his mother died.

"Tonight," was all she said, then she was gone.

Gavin was briefly stunned by the encounter, but he turned his attention back to his surroundings, and his thoughts fled elsewhere. With longing he pressed a hand over the cold stone wall. This had been his home. The memories were full of irony. He blessed thoughts of his mother, treasuring her laughter and courage, while he cursed the reality of their life here. Ten years of exploring the world beyond this tower had made him realize just how wretched their existence had been. Feeling the urge to sit down and cry himself, Gavin forced his mind to the present. It was his meeting with Lady MacBrier that he anticipated.

Anya ran through the trees and didn't slow down until she reached the stable. She chatted casually with Robbie, the old stable master, hearing the sweet normality in her own voice that hypocritically concealed the turmoil of emotions seething within. The soreness she felt with each movement wouldn't allow her to forget what had passed between her and Cedric last night. The memory of it even pushed away thoughts of her brief encounter in the tower. Normally such a thing would have spurred her imagination and daydreams, but today it meant nothing.

"Are ye well, lass?" Robbie asked intently, startling her from her thoughts. "Ye dinna seem quite yersel' t'day."

Anya attempted a smile. "I'm fine, really. Just had a bad night."

He raised a skeptical brow, but Anya flippantly passed it off. She forewent her usual time with the horses and returned to the house for breakfast to find that Brierley was alive with excitement. Even back in the kitchen, where the servants ate quickly in order to be about their preparations for the arrival of this evening's guests, it was difficult not to feel a sense of anticipation. Normally, Anya would have been caught up in the excitement to some degree. But oppression was all she could feel as she sat to eat, picking at her food with little interest.

"I thought ye liked m' bannocks," Mrs. MacGregor startled her.

"Oh," Anya apologized, "they're wonderful as always. I just . . . had a bad night."

"Ye didna sleep well?" she asked, wiping her plump hands on her apron.

Anya nodded and attempted to eat, knowing she would need her strength to make it through the day. She glanced around the big table, where a handful of maids and livery servants were still eating and chatting. She didn't want any fuss made, especially in front of them. Most of them knew she had not been born a servant, which made her not quite fit in—even with those who were now considered her kind.

"If ye have trouble sleepin' again, let me know and I'll give ye somethin' tae help."

"Thank you," Anya said with her mouth full, wishing such a thing could begin to ease her problem. She almost considered telling Mrs. MacGregor what had happened. She knew she would get some much-needed sympathy, but she feared the long-range repercussions of such a confession. No, it was better left unsaid, even to the woman who came closest to being her friend. Anya felt herself flush red just to think of her plight.

Mrs. MacGregor apparently took notice. "Are ye certain ye're feelin' fine, lass?" she asked, pressing a hand to Anya's face. She was rather knowledgeable with medicine, and she was the one called upon if any of the servants became ill or injured. Rarely was a doctor summoned. Although Mrs. MacGregor's official duties mostly pertained to the kitchen, all the servants knew she was capable in many other areas, as well.

Anya had been taken under Mrs. MacGregor's wing many years back, and by her side she had learned skills related to cooking, cleaning, organizing, and medicine. Mrs. MacGregor had often told Anya what a shame it was for her to be confined to doing the scullery, when she had such talents. But Anya had long since given up hoping for anything beyond this. Even her dream of being swept away by some handsome man who would marry her and free her from all this was now dashed. No man would want her in this condition, used and tossed aside. Such dreams had been preposterous in the first place, she reminded herself. She was a prisoner of Brierley, as much as if she were chained to its walls.

"I say," Mrs. MacGregor raised her voice when Anya made no response, "are ye feelin' all right?"

"Yes, of course," Anya replied, attempting a smile.

Mrs. MacGregor looked dubious, but seemed to catch the hint that Anya wanted to be left alone. "Be sure to put some balm on those hands b'fore ye leave," she added before turning away.

Anya decided she could eat no more, and rose to retrieve the jar of hand balm from a shelf she could barely reach by going on her tiptoes. She took out a frugal amount, fearing it might be gone forever if she used it up too quickly. She was rubbing the cooling balm into her dry, aching hands when Effie MacBrier came into the kitchen and sat down.

"Effie likes porridge and bannocks," she said in her typical way.

"There's m' lass," Mrs. MacGregor beamed toward Effie, who showed no response. "I'll have yer breakfast in a wee minute."

"Time for breakfast." Effie looked at the watch that hung around her neck on a gold chain. "Effie likes porridge and bannocks."

Anya sat close beside Effie, feeling a welcome reprieve from her turbulent thoughts. "Good morning, Effie." She squeezed her hand. "It's Anya."

"Anya likes to play games." Effie greeted each person she knew with a brief summary of what she related to them. Anya had played games with Effie back in the days when the Earl had taken them on excursions together, and they'd had such fun.

Effie was much older than Anya, but the condition she had been born with made her much like a child in most respects, even though she made up for it with her acute memory and artistic abilities. Branded a burden, Effie had been more or less shunned by the remaining MacBriers after the Earl's death. But many of the servants loved Effie, and she had found a comfortable life among them, where she was looked after and cared for. Effie was one of the few bright spots in Anya's miserable existence. They often shared meals, and Anya enjoyed spending time with her when the work was finished.

"I would bet that th' two o' ye'll be peepin' in on the ball t'night," Mrs. MacGregor chuckled.

Anya hadn't even thought about it. Right now, she didn't feel at all like observing the MacBriers while they flaunted their money and power to their guests. But spying on MacBrier socials was something she and Effie had done together for twelve years. She felt certain Effie would not let her out of it.

"Effie likes to spy." She focused her attention on the breakfast placed before her, took a bite, and went on. "Effie likes to spy at parties. Pretty dresses. Pretty music. Effie likes to spy."

"Anya will come to get you after dinner," she said carefully. "Wait here after dinner. Do you understand?"

"Effie wait here after dinner," she repeated. "Effie likes to spy."

"I must do my work, Effie. Be a good girl today."

Anya glanced to Ellen, a front hall maid, who nodded as she said, "I'll be takin' Miss Effie with me tae gather flowers."

Anya kissed Effie's cheek and rose to replace the jar of balm. She barely had it in place when Una entered the kitchen like a lioness on the prowl. Anya shoved it far back onto the shelf, her heart pounding as she feared the old woman might find out it was there.

Once Una's presence was realized, everyone became silent, pretending to be so busy eating they didn't even have time to look up. Anya felt a degree of comfort to be reminded that she wasn't the only one who hated Una.

From what the Earl had told her, Anya knew that Una had come here long ago, accompanying Lady Margaret and her daughter, Malvina, not long after Margaret's husband had died. They had come to visit Ishbelle, the Earl's first wife, Margaret and Ishbelle being cousins. The purpose of their visit was to attend the birth of Ishbelle's first child. Margaret and Ishbelle had been close since childhood, and Una had been with Margaret since before her birth—a servant who had become more of a constant sentry, so thoroughly involved in Lady Margaret's life that Anya felt certain it must be stifling. Una certainly made Anya feel stifled, but Lady Margaret likely deserved it. In truth, they deserved each other. They were both cruel and manipulative, as far as Anya could see.

Apparently because of her experience at midwifery, Una had attended Lady Ishbelle when she gave birth. But Ishbelle died bringing Effie into the world, and less than a year later the Earl had married Margaret. Nothing had ever been the same since, according to those who had seen the changes firsthand. Margaret swooped down upon Brierley like a vulture, with Una always at her shoulder. And some even said that Ishbelle's death had not been purely accidental. Margaret gave birth to Cedric a couple of years after the marriage. But the Earl took to drinking too much, and according to Mrs. MacGregor, it was only when he had received Anya as his ward that he began to show some life and dignity again. But in less than two years the Earl had been murdered, and what little Margaret had not controlled before then fell into her hands. Of course, Cedric had rightfully inherited the title, though he was so controlled by his mother that it was really she who ruled this wretched place. But then, it was apparent that Una ruled Margaret. And it was Una who Anya truly feared. As a child, Anya had believed she was a witch. Though she had grown up to lose her belief in such things, it still described Una well.

Mrs. MacGregor turned to see the reason for the sudden silence in her kitchen. Her eyes filled with barely concealed hatred when they fell upon Una. "What can I do for ye?" she asked tersely.

Una moved close to Mrs. MacGregor and spoke too quietly for anyone else to hear, then she left and the mood immediately lightened. Anya gave a wave in Mrs. MacGregor's direction and headed up the back stairs, pausing to make certain that Una had gone the other way.

With habitual lack of enthusiasm, Anya set to her chores. She began by going through the bedrooms to empty and clean the chamber pots, pausing at each opportunity to wash her hands. Her next duty was to go back through the same rooms and clean around the fireplaces, where fires were only lit to take off the morning chill during these unusually warm summer days. When that was finished, she went to the kitchens, where her favorite chore was scrubbing the pots and pans until they reflected the sun that shone through the west windows. She hated the scrubbing, but at least her hands stayed clean, and she often had Mrs. MacGregor or one of the other maids to talk with.

The work was always oppressive for Anya, but today it was accompanied by echoes of Cedric MacBrier's taunts pounding through her head. Each time she thought of his cruelty, the chains that seemed to bind her tightened without mercy, until she thought she would scream.

Anya was relieved to finally stop for dinner. She ate with Effie, then they sneaked up the back stairs to the upper front hall. The family gallery was located here, and she paused as always to gaze at the portrait of the late Earl. She sighed nostalgically and moved her attention to a darkened piece of glass that was set for the purpose of watching the ballroom below. The peep had been intended for children who were too young for such social events, and at one time, that was what Anya had been. She had watched the MacBrier social life with a dream that she would one day be a part of it. But she had long since passed the age of coming out, and still she remained behind the glass, hidden beneath the guise of a servant girl.

As the guests began filtering in, Effie and Anya pressed their faces to the glass and quietly watched. Anya's thoughts fled unwillingly to

Cedric, but she tried to smother them, unable to bear the hurt. Her mind turned to Malvina as she watched her enter the ballroom, dressed as always in the finest, most fashionable gown available. "She's still ugly," Anya muttered under her breath. "No amount of money will change that. Why doesn't she just admit no one will marry her and give up? She's been an old maid for over ten years now."

Despite the difference in age between Anya and the Earl's step-daughter, they had always been competitive. Or rather, Malvina had shown a competitive nature toward Anya. Anya had never cared—at least not until she had been pushed from their world into this one, and Malvina had never ceased to taunt her about it.

"She's still ugly," Effie repeated, and Anya giggled, which helped, if only for the moment, to push away the reality.

Gavin emerged from the forest just after dark and moved stealthily around the house. Rounding the southeast tower, he hovered close to the wall, watching as carriage after carriage rolled beneath the gateway and finely dressed ladies and gentlemen stepped down, disappearing through the portals of Brierley.

Taking a deep breath, Gavin moved unobtrusively toward the entrance, waiting for a large group to arrive. With amazing ease he slipped among them and found himself in the front hall. He couldn't resist the urge to stop and just look around. It was incredible to think that he had grown up on the other side of this very house, and yet he'd never seen any of this before; it was like an entirely different world. In truth, it was.

Gavin moved casually through the crowds into the ballroom, taking care to hide his fascination for all that surrounded him. He had certainly done his share of socializing in the past ten years, and had seen many fine homes, but never had he dreamed that anything so large, so elegant, so . . . magnificent really existed. What about it left him so intrigued? Surely this charade that people played out behind their wealth did not impress him. Yet he couldn't help feeling drawn into the excited buzz of the chatter, spellbound by the eloquence of dancing couples floating over the polished checkerboard floor in time to the music.

For more than an hour, Gavin silently mingled, observing this life, so close to him, yet so foreign. In time he located Cedric MacBrier, and couldn't help watching him closely. What did he feel? Jealousy? Certainly not for this kind of life. But still, it was jealousy; he had to admit it. He envied Cedric for being James MacBrier's son; not his heir, but his son. Although he had to wonder if his feelings stemmed more from an innate need to have a father figure he could connect with and look up to. And there was no doubt that he felt a great deal of respect for the Earl, knowing that he'd never shared an inappropriate relationship with his mother.

To look at the Earl's son now, it took little effort to realize that he and Cedric were as different as the sun and the moon. Cedric was slender and fair, to the point of almost appearing sickly. Even so, the young man seemed healthy and strong, and Gavin supposed that women might find him attractive. Still, Gavin was not impressed.

While he continued moving through the crowds, sipping champagne and sitting for a time against the wall, he recalled the hours he'd spent as a child, spying on those who came and went from Brierley. A particular path through the forest was frequented by these people when they rode, and there was a certain shady spot used as a common resting place. In his eighth year, Gavin had found a tree with a smooth and comfortable limb, situated perfectly so he could see and hear all that went on below without ever being noticed— especially in the summer when the lush, flat leaves clustered together to conceal him completely. He was still amazed at how much he had learned by eavesdropping. And from his tree, Gavin had become familiar with the MacBriers.

Of course there had been the Earl. And then there was his wife, Lady Margaret, who was difficult to read, but for the most part seemed cruel and malevolent. And there was Margaret's daughter from a previous marriage, Malvina, who was homely to put it in polite terms, and no amount of expensive clothes and jewels could hide it.

And then there was Cedric—son of James and Margaret MacBrier, born to be earl of all this. From a distance, Gavin had hated him. It was a relief to know that his original judgments had not been far off. Cedric MacBrier was so shallow, so transparent, that it took little time in observing him now to see what kind of man he really was. By his arrogance and self-motivated conversation, Gavin could tell his loves were money and power—and the place he held in the midst of both. By his flirtations, so syrupy and lurid, Gavin knew his scruples were likely atrocious—if he had any at all.

Becoming bored and disgusted, Gavin turned his attention to Malvina after Cedric had exchanged brief, heated words with her. She was obviously still unwed by the way her eyes turned upon anything in a kilt or breeches who wasn't attached. Gavin was surprised to feel Malvina's eyes on him. She attempted a coy smile that made him cringe, but he couldn't resist the opportunity. Deftly he swept her hand into his and bent to kiss it. "What a pleasure, Miss . . ."

"MacBrier," she stated. He was surprised that she'd taken on her stepfather's name—likely for the prestige.

"Of course," he smiled. "It is a pleasure."

"And you?" she asked. "I've not seen you here before."

"I've not been around," he said as she placed her hand over his arm, attempting to urge him to the dance floor.

Gavin had no desire to dance with a woman like Malvina, who had the charm and grace of an old sow. "How about a drink?" he said, steering her the other direction.

"I didn't catch your name." She set her eyes on him as if surveying a prime cut of meat on a butcher's hook.

"Gavin Baird," he stated. She attempted that coy smile again, which made it evident the name meant nothing to her. He doubted it would have the same effect on Margaret MacBrier, and he decided to pursue his purpose quickly. He couldn't bear her company for long. "I haven't seen your mother here yet. I'd like a word with her."

Malvina did a poor job of covering her disappointment. "Wait here. I'll go and find her."

Gavin sipped his drink and tried to pretend his heart wasn't pounding, knowing he had only moments before facing the Lady of Brierley. He glanced up and caught sight of a small pane of dark glass that blended easily into the ornate decor rising to the ceiling. A shadowy movement behind it caught his attention. Focusing more carefully, he distinctly saw two heads leaning against the glass, moving occasionally closer together as if to exchange conversation. He wondered what poor souls were sentenced to view all of this from a distance. Children? To his knowledge, there were none at Brierley. Servants? Perhaps, but not likely. The question was obliterated by a terse feminine voice.

"Malvina informs me that you wish to see me." Lady MacBrier stood before him, every bit the essence of lavishness he had expected.

When their eyes first met, Gavin couldn't find the words he wanted to say. He felt lost for a moment. He caught something in her eyes that seemed afraid, but quickly became unreadable.

"Lady MacBrier," he said at last, nodding slightly.

"Malvina tells me you are Gavin Baird." The name pressed through her lips with contempt.

"That's right." He watched as she glanced quickly away to meet the eyes of a familiar stone-like face, standing nearby in the doorway to the hall. Gavin knew well who Una was: Lady Margaret's nurse from birth, nanny into adulthood, and constant, doting companion to this day. In Gavin's days of spying, Margaret had never ventured into the woods without Una, and Una rarely did anything—except check in on Jinny and her son—without Margaret. Gavin hated them both.

"What do you want?" Margaret hissed under her breath.

"A word alone," he stated, trying to sound stern.

Margaret glanced around nervously, as if seeking some kind of escape from this encounter. Una's expression apparently told her there wasn't one. Margaret nodded toward the hall, then she turned in that direction and Gavin followed. The hall was long and sparsely lit, most likely to discourage visitors from exploring. At last they entered what appeared to be the library. Una slipped silently through the door before Margaret closed it.

"I was hoping we could speak alone." Gavin glanced toward the old woman, who hadn't changed a bit in ten years—except that she looked twenty years older. She still wore grey from neck to toe, which closely matched the color of her tightly pulled hair and the stern expression carved into her colorless skin.

"We are," was all Margaret said before she turned to face him. "Now, what do you want? You have no business or right coming here."

"Oh, but I do." He smiled and sat down, stretching out his legs and crossing them at the ankles. He'd waited ten years for this moment.

Anya was lost in her musings about how things might have been when her eye caught a stranger, someone she'd not seen before. Or had she? There was something familiar about him. She puzzled long and hard over it before she realized it had to be the same man she'd met this morning in the tower.

She had always preferred seeing men in breeches, but she couldn't help thinking how fine he looked in a kilt. He wore a matching plaid broached to his shoulder, hanging nearly to the floor behind him. Her curious gaze followed him while she wondered what he was doing here. He was apparently alone, and it wasn't until he came across Malvina that he appeared to speak to anyone at all. Without understanding why, Anya nearly seethed as she watched him kiss the homely woman's hand. "That little witch, Malvina, tries to set her hooks into every single man that passes her way," she hissed.

"Little witch," Effie repeated. "Malvina is a little witch."

"Oh Effie," Anya implored, "you mustn't repeat that. I'd be in such trouble."

Anya knew it didn't matter. Effie couldn't understand her plea, but it made little difference. Things couldn't get any worse.

Anya turned her attention back to the ballroom. She searched for the dark stranger, and was relieved to see him standing alone until she realized he was looking at her. How ridiculous, she told herself. No one could possibly see through the dark glass, and he was too far away to see anything even if he could. But still, she felt certain he was looking directly at her. Anya felt a little unnerved, but her thoughts shifted as Lady Margaret approached him.

"What on earth does she want?" Anya muttered.

"Ten o'clock," Effie announced, looking at her watch. "Time to dress for bed. Must go to bed. It's ten o'clock."

Anya glanced back to find that the stranger was gone, and she couldn't help feeling disappointed. "Come along, Effie. Let's get you to bed."

"Need a book," she said as they headed for the stairs. "Need to read before bed."

"Have you finished the last one already?"

"Yes. Need a book."

"Very well," Anya agreed, and turned down the back stairs toward the library to help Effie find a book. Otherwise, there would be no peace.

Approaching the door, Anya was surprised to hear voices raised in anger. One was undoubtedly Margaret's, and the other a deep male voice. It had to be the dark-haired stranger—with the brown eyes, she recalled from seeing them in the sun this morning.

When Effie became aware of the argument, she seemed agitated. Anya quickly pulled her into an alcove and whispered gently, "Let's be very quiet, so Mama won't hear us, or she'll get angry."

The statement had little effect on Effie. When Anya heard the library door opening, she had no choice but to clamp her hand over Effie's mouth while she whispered reassuring words into her ear, pretending to play a game. Anya tried to listen intermittently to the argument, but she caught very little. As the door slammed and heavy footsteps receded down the hall, Anya peered around the corner to get a glimpse. It was no doubt the same man; even in the dim light, she could tell by the way he wore that kilt. And the plaid flew out behind him as he hurried away. Again Anya wondered who he was and why he was here, then she asked herself why it mattered to her. She waited patiently until Margaret and Una left the library and returned to the ballroom, grateful that Effie was going along with the game. If Effie became afraid or upset, there would be no hiding her. Quietly they slipped into the library, and Anya scanned the shelves quickly in search of something Effie hadn't read.

"Bad man," Effie began muttering. "Bad man yelled at Mama."

"He was angry, Effie. That doesn't mean he is bad."

"Bad man yelled at Mama," she muttered. "He's a bad man."

Anya gave up trying to explain and handed Effie a book. "You'll like this one," she insisted, and ushered her back upstairs.

With Effie left to her reading, Anya returned to the peep, hoping the stranger had gone back to the ballroom. He was nowhere to be seen, and Anya realized she was tired. Finally resigning herself to turn away, she gasped to find Cedric behind her. He laughed, then wrapped his arms around her.

"Let me go!" she insisted, fearing he wanted to repeat last night's horrible episode.

"What's the matter, Anya? I thought you liked me."

"I hate you!" she retorted.

"But I like you."

"Only because you think I'm some cheap toy. Now let go of me." She finally squirmed out of his arms. "You fiend!" she spat, once she could look him in the face. "Don't you ever lay a hand on me again, or I swear I'll kill you."

"Do you think you could?" he laughed.

"Then I'll kill myself," she retorted. "I would rather die than be subjected to you again. See how your conscience could rest with that—if you even have a conscience."

"Oh, but I do," he laughed. "And you, my dear, have a great deal of spunk. More than I ever imagined."

Anya looked him over in the dim light of the hall sconce. Yesterday she would have claimed to love him. Perhaps she had hoped, somehow, that he might be the one to rescue her from all this. But now his smooth blond hair revolted her, as did the pale blue of his eyes, full of triumph and arrogance. The true knowledge of his motives tore at her insides like a vulture tearing at raw flesh.

"I hate you!" she snarled and he laughed, as if her rage only proved his last statement. "How dare you! You have taken the only thing I had left in the world that was mine!"

"I was just having a little fun." Cedric smiled like the devil and touched her chin.

Anya jerked away. "At the expense of all I hold dear?" she hissed. "And what if there are results?"

"Results?" he echoed, as if such a thought were preposterous. "Don't be silly, my dear. You can't get pregnant from one encounter. But we could try again," he smirked. "Although I think I would prefer a little cooperation. You gave me some pretty nasty bruises last night."

Anya became so furious, so humiliated that she wanted to tear his eyes out. But all she could do was turn and run, while his wicked laughter followed. She didn't stop running until the door to her attic room was shut tight and locked, but echoes of Cedric's laughter stormed through her mind far into the night. With fury she pounded her pillow with her fists and cried until it was far too damp for comfort. She felt like a prisoner here, taunted and tormented day in and day out. Far worse than the menial chores she was forced to perform was the cold steel of piercing eyes that hopelessly weighed her down at every turn. Like chains about her ankles, the sinister remnants of the MacBrier family held her hostage.

She wanted desperately to leave Brierley, but there was nowhere to go. She would likely starve before finding any opportunity for employment, and who would hire a girl who came to apply dressed as she was? It was simply no good. She had to stay or die. But at the moment, she almost preferred to die.

Chapter Two

The Escape

Gavin quickly changed his clothes, bundled his things together, and locked the door to the tower rooms. With purpose he moved through the forest toward the clearing where he had left his horse tethered near a ravine. He was grateful for his knowledge of the terrain; his mind was still seething, and he hardly paid attention to where he was going.

Lady MacBrier was far worse than he had remembered. He'd never seen so much hatred and belligerence in any one person. No amount of reasoning could convince her that he was not the Earl's son, that he had no ulterior motives. He only wanted to be present when the safe was opened. Was that too much to ask? If only the Earl were still alive!

Gavin was almost to the clearing when he realized he was being followed. Would Margaret MacBrier really be so low as to have him hunted down? He dismissed the thought as an absurdity, but moved quickly through the trees, relieved to see the horse nearby. With little thought he ran the distance, stuffed his bundle into the saddlebag, and mounted, turning briefly to assure himself that he was alone in the clearing. But the moment he heeled the stallion into a gallop, a shot was fired without warning, and he felt burning pain tear into his left shoulder. The horse reared back and Gavin rolled to the ground, too stunned to think clearly.

He couldn't believe it! The MacBriers had actually sent someone out to kill him. And that someone could shoot well enough to hit a moving target. Was what he possessed so valuable? The Earl had said some would kill to have it, but Gavin hadn't taken him literally.

Attempting to get control of his thoughts, trying to ignore the pain, Gavin was relieved to see his well-trained stallion hovering nearby. His only hope was to mount again and get out of here. But could he do it with his shoulder throbbing and his shirt turning sticky with blood? Not to mention the likelihood that someone was still in the trees, waiting to finish him off.

"Please, God," he murmured, "just get me out of this alive. That's all I ask."

With nothing spurring him on but faith and desperation, Gavin crawled over the ground toward the stallion. Mustering a burst of energy, he rose to mount. One leg was barely in the stirrup when a second shot rang out and Gavin reeled backward, his thigh catching fire from the inside out. The stallion bolted away, and Gavin found himself too consumed by the pain to even move. Heavy footsteps approached, and he knew his life was over. Instinctively he remained still, praying he wouldn't be shot again.

"Too bad," a gruff voice chuckled to himself, "what happens tae poachers 'round here."

He kicked Gavin to roll him over on the ground. Gavin held his breath, wanting only to be left for dead while he still had any strength at all. He felt rough hands pulling at his fingers, and realized this thug was looking for the ring. As he was thoroughly searched, Gavin was grateful for the instinct he'd followed to leave it hidden at home. He wondered for the first time what might have happened to the other ring. Hadn't the Earl told him it was one of two? Didn't the MacBriers have the other?

"Too bad," the thug repeated and laughed, his search apparently done. He kicked the inert form again, and Gavin's life passed before his eyes as he felt the ground fall out from under him. Only then did he recall the ravine.

"Please, God," he muttered too softly to be heard as his body rolled over the edge.

Anya slept at last. Her dreams were full of soft beds covered with fine linens and hot baths scented with lavender. She dreamed of pretty dresses and hair hanging free, of hands soft as rose petals, and sunrises that brought hope rather than the despair of facing another day's back-breaking, hand-cracking work.

A childhood memory filtered through her dreams, taking her back to a time when life had been as only her dreams were now. The forest felt so real. The smells and sounds struck her as if the years had fled. She was a girl again, clad in a riding habit of blue velvet. Oblivious to how far she had strayed on her own, she thought of nothing but the enchantment of the forest as she rode her own Shetland.

She hadn't known what spooked the little horse, only that she fell and it bolted away, leaving her alone and frightened, and too sore to move. And then she saw him. He was little more than a boy, but his arms felt strong and capable as they lifted her up, and she wearily rested her head on his shoulder as he promised to see her to safety.

Her next awareness was the smell of the stable and Robbie's comforting voice as he told her everything would be fine. Her rescuer was gone, but Anya had always wished that such a thing might happen again. She had daydreamed and longed and hoped for ten years that such a rescue might happen to her now. But only in the oblivion of sleep did it even seem possible. Still, to this day, Anya remembered that face.

"That face!" she heard herself say. Then her heart sank as the reality of her darkened room assaulted her senses. She tried to recall her dream, knowing that its peace had been such a comfort. But her mind was too clouded by the present to pull the pieces together.

Anya's chapped hands ached. She opened and closed her fingers in an effort to ease the pain, knowing that nothing would. She turned her face upward to gaze into the blackness, longing still to escape from all of this. But the absurdity of her wish forced her to face the reality. She was sentenced to life at Brierley.

It was far into the night before Anya came to the conclusion that she must put her encounter with Cedric behind her. There was no other choice if she was to live with any degree of sanity. He was likely right: she wouldn't be pregnant after just once. With a determined effort, she pushed it all deep enough into her mind that it couldn't be felt. Then she fought for something else—anything else—to think about.

Her thoughts turned to the stranger at the ball and his argument with Lady MacBrier. Putting together what little she knew, Anya couldn't help feeling intrigued, if only to know that someone else hated the MacBriers as much as she did. Though she had only caught brief phrases, she knew their argument had something to do with the Earl. The fresh reminder of his absence left her feeling empty. As her longings for her great-uncle deepened with the night, she began to wonder if this was all she would ever have in life. Perhaps it wouldn't have been so difficult if she had never known anything else. But memories of the life she had once enjoyed haunted her on nights like this. She couldn't help longing for something more—or perhaps someone. Someone like the Earl, who cared whether or not she was here. Someone to protect her from people like Cedric.

It was earlier than usual when Anya rose, giving up on sleep at last. She dressed quickly and went straight to the stable, as she often did before settling in to her duties. Of course she was not allowed to ride, but she enjoyed visiting with the horses, and Robbie was usually there to share some good conversation. As early as it was, she knew Robbie would still be eating breakfast with the first shift in the kitchen. But she needed this time of solace to settle the thoughts that had hung with her through the night.

The dawn sky was clear and brilliant, but Anya hardly noticed. The stable was almost dark, and she took the liberty of throwing open the shutters. Then she greeted each of the horses with some hand-fed grain and a light pat on the nose. She heard an unusual sound, but it was muffled by a horse's snort of pleasure at her attention. Perking her ears to listen more closely, she felt her heart pounding inexplicably.

"Robbie." She distinctly heard a voice, gruff and strained. "Is that you?"

Anya glanced in every direction, afraid to admit that she wasn't who she was thought to be. Looking down, she saw splotches of blood in the straw, and followed the trail to an unused stall. Peeking over the edge, she held her breath to see a man with his face buried in the straw. He was curled on his side, his right hand clutching his left shoulder, while his left hand was pressed against his left thigh. Blood oozed between all ten fingers.

"Good heavens!" she gasped, and he looked up in fear at the sound of an unfamiliar voice. Anya caught her breath again. It was *him!*

"Who are you?" Gavin struggled to sit up and groaned, not seeing clearly enough to know she was the woman he'd met just yesterday morning in the tower. Anya stood in silence while he began to pray aloud, "Please God, don't let her be one of them who wants me dead. It would be such a pity after all the trouble I took to get here." He groaned again, and gave up any effort to move as his face slammed back into the straw. "Please, God," he continued, "don't let them find me. I must have left a trail of blood as plain as day, but please don't let them find me!" He opened his eyes and turned them weakly toward Anya again. "Well?" he moaned. "Either kill me or take pity. I can't bear the suspense."

"Forgive me," she said at last, kneeling beside him. "I was just so . . . surprised." She attempted to look at the wounds, but his hands were nearly frozen over them. She thought it best to leave them be until she had something to dress them with. "I won't tell anyone I found you, if that's what you fear. But I'm afraid I can't do much about the trail you left."

"I'll leave that up to someone with more ingenuity." He tried to chuckle, but it turned into another groan. "Oh, please, God," he muttered, glancing toward the ceiling, "like I told her, just kill me or take pity."

"I think He already has," Anya tried to assure him. "Wait here," she implored, coming to her feet, then she laughed at herself. "I suppose you won't go anywhere."

"Not in the next few minutes. Wait!" he added as she turned to leave. "Do you know the stable master? Robbie?"

"Yes . . . yes, of course."

"Get him. He's the only one who can help me. And please, whoever you are, I'm begging you not to tell anyone else."

"I'll get Robbie," she said with empathy. Gavin took it as an acceptance of his plea before his head dropped like dead weight into the straw again.

Anya nearly ran from the stable, then told herself she must be more discreet. Her mind was racing with questions, and there was only one answer that made any sense. For some reason, Margaret MacBrier hated this man enough to try to have him killed. Was it possible? The situation was too obvious to be otherwise.

Casually she walked toward the side door of the house, noticing the trail of blood that came from the direction of the forest. She found Robbie along with some others eating breakfast, and she casually opened a cupboard where medical supplies were kept. As she pulled out some bandages and disinfectant, Mrs. MacGregor predictably questioned her.

"One of the horses has a cut on the hock—from a nail in the stall, it appears." She was proud of herself for the casual tone.

"Why dinna ye let me see tae that," Robbie offered.

She turned to him and smiled. "Finish your breakfast, I'll—"

"I'm dun," he announced, and stood from the table to follow Anya out the door.

"I lied," Anya said.

"Aboot what?"

"There is no ailing horse. It's a . . . Good heavens!" She glanced skyward and couldn't believe her eyes. The clouds were rolling in so thick and black that it seemed they would burst at any moment. "That storm certainly moved in quickly."

"Aye, it did," Robbie agreed. "Now aboot this lie?" he persisted.

"There is a man bleeding to death in one of the stalls. He asked for you." Robbie moved to run toward the stable, but Anya placed a hand on his arm. "I suspect we should appear discreet for his sake. Let's make this hurt horse story look good." Robbie nodded and walked patiently with Anya into the stable.

"Gavin!" he cried upon seeing the patient. "What in heaven's name have ye dun tae yersel'?"

"Robbie," he smiled, more weakly than before. "I saw an angel of mercy a while ago and thought I was dead. Now I know I'm alive. You're still as mean and ugly as ever."

Robbie laughed, but Anya saw the concern in his face as he motioned for her to help tend the wounds. "Answer m' question, lad," he insisted. Anya realized Robbie was trying to distract him from their attention to the bullet hole in his thigh.

"I had the audacity to visit Lady MacBrier last evening," he muttered. Anya knew her assumptions had been right. "Before I left the estate I was shot, searched, and kicked into a ravine by some thug who muttered something about poachers, as if he'd told himself a joke."

"I get th' idea," Robbie muttered. "Shut up and save what wee bit o' strength ye've got left."

"Bullet went straight through," Anya reported quietly to Robbie. She pointed to the blood in the straw beneath his leg. "He's bleeding more out the back. The pressure of his hand has slowed it down here."

Gavin appeared concerned at their whisperings. Robbie said in a jovial tone, "Ye're a lucky devil. Anya here knows what she's doin' when it comes to doctorin'. Ye might get out o' this alive yet." Gavin lifted his head feebly to look at Anya. She felt his eyes focus on her and saw the recognition in them.

During Gavin's struggle to climb out of the ravine and get to the stable, he'd found his mind recalling that sweet face he'd seen only briefly in the tower rooms. It was like the face of a child with eyes that had seen a thousand years. He had to admit that something about her had intrigued him. She had clung distinctly to his memory. He'd wanted to live just to see that face again, if nothing else. And here she was. Could he be hallucinating? He prayed that he wasn't.

Thunder sounded outside, and rain began to beat on the roof. Gavin glanced toward the ceiling and muttered a quiet "Thank you, God."

"For what?" Robbie asked.

"For washing away his trail," Anya provided, marveling at such a rapid and obvious answer to a prayer. Could it just be coincidence? Somehow she didn't believe it was. His prayer had been too sincere, too confident. She quickly took Gavin's hand and put the back of it to his mouth. "Bite this," she insisted. "I don't want you to scare the horses." With no more warning, she poured disinfectant into the wound. Gavin bit and groaned and writhed all at once.

"I thought you said she was good," he breathed hoarsely.

"I didna say she was gentle," Robbie laughed, but Anya caught the undertone of concern. Whoever this Gavin was, he meant something to Robbie. Gavin's pale, drawn face and continually weakening voice were obvious signs that this was no small thing.

"How did you manage to get here?" she asked while bandaging his thigh.

"A lot of praying," he muttered gruffly.

"Is that how you got out of the ravine?" She could hardly believe he'd made it here alive.

He closed his eyes and rolled his head to the side. "I caught an out-hanging tree with my good arm."

"It must o' been th' prayin'," Robbie inserted, and Anya silently agreed.

With Gavin's thigh bandaged tightly, she turned her attention to his shoulder. He met her eyes briefly, and something stirred in her that made her glad she had been the one to find him.

"This one just grazed the muscle," she reported to Gavin. "You're very lucky. I doubt you could survive digging out a bullet with all the blood you've lost."

"Thank you, God," he rasped, but Anya felt certain it was heard.

Again they went through the painful ritual of cleansing the wound. Anya gently wrapped it while Gavin turned his attention to Robbie. "I can't stay here."

"Such a smart lad," Robbie teased.

"Can you get me home, Robbie?"

"Once it's dark . . . I can get ye home. But answer me this, lad. What are ye gonna do when ye get there? Ye canna make it in this condition alone. An' ye'll be worse by th' time we get ye there. I canna stay with ye. I would if I could. But I canna do it."

Anya felt Gavin's eyes on her. He said nothing and his expression remained unreadable, but Anya heard herself saying, "I can go with him."

"Nonsense, lass," Robbie protested. "Ye canna just leave here and—"

"Oh, of course not," she said sarcastically, handing him the left-over bandaging. "How could I possibly leave behind all that I have here?"

A contemplative silence accompanied sporadic glances among the three as Gavin seemed to leave his fate up to them.

"It wouldna be easy," Robbie told her. His tone of voice indicated he'd like to talk her out of it, while his eyes seemed to hope his efforts would fail.

"You know I could handle it. After what I've done here, I believe I can handle anything."

"She's right there, ye know," Robbie nodded toward Gavin, whose eyes turned again to Anya with a sense of gratitude and a hint of pleading.

"Well," Robbie came to his feet, "I dinna see any options. I'm th' only friend he's got, an' ye're th' only one I would trust with him."

Anya felt an unexplainable thrill at Robbie's consent. She immediately began planning how she would leave this dreadful place in the dead of night, and no one would ever miss her. She had no idea where any of this would end, but it was the closest she'd come to freedom or adventure since the Earl had died. Anything would be better than being here—under the same roof with Cedric MacBrier. This was the perfect opportunity to really put it all behind her, once and for all.

"Where are you going?" Anya asked Robbie.

"Tae bandage th' horse that was hurt." He winked at her and moved away.

"Thank you," Gavin muttered. "I'll make it up to you." He wondered if he ought to tell her that it was possible to find someone else to care for him. He did have at least one other friend in the world. It would be difficult, but it was possible. For a moment he nearly said it, but something stopped him—the same something that had kept her image vivid in his mind since he'd last seen her.

Anya only smiled and came to her feet. "I'll be right back." She returned with a bucket of water and a rag. She immersed the rag and wrung it out, then wiped gently at Gavin's face to remove the sweat and dirt of his ordeal. He opened his eyes at her touch. "It's cold," she said, "but it might help you feel better."

"Thank you," was all Gavin could think to say. His eyes wanted to close. He felt so tired, so weak. But he forced them to stay open. He wanted to watch her. He marveled at the simple beauty of her face. He thought of Malvina, adorned in the best of everything, while her homeliness was still blatantly obvious. And here was this woman. Her clothes were tattered and worn, and the scarf she wore tightly around her head was anything but becoming. Still, she was beautiful.

He couldn't tell if her eyes were green or blue. Perhaps a little of both. But the pain in them was evident. He wondered what had happened to put it there. He pondered the feeling that there was something incongruous about her. Then he realized that her speech and manner didn't match up with a scullery maid. It didn't make sense, which intrigued him all the more.

Anya realized Gavin was watching her, but she kept her eyes on her work. She took one of his hands and put it into the water, rubbing between his fingers to wash away the caked blood. She dried his hand on her apron and proceeded with the other. She met his eyes again, and suddenly grasped the reality of what she had agreed to do. Had her desperation to get away from Brierley made her commit to something foolish? She looked again at Gavin, whose eyes were closed now, and decided that her cause was worthy.

"I must go now," she said quietly, and his eyes responded. "I need to see to my work as usual so that no one will suspect. I'll see you tonight . . . when we leave."

He gave a slight nod and closed his eyes again. Anya glanced at him, took a deep breath, and hurried toward the house. After break-fast, she went quickly upstairs to begin her work. With more vigor and enthusiasm than she'd felt in years, she did everything required of her and more, thinking perhaps this alone might make someone miss her.

She thought of the people she would be leaving behind. Even though she had a certain rapport with many of the servants, the only ones she would really miss were Mrs. MacGregor and Robbie. She certainly wouldn't miss Lady MacBrier, or Una, or Malvina. And especially not Cedric. But what about Effie? Anya's heart dropped a little. She quickly reminded herself that the others loved Effie as well, and she would be taken care of. But still, she would certainly miss Effie.

Her thoughts turned to Gavin. She recalled their brief encounter in the tower, watching him at the ball, and hearing him in the library late last night. Was it merely coincidence that she had crossed his path so many times? And now this stranger called Gavin was about to become the center of her life . . . at least for now.

When her work was done, Anya sought out Effie, spending a long evening with her, trying to make her understand as much as possible that she was going away, but that didn't mean she didn't love her. When they parted, Anya quickly tried to push the regrets behind and feel only the anticipation of what lay ahead. She had no idea what might happen once Gavin recovered—or if he didn't. Would she come back to Brierley? Or perhaps find a position elsewhere? Anya forced herself to think only of now. She would cross that bridge when she came to it.

Feeling restless, but knowing they would not be leaving for some time, Anya went quietly down the back stairs and through the darkened house to the library. By the light of a single candle, she found the slender book at the far end of a shelf, pushed between two novels as if it were insignificant. She pulled it down and knelt on the floor to turn through the pages with a certain reverence. She doubted that anyone else knew this was here, or they likely would have destroyed it. Anya was grateful they hadn't. Her great-uncle's journal was priceless to her; she had read it many times in the dead of night. His life had been tragic in a sense—the way he'd lost his first wife and his life had fallen apart. And then there were the entries about herself. To read them gave reality to what they had briefly shared in her childhood.

The bizarre thing about the Earl's journal was the way three pages had been torn out following his last entry. Anya had wondered and speculated over it endlessly. She was certain it had something to do with his death, but it was a question that would likely be forever unanswered.

Carefully Anya closed the book and returned it to the shelf. She was tempted to take it with her, certain it wouldn't be missed, but her sense of honesty overruled. It didn't belong to her, so it had to stay.

Realizing what time it was, Anya hurried back upstairs to gather her things. Her heart pounding with anticipation, she wondered where all of this would take her. But for now it didn't matter. She wanted only to escape.

Chapter Three
Angel of Mercy

Anya only needed a few minutes to gather everything she owned. Beyond the uniform she wasn't wearing, a worn nightgown, and some underclothing, there was only a hairbrush and the little doll, now old and ragged, the Earl had given her the day she'd arrived at Brierley. Bundling it all together in a sheet, Anya threw her cloak around her shoulders, extinguished the lamp, and headed down the stairs with a sense of good riddance.

A high moon guided her to the stable, where she found Robbie readying the horses. She wondered why he had only saddled two, until she took one look at Gavin. If not for his shallow, labored breathing, she might have believed he was dead. He would not be able to ride alone.

"How is he?" Anya asked quietly and handed her bundle to Robbie.

"Th' bleedin' finally stopped a bit ago, but Ah wonder how he'll tak' th' ride."

Anya knelt beside Gavin and set a hand to his brow. Startled brown eyes shot open, then filled with relief when he saw her hovering above him.

"It's all right," she whispered. "We'll have you home soon."

A barely perceptible lift of his chin was Gavin's only acknowledgment. Robbie took hold of Gavin's good arm and hoisted him to a sitting position.

"Ah'm gonna need yer help, lass," Robbie said, and she braced her arms around Gavin's waist, allowing him to lean his weight against her as he came unsteadily to his feet with a stifled groan.

"How ye doin', lad?" Robbie asked lightly.

Gavin flicked a smile toward the older man. "I've seen better days."

Anya felt Gavin exert all the strength he could muster as he was helped into the saddle. He leaned forward unsteadily, and she feared he might fall until Robbie mounted behind him to offer support.

A partial moon moved in and out of wispy clouds, giving Brierley a haunted appearance as they rode slowly past. Anya situated herself more comfortably into the saddle and breathed in the freedom of the brisk air. "Take care, Effie," she whispered to the night, then turned her attention to whatever might lie ahead as she followed Robbie silently into the forest.

What Robbie had said was normally an hour's ride took more than three with their wounded passenger, who passed out after the first mile. Anya found it difficult to stay awake the last hour, and she began to ache from the tedious plodding of the horse beneath her.

"It's just up ahead, lass," Robbie finally called over his shoulder. Anya straightened her back, attempting to focus her eyes on what would be her home for the coming weeks. One moment there was nothing but trees, and the next, a cottage-like house loomed before them. It was difficult to discern any detail in the darkness of the surrounding forest, but it had a quaint feel about it that Anya liked already. Robbie halted and motioned for her to come beside him. He set a key into her hand, and she dismounted on unsteady feet.

"Why dinna ye see if ye can get th' hoose open, an' we'll get th' lad tae bed."

Anya struggled for a minute with the lock, then she felt the key turn and the door moved on quiet hinges. She immediately had to move aside and let Robbie pass with Gavin over his shoulder. Anya closed the door and followed them through the darkness, realizing that Robbie must be familiar with Gavin's home to find his way to the bedroom so easily. She located the bed and turned it down. Robbie relinquished his burden with a groan and mumbled, "It's a good thing Ah'm not as old as Ah look."

She heard him fumbling in the dark to find a lamp, and a moment later the room became illuminated with a yellow glow. Robbie pulled off Gavin's boots and tossed them aside before he left to unload the horses. Anya turned to absorb her surroundings and felt a rush of reality. Gavin was as white as the sheets beneath him, and a cold dread trickled down her spine. What if he didn't survive? What would she do then?

Convincing herself to keep a bright outlook, Anya concentrated on becoming acquainted with her new living quarters. At first glance, the bedroom seemed elaborate in relation to the size and structure of the house. The floor was gleaming, polished wood, with identical woven rugs on either side of the bed. Intricately carved floral designs enhanced the wood of a large bureau and mirror, where two lamps sat on either side of a basin and pitcher. The wardrobe matched the bureau, and the walls were papered in cream pinstriped with red. A large fireplace was inlaid with mosaic tiles of the same colors, coordinating with the rugs and the tapestried cushion on a rocking chair near the window, where creamy drapes hung. On the carved mantel sat a brass clock, unwound, between two brass candlesticks. The brass bed, its linens entirely white, was situated beneath a painting of the lion lying with the lamb. From the books scattered over the bedside tables, Anya surmised that Gavin was an avid reader.

Her eyes went again to the central focus of the room. She touched Gavin's brow to check for fever. He showed no response to her touch, but she found a faint pulse. She lifted the covers to his chin, then took up the lamp and moved to explore the remainder of the house. She quickly realized that the bedroom was the largest room. Inside the front door was a tiny entry hall that led into a parlor decorated much like the bedroom, except with more blues. She found Robbie in a large kitchen with many windows that she felt certain would fill the room with light in the mornings. She watched for a moment as he added supplies to an already well-stocked pantry. Robbie winked at her and disappeared out a side door, near a bay window where a dining table and four chairs fit nicely.

Anya ran her fingers over a large work table and the brightly polished water pump, finding pleasure imagining herself in charge of such a kitchen. Behind the kitchen and just off the bedroom was a separate bathing room with a huge bathtub, fluffy towels stacked near an ample supply of soaps and shampoos, and a little stove for heating water.

"Ah, there ye are, lassie." Robbie startled her, and she followed him into the kitchen. "Ah've checked aboot, and it seems there's plenty tae keep ye goin'. There's wood stacked ootside," he pointed toward the side door, "and Ah brought what ye'll need to keep th' wounds proper."

Anya nodded firmly, hating the realization that Robbie was leaving her alone here with a man who was half dead.

"Now," he lifted a finger, "if there's anythin' ye're needin', there's a village twenty minutes sooth on foot. Just follow th' road ye see past th' trees in front." She nodded again. "They set th' market oot on Wednesdays, and ye can get nigh anythin'."

Robbie walked into the bedroom and opened a drawer in one of the bedside tables. "Aye, here's some cash tae get ye by. Ah think that's all ye need tae know."

"Thank you," she said feebly.

"It's Ah who should be thankin' ye, lass. Ah dinna ken what we'd a dun withoot ye."

Anya glanced warily to Gavin's unconscious form, and Robbie's eyes followed. "Dinna ye worry, lass. He's a strong 'un. He'll make it through."

Robbie walked toward the door and she followed. "Now, ye'd do well tae keep the door locked. Ah'll check back as soon as Ah can. Ye're a good woman, Anya," he added with a fatherly hand on her shoulder. "Ah'll be prayin' fer th' both o' ye."

Anya wanted to beg him to stay, just until morning. But she knew he would be missed if he didn't return now, and she had to face this sooner or later. She reminded herself that she had volunteered to help. It couldn't possibly be as bad as living at Brierley.

It wasn't until Robbie had gone and Anya had made certain both doors were locked that she stopped to ponder his warning. If someone had tried to kill Gavin, did they know where to find him now? She found the thought worth ignoring for the time being.

Setting her mind to the tasks at hand, Anya turned her attention to Gavin. She changed the dressings on his wounds, relieved to find less blood than she had anticipated after the journey. She felt concerned when Gavin showed little reaction to the disinfectant. But she concentrated on the present and dedicated herself to doing all she could to save him. She would face the future when it arrived.

Her next need was to get some sleep. With only one bed available, and the parlor sofa too far away to attend her patient, Anya found extra blankets and prepared a makeshift bed near the fireplace. She contemplated building a small fire to take off the chill, but exhaustion favored going without it. She changed for bed in the bathing room, checked on Gavin once more, then doused the lamp and slipped between the blankets, falling into a sound sleep before she had time to think about what tomorrow would bring.

Anya's next awareness was the distant sound of bleating sheep. Half asleep, she listened as the herd moved closer, until the noise became almost deafening. She could hear the shepherd's whistle and the dogs' barking as they responded to the commands. This sign of simple, untroubled living gave her peace, and she drifted off again as the herd moved on up the road.

She guessed it was almost noon when she woke again. She wasn't used to waking up in such brilliant sunlight, and it took several minutes to adjust her eyes. Realizing how many hours she must have slept, panic sent her to Gavin's side. Finding evidence of his breath and pulse, she sat on the edge of the bed and sighed. So far, so good. Assured that the bleeding had stopped, she set herself to getting her surroundings in order, if only to avoid worrying over his unconscious state.

Once dressed, Anya had to admit she was famished. She made a mental list of what to do while she sat in the sunlight of the bay window, eating dark bread, cheese, and hot tea. Again she went through the house to acquaint herself with it more fully. She found it a bit dusty, but in fairly good order. And she was pleased to find enough of everything they needed to last at least a week or two.

After dusting and straightening a bit, Anya checked on Gavin and found him resting well. The urge to take a hot bath was just too much to resist. While the water heated she contemplated the luxury, trying to remember the last time she had been able to clean herself with anything more than a basin of water in her attic room. The bath proved to be a worthy indulgence, and she felt almost guilty for enjoying herself so thoroughly while her purpose for being here lay on the brink of death in the other room. Unwillingly, her mind went to Cedric. She winced inwardly at the thought of how he had marred her life. It was too bad she couldn't just wash away what he'd done to her. Knowing such a thing was futile, she switched her mind to the reason she was here. Thoughts of Gavin forced her out of the cooling water to make certain he was all right.

She decided laundry was the next task. While gathering what needed washing, Anya hung her cloak in the wardrobe and paused to admire the clothes hanging there. Gavin was not a man of many possessions, but what he had was fine. She lingered over a kilt and plaid, recalling how he'd looked walking down the hall at Brierley, dressed in his finest. Drawing herself back to reality, she found an empty bureau drawer and took the liberty of putting her few belongings into it.

With the laundry hung outside on the line to dry, Anya was struck with the thought that Gavin was also in need of a cleaning. Removing the covers from his still form, she contemplated the possibility of mending the clothes that had been damaged by bullet holes and his struggle to get back to the stable. But a closer examination proved it would be futile, especially when he had plenty of clothes to get by with. Relegating them to rags made the task easier, as she was able to cut them away with scissors and not worry about the damage. She was grateful for his unconsciousness as she pushed his shirt aside. It would have been difficult to explain to him why she gasped and put a hand to her suddenly pounding heart. The last thing she had expected to see was a conspicuous birthmark on Gavin's right shoulder. But once she came to accept it, everything made perfect sense.

"It's true," she whispered aloud, reaching out a hand to touch it, convincing herself it was real. The reality brought on a mixture of emotions. But looking at Gavin's face, absorbed in peaceful oblivion, she felt somehow privileged to be here. Knowing who and what Gavin was left her feeling an unspoken bond with him. Yet she'd hardly exchanged a handful of words with him. Unconsciously she pressed a hand to his face. Now that she was looking for it, the resemblance was evident, if not strong. There was no question that Gavin was James MacBrier's son. And while it was not easy to think of the Earl fathering an illegitimate child, she knew his life had been difficult and she couldn't find it in her heart to judge him.

Anya's mind went to a childhood memory. She lost track of the time as she sat with her hand pressed to Gavin's warm cheek, while in her mind she saw herself as a child in green velvet, absorbed in the book spread over her lap. It was filled with names and dates going back many years. A vibrant James MacBrier sat beside her, pointing out the direct bloodline of each Earl of Brierley down through the decades. She accused him of teasing her when he said that each of these men had been born with a mark that proved their birthright. The Earl had said nothing. He only unfastened the top two buttons of his shirt and pushed it aside to show her the mark of Brierley. Anya remembered little else of the day, except that her great-uncle had said something cryptic about fearing Brierley would fall in the coming years, due to circumstances he didn't understand.

Gavin shifted slightly and startled Anya to the present. Reverently she touched the mark once more, wondering what it might be like if Gavin were the Earl of Brierley—instead of Cedric. Reminding herself not to get caught up in childish fantasies, she forced herself to get on with her chore. She carefully cut away the tattered shirt and breeches, leaving his underclothing in place, allowing him to maintain his modesty. The experience of bathing a patient was not new to her. On a number of occasions she had assisted Mrs. MacGregor in the care of servants when they were ill or injured, and she approached it with matter-of-fact efficiency.

With Gavin's wounds cleaned and dressed, Anya contemplated trying to put him in a nightshirt. Logically he was too heavy to dress without help, and a nightshirt would also make it difficult to get to the shoulder wound. She left him as he was, and tucked a warmed blanket up over his shoulders.

Anya hummed lightly as she washed out the tattered clothes and cut them into rags. The chore might have been enjoyable if not for the constant ache of her hands, especially when they were in and out of hot water. She wished she had thought to get some hand cream from Mrs. MacGregor before she'd left, and made a mental note to get some when she went into town.

She ventured into the yard once more to hang the rags with the other laundry on a line stretched between two trees. A small stable sat near the house, and she investigated to find it void of any animals.

Reasoning it out, she decided Gavin likely had a horse that had been lost in his recent caper at Brierley.

Thinking on her discoveries of this day, Anya stopped to realize that something was bothering her. She knew now that the rumors were true: Gavin was the Earl's son. Then was it also true that Gavin had killed the Earl? The thought made her nearly ill. But pondering it further, she decided that Robbie would not be so fond of Gavin if such a thing were even remotely possible. She decided to get to know Gavin on her own before making any judgments one way or the other.

When the work was completed and all was in order, Anya checked again on Gavin to find his condition unchanged. She built a small fire in the bedroom and crawled gratefully into her bed on the floor. Never had exhaustion been so gratifying. She felt at peace here. It was a pleasure to have diversified tasks instead of doing the same cumbersome jobs over and over. And she enjoyed benefitting personally from her efforts. She found herself praying that she would never have to go back to Brierley, then wondered when she had begun doing such a thing. She couldn't recall praying since the Earl died, and decided that her brief association with Gavin had restored her faith in prayer. Praying that Gavin would show some improvement tomorrow, Anya drifted off to sleep, grateful to have left Brierley in her past. She didn't bother to contemplate the future.

Suddenly Anya came awake, her heart pounding. She wondered why. She waited, her ears attuned to the stillness of the house, listening for a clue. A deep moan came through the darkness, and she hurried to Gavin's bedside.

"Gavin," she spoke close to his face, but he only groaned again. Putting a hand to his brow, the evidence of a burning fever made her heart sink. "Please, God, no," she whispered.

With a lamp burning low, Anya stayed near Gavin through the night and into daylight, bathing him with tepid water and doing everything in her knowledge to fight the fever. But still it raged on. He writhed in apparent pain and muttered indecipherable phrases. Anya could only attempt to comfort him, not certain if he was even conscious. During brief intervals of peace, she rested with her hand against his face to monitor his temperature. The reality muddled into her dreams as she wondered about Gavin. What kind of man was he? What was his involvement with the MacBriers, and why had he ended up in this condition after his confrontation with Lady MacBrier? She felt angry on his behalf for what they had done to him. Then she found herself crying to see such a fine man in this miserable, helpless state.

By early afternoon, Gavin's skin felt only slightly warm, but the house was in shambles. Wet towels were draped everywhere, and the kitchen showed evidence of her hurried attempts to ease her growling hunger and return to his side. Evening brought his fever up again, and Anya cried more fervently. She began to ask herself what she would do if he died. Beyond the tragedy of his loss, she couldn't imagine how she might deal with the circumstances. As he went in and out of delirium, she spoke aloud to convince herself more than him that everything would be all right. He would make it through this. He had to!

"Come on, Gavin," she whispered against his face, brushing her fingers through his hair, smoothing the sweat from his brow. "You can make it. I know you can make it."

Exhaustion moved her onto the bed beside him, just close enough to keep a hand against his face. She didn't realize his fever had broken until she awoke to sunlight and found him resting peacefully. With a sigh of relief and a prayer of gratitude, Anya found fresh ambition despite her lack of sleep. She quickly put the house in order. After bathing and doing up the laundry, she bathed Gavin to cleanse away the stickiness of the fever sweat. She noticed his face turning darker with growing stubble, but she wasn't about to shave an unconscious man.

With everything in order, Anya went to the bookshelf in Gavin's parlor and found a novel that looked intriguing. The house felt stuffy, so she opened the bedroom window a little and sat in the rocker to read. Every few minutes she got up to check on him, fearing he was either going to wake up or die. Finally she just settled herself against the headboard to read, one hand pressed to the base of his throat where the slightest pressure assured her his blood was pumping.

Somewhere on the brim of coherency, Gavin had the sensation that he'd passed through hell. Burned and scarred by memories and realities, he somehow emerged, escorted to heaven by the voices of angels. The brilliancy was something he felt unprepared to face, and he willingly backed away, only to hover in a seemingly endless limbo, where heaven and hell met near the earth, each crying out for its own claim on his soul. And then in an instant he was here.

Here! He inhaled the familiarity and pushed against his eyelids, knowing he had to see it to believe it. Blinding light was all his eyes perceived before they won out and closed tight. He wondered for a moment if heaven had triumphed and he was dead after all, but it took only the slightest movement to assure himself that his body was very much alive—and hurting.

Gavin felt certain he was home, though he couldn't recall getting here, and he wasn't even sure where this nightmare had begun. The bed beneath him felt familiar and secure, but he sensed something unusual. Shifting slightly, he realized he was not alone. With fresh motivation, Gavin pushed open his aching eyes. Once they adjusted to the sunlight, peace washed over him to know it wasn't a hallucination. He *was* home. This was his bedroom. It all felt right. Turning to take in the full spectrum of his surroundings, Gavin became conscious of the hand against his throat. His eyes focused first on tiny bare feet against the blanket, peeking from beneath the hem of a dark skirt. His gaze moved up over an aproned hip, where an arm lay against an open book. Making an effort to shift his aching shoulder, he saw her face and the memories came flooding back. Perhaps it hadn't all been a dream. The hell part was easy to recall. And he could well imagine this lovely angel of mercy hovering with him between life and death. He watched her as she slept, her head propped against the headboard, a gentle hand unconsciously pressing against his throat. Even in sleep, she seemed somehow aware of him.

Just this side of a dream, Anya pressed her fingers to Gavin's skin and felt his pulse quickening. She could almost imagine it racing, only to come to a dead stop. With a panicked gasp she lifted her head, praying inwardly that he would not leave her now after holding on this long. It took her a moment to realize that he was looking at her. Then, without thinking, she pressed the side of her face to his in some semblance of an awkward embrace, laughing with pure relief.

"Oh," she said close to his ear, "thank God. You've made it." She drew back and smiled at him, pressing a hand against his flushed cheek. "Thank God," she repeated.

"Amen," Gavin muttered, feeling like his mouth was full of desert sand. Her grin brightened, and he couldn't help smiling. "You stayed," he whispered. "Thank you."

"I'm just glad you didn't die." She brushed her fingers over his brow, pushing back a stray lock of dark hair. Gavin took notice of her attention and Anya drew back self-consciously, wondering if it was inappropriate now that he was awake. On the same thought she slipped off the bed and stood, wringing her hands tensely. She had come to feel so close to him. And now, with his big brown eyes regarding her intently, she had to admit they were strangers.

She attempted to explain her behavior. "I was so worried. You've been unconscious for days, and you had such a dreadful fever, and . . ."

"And thanks to you, I'm alive," he said when she faltered.

Anya looked down shyly and cleared her throat. Gavin moaned as he attempted to move, and she rushed to his side in concern. "You must be careful," she said. Their eyes met as she situated the pillows to make him more comfortable. "Is that better?" she asked.

"Much," he said with a raspy voice. "Thank you."

"You must be thirsty." Anya backed away a few steps and he nodded. "I'll just get you a glass of water, and . . ." She hurried away without finishing.

Gavin shifted slightly, and the pain in his leg throbbed more intensely. On a hunch, he moved his hand down over the blankets and held his breath until he was assured that his leg was still there. That was a relief, he decided just as the woman returned with a glass of cool water. Without speaking, she deftly lifted his head and pressed the glass to his lips. His dry mouth absorbed it like a sponge, but he was amazed at how the effort to drink drained his strength.

"Take it slowly," she whispered, then asked if he'd had enough.

Gavin nodded feebly, and she gently guided his head back to the pillow. "I'm sorry," he spoke more easily now, "but I don't remember your name. I think I heard Robbie say it, but . . ."

"Anya Ross," she provided, setting the glass on the bedside table.

"May I call you Anya, or does it have to be Miss Ross?"

Anya straightened her shoulders. "Whatever you wish, my lord."

"Why do you call me that?" he asked, raising an eyebrow.

Anya smoothed invisible wrinkles out of her apron, contemplating her implication in light of his obvious identity. Noncommittal, she replied without looking at him, "That is what I have called all the men I have served."

"Does that put me into the same category as those snobs at Brierley who go about with their noses in the air?" Gavin's voice held a definite edge.

"It was not intended to." She met his intense gaze and wondered why he would seem so offended.

Gavin only smiled. "I assume Robbie told you my name."

Anya nodded, then she added without thinking, "Just Gavin?" She saw his expression falter and immediately regretted asking. "I'm sorry," she stammered. "I was just . . ."

"Why should you apologize?" he asked tersely, though it was more her expression than the question itself that made him certain that she knew. "It's not your fault or mine that I have only my mother's name. I am what they call an accident of nature." Gavin paused to note her widening eyes. "But you knew that, didn't you." It was not a question.

"I suspected," she had to admit.

"And how did you suspect?"

While Anya pondered a response, she noticed his eyelids drooping and acted quickly. "You must be exhausted. It will take time to get your strength back." She fluffed his pillows a little and tucked the blanket over him. "You rest now, and then I'll see that you get some nourishment."

She expected him to argue, but he only watched her leave the room. When she peeked in minutes later, he appeared to be sleeping soundly. Anya sat at the kitchen table to gather her wits. She wondered how she would manage caring for this man over the coming weeks if he persisted with his bold questions and unyielding eyes. And he'd barely been conscious ten minutes. Deciding that for the time being she was in charge and she'd better act it, Anya made up her mind not to allow him to intimidate her. By the time he was strong enough to take control of his home again, she would be prepared to move on.

Knowing she must concentrate on the present, Anya rose to prepare some broth. Gavin would be hungry, and she needed to care for him. At this moment, nothing else mattered.

She was sitting in the rocking chair, reading, when he awoke again early in the evening. She felt his eyes on her before he made a sound.

"How are you?" she asked, setting the book aside.

"Thirsty," he said, and she was quick to help him drink. He finished what was in the glass and asked for more.

"That's a good sign, I think," she said, setting the glass aside. "Now, it's time we start getting your strength back. Let me help you sit up, and I'll get you something to eat."

Embarrassed by his dependency on this delicate woman, Gavin attempted to sit up on his own, declaring firmly, "It's all right. I think I can manage."

"I wouldn't do that if I were . . . you." She added the last as his body slammed down onto the bed and he looked up at her with a sigh of disgust. "That's what happens when you lose blood, my lord. There isn't enough flowing in your veins to do much of anything. So just accept it. I don't appreciate stubborn patients."

Gavin said nothing as she propped him into a near-sitting position with several pillows. "Is that all right?" she asked. He only nodded.

Anya left the room, and Gavin cursed inwardly. Already he hated this. He hated the pounding in his head and the immense heaviness that left him practically helpless. And now that he was sitting, he glanced down to see the sheet lying idly about his waist. Warily he lifted it, then sighed in relief to see that he was modest to some degree. Still, he hated this more by the minute. But presently, it seemed, he had little choice but to live with it. He reminded himself that he should feel grateful just to be alive.

Chapter Four
Questions

When Anya appeared with a dinner tray, Gavin tried to comprehend the care she had given him while he'd been unconscious. He hardly knew what to say, but he felt decidedly uneasy at being so thoroughly dependent. Without a word, she set the tray down and sat close by to help him. Gavin took the spoon from her and announced quietly, "I think I can manage myself, thank you."

Anya nearly protested, but she only lifted her hands in resignation, knowing it wouldn't take long. She found his pride a bit unreasonable when he'd nearly collapsed a few minutes ago from trying to sit up. After two spoonfuls he dropped the spoon on the tray and sighed. "So, now you're going to feed me like a baby."

"Just until you get your strength back." She smiled, and his discomfort lessened slightly. "If you stay down and do what you're told, you'll be on your own much sooner, my lord."

"I am not your lord," he said between spoonfuls.

Anya glanced at him warily. "Then what would you prefer that I call you?"

"Gavin would be fine," he said, and she made no comment. Hating the silence, he added, "This is good . . . as far as broth goes."

"I'm not such a bad cook," she admitted.

"So far I have an accomplished nurse, an excellent housekeeper, and you can cook as well. Now, why would I be so fortunate as to be found half-dead by a woman with such diversified talents?"

Gavin meant it as a compliment, but her eyes told him that was not how she'd taken it. With an indignant tone she informed him, "Mrs. MacGregor taught me much."

"Mrs. MacGregor?"

"She was the head cook at Brierley, though if not for her, the household would fall apart. She kept the housekeeper on her toes, and if there was a problem, she handled it. She was very good to me, and allowed me to work with her in many things, so I could learn."

"Obviously you learned well," he said, but she made no response. Observing her more closely, the incongruities he'd once noticed came back to him. He couldn't help being curious. Her face shone with purity and youth, while her eyes looked hard and cynical, as if she had seen a lifetime of harsh living. He didn't doubt that being a servant at Brierley could be a hard life. But the disturbing thing was her voice. Anya Ross spoke with an educated refinement that made the scullery clothes she wore as out of place as a fish in the desert.

"And did Mrs. MacGregor teach you to speak like a lady?" he asked.

Anya was so shocked she couldn't think how to react. She felt somehow afraid, and wondered why she didn't want him to know the truth. Reminding herself not to let him intimidate her, she answered firmly, "I learned to speak long before I came to Brierley, sir. Personally, it's something I've never thought about."

"And tell me, Anya," he said while she carefully tipped the bowl to spoon out the final drops, "what brought you to live at Brierley?"

Anya looked at him sharply. If he wasn't mocking her, he was prying into her private life. Without a word, she gave him the last spoonful and went into the kitchen. A minute later Gavin called, "You didn't answer my question."

"I'm eating my supper, if you don't mind," she called back. "And I'm not going to talk with my mouth full."

Gavin didn't have the strength to holler back. He felt a bored frustration settling in already, and he knew it would only get worse. While this Anya blatantly avoided him, he attempted to see if there was anything on the bedside table worth reading. But he hardly had the strength to even reach it. When she finally returned, he occupied himself with watching her every move as she straightened the room and closed the drapes. She lit a lamp and built a fire without so much as a glance in his direction. While she folded a pile of clean linens at the foot of the bed, he finally spoke up. "You have a way of avoiding conversation, Anya Ross. Is there a reason why you don't want to talk to me?" She looked as if he'd asked her to do something criminal.

"As I see it," she explained, "you and I are practically strangers. I have committed myself to keeping you alive. Beyond that, anything else is pointless."

"Have you ever heard of casual conversation for the sake of it?" he asked wryly. "Don't you ever get lonely with no one but yourself to talk to?"

"I learned to deal with being lonely a long time ago."

"Really? You must tell me how you did it. Personally, I've never gotten used to it."

"This is a ridiculous conversation. As I said, we're—"

"Practically strangers. Yes, I know. Even though you've sat almost constantly by my bedside for days."

Anya wanted to ask how he knew she had attended him so closely, but she retorted with, "I know absolutely nothing about you. I don't even know your name."

"Baird," he stated. "My mother's name was Jinny Baird, and I think you know a lot more about me than you're letting on." She looked briefly panicked. "Ah, so we come back to one of those questions you've managed to avoid. You knew I was illegitimate, didn't you, Anya? I didn't tell you, and I know Robbie didn't tell you. You could squeeze blood out of a rock easier than you could get gossip out of old Robbie. So, how did you know?"

Gavin could see in her eyes that she was contemplating an exit. But he stopped the attempt with a firm, "You can walk out now if you want, but like it or not, you're going to have to face me. And I refuse to be fed by a woman who won't even answer a simple question."

"Watch your tongue, Mr. Baird, or you may be left to your own resources. Just see where that leaves you."

"I daresay I could find at least one person out there who would take care of me for a price."

"And how do you figure you'd go and find that person?"

"That's a good point." He almost smiled. "But tell me this: where were you planning to go when you leave here?" Her eyes turned hard before she looked away. "And that brings us to another unanswered question. What were you doing at Brierley, and what made you so anxious to leave?" Anya sighed but hesitated still. "Why don't you just talk to me and get it over with?"

"Fine," she nearly snarled. "My parents died when I was a child, and I was sent to Brierley. I remember very little of my life before that. Satisfied?"

"No. I want to know why you're so defensive about—"

"Ooh," Anya interrupted, infuriated and frustrated, "you're as arrogant as your father." To Anya, it was something of a compliment. James MacBrier's arrogance had always been endearing as far as she had ever seen. But it was immediately evident that Gavin not only misinterpreted the comment, it was not the right thing to say.

"My father?" He gave a bitter laugh. "And what would you know about my father?"

Anya huffily refolded a towel that had fallen to the floor. "It's no secret."

"Ah," his voice filled with enlightenment, "you've been listening to Brierley gossip."

Anya lifted her chin, deciding she could be equally as bold and obnoxious as her patient. "Is it gossip?"

"What you're really asking is, am I the Earl's son? And the answer is *no*. I am not."

Anya's eyes moved unobtrusively to the birthmark. She felt certain there was something he wasn't admitting to.

"Disappointed?" he asked. "My mother was a servant girl, and my father was a livery boy who deserted her when she got pregnant." He paused and willed his voice to remain calm. "What else does the gossip say about me?" Anya hesitated. "Come on, Miss Ross. Let's get past the formalities and get it over with."

Anya could see his strength draining away, but she felt certain he would refuse to rest until she answered his questions to some degree. "All right," she said. "If you'll promise to stop wasting your strength on petty issues, I will tell you." Gavin nodded, and she took a deep breath. "There has always been talk of a boy born and raised in the forest tower with his unwed mother." She saw his eyes turn down, and a muscle in his cheek twitched. "They say he is the Earl's son; that the Earl had a relationship with this woman, and—"

"All of it's true," he interrupted, "except that the relationship my mother shared with the Earl was platonic."

"But—" Anya began to say, but he broke in again.

"It doesn't matter what you heard or how it may appear, Miss Ross. I don't know who my father is, but I know who he isn't."

Anya was tempted to openly question the birthmark, but his adamance made it clear that pressing the issue further would likely make him angry. He was obviously sensitive about the subject.

"And what else do they say?" he asked calmly, but with hard eyes.

Anya wondered whether or not she should tell him. But under the circumstances, it was likely he already knew. "They say that you killed him, and . . ." Anya stopped when his face went even whiter than his already ghostly pallor. "You didn't know," she added softly, with regret.

Gavin didn't know what to say. How was he supposed to know? He hadn't even been in the highlands for most of the last decade, and his only contact with Brierley was a close-lipped old man who claimed it was better that he remain ignorant of senseless gossip. But was it ignorance that had set him up to be shot and left for dead?

He couldn't believe it. He thought of all James MacBrier had done for him. Gavin respected him. And now he realized that all these years he'd been dubbed the Earl's murderer. But he should have guessed. Didn't he leave Brierley right after it happened? Hadn't he carried away possessions the Earl had said others would want?

"I'm sorry," Anya whispered, seeing unmasked pain come into his eyes.

Gavin looked up, startled. Her guard was down. Her eyes were soft with compassion. "I practically forced it out of you, didn't I?"

"I didn't realize I was the bearer of bad tidings."

"Neither did I." He chuckled dryly.

"You'd do well to get some rest."

Gavin nodded and watched her walk out with a pile of folded linens. He relaxed against the pillows, and a familiar turmoil rose inside of him. It had always been this way. No matter the years or his efforts, Brierley always came back to haunt him. And just when he'd decided to confront it head on and be free of it forever, it had nearly cost him his life. And now this. If it was rumored that he'd killed the Earl, would he ever be completely free of the taint of Brierley?

Wearily he closed his eyes in an effort to be free of thoughts he could do nothing about. He realized that he had no choice but to let go of the Earl's request to have the safe opened in his presence. It was not worth dying for. He wondered briefly if they had already opened it somehow. Perhaps they had the other ring. Una had seemed to know what the safe contained, though Margaret had seemed ignorant. Still, there was something in their attitude that made Gavin certain they didn't want that safe opened—with or without him present.

Gavin opened his eyes to find Anya sitting on the edge of the bed. "I need to change the dressings," she said quietly, and he nodded. He found it enjoyable to observe her as she attended to his shoulder. He wasn't terribly fond of the situation he was in, but he decided it could be worse. She could look like Malvina. If nothing else, it was a pleasure to watch her.

When Anya poured disinfectant into the wound, Gavin stiffened and cursed under his breath. "Is that necessary?" he demanded when he finally relaxed.

"Cleansing wounds is painful, Mr. Baird. But once they are cleaned and treated, the healing can begin. Better that than dying of gangrene."

"I must admit," he said more softly, "I was grateful to find my leg still there."

"Well, I likely would have let you die before I'd have cut it off myself." She smiled, hoping he would know she wasn't completely serious.

Impulsively, Gavin reached up a weak hand to touch her face. She paused and looked at him in question. "Thank you, Anya," he said gently. "I owe you my life."

"It was my pleasure, actually," she replied, and proceeded to dress the wound.

"Your pleasure to save my life, or to leave Brierley?"

"Do you ever run out of questions?" she asked, moving down the bed to push the sheet aside just enough to expose his bandaged thigh.

"Sorry," he chuckled. "I suppose I've had a . . . bad week."

"Indeed." She smiled, then poured disinfectant into the wound.

Gavin clenched his teeth and cursed again. "What are you doing down there, woman? The shoulder didn't hurt that bad."

"Your shoulder didn't have a hole clean through it. Now, stop being such a baby and hold still."

Gavin held his breath until the sting began to ease. "You didn't answer my question," he said while she bandaged it.

"What question was that?"

"Was it a pleasure to save my life, or to leave Brierley?"

"Both, actually," she stated and finished her task. "You'd better rest now. Is there anything else I can get you before I go to bed?"

"No, thank you," he said, feeling as if he was lying when he added, "I'm fine."

Anya adjusted his pillows so he could lie back farther, then she doused the lamp and left him alone. Gavin had never felt so completely exhausted, but sleep eluded him as he listened to the evidence of Anya in the other room.

With the house in order, Anya changed for bed in the bathing room, then slipped quietly through the darkness into her bed by the fireplace. As tired as she was, she found it difficult to relax. The sound of rustling sheets let her know Gavin wasn't asleep, and she asked quietly, "Are you all right?"

Gavin wanted to tell her that if he was all right, he wouldn't be lying here, bound to this bed, completely dependent on a beautiful woman. "I'm fine," was all he said.

"Good night," she said in a voice that made him realize he hadn't dreamt he'd heard angels in his unconsciousness.

"Good night," he replied, and gradually the tension dissipated into mutual slumber.

Anya awoke with a gasp and realized Gavin was moaning. "Please, God," she prayed aloud, hurrying to his side, "not more fever." She was relieved to find his skin cool. But he made no response to her touch, and his moaning persisted. She shook him gently, but his nightmare continued. "Gavin." She took his face into her hands and shook it. Still he showed no response. He only seemed more distraught, and somehow afraid. "Gavin!" she nearly shouted, and he came awake with a breathy moan.

It took a moment for Gavin to bring his mind from the illusion of his dream to realize he was in his bed.

"Are you all right?" Anya whispered through the darkness, and he was startled by how close she was.

"I was . . . dreaming," he said, conscious of the warmth of her hands against his face. He was surprised at their roughness, which didn't coincide with her gentle touch.

"Yes, I know," she said in that angelic voice. "Do you want to talk about it?"

"Not especially," he answered, and she began to draw away. Instinctively he took hold of her arm, and she became still. "But . . . maybe I should," he added, if only to keep her near. She waited patiently for him to begin, but he became aware of something unusual near his head. Turning to investigate, Gavin felt her hair brush over his face. It smelled clean and sweet, and he nuzzled closer, trying to recall the last time he'd had a woman so near. He honestly couldn't remember.

"Gavin," she said, "are you . . ."

"I'm fine," he said, "I just . . . well, it was like the night I was shot. I could feel myself falling into the ravine, over and over. That's all, really."

"It must have been terrifying." Her voice was sweet with compassion. He could think of nothing else to say. "Will you be all right now?"

He wanted to tell her no. He wanted her to stay close by so he could absorb the comfort she so freely offered. "Yes, of course," he said, and hesitantly let her go.

Anya crawled back into her bed on the floor, but sleep evaded her far into the night. She wondered endlessly why their brief encounter in the dark left her feeling changed somehow. It might have been a comfort to know that she was not wondering alone.

Gavin's second chance at life fell into a routine that he wasn't terribly fond of. He hated the heaviness in his limbs that made it difficult to even think about moving, and the pain didn't help. But worse, he hated his total dependency on another human being. He couldn't remember a time when he had been this dependent on his own mother. Anya assured him that she was quite accustomed to doing everything he needed, and for the most part she didn't seem to mind. But he was mortified, and her assurance that she had done worse in her day was not a comfort.

Altogether, it was not an enjoyable situation. But Gavin's mother had taught him to look for silver linings in the clouds. In this case, they weren't difficult to find. It truth, it wasn't bad being coddled by a pretty woman. He often wondered over this Anya. Where had she come from, and why had she been willing to leave everything behind to be here with him? He thought of his encounter with Lady MacBrier, and wondered how she treated her servants—one in particular. If he thought too hard about the MacBriers and what had happened when he'd attempted to make a deal with them, he became downright depressed. Instead, he concentrated on Anya. She managed to keep busy, and it was only when she fed him that they shared any opportunity for conversation. There was so much he wanted to ask her, but he quickly realized he had overdone it that first day, and he held back for the time being, hoping she would learn to trust him. He often caught glimpses of the pain in her eyes, and he nearly ached to know its source. Instinctively he wanted to take that pain away. Perhaps it was the sense of fairness he'd been raised with that made him want to somehow repay her for all she'd done for him. But that would never happen if she didn't learn to trust him, and he reminded himself not to get overzealous.

Gavin's curiosity left him frustrated as she flitted in and out of the room like a mother hen without one moment to waste. He hated that dreadful uniform she wore, and he wondered what she'd look like in something like a blue day dress. Or perhaps with a tartan plaid wrapped about her shoulders and her hair falling down her back. It was her hair that bothered him most, simply because he'd never seen it. He suspected it was blonde when he saw an occasional wisp that escaped from beneath the scarf she wore tightly around it. And he often thought of how it had felt against his face in the darkness. But his curiosity over her hair was overshadowed when he began to notice her hands. She never held them still long enough to give him a good look, but he could swear they were the hands of an old farm woman. They didn't match the rest of her, any more than her eyes did.

"I believe you're getting a little color to your face," she announced one morning as she sat to feed him breakfast.

"How can you even see it, when I'm long overdue for a good shaving?"

"All in good time," she replied. "I can't do everything at once."

"And you'll notice I've been a good boy. I've not asked you a single question for days."

"Yes," she smiled and gave him a spoonful of brose, "I had noticed it was rather peaceful."

"Am I still as arrogant as the Earl?" he asked.

"Which one?" she retorted, and he could have sworn that for a moment the pain in her eyes deepened.

"I believe when you brought it up before, you were referring to James MacBrier."

"I meant it as a compliment, really." She gave a slight smile. "Actually, I was rather fond of him."

"You knew him?" Gavin leaned forward a little.

Anya was surprised by his enthusiasm. "Yes, although I was very young when he died. Brierley has not been the same since."

"I can believe that." He dutifully swallowed the offered brose and asked, "How old were you when you came to Brierley?"

Anya looked at him warily, but decided there was no reason to take offense. "I was nine," she answered. "The Earl died two years later."

"Why Brierley?"

"Are we making up for lost time?" she asked tersely in reference to his rekindled curiosity.

Gavin ignored her. "Why were you sent to Brierley when your parents died?"

Anya consciously swallowed her emotion and managed a steady voice. "My last remaining relative was there." She cleared her throat. "Could we talk about something else, please?"

"Like what?" He leaned back on the pillows and folded his arms.

"Like you, for instance. Why did you live in the forest tower, and what made you decide to leave?" She smiled. "I can ask questions, too."

"So I see," Gavin said with an edge, figuring he deserved this. He had no desire to talk about such things, but he wondered if opening up about himself would help her trust him enough to do the same. And perhaps if she talked about the cause of her hardened eyes, she might be able to put it behind her. He felt certain her reasons for leaving Brierley had little to do with just wanting a change of scenery.

"As you already figured," he began, "I grew up in the forest tower of Brierley with my mother. I left when I was sixteen because she died, and it was made clear they were not going to take care of me the way they had my mother. I tried for some time before that to find work in the area, but it never lasted, because each of my employers somehow came upon bad luck as a result of my being there."

Anya hesitated with the spoon halfway between the bowl and his mouth. "You mean . . ."

He clarified. "Apparently they didn't want me to make it on my own, at least not anywhere on or near MacBrier land."

"By *they*, I assume you mean Lady MacBrier and that . . ." Anya hesitated, certain it wasn't proper to voice the words that came to her mind.

"And that witch who follows her around like a lap dog," he finished for her with a bitterness in his voice that she easily related to. "Yes, that's who I mean."

"But why did they care for your mother? If she was only a servant girl, why didn't they just send her packing?"

"That's a question I often asked myself growing up. From what I have gathered, the Earl came to care for my mother after his second marriage turned sour." Gavin saw suspicion come into her eyes, however subtle. "I know what you're thinking, but it's not true. I overheard them talking, and—"

"Who?"

"My mother and the Earl." Gavin didn't like this conversation. He'd never spoken so openly about this with anyone. But instinctively he trusted her. "They had no idea I was listening, Anya, and it was evident from the conversation that I was not the Earl's son. Later, he told me himself that they had been good friends. It was very evident that their relationship had been platonic."

Anya glanced down, embarrassed by his boldness. While she scraped the last spoonful of brose from the bowl, she asked quietly, "Then why were you kept hidden at Brierley?"

"Because Lady MacBrier thought it was true, and Una wanted us where she could keep an eye on us. She promised that my mother would be provided for in return for keeping quiet. My mother didn't break that promise until the day before she died, when she sent me to get the Earl."

"You mean . . . he didn't know?" she asked breathlessly.

Gavin shook his head. "He was furious. My mother told him the circumstances and made him promise that I would be provided for."

"And did he?"

"He gave me this house." Gavin looked around with a flicker of yearning in his eyes, then he turned directly to Anya. "And he gave me a box of jewels that he said would be ample if I used them wisely. I was astounded to learn the value of some of them, but I only sold the less valuable ones and made investments. The rest of them are put safely away. He was a kind and generous man, and one of my biggest regrets is not having the opportunity to know him longer." Gavin looked down and swallowed the emotion. "He was killed that very night."

Anya didn't realize there were tears in her eyes until she blinked and they splashed onto her face. The story didn't completely make sense, but the tragedy of it was evident. She felt sad for the Earl and his tragic death. And she felt sad for Gavin. She wondered why his mother had lied to him. Was it possible that she and the Earl had vowed to keep it a secret and never to speak of it, even between themselves? Or perhaps . . . Yes, it made sense. It was well known that the Earl was a heavy drinker. Perhaps he just didn't remember, and Gavin's mother had kept her silence to avoid any problems.

But now it didn't matter. Gavin's life had been made better by the Earl's hand. And with the Earl dead, there was no point questioning something that she knew was painful for Gavin. His eyes made that evident. She wished she could tell him just how deeply his confessions affected her, and how grateful she was to be here, sharing these few weeks of her life with him. They had something very special in common. They both loved James MacBrier and missed him terribly.

Gavin heard Anya sniffle, and looked up to see her wiping her face with the corner of her apron. He wanted to question her emotion, certain his story wasn't worth crying over. But he had seen how easily her defenses came up, and he didn't want to embarrass her. He pretended to look the other way until she got control of her silent tears, then he said, "Open the top middle drawer in the bureau. There's something I want you to see."

Anya stood and did as he asked.

"It's near the back, at the right; an old piece of paper."

"This?" she asked, holding it up.

"Yes," he said, then added, "Read it."

Anya fought to keep her emotion from rising again as she read the simple lines of poetry, signed by James MacBrier. She blinked back the tears and looked at Gavin in question.

"My mother died with that in her hand," he stated. "That was how the Earl felt about her. It was as if he loved her so much, he was determined to do nothing to bring pain into her life."

Anya quietly returned the paper to its resting place and closed the drawer. She couldn't help feeling the poignancy of what he was telling her. But still, it made no sense in light of other facts. Not knowing how to explain her confusion, she said nothing.

"Now it's your turn," he insisted.

"What?" she asked, caught off guard.

"Now you know why I was at Brierley, and why I left. It's your turn."

"I already told you why I was there."

"Yes, but you didn't tell me who this relative was that made it possible for you to live such a life of leisure at Brierley."

His sarcasm was evident, but Anya felt certain he had no idea how close to the truth his implications were. If the Earl had survived, her life would have been much different.

When she said nothing, he persisted, "And you didn't tell me why you left."

"I left to save your life, Mr. Baird."

"I'm not complaining, but I suspect there was more to it than that."

"You don't know what you're talking about," she insisted, bending to remove the breakfast tray.

"That's true. I don't. That's why I have to ask so many questions."

"Don't you have anything better than me to occupy your mind with? Can't you find something else to think about or—"

Anya gasped when he took hold of her arm. "No, I don't," he insisted, sounding almost angry. "Because if I don't think about you, Anya, I have to think about the fact that the MacBriers want me dead. I can hardly close my eyes without hearing that gun go off and feeling the pain. If I'm not thinking about you, I find my mind wandering to the hours it took me to get from that ravine into the stable where you found me. I have to wonder why they hate me so badly, and why God made it possible for me to survive. My whole life has been a string of unanswered questions, Anya. And now, when I thought I could put it behind me, I have nothing but more unanswered questions."

Gavin finished his little speech and realized the fear showing in her eyes had intensified. He relaxed his grip, and she took an abrupt step backward. He was about to apologize when she snapped, "And so you taunt me with questions about myself?"

Gavin reminded himself to keep this light. "I'm curious—and I'm bored. Is there a problem with that?"

"Well, I've got work to do. I haven't got time for idle chatter," she huffed and went to the kitchen, already dreading having to feed him lunch.

Gavin hit a fist against the bed and sighed in exasperation. Is that what she considered the confessions of his life—idle chatter? He didn't understand how the most caring, compassionate woman he had ever known could be so infuriatingly rude. But he wasn't going to stand for it.

Chapter Five
healing

Anya had barely finished eating her lunch when Gavin called from the bedroom, "I'm starving in here. You're neglecting me."

A few minutes later she appeared with his lunch, and he grinned. "It worked. I thought it would make you ignore me until supper."

"It was tempting," she retorted, but Gavin could see a touch of barely concealed humor in her eyes. While he watched her with growing interest, he wondered what was happening to him. There was no denying that he had become practically obsessed with her. He could rationalize it away as an excuse to ease his boredom, but instinctively Gavin knew his interest in Anya had more to it than that.

Gavin said nothing as Anya fed him, but his eyes remained fixed on her face until she nearly trembled from the intensity of his gaze. "Well, don't just sit there and stare at me," she finally said.

Gavin chuckled. "You get angry because I talk too much. Now I don't talk enough. What does a man have to do to make you happy, Miss Ross?"

"Just eat this and get some strength back so you can feed yourself."

"No one will be happier than I when that day comes, I can assure you."

"I don't know," she smiled wryly. "I daresay my sentiments would be close to it."

Gavin chuckled again. "So," he said, "tell me about this relative of yours at Brierley. Man or woman? Did they treat you well, or—"

"Mr. Baird," she interrupted, "did it ever occur to you that perhaps there is simply nothing worth mentioning about my life or my circumstances? I have worked as a maid for the MacBriers for what seems a hundred years. I'm afraid I don't have the colorful background that you do."

"Colorful?" He chuckled dubiously. "If my life has been colorful, I will take black and white, thank you very much. What my life has been is lonely, and sometimes very bitter."

Anya sighed, feeling empathy for his words. "Brierley seems to have a way of doing that to people."

"And I thought it was just me," he said, not completely serious.

"Don't flatter yourself."

"Tell me about it, Anya."

"You are the most obnoxiously curious person I have ever met, Mr. Baird."

"That's what my mother used to say," he laughed.

"And did your mother tell you that curiosity killed the cat?"

"Actually, she told me that if I wanted to know something, I had to ask."

"And did she always answer you?"

"No."

"I think I like your mother."

"I always did." He smiled, and Anya took the tray to the kitchen.

With the house in order, Anya helped Gavin wash up. She remained quiet, and was grateful that he did as well. When he was relatively clean, Anya complied with his request for a shave. She was glad she'd done this before so she could approach it with a degree of confidence. With that finished, she decided it hadn't been so bad after all. Impulsively she offered, "Would you like me to wash your hair for you?"

"That would be fine," Gavin replied, trying not to sound as enthused as he felt. He enjoyed having her play in the lather on his head. Watching her face, he felt an urge for mischief.

It startled her when he took hold of her wrist, and she was surprised by the strength in his grip. She looked at him in question, and for a moment she felt afraid. There was something in his eyes that reminded her of the way Cedric used to look at her, and she tried to twist out of his grasp.

Anya's reaction surprised Gavin. The fear in her eyes didn't make sense until he recalled their first encounter in the forest tower. Trying to perceive where the fear was coming from, he mustered what little strength he had to hold on to her, saying as gently as he could, "It's all right, Anya. I'm not strong enough to hurt you. And I wouldn't even if I were."

"I know," she said, but her eyes disagreed.

Attempting to lighten the mood, Gavin carried out his original intention and pushed her lathered hand to the side of her face, startling her into an embarrassed laugh. "You're a scoundrel, Gavin Baird," she giggled, and lightly slapped his face with the other lathered hand.

Gavin laughed. "And you're more beautiful than ever when you laugh." He wiped the suds from her face. "Though I think I prefer you without this."

Anya realized he'd given her a compliment that couldn't possibly be misconstrued as mocking. She met his eyes and briefly lost all sense of time. Gavin wiped his hand on the towel draped over his shoulder, then reached up to touch her face again. "So soft," he whispered, and for a moment Anya just closed her eyes, allowing herself to become lost in a fantasy that she knew could never be. She felt his thumb move over her lips, as if to test them, and the reality came back to her.

"You're dripping all over the bed, my lord," she said lightly and began to rinse his hair, holding his head above the basin. He smiled warmly at her, but she reminded herself this was only temporary. When Gavin Baird got up out of his bed and walked, he would go back to whatever life he had enjoyed before this had happened. And she would move on. She felt certain he would be willing to help her find a position elsewhere, and she could leave Brierley behind forever. Even if she chose to indulge in any romantic fantasy that included Gavin Baird, it crashed into reality with the memory of Cedric MacBrier. He had ruined her, and she felt certain that if Gavin knew the truth, he would not be so apt to indulge her with his intimate glances and kind words.

As always, Anya forced her mind to the present and pushed all else away. She fluffed his hair with a towel until it was almost dry, then she combed it through.

"Where did you get these beautiful curls?" she asked lightly, reminded of James MacBrier.

"I can't tell you," he replied, then he motioned toward the wardrobe. "Hand me some breeches, woman."

"You're not strong enough to get out of that bed," she insisted.

"No," he admitted, "but I'm strong enough to wear some breeches, and I'm tired of hiding beneath a sheet."

Anya sighed and looked through the wardrobe until she found a pair of black breeches that looked well-worn and comfortable. She tossed them to Gavin. "Do you want me to help you?"

"Not particularly," he admitted, "but I don't think I have much choice."

"Thank you," he said once he was situated. She noticed he looked sleepy.

"I'm going to take a bath while you get some rest," she told him.

Gavin nodded and drifted easily to sleep. He awoke to the sound of water being poured into the bathtub. The door between the bedroom and bathing room was left ajar. He couldn't see anything, but he could hear enough to imagine Anya letting her hair down to lather it the way she had his. Feeling habitually bored, Gavin opted for a little conversation. "Anya?"

It took her a moment to reply. "What?"

"Is your hair still wrapped up in one of those ridiculous scarves?" he asked.

"Do you ever run out of questions?" she asked, but didn't sound irritated as she often did.

"Never. Tell me about your hair."

"It's in the water with the rest of me. I thought you were tired."

"I was. I took a nap. Now I have the urge to get up and run around the house a few times. Want to join me?"

"When you get up, we will *walk* around the house. In the meantime, I'm bathing."

Gavin left her to her luxury while he fantasized about her walking into the room, her wet hair hanging down her back. It was not a surprise, but definitely a disappointment when she finally emerged in one of those dreadful uniforms. Her hair was concealed as usual.

"Funny," he said, "you don't look any cleaner."

"Neither do you," she retorted. "Roll onto your chest, and I'll see if I can rub some of the stiffness out of your back muscles before I cook supper."

"Yes, my lady," he grinned.

Anya wanted to apologize for the roughness of her hands, but she had no desire to open the subject. He didn't seem to mind, so she said nothing. She tried to detach herself from this desire she felt to be close to Gavin by recalling the many times she had done this task for others and felt nothing. Never had she found caring for another human being so personally fulfilling.

When Anya had repeatedly massaged every muscle in his back and shoulders, taking care to avoid the wound, she announced, "I think that's about all you're going to get out of me for one day, Mr. Baird."

"You do work hard for me," he said softly. He looked so relaxed that she felt certain he was almost asleep.

"All for a good cause," she teased, and rose to leave. Before she could grasp his intention, Gavin rolled onto his side and caught hold of her arm, forcing her to sit back down. Anya saw the color drain from his face, and he breathed as if he'd just run a race. But he managed to keep her from moving. Anya tried not to feel panicked, but his male aggression encouraged memories of Cedric's barbaric advances, and she winced slightly.

"What's the matter?" he asked gently. Anya only shook her head, her eyes wide with some kind of fear. "You know I don't have the strength to keep you here. You can go if you want, but I was hoping we could talk."

"We can talk without being quite so close, Mr. Baird," she replied with a barely discernible quiver in her voice.

"Don't you ever get lonely, Anya?" he asked. "Don't you ever just want to be close to someone?"

"No," she insisted. Her experiences with any kind of closeness had always ended in pain. Everyone she had ever cared for with any depth had either left her or inflicted abuse.

Gavin searched her eyes and wondered freshly over the pain etched in them. Instinctively wanting to ease it, he set a hand to her face, but drew it back quickly when she groaned and recoiled as if his touch had burned her. At first he felt hurt. He wanted to ask her if he was so repulsive, or if she simply didn't like him. But briefly contemplating all he knew, he felt a puzzle vaguely falling together in his mind.

"Anya," he whispered, but she made no response. "Look at me," he insisted, and she turned quickly, dutifully, as if she feared he might punish her if she didn't. The reaction only deepened his theory as he asked, "Anya, has someone hurt you?"

For a moment her eyes looked misty and afraid, then they turned hard as she flippantly retorted, "I have no idea what you're talking about."

Gavin contemplated the situation and felt certain that drilling her with questions on such a subject would accomplish nothing. Instead, he approached the matter from a different angle. "Have you ever been kissed, Anya?" he asked.

"Yes, I have," she insisted, "and it was brash and revolting."

She attempted to gather her wits before she made a fool of herself any further. She couldn't begin to make any sense of the turmoil of emotions going on inside her. How could she so thoughtlessly put Gavin's apparently genuine affection into the same category as Cedric MacBrier's brutish behavior? Instinctively she trusted Gavin, and she knew she wasn't being fair. But Gavin put it all into perspective when he set a hand on her arm and responded to her cynical statement. "Then so was the man who kissed you."

Anya turned to meet his eyes and found so much she wanted to say. But before any words could form, he added, "Let me put it this way, Anya. Have you ever been kissed by a gentleman?"

"What are you implying, Mr. Baird?" She went to the wardrobe to find him a shirt, deciding she'd had enough of constantly viewing him without one.

"I'm not implying anything," he said, finding this amusing. "I simply asked you a question."

She tossed him the shirt, and he smiled as if he sensed her reasons for giving it to him. "You speak to me of kissing, then you try to tell me you're not implying something. If you're trying to convince me that *you* are a gentleman, then why do you—"

"Actually, I *am* a gentleman, Miss Ross, and if you'd come back over here, I'd prove it to you."

Anya only had to glance at his face to be certain they were still talking about kissing. It seemed so preposterous that she wanted to laugh. Instead, her eyes were drawn to his while she wondered what it might be like. She helped him put his left arm into the shirt sleeve, and her thoughts brought on a quiver somewhere in her stomach. She was trying to talk herself out of this desire she had to take him up on it when a pounding at the side door made her heart race.

Gavin chuckled at the way she started. "That's Robbie," he said to calm her obvious fear.

"How do you know it's not one of Lady MacBrier's thugs, wanting to do in the other leg?"

"Nobody knocks like Robbie," he said.

A moment later they heard the old man call, "Are ye in there, lass?"

Anya took a deep breath and went to the door, hoping she didn't appear as flushed as she felt. Robbie laughed and took her shoulders into his hands.

"Ye're lookin' fine, lass. Gettin' away from that hoose is doin' well for ye, Ah ken."

"I must admit, it's true," she said. "Come in. Would you like some coffee, or—"

"Nah," he pushed a hand through the air. "Ah just came tae see how ye was gettin' on. And how's th' lad?"

"Go see for yourself." She smiled and motioned him toward the bedroom.

Robbie laughed while Anya hovered in the doorway, watching the reunion of lifelong friends. "Ah telt th' lass ye were stubborn enough tae stay alive."

"If only to cause you trouble, old man," Gavin laughed. They shook hands, and Robbie tousled Gavin's hair as if he were just a boy.

"Ye're lookin' a wee bit better than th' last time Ah saw ye." Robbie winked toward Anya. "Is he givin' ye any trouble, lass?" he teased.

"None that I can't handle," she replied, her eyes sparkling.

Gavin smiled at her. "Who is giving who trouble? The woman feeds me nothing but brose and broth, and expects me to get my strength back."

"All in good time, Mr. Baird." She folded her arms and smirked at him. "You'd best watch your tongue, or I'll be watering it down."

"'Twould serve ye right, lad," Robbie bellowed. "Ye'd do well tae treat this 'un like a queen."

"That's likely good advice, my friend," Gavin said as if she weren't there, though his eyes didn't leave her for a moment. "With any luck, I'll be stuck in this bed forever, and she won't be able to leave."

Anya looked down at her bare toes where they peeked out from beneath her hem against the cool wood floor.

Silence hung tensely in the air for a few moments. For the sake of conversation, Gavin asked, "So, how is Brierley these days?"

Robbie laughed and slapped his leg. "It's settlin' a little now, lad. But Ah must say ye had the lady mighty stirred up there by th' way she went intae a fit o' nerves."

Anya smiled and caught Gavin doing the same. It was all amusing until Robbie added, "An' if that weren't enough, the lady nearly rose th' roof when she found th' lass here missin'."

Anya was caught so off guard she didn't have time to think of acting innocent. Her eyes widened with guilt, only to find Gavin staring at her as if he'd caught her in an act of theft.

"Ah dinna think Ah've ever seen her s' fit tae be tied since th' day they buried th' Earl with that ring still on his finger."

Robbie chuckled and rambled on, while Gavin's eyes seemed to bore into every part of Anya's soul in search of what she was trying to hide. Unable to bear it any longer, Anya returned to the kitchen to heat some soup. Robbie finally emerged from the bedroom, declining her invitation to stay for supper. He told her he had found Gavin's horse and had left it in the little stable. After reminding her to see that it was cared for, he made certain all was well and she had what she needed. Then he left as quickly as he'd come, and Anya locked the door behind him. Her first thought was dread at having to feed Gavin his supper, but before she had a chance to even turn around, his voice boomed from the other room.

"Anya!" he called. She contemplated ignoring him, but somehow she knew there would be no peace. Facts be faced, this was his home, and she was eating his food. And he'd been right when he'd said she had nowhere else to go, at least not yet. And even if she did, she couldn't desert him. He needed her.

"Yes?" she asked quietly, coming to stand in the doorway.

"Maybe you could explain that to me," he said casually.

"Explain what?" she asked, perfectly innocent.

"All right, Anya. We'll do this the hard way. First of all, you come and sit down—right here." He pointed to the edge of the bed next to him.

"And if I don't?" she defied him. "Will you chase me down and beat me?"

"I may be bedridden, but I can certainly make your life miserable. Now sit, or you can go back to Brierley this minute."

Anya wanted to tell him he couldn't manage without her, but she could only think of how going back terrified her. She felt certain he knew that, and she obediently sat down, folding her hands in her lap.

"I have given you most of my life history," Gavin began firmly. "Fair is fair. Now I've got a question for you."

"And what might that be?" she asked nonchalantly.

Gavin leaned back and folded his arms over his chest. "Why do you suppose Lady MacBrier was so upset over losing a scullery maid?"

"I haven't a clue," she said lightly, but Gavin knew by her eyes that she was lying. "Perhaps it's difficult to find help these days for—"

"Anya," he mustered all the strength he had and took hold of her arm, forcing her to face him, "you are keeping something from me, and you're hurting yourself by doing it. I want to know what it is." Anya said nothing, and he leaned toward her. "What do you know about them that made Margaret MacBrier so unwilling to let you go?"

Anya's eyes widened. She'd never looked at it that way before, but in a sense, it was true.

"That's how they work, you know." His voice lowered to a hoarse whisper. "I used to wonder why they didn't just send my mother and me away, but I believe Una prefers to keep those who might threaten her darling Margaret right under her thumb, where she knows exactly what they're up to." He paused, but still she said nothing. "Tell me, Anya."

"What business is it of yours?" she insisted.

"I care, Anya," he said almost angrily. "Tell me, is there anyone else in your life who can say the same?"

She was going to tell him about Robbie and Mrs. MacGregor, but she had a feeling he would disregard the surface relationships she had found there. Part of her wanted to believe he cared, that he could help her. But the thought of facing what her years at Brierley had done to her seemed more than she could bear.

"Why are you doing this to me? Can't you see I'm trying to put all of that behind me?"

"You're not putting it behind you," he retorted. "You're hiding from it."

Suddenly terrified, Anya rushed from the room, ignoring the way Gavin called after her.

"Don't you walk out on me!" he shouted, but he only heard the side door open and slam shut. "Blast!" he muttered and drove a fist into the bed. His anger toward Anya quickly faded as he wondered how he could be so stupid. She would never come to trust him if he didn't learn to be a lot more gentle and a little less arrogant. When she didn't return for quite some time, he began to wonder if she would have actually walked out on him for good. Wondering where she would go if she did, Gavin turned his mind to prayer on her behalf. He needed her, and whether she believed it or not, he felt sure she needed him, too.

Anya wandered into the little stable, telling herself she needed to check on Gavin's horse. It was a good excuse to escape the little house that suddenly seemed to suffocate her. But was it the house? Or was it Gavin? She groaned at the thought and gently patted the stallion, whispering kind words that soothed her own nerves. Noting that Robbie had already fed and watered the horse, Anya knew there was no good reason to be out here. She felt guilty to think how she'd run out on Gavin, when she knew instinctively that his intentions were noble. He was arrogant and brash at times, but she couldn't deny the kindness he'd shown her. She thought of the stories he'd told her of his own past, and felt sure he would understand the things she had suffered. She *wanted* to unburden herself, but it all seemed so humiliating to even think about. Not to mention the pain. But then, Gavin had let her know that such pain was not unfamiliar to him. She wondered why she felt such a closeness to him, when in many ways she felt they hardly knew each other. The answer was easy: Brierley. It bound them together in more ways than he realized. Didn't that make them the ideal friends? Wasn't that what she needed—a friend? Of course she knew that it could be no more than that—not in the long run. But perhaps he was the right person at the right time to help her cross her own barriers and face up to the truth of her past.

While Anya's thoughts whirled in turmoil, she noticed a saddle and saddlebags that had not been here when she'd investigated the stable before. They must have been on the horse when Robbie found it. Looking more closely, she felt a sudden chill at the spattering of blood on the fine leather. Gavin must have been on the horse when he was shot, she concluded. She found traces of blood on the saddle-bags as well, and felt something tear at her. With determination she picked them up, shut the stable up tightly, and returned to the house. Whatever came of this, she knew that Gavin needed her. And if she admitted to the truth, she felt certain she needed him, too.

Gavin sighed audibly when he heard the side door. He looked up a moment later to see Anya standing close by. Their eyes met as she tossed his saddle bags onto the bed. He glanced at them, then back at her, wondering what to say.

"Robbie found your horse. I just checked on him. He seems to be doing well."

"Thank you," he stated.

"There's blood on the bags," she mentioned, "and the saddle, too." He said nothing so she added, "I didn't realize you were riding when it happened."

"I was trying to mount," he stated. Anya squeezed her eyes shut briefly as a vivid mental picture assaulted her.

Gavin watched her carefully, warmed by her unmasked emotion on his behalf. He searched for the right words, but all he could think to say was, "I'm glad you came back. I was afraid you had left me for good."

Anya looked up in alarm. "I hope you know I could never really do such a thing."

"I'm glad to hear that," he chuckled tensely, wanting to get past these barriers. "Though at moments I wouldn't blame you. After all, I can be as arrogant as the Earl."

"He was endearingly arrogant," she said in a way that didn't ring true to a scullery maid's appraisal of an earl.

"I'm sorry, Anya," he admitted so humbly that she almost felt like crying. "My intention was not to upset you."

"I know," she admitted, absently smoothing her apron. Fearing the direction this conversation was going, she quickly found a distraction, motioning toward the saddle bags. "Would you like me to empty them out and—"

"Please," he said gently. "I don't even remember what's in there."

In one side Anya found the typical contents of a man's saddle bag and put them away. As she opened the other side, her turbulent thoughts recalling Gavin's encounter at Brierley suddenly got the better of her. She wondered why she should be feeling such intense emotion on his behalf. Carefully she pulled out the tartan plaid and kilt she had seen him wearing that night at Brierley. The yards of blue-grey fabric tumbled over the bed. Their eyes met again, but neither of them spoke as she folded it carefully and put it away, along with the empty bags.

"Thank you," he said when the task was completed.

"You must be hungry," she said, feeling some relief to think of escaping his watchful eyes, if only for a few minutes. Recalling where their conversation had ended earlier, she felt all the more eager to put it off. "You can start eating more variety now, I think. I've got some soup simmering, and I'll just—"

"I don't want to eat right now," he said, and she stopped in the doorway, her back to him. "Anya," he added so gently she couldn't help but turn around, knowing her hope for escape was dashed. "Will you please come sit down and talk to me?"

"But supper is—"

"It'll wait," he insisted kindly, holding his breath, wondering if she would storm out of the room and leave his plea unanswered as she had done in the past. He almost felt afraid himself as she resolutely came to the edge of the bed and sat down. Noting the visible trembling of her hands, Gavin tried to comprehend the courage it was taking her to face what she knew he was going to ask.

"Anya," he said, touching her arm briefly, "you don't have to talk to me if you really don't want to, but . . ." She looked at him with something almost pleading in her eyes that gave him the will to go on. Instinctively he believed she wanted to be free of whatever caused her pain. "Do you want to know what I think?" he asked, but didn't wait for a response. "I think it's bottled up so tightly inside of you that it threatens to explode if you even think about it. It's like a festering wound that will never heal if you don't clean it out and treat it."

Gavin's voice softened further. "Anya, tell me," he nearly pleaded. He brushed the back of his fingers over her flushed cheek. "Tell me about it, Anya, and I'll throw it away. Give me your pain and I'll bury it, once and for all."

"Why are you doing this?" she asked, her fear turning to awe. Then she bit her lip to stop its trembling.

"You saved my life. I can only attempt to repay you."

Anya tried to come up with a reason—any reason—not to tell him. When she couldn't think of one, the words began to form in her head, and with them came the pain. Unwillingly she pressed a hand to her brow, as if it might hold back the pounding that threatened to explode.

Through the silence, Gavin's gentle voice helped urge Anya past her fears. "You once told me," he whispered, "that cleansing wounds is painful, but once they are cleaned and treated, the healing can begin."

"Did I say that?" she chuckled in an effort to choke back the tears, but it turned into more of a sob.

"I'm living proof," he replied.

Anya swallowed hard and bit her quivering lip, though she didn't dare open her eyes for fear of the tide breaking through. "Perhaps you're right," she had to admit. "It's just that . . . over the years I have begun to wonder what's right and what's wrong, and . . . in truth, Gavin, I fear you will think badly of me, or . . ."

"Pasts are not for judging the present," he said when she faltered. "I try to be living proof of that, too."

"You don't strike me as a man ashamed of his past," she said with a more steady voice.

"Not ashamed, perhaps, but . . ." Gavin felt the conversation turning back to him. He wanted to steer it toward Anya, but wondered if more confessions on his part would help her open up. "Anya," he shifted a little closer and absently moved a gentle hand over her arm, "I know how it feels. I've been there. I've felt those cold MacBrier eyes weighing me down at every turn, piercing me through like a dagger. I've been away ten years, and still I'm not free of it.

Sometimes when I think of what they did to me, to my mother; the way we lived . . . banished from the world as if we were lepers, and . . ." He lowered his voice, forcing his mind back to the present. "When are you going to stop trying to hide from me? Haven't you learned by now that you can trust me?" He lifted a hand to briefly touch her face. "Is there anyone better than I who could understand how you feel?" Her eyes widened at this. "Tell me, Anya."

Anya nodded to indicate she would, but the hand pressed to her brow made it evident she needed time. Gavin waited patiently, trying to stay close without threatening her narrow realm of security. He didn't know what he'd expected her to tell him, but the words that came out in those first broken phrases sent his heart into his throat, where it threatened to choke him.

"I was sent to . . . Brierley, to . . ." She gave a little sob, and tears leaked out beneath her closed eyelids. ". . . to be the ward of . . . my great-uncle." Anya put a hand to her heart and bit her lip again. "My mother was . . . born a . . . MacBrier." She heard Gavin suck in his breath, but she attempted to ignore it. "Her father was . . . a brother to . . . James MacBrier."

As the pain rushed up to hit Anya between the eyes, she knew she'd been struggling these many years to push away the truth of what she'd just admitted, as if it might make what she had become more bearable. But the sob that broke into her throat, escorting the pain into the open air, made it evident that it was true. The reality of who she was and what she'd been forced to become was more than she could bear.

Gavin watched in stunned silence as Anya nearly howled toward the ceiling, then fell apart in her pain. Even as he had tried to imagine what was hurting her, he would never have dreamed she was a MacBrier. But now, all the incongruities suddenly came together. She should have been adorning drawing rooms and showing off the latest fashions. And she was living her life hidden in servant's garb, working away the pain beneath the heel of a power that should have been hers.

When he finally came to his senses, Gavin found Anya doubled over in anguish, crying beyond control. He only touched her shoulder and she curled up close to him, holding one hand to her side and the other over her face. While she sobbed, Gavin wondered what explanation could possibly justify this madness. The more Anya cried, the more she clung to him, as if he were a lifeline. He couldn't comprehend what kind of loneliness she had been enduring to bring on such emotion when, in actuality, he had given her so little reason to trust him. But it was easy to put his arms around her. And the part of him that ached for the circumstances of his own life, marred by the same source as Anya's pain, brought forth emotion of his own. He remembered his mother telling him that the circumstances he'd been born into would make him strong. And despite the difficulties, he felt gratitude for all that was good in his life. He knew his mother had instilled in him the strength to face it. But the woman in his arms had faced far worse, and her tears were evidence that it had broken her.

When her sobbing quieted to an occasional sharp breath, Gavin lifted her chin, and she reluctantly faced him with swollen eyes. "I'm sorry." She wiped at her face. "I didn't intend . . . to . . ." Her words faded into a sniffle.

"It's all right," he whispered, and Anya recalled the analogy of cleansing wounds. She wondered why he was so good to her, so patient. She wished she could stay here in his arms forever. Not since before the Earl died had she felt such comfort.

Though Gavin hesitated to ask, he figured as long as she was unburdening herself, she might as well have it over with. She relaxed her head against his shoulder and he said gently, "What happened, Anya?"

Anya sniffled and sat up straight, absently smoothing her apron while Gavin leaned against the headboard and folded his arms.

"Being sent to the Earl," she began, "was the best thing that ever happened to me—at least at the time. I must confess I hardly noticed my parents' deaths, mostly because I hardly knew them in life. They were rarely at home, and I was left constantly in the care of tutors and governesses. Even when my parents were home, it seemed they hardly took notice of me." She gave a bitter little laugh and stared at the floor. "I remember my governess scolding me because I showed no reaction when I was informed of the accident. A few days later, I was sent to Brierley. I remember being afraid at first, but when I stepped out of the carriage, I felt as if I were part of a fairy tale. Brierley was like a castle to me."

Anya sighed, and a nostalgic smile touched her lips. "The Earl was kinder to me than anyone had ever been. He kept me close to him in many of his activities, and we came to share a special bond. I later learned that he had become a heavy drinker in the years after his first wife died, but they say he all but stopped when I came. Mrs. MacGregor told me those were the only happy years Brierley had seen since Lady Ishbelle died. And then . . ." She drew a sharp breath. "Then he was gone. I cried for days. He was the only person in my life who had ever truly loved me. I felt so afraid and alone, but I never dreamed . . ."

Gavin saw her lip tremble as she hesitated. She put a hand to her brow. He could see the pain rising again.

"What?" he urged. "Tell me, Anya."

"Soon after the funeral, Lady Margaret came to my room. Of course, Una was with her. They informed me that my parents had died with heavy debts that the Earl had paid off. Until that day, I had heard nothing about it. She told me it was time I began earning my keep. They took away most everything that was mine, and they put me in the darkest, dampest room in the house, and set me to the lowliest chores." Anya finally looked up at Gavin, and with an emotionless voice said, "And that is where I stayed until I found you in the stable."

Gavin reached up to touch her face, empathy filling his expression. "My savior," he whispered. Anya looked away, and he attempted to lighten the mood. "You're a regular Cinderella." She looked up at him in surprise, and he smiled. "Or should I call you CinderAnya?"

Anya looked at him and felt the world fall away. With a glance and a few simple words, Gavin could almost make her believe that he could do as he'd promised: just take her pain and throw it away.

Gavin watched her eyes turn deep and dreamy until the tension was so thick he could almost touch it. Impulsively he added with an embarrassed chuckle, "Don't look at me like that, Miss Ross. I'm no Prince Charming."

Anya realized her eyes were betraying her and she looked away, clearing her throat tensely.

"Imagine that," Gavin added lightly, "a woman like you associating with a man like me."

"What's that supposed to mean?" she demanded.

Gavin grinned. "Me, a man without a name, and a trail of nasty rumors behind him. And you, a MacBrier."

"I don't feel like a MacBrier," she retorted.

"It would seem much of the good blood died out with the Earl," he added.

Anya looked at him and smiled. She knew he didn't believe he was the Earl's son, but she chose to say anyway, "You're so much like him."

"Like who?" Gavin chuckled.

"The Earl. You remind me of him, in a way."

"I hardly knew the man."

"But your mother did," she replied with confidence, though she felt certain he didn't grasp her full implication.

Gavin smiled. "Thank you, Anya."

"All I did was get your shirt all wet," she said, wiping a hand over his damp shoulder as if she could dry it.

Gavin took her hand into his and felt an urge to kiss it. But an unexpected panic returned to her eyes, and she pulled away before he had a chance to wonder why.

"It's getting late. We'd best get some supper," she said, and hurried into the kitchen.

Chapter Six
hands

Gavin waited patiently for Anya to return and feed him. Wondering why she had become so skittish when he'd tried to hold her hand, he watched them very closely. After all she had confessed, why would she be so concerned about her hands?

When he nearly had his fill of the light supper she served him, he decided to just ask. "Why don't you want me to see your hands?"

Sure enough, her eyes filled with panic. "They're ugly," she stated, and continued to feed him.

Impulsively Gavin grabbed her wrist, and the spoon dropped to the tray. He expected her to jerk it free; they both knew he didn't have the strength to stop her from doing it. But she only gazed at him, something near to terror filling her eyes as he drew the delicate hand closer to get a better look. Her skin was so dry he could see every detail of its flaky white surface. There were signs of freshly dried blood in many of the knuckles where they had cracked.

"They say," he looked at her face and touched the back of her hand to his lips, "that a woman's hands tell the story of her life. What does a woman do to get hands like this?"

Anya jerked her hand free and came to her feet.

"Despite it all," he said, "you have a difficult time answering a simple question."

"The work I had to do was very hard on my hands," she stated, picking up the tray. "I had to wash them many times a day, and the soap and water dried them terribly."

"Thank you," he said, and she left the room. But he still didn't know why the condition of her hands was something painful for her to talk about.

Inevitably she returned to ask the daily question, "Is there anything you need before I go to bed?"

"Just one thing," he said and patted the bed beside him.

Anya knew what he wanted. In spite of the kindness he'd shown her, she found the prospect of facing this difficult. But her emotions were drained and her strength gone with them. She didn't have the will to argue, so she sat dutifully and gave him an almost defiant glare.

"Why are you ashamed of your hands, Anya?"

"I told you. They're ugly."

"Why?" he asked, and she looked away sharply.

"You're right. They tell the story of my life, and it's not very pleasant."

"But it's no fault of your own," he protested.

"Perhaps not, but they still represent what I have become."

Gavin took her hands into his. She looked at him warily and curled her fingers under. But she didn't try to pull away.

"Surely you've had something to put on them that helps," he said, rubbing his thumbs gently over the backs of her hands.

"I did at first," she said quietly. He looked into her eyes, sensing that she was admitting something difficult. "A few weeks after the Earl died, Una came to my room. She just walked in without even knocking . . . said she'd come to look at my hands. She told me I had lost my right to have the hands of a lady, and my hands were proof that I was not earning my keep. She took away my hand balm and told me if I wanted such luxuries, I'd have to earn them." Anya sighed. "Mrs. MacGregor kept some balm in the kitchen for me, but I had to be careful about using it, or . . ."

She didn't finish, but Gavin nodded to indicate he understood. The old woman was mad at the very least. And at the moment, Gavin felt the urge to track her down and strangle her. But looking at Anya, he knew, for her as well as himself, that nothing so brash would ever change the past. Still, he could change the future. And he could start now.

In a gesture of acceptance he lifted one of her hands to his face, holding the palm to his cheek while he watched her eyes. He saw her expression of panic before he felt the texture against his face that told him something wasn't right.

Anya saw the realization come into his eyes, and she attempted to jerk her hand free. The color drained from his face and his grip weakened, but he managed to hold onto her long enough to turn her palm to his view.

For a long, silent moment, Gavin just stared. He blinked several times to convince himself he wasn't seeing things. Then he gently touched the scarred welts carved into her flesh. Without speaking, he took her other hand and found the palms identical. The full picture became clear, and Gavin felt emotion burning behind his eyes. "And did Una give you these?" he asked, his voice cracking.

Anya squeezed her eyes shut and tears trickled out. She curled her hands into fists and put them against her face. "I . . ." she began with a gentle sob, "I . . . worked so hard. I did . . . everything . . . she told me to do, but . . . but it was never enough. She . . . she . . . called me horrible names . . . and she told me . . . it was time I . . . learned my station . . . in life." Anya swallowed hard and gained a degree of control. "She told me if I didn't hold my hands up, she would put the scars where they wouldn't be so easily hidden."

Gavin winced, and an empathetic groan came from his throat. With a distant voice, Anya finished, "Mrs. MacGregor helped me keep them wrapped. But I had to keep working, and they festered until I thought I would die." Again their eyes met. "So you see, it was made very clear to me exactly what my hands represent. I will never be free of what Brierley has done to me."

"Anya." Gavin took her hands into his and squeezed them. He looked at her deeply, and she saw moisture gather at the corners of his eyes. "My sweet Anya. Do you know what it means to me to hear someone else say those words?"

Anya was speechless. Words seemed trite to express what she was feeling. But his eyes told her he felt it, too—this unspoken bond that life's hardships had given them. Fresh tears came as she watched him press his lips into each of her palms, as if his kiss could take away the pain. She met his eyes and almost believed it had.

"Come here, Anya," he said, motioning for her to move closer.

"Why?" she asked skeptically when he gave her a wry smile.

"If I was any kind of a man, I'd take you in my arms and give you a hug. Heaven knows we could both use one. But frankly, I'm worn out. So you're going to have to come over here and help me out."

Anya didn't have to ask herself if she trusted him, and there was no question as to whether or not she wanted to be close to him. He'd already proven himself capable of filling a void in her life that had been empty since the death of James MacBrier. With little hesitation, she eased closer and settled her head onto his right shoulder as they shared an awkward embrace. Gavin put his arm around her and relaxed against the pillows propped behind him.

"That's better," he said, brushing his lips against her brow.

"Why are you so kind to me?" she asked quietly.

Gavin thought of a hundred ways to answer her question, but instead he turned it around. "Why did you save my life?"

Anya lifted her head to look at him. She could have told him it was only to escape Brierley, but she knew in her heart that from the moment she first saw him it was much more. She feared that the future could not hold them together, and she reminded herself that what they shared was something perhaps right for now, but not for always. Even so, it was only now that mattered. He was helping her cross the bridges between Brierley and her life ahead. They were two lonely people with a common enemy.

The questions remained unanswered, but Gavin took it upon himself to escort her one step closer to freedom from her past. With effort he lifted his aching left arm and pushed the scarf from her head. Anya gasped and attempted to stop him, but it was too late. Gavin watched in awe as a mass of golden hair fell in waves to hang far below her shoulders. He couldn't resist the urge to touch it, then he pushed his hand into it, exploring it, savoring it, while Anya kept her face timidly against his shoulder.

"And you've been hiding this for ten years?" he asked with a huskiness in his voice.

Without looking at him she said sadly, "Una told me if I didn't keep it out of the way, she'd have it cut off."

"The old witch," Gavin muttered, but his tone made her laugh as she looked up at him.

In that moment, it all came back to him. The expression, the eyes, the hair. Together they made the memory clear. A grin spread over his face as he exclaimed, "It was you!" Anya's eyes filled with question and he clarified, "You were just a child. I found you in the forest and carried you back to the stables."

Anya smiled. "I remember. I fell off my pony, and . . . Was that really you?"

Gavin nodded. "I used to watch you riding with the Earl. I'd forgotten until now." His eyes softened. "But you've changed." Her expression faltered until he added, "You're more beautiful now than I would have ever imagined when you were a child."

Anya held her breath when he bent to kiss her. For a moment she felt afraid. For a moment she thought of Cedric. The moment passed quickly as she became consumed with nothing but Gavin, and she wondered how long she had been wanting this deep inside. At first he kissed her meekly. He drew back slightly, and their breath mingled along with their eyes. He kissed her again. Anya felt it turn warm and alluring. But his ardor faded with his strength, and he sank back onto the pillows.

Hesitantly Anya drew back in silent question. Gavin's lips parted to draw a sustaining breath. His eyes sparkled with eager invitation, and Anya was quick to comply. She felt a hand move into her hair while their kiss turned to something she had never dreamed existed in this worldly sphere. From it she drew peace. There was generosity in his affection. She felt renewed rather than depleted. Adored, not degraded. The pain that had weighed upon her so heavily seemed to flow into him, as if he could toss it to the wind.

Gavin was pleasantly surprised by Anya's eager response. He didn't believe he'd ever found kissing a woman so pleasant, despite his being as weak as a baby. Inwardly he cursed the lack of strength that made it impossible to put his arms around her, though he knew in truth that his weakness only made it easier to refrain. Suspecting she had suffered still more than she'd admitted to, he instinctively knew Anya deserved time and commitment. She deserved to be treated like a queen, MacBrier blood or no.

Anya drew back breathlessly and slowly opened her eyes. Gavin smiled, and she put her face timidly to his shoulder.

"Your heart is pounding, Mr. Baird," she said with a hand against his chest. "You should not be exerting yourself like that in your condition."

Gavin chuckled and brushed his lips over her brow. "I was just lying here."

The barely detectable humor in his voice reminded her so strongly of James MacBrier that she had to raise her head and look at him. He only grinned and kissed her nose.

Anya relaxed her head against his shoulder, relishing the security she felt. She tried to recall the last time anyone had just hugged her for the sake of it. Mrs. MacGregor might have done it a time or two. But beyond that, James MacBrier had been the only person to ever show her genuine affection. Was that why being in Gavin's arms reminded her so much of him? Again she raised her head to look at him. He gave her a questioning smile, and she relaxed.

"Why do you keep looking at me like that?" he asked, rubbing a gentle hand up and down her arm.

Anya considered ignoring the question, but she reminded herself that she had come beyond that. She wondered how to explain it without offending him. "It's just that . . . well, there are moments when you remind me of James MacBrier."

"That's something of a consolation, I suppose." He chuckled and pressed his lips into her hair. "I always *wanted* to be his son."

Anya seriously considered telling him what she knew about his birthmark that he apparently didn't know, but she decided now was not a good time. They'd already had enough drama for one day. Instead she asked, "If you only met him the day before he died, then how could you have wanted to be his son?"

"Let's just say I observed much from a distance." Anya kept her head against his shoulder, but shifted so she could see his face as he told her about the tree in the forest where he had spied on the MacBriers. She laughed as he told her some of the things he'd seen and heard from his lofty view, and she was amazed at the insight he'd gained into these people from his distant observance. She felt somehow comforted to hear him speak of Cedric as a shallow, unscrupulous cad. And she nearly fell off the bed with laughter when he told her that Malvina was so homely she could put a warthog to shame.

"Of course," Anya said when she had wiped the tears of laughter from her eyes, "if Malvina were a kind person, her appearance would make no difference."

"That's likely true," Gavin admitted. "But she's too much like her mother, as is Cedric."

"It's too bad you couldn't have been the Earl of Brierley," she said, a bit too seriously.

Gavin chuckled uncomfortably and looked away. "I have no desire to be any such thing."

"But you said you wanted to be his son, and—"

"His son, yes, but not the Earl. I have no desire to *ever* return to Brierley, in spite of what the Earl asked me to do," he added sadly.

"And what is that?" she asked in a tone of surprise that made him realize she didn't know what he was talking about. Glancing at his right hand where it rested on Anya's arm, he realized for the first time since he'd gained consciousness that he was not wearing the Earl's ring. He'd worn it every day for ten years, but he'd taken it off as a precaution when he'd returned to Brierley.

"Will you get something for me?" he asked.

"But you didn't answer my question," she said in an attempt to mimic something he'd said to her many times. Gavin chuckled.

"I have every intention of answering your question," he said, "but I want to show you something first. It's behind the right front bureau leg, on the floor." Anya knelt on the floor and probed with her fingers. "It's wrapped in a piece of rag. Can you . . . Yes," he swallowed hard as she stood with it in her hand, "that's it."

Anya handed him the object and watched him unwrap it, wondering what might warrant hiding it in such a way. She caught her breath as the ring came into view and he slid it onto the third finger of his right hand. She recognized it as the ring the Earl had worn, but she didn't know how to ask why he had it. She was relieved when he explained.

"The night before the Earl died, he gave me this. He said it was one of two. Until today, I didn't know what had happened to the other one."

"Today?"

"Robbie mentioned that Lady MacBrier hadn't been so upset since she found out they'd buried the Earl with that ring on his finger."

"So he did." She recalled now that it had become lost in the other things Robbie had said. "It must be very valuable, then," she said, fingering it idly, liking the feel of Gavin's hand.

"It's valuable because it's the key to a safe at Brierley." Anya's eyes widened as she sat again on the edge of the bed. "He told me it contained a treasure that only I could appreciate, and he asked me to be present when the safe was opened. It took me ten years to realize that he wouldn't have said that if he didn't want me to do it. So I went back to Brierley and told Lady Margaret I didn't want anything the safe might contain; I just wanted to be present when it was opened. We argued, but Lady Margaret was adamant. Of course she was just acting as a puppet on Una's strings. They insisted the real treasure had been stolen before the Earl's death, and the safe's contents were better left alone." Gavin's eyes turned distant. "And then they tried to kill me."

"Don't you worry they'll come looking for you, or at least the ring?"

"Well, I assume they believe I'm dead," he stated. "But putting the pieces together, I don't think they really want the ring. What they want is for the contents of that safe to never see the light of day. I doubt that anyone beyond Lady Margaret and Una are even aware of it. But they seemed to know what was in it; at least Una did." He met her eyes sadly. "At this point, I believe it's something better forgotten."

"You don't mean that," she guessed with a degree of confidence.

"No," he chuckled tensely and tightened his embrace, "but there's nothing I can do about it, Anya. My life is worth more to me than that. If they think I'm dead, let them think it. I like my life just the way it is."

Anya smiled up at him. "And how is that?"

"With you here by my side," he said with so much tenderness that she was almost moved to tears. Was it possible that he had grown to care for her so much? Whether or not he had, she reminded herself that he had lived a full life before this, and when it was over, he would go back to living it.

"And what of your life before you returned to Brierley?" she asked.

"What of it?"

"You've told me nothing of what you've done in the years since the Earl died."

"Well," he drawled, wondering where to begin, "I've done a lot of traveling. I even went to America for a while."

Her eyes widened with interest. "Was it as incredible as they say?"

"It was worth seeing, and I enjoyed it. But I was always glad to come back here. The highlands are my home, even if there was never anyone here to call family."

"Is there no one?" she asked.

"Oh, I have a few friends here and there, but . . ." He drifted off with a hint of sadness, and Anya tried to distract him.

"What else did you do?" she asked with interest.

"I attended the University of Edinburgh. I did rather well, actually, especially considering the only other education I had was from my mother."

"She must have been an incredible woman," Anya commented, feeling admiration for any woman who could raise a son as good and kind as Gavin Baird.

"She was," he agreed. "You remind me of her, in a way, though I can't say exactly why."

"Perhaps it's the way I feed you." She smiled impishly.

"You do take good care of me." He strained to lift his left arm, just so he could touch her face.

"It's my pleasure," she said, looking into his eyes, wishing she could read his motives. Everything felt so good and right between them that she found her mind wandering to a vision of spending the rest of her life here with Gavin Baird. But the fantasy was squelched by a memory. Hadn't her life been too good to be true when the Earl died and all of it had been shattered? She reminded herself not to get too attached. She enjoyed being with Gavin, and it was evident that he enjoyed her company as well. But it was temporary. This would all be in the past one day, and life would go on. The uncertainty of that was unnerving, but the confidence she had gained in talking with Gavin prompted her to approach something she had been considering in the back of her mind.

"Gavin," she said, resting her head again on his shoulder, if only to avoid looking at him.

"Yes, my sweet," he said quietly.

"When you get your strength back, and you're able to take care of yourself again . . ."

She hesitated, and Gavin wondered if her thoughts were wandering to the same places as his. At this moment, he could not comprehend ever being without Anya again. Perhaps that was the very reason her next statement caught him so off guard.

"Do you think," her voice picked up a nervous edge, "that you would be able to help me find a . . . position . . . elsewhere . . . so I could—"

"What in heaven's name are you talking about?" he asked so abruptly that she sat forward, her eyes wide. "You're a MacBrier, for crying out loud. When this is over, you could do anything you like, Anya. You could—"

"I don't think you understand. I don't want that kind of life. And even if I did, it's beyond my reach. I just want to find work that I can enjoy and be appreciated for my talents. All I ask is that you—"

"Do you hear what you're saying?" he asked, trying to keep the anger out of his voice. "Do you think James MacBrier intended for you to spend the rest of your life as a servant to others, and—"

"It doesn't matter what he wanted. He's long gone, and nothing will ever—"

"He might be gone," Gavin lifted a stern finger, "but his resources are not. You can rest assured, Miss Ross, that when I get back on my feet, I will move heaven and earth to be certain that you are cared for, but I will *not* find you a position." His voice lightened slightly. "Haven't you ever considered the likelihood of marrying and having a family? You're a beautiful woman, Anya, with much to offer. I can assure you that—"

"I used to think such a thing was possible," she interrupted curtly. "But not anymore."

The look in her eyes made Gavin certain she had yet to unburden *all* of her pain and fears. "I wouldn't be so sure, if I were you," he said.

Gavin's words were full of that tender kindness he had proven capable of. Their eyes met in tense silence while Anya debated whether to run in the other room and hide, or bury herself in his embrace.

"You are worth so much more than that, Anya." His voice was strong with conviction. "You are not the woman Una has tried to convince you that you are. You are a woman with innate dignity and refinement. You have noble blood, Anya. You should live like a lady."

"You don't understand, Gavin."

"You're right. I don't understand."

"I won't have you taking care of me for the rest of my life, just because—"

"Because you saved my life? Because the Earl left me with more money than I could spend in three lifetimes? I wouldn't be much of a man if I *didn't* take care of you, one way or another."

Anya looked at the floor and fidgeted with her apron. "I'm tired of feeling like a . . . a . . . burden . . . or—"

"You will never be a burden to me, Anya, I can assure you."

"Don't be making promises you can't keep, Mr. Baird," she nearly snapped.

"If you really knew me, Anya, you would know I *do not* make promises I can't keep."

"That's just it, Gavin. We are little more than strangers. You have no business talking of the future as if—"

"Your memory fails you badly, Anya." His voice picked up an edge of the frustration he was feeling. "Is my affection so easy to forget?"

"A little thoughtless affection changes nothing," she retorted. "You and I both had a life before this, and when this is in the past, we will both—"

"Is that what you call it? You had a *life* at Brierley?" His sarcasm didn't begin to express his bitterness for what he had learned about her today. "What you had, Anya, was an existence. You were existing because the only other option was to die. My mother existed for *me,* and I truly believe that once she knew I could care for myself, she was grateful for the opportunity to die. And as for me, you have no idea what *my* life was like before this. It may not have been miserable, but it was still just *existence.*"

He nearly spat the last, leaving Anya to wonder what he was really trying to tell her. She didn't dare hope that he might want to share more with her than he already had, but she felt tempted to test it. In a gentle voice she said, "You seem to be implying that something beyond this will exist between us."

Gavin looked at her hard. He didn't want any question that he meant it when he said, "Whether we are friends or sweethearts, Anya, I can assure you that something very strong will always exist between us. We have too much in common, too much that binds us together, for our lives to ever be the same again."

Stunned and uncertain, Anya futilely searched for a response, aware that her breathing was strained, her heart was racing. Suddenly overwhelmed by her own feelings, she rushed from the room, wishing with all her might that Gavin Baird would find a way to convince her damaged heart that what he'd just said was true.

Chapter seven
Anya's Bluff

For reasons she didn't understand, Anya tried to pretend that nothing had changed. She made great effort to remain expressionless in Gavin's presence, and she was grateful when he began to feed himself. She felt certain she couldn't bear the eye contact.

It was a disappointment to rise on Wednesday and find it storming. Anya had been looking forward to getting out of the house. But in analyzing their supplies, she realized it was pointless to go to town in this rain when they could easily get by. So instead she stayed in the house with her feelings, under Gavin's watchful eye and imposing presence.

She kept asking herself why he had done it—all of it. The gentle words, the compassion, his attention to her hands, her hair. And the kisses. Those sweet, beautiful kisses, unlike anything she had ever known in her life. Just to think of his lips over hers left her fluttery, and occasionally a silent cry of joy surged through her. She felt too unsure of her feelings to look Gavin in the eye, but she was too caught up in them to notice the change in him.

As days passed, however, Anya began to feel the changes in herself. It first began when she caught her reflection while passing the bureau mirror. She had not even had a mirror at Brierley, but often while working in the bedrooms she would catch a glimpse of her reflection, always hating what she saw. But something had changed. Perhaps it was her hair; there was no doubt she looked different with it down. But if she was honest with herself, she had to admit it was something more, something wonderful.

It didn't take much for Anya to figure that Gavin had been responsible for these changes. He was continually showing gratitude for all she had done for him. But did he have any idea what he was doing for her? She felt alive again. Only because he cared. It was simply that. She knew Gavin cared.

Then what was she afraid of? Surely not Gavin. Yet she could hardly face him. More than a week had passed since her deep confessions to him, and Anya found that she missed the affection they had shared. And the conversation, the friendship. Yet she felt certain the distance between them was her own doing, and she wondered why.

With supper cleaned up and the house in order, Anya went to bed as usual. Shortly past midnight the wind began to blow while she lay silently awake, wondering if Gavin was sleeping. Thunder began to rumble in the distance, and she rose to close the window.

Anya got back into her makeshift bed without a word, but Gavin couldn't help noticing her silhouette against a flash of lightning. He wondered if Anya had any idea how he had become obsessed with her. Did she begin to understand that the emptiness in his life was somehow lessening, simply by her presence in his home—and in his life? How could she, when she wouldn't even look at him?

Gavin had hardly taken his eyes off Anya each moment she was within his view, but days had passed with hardly a mutual glance. Even when she consented to help him shave, she hardly looked directly at him. He wondered what she was trying to hide. Or perhaps she was just hiding from him. Had his boldness left her so uneasy? Had he misinterpreted her kindness as something more? Did she believe his intentions were somehow dishonorable?

Anya became increasingly restless as lightning illuminated the room in brief spurts. She didn't feel afraid, but she was certainly not at ease. When lightning flashed and thunder rolled simultaneously, she couldn't suppress a startled gasp.

"Anya," Gavin's voice rang through the dissipating thunder. He was relieved to have the silence between them broken.

"Yes?" she finally answered, embarrassed by her outburst.

"Are you afraid?"

"No. Just startled."

Her words sounded final, and he remained silent while the thunder ushered in a gentle rain that gradually became a downpour. Anya felt chilled, but she didn't have the motivation to get up and build a fire. She just tried to roll up tighter in the blankets and fall asleep.

Gavin sensed Anya's restlessness and called to her again. "You're cold, aren't you."

She hesitated. "A little."

"If I thought I could move that far, I'd gladly offer to trade you places."

"Don't be silly," she insisted. "I'm fine."

"No, you're not. You're cold and—"

"I'll build a fire," she said, sitting up, actually relieved to have something besides silence passing between them.

Gavin sighed loudly and had to admit, "You must believe me when I tell you that I truly wish I had the strength to do it for you."

"I know," she said gently, and he felt certain she understood.

They chatted about trivial matters while she went about the task. When she had an adequate fire going, she crawled back into her bed, feeling much better for more than one reason. She felt warmer, yes. But she also felt the evidence of Gavin's caring, even though she could still feel a tension in the air between them. She was just wondering how to dispel it when he said, "It's nice to have you talk to me, you know. I was beginning to wonder if, for some reason, you didn't trust me."

Anya felt briefly alarmed, wondering if that was somehow the impression she'd given him. Reminding herself there was nothing to be afraid of, she impulsively tried to close the gap she'd unintentionally created. "Why should I trust you after the way you kissed me last week?" she teased.

Gavin felt immense relief to hear her admit what had happened between them. "Because it was a gentleman's kiss," he replied, "and a true gentleman always keeps his word."

Anya knew what that made Cedric MacBrier. "Thank you," she said softly.

"For what?" he asked.

"For being a gentleman," she said, "and for . . . being patient with me."

"It's my pleasure, actually," he whispered. Then only the rain was heard for the remainder of the night, singing them both into a peaceful sleep.

Gavin awoke and realized Anya was still sleeping. He was normally awakened by sounds of her busily working in the kitchen. He couldn't resist the urge to shift just enough to get a clear view of her where she lay near the fireplace. Did she have any idea how beautiful she was with her hair strewn over her pillow, like some kind of angel?

Anya stretched herself awake and realized by the angle of the light that she must have slept longer than usual. Then she opened her eyes fully, and found Gavin staring at her from across the room. She flushed crimson and hastily pulled the blanket up to cover her prudishly modest nightgown.

"Good morning," he said with a smile that held no hint of mischief. But she kept the blanket wrapped tightly around her as she hurried into the other room to change. Once alone, she leaned against the wall to catch her breath. It wasn't so much her embarrassment that bothered her as the feelings his attention evoked.

"Ooh," she said aloud, scolding herself inwardly for becoming emotionally involved. She now knew the source of her fear. Once Gavin could care for himself, his interest in her would wane and she'd have to move on. There was no sense getting caught up in this, only to have to let it go.

She quickly dressed and prepared breakfast, grateful that today was Wednesday. Going into town would allow her to get away and see all of this from a clearer perspective. She silently took Gavin his meal, then cleaned the kitchen so she could hurry.

When Anya came to retrieve the tray, Gavin took note that she was apparently going out. "Off to market?" he quipped.

"How observant you are," she replied on her way to the kitchen. She returned the tray bearing bread, cold meat and cheese, and plenty to drink while she was gone. "That should keep you from starving until I return," she said, then went to the tiny drawer in the bedside table where Robbie had told her the money was kept. She was surprised at how much there was, but she kept a straight face as she counted out a few notes, ample for what she needed.

"Wait a minute." He sat up, apparently insulted. "What do you think you're doing?"

"I'm sorry," she said, dropping the notes to the tabletop. "Robbie told me to use what I needed, and . . . I just assumed that . . ." Their eyes met silently for a moment while Gavin tried to look mean and Anya tried to guess what was bothering him. Was it having a woman go through his money—or taking free rein with it? "Did I take too much?" she asked, attempting to put some back.

"On the contrary," he said at last, "I don't think you took nearly enough."

"Oh, this is plenty," she insisted, now more puzzled. "All I need is . . ."

"Some new clothes," he inserted. Anya began to protest, but he pulled the money from the open drawer, counted out several notes, and slapped them into her hand. "I want you to stop at the tailor's and buy new everything, including enough dresses that I don't have to see you in the same one twice a week."

"I couldn't possibly. Do you have any idea how much that would cost?"

"I could guess," he said, glancing toward the notes in her hand. "That should cover it, I think. And get something to put on those dreadful hands."

Anya looked at the money and felt certain she couldn't spend that much if she tried. "Gavin, I can't possibly spend your money to—"

"Whose money is it?" he asked pointedly. She looked at him in question, and he gave a firm nod that took her mind to their conversation concerning the Earl. Anya glanced at the notes in her hand as he continued. "That money was your great-uncle's. If he were alive, he would have spent a lot more of it on you."

"But, Gavin, I—"

"If you must be so proud, consider it a partial payment for all you've done for me."

"But, I—"

"Don't argue with me!" he actually shouted. "In ten years I haven't spent a tenth of what he gave me, so don't stand there acting like you're taking something hard-earned. And you'd best do as I say, or I'll burn those atrocious uniforms of yours." Anya opened her mouth to retort, but he sternly added, "You spend every single bit of that, woman, or I'll send you back to Brierley."

The statement ended her protests, but Gavin wished he hadn't said it by the look that came into her eyes. Silently she turned and left, but her absence started Gavin contemplating the circumstances. He thought of his mother and tried to compare Anya to her. Foremost in his comparison was a measure of feelings. Not since Jinny Baird died had he felt a desire to care for someone, to be there for their needs, to share his hopes and dreams. But beyond that, his feelings for Anya were different. To look at her, he felt something he could never have felt for his mother. He had traveled far and had seen a lot of women, but he'd never known a feeling like this.

"Is it love?" he asked himself aloud, knowing she was long gone. Now that the word had escaped him, it didn't seem so bad. There was no doubt that he loved his mother. Surely what he felt now was no less than that.

Gavin thought about it long and hard, deciding that he had no intention of playing games with this. He was not going to leave the future beyond his recuperation to chance. If he loved her, so be it.

With a basket over her arm, Anya set out in the direction Robbie had told her to go. It felt good being outdoors to do more than hang the laundry or feed the horse. She walked at a comfortable pace, taking time to absorb the lush Scottish countryside surrounding her.

She had barely come around the bend in the road when a broad strath opened up before her. From here she could see a quaint village nestled at the base of it. She knew it was likely many miles in any direction to find anything but a few scattered farmhouses. The seclusion of the little village left her intrigued.

She learned by a sign at the edge of town that it was called Strathnell, and had a population of six hundred and three, recently crossed out and corrected to six hundred and five. It wasn't difficult to find the market square. By the bustle and noise, Anya felt certain that at least six hundred of Strathnell's residents were present. The few not here were likely at home with those new babies that had probably forced the change on the sign.

Anya realized she hardly knew what to do. It had been years since she'd been to a market, and then she had been with the Earl, who had

purchased her a pink scarf and some shortbread. She wandered idly
and observed enough to feel confident that she could handle it, then
she went from one end to the other, purchasing all she needed for the
kitchen, including fresh vegetables, some herring and salmon, and hot
scones. She splurged on some shortbread and a jar of marmalade,
then sought out a vendor who sold her a jar of hand balm. He took
notice of her hands and offered her a good price for two jars. She
accepted the offer.

With her purchases made, Anya looked at the money left and
recalled Gavin's instructions. She had been so caught up in the excitement of the square that she'd almost forgotten. She was tempted to
ignore his demands and just go home. She had everything they
needed and more. But something in her ached to feel something
against her skin that had not seen her toil at Brierley.

With little effort she found the tailor's shop on a side street, where
a dark man's suit and a lavender day dress were displayed in the front
window, behind a sign that claimed them as the latest fashion. The
clothes were conservative compared to what she had seen at Brierley,
but she assumed a tailor could never sell anything that wasn't, in a
town like this.

Gathering fortitude, she stepped inside and a little bell above the
door tinkled to announce her arrival. A young woman stepped out
from behind a curtain with a child barely old enough to walk
following close behind.

"Can I help ye, lass?" she asked in a jovial tone, showing by her
expression that it was unusual to see someone she didn't recognize.

"I need to purchase some dresses, and . . . other things." She
cleared her throat.

"Ye've come tae th' right place," she announced proudly. "If it's
underthings and such yer needin', I can help ye with that, and then I
can fetch m' father. He can make up anything tae catch yer fancy."

"That would be fine," Anya said, and was soon overwhelmed
with attention. She was amused by the tailor's daughter, and pleased
by the way she discreetly managed to gather everything that Anya
needed for underclothing without making a fuss. She also insisted
that Anya take two pretty but conservative nightgowns, which were a
must.

The tailor himself soon appeared, and Anya smiled as he bent gallantly before her. "Ah, it would be a pleasure tae see one as pretty as ye, lass, dolled up in the finest. Let us get ye measured, and I'll get makin' whatever ye please right away."

"Do you have anything already made," she asked, "that I could take with me?"

"There's th' dress in th' window," he stated, "and another that's sim'lar in yellow. They mightna fit ye perfect, but I would say they'd do until we can get ye fitted."

"That should be fine," Anya agreed, then she let herself be measured and shown swatches of fabric until her head spun. And then she had to choose styles from several drawings. When they were finally finished, Anya chose to wear the lavender dress home, and the tailor's daughter insisted she take the hair combs that had been with it in the window display.

Anya finally left the shop, agreeing to return next week to pick up her order that had been paid for in full. She felt like someone else as she stepped into the open air with a light heart to match her step. But she'd hardly gone twenty paces when her eye caught something in a different window that made her stop and go inside. Gavin had said to spend all of the money.

"Excuse me," she said to the stodgy little man behind the counter, "could I see that cane there, the one in the window with the gold handle?"

"What, this one?" He brought it forth as if it were a king's scepter.

"Yes, thank you." Anya examined it, certain it was perfect. Gavin would need something to help him get around until he healed completely, and she thought it would be nice to have a cane so fine for the purpose. It suited him. She inquired as to the price, and was relieved to find that she had plenty.

Her excursion ended with a brief stop to purchase a handful of books that she hoped Gavin would like. And she was almost proud of herself to realize she had spent all but a few shillings.

As Anya headed home, burdened with her purchases, she thought deeply on the situation. How could she deny the way all of this made her feel? Was it wrong to enjoy Gavin's attention, even if it didn't last? Before she arrived, she had made up her mind to stop worrying about the future, stop thinking about the past, and just enjoy today for what it was. These memories could last her a lifetime.

By the time Anya returned, Gavin was feeling comfortable and confident with his discovery. He heard her setting packages down in the other room and putting things away. His heart beat rapidly, anticipating her coming into the room. When she finally did, his heart raced for a moment then came to a dead stop.

Anya held her breath, waiting for his approval of the dress she wore, with the matching combs pulling her hair back on the sides.

"You are beautiful," he finally said, and Anya believed he meant it.

"It's been so long," she said, trying to suppress the joyous way it made her feel to be treated this way. "Thank you, Gavin."

"It's my pleasure," he smiled warmly.

"And why is that?" she persisted.

Gavin took a deep breath, but didn't hesitate even slightly. "Because I love you, Anya."

Anya looked shocked, which he had expected, then she turned her back to him, which he hadn't. He felt suddenly vulnerable, and wondered if he should have said it.

Meanwhile, Anya's heart was beating so fast that she felt certain it would stop and end her life here and now. What could she say? How could she possibly react to such a statement? "Don't be ridiculous!" she said at last.

"Is it so ridiculous," he asked, "for a man to admit to his feelings?" He told himself it likely was. Had he been a fool to think that such directness was the right way to handle it? How would he know? He'd never done this before, and no one had ever told him what to do. "Anya?" he said when she made no response. Still she didn't move. "Look at me!" he insisted.

Anya's mind was so full of a thousand tumbling thoughts that she couldn't bring herself to respond. Could he possibly be serious? Or was he just toying with her—the way Cedric had? Cedric had told her he loved her. The thought made her cringe. It didn't seem in Gavin's character to lie to her. But even if he believed he loved her now, would it last?

"Anya!" he repeated. "If I could get out of this bed, I would force you to look at me. But I can't!"

She turned toward him. "I'm sorry," she laughed tensely, "it's just that . . .well, I mean, it's common for a patient to feel that way about a nurse." Gavin's expression faltered. "You're likely feeling . . . vulner-able . . . and dependent . . . on me. I daresay it will . . . pass." Inwardly, Anya prayed it would not, but she couldn't afford to set hopes on an infatuation that might well be gone when he had his strength back.

Her words hurt, and Gavin fought to find a reply that might save his pride as well as his feelings. Perhaps she was right, but then . . . maybe she wasn't. "All right," he said at last, "we'll talk about this again when I get out to chop some wood." Anya nodded in agreement, but she couldn't hide the brief disappointment that came into her eyes.

"And tell me, Anya," he persisted, "disregarding any feelings I might have, what did you plan to do when I don't need you anymore . . . to take care of me?" he added to clarify what he considered an important point.

"Perhaps I'll go back to Brierley," she mused.

"I don't believe that for a minute. You wouldn't unless you absolutely had to."

"I thought of putting out an advertisement. I have talents that could be useful. But if I can't find a position somewhere, I might absolutely have to."

Over my dead body, Gavin thought to himself, then he added aloud, "Is that all you can see yourself as—a servant?"

"That is what I am."

"It's not what you were born to be." His voice contained a hint of anger. "Granted, I don't have a lot to offer here, but it beats perdition out of working for people like Margaret MacBrier. Doesn't it?"

"What you have here is wonderful, but . . ."

"But what?" he insisted when she faltered.

"I can't stay here under these circumstances and take advantage of your . . ."

Gavin's eyes went hard and Anya turned away again, not liking where this conversation was going. She wanted so badly to tell him how much his words meant to her, how she hoped the feelings behind them would not change. She wanted to tell him that the feeling was mutual. But Cedric MacBrier and his deceitful methods, disguised as love, came back to her. Anya scolded herself. She had made a vow to put that behind her. Gavin was different. Of that she was certain.

"You know," she said, and his eyes softened at her tone, "they also say that it's common for a nurse to feel a certain . . . affection for her patient. Perhaps we should discuss this when we can stand to face each other as man and woman."

Gavin smiled, and Anya nearly melted under the power of his eyes. She turned timidly away and was relieved when Gavin broke the tension by saying, "Show me what else you bought."

Anya hurried to the kitchen to gather her packages, wondering if she should try to ignore what had just passed between them. But she didn't want to. Hadn't she just told herself to enjoy this while it lasted? And it was all so wonderful, how could she help but enjoy it?

She returned with an armload of packages that she dropped on the foot of the bed. Gavin watched with satisfaction as the scullery maid began to transform into the girl she had once been. He laughed when she rolled up the old uniforms and threw them into the bottom of the wardrobe. She modeled her other dress, explaining that the others would be ready next week. Gavin liked the way she looked in yellow; it matched her hair and made her look like sunshine personified. She showed him everything except her new underthings, which she discreetly slipped into a drawer. Then she brought out the books. Gavin was surprised that she had thought of such a thing, not to mention that she seemed to know his taste. "Thank you," he said with warmth.

"I thought it might help pass the time."

Anya was tempted to show him the cane, but on impulse she decided to wait. She would surprise him with it when the time was right.

"Oh," she remembered, reaching into her pocket to pull out a few coins, "the change." She dumped the shillings into his hand.

He smiled with approval, then changed the subject. "I could use another shave. I feel like a hibernating bear."

"Perhaps you are," she quipped, and Gavin smiled to see the teasing in her eyes. Anya left to gather his shaving things, and was soon sitting beside him with a basin of hot water on his lap.

"I could probably do it myself," he said as she began to soap up his face.

"Then why don't you?" she asked, holding out the brush.

"Because I don't want to," he smirked. "I like the way it feels to trust you while you hold a blade at my throat."

"What if I miss?" She set the soap aside and picked up the long, straight blade.

"It would be a shame, after all your efforts to save me thus far."

Anya only smiled. Gavin remained silent while she carefully slid the blade over his face and throat. He moved the muscles in his face accordingly, and she occasionally smiled at his appearance. But each time their eyes met, the tension deepened a little further. Gavin's confessions hung over them, making each breath, each glance, each touch seem to hold an unspoken meaning.

Anya was proud of herself for finishing without a nick, then she dried his face and rubbed it with shaving lotion, realizing the scent intoxicated her. The lotion stung the cracks in her hands, but she ignored it, concentrating on the feel of his face and the look of love shining from his eyes.

Before she was finished, Gavin took her face in the same manner and kissed her. Anya felt relieved to have it happen and longed for it to go on, but the sting in her hands began to burn and she pulled away quickly, feeling awkward as she appeased the question in his eyes. "I have to wash my hands."

It only took a moment for him to figure that what made his face tingle was likely painful to the open cracks in her skin. "And yes," she called from the kitchen, "I got something for my hands."

"Good," he called back. "When you finish, bring it here."

Anya tidied up the shaving mess, then handed him the jar of balm. "Does it require your approval?" she asked.

"No," he patted the bed to indicate that she sit, "but perhaps my assistance." Without permission, he took one of her hands and put what she considered a ridiculous amount of balm onto it. Anya sighed at the cool, softening relief of the cream, and found she was fascinated by the gentle care with which he rubbed it into every crack and crevice, over and over, until the entire amount was gone, soaked into her hand like water into a dry sponge.

He repeated the process with her other hand, and Anya assumed he was finished until he took up the first hand and started over.

"What are you doing?" she asked.

"Making up for lost time," he said without taking his attention from her hands. Anya couldn't argue, as she was certain her hands well needed it, and she was thoroughly enjoying the experience. She watched her hand in his until she glanced up and found him watching her. She wanted to look away, but something in his eyes challenged her. She was more relieved than she wanted to admit when he leaned forward to kiss her. And she couldn't deny how thoroughly secure and safe it made her feel.

"Anya," he touched her face in adoration as he eased back to look into her eyes, "my feelings will not change. You know that, don't you?"

"I know no such thing." She pulled away abruptly, and Gavin scolded himself inwardly for being so bold—again. But at least *he* was being honest with himself.

"Are you trying to deny the feelings between us?" he asked, certain he would regret saying this as well.

"Feelings have nothing to do with it!"

Gavin felt insulted. "What are you accusing me of being?" Anya stood up and began putting things away with a little too much vigor. "Answer me!" he demanded.

"You're a man!" she retorted. "And the fact that you find pleasure in . . . in . . . kissing me that way does not mean you love me."

"That," he pointed a finger at her, "is where you are wrong, Anya Ross. And I will prove it to you."

"Fine," she slammed the wardrobe closed, "but in the meantime, mind your manners." She left the room while Gavin wondered whether he should bless or curse the time he'd just spent with her. He had heard that women were difficult to understand, but this was ridiculous. She had been a purring kitten one minute, a rabid tigress the next.

Anya prepared dinner with a vengeance, scolding herself for getting so caught up in these feelings, and then making a fool of herself when confronted with it. What was happening to her? But while she fumed, she prepared a meal for Gavin beyond anything she had fed him so far. She prepared the herring by dipping it in oatmeal, using a recipe that Mrs. MacGregor had claimed was a delicacy. She prepared a vegetable dish to accompany it, then reheated the scones and made soup as well. She set it all out on a tray to look attractive, then carried it to the bedroom and set it over his lap. Gavin looked over the fare with approval, then he turned expectant eyes upon her.

"I'm sorry I yelled at you," she heard herself saying, wondering when she had lost control of her own senses.

"I'm sorry I couldn't resist kissing you," Gavin said, even though he wasn't. Anya nearly blushed at the memory and turned away to hide it. "This looks wonderful," he said, changing the subject. "It smells better than wonderful."

"I hope you enjoy it," she said, then hurried to the kitchen to eat her dinner out of his view.

As the days wore on, Anya avoided Gavin's gaze. She asked herself why, but had no answer. Perhaps she simply didn't want to get her hopes up. It was as she had told him: they could not base a lifetime on feelings established under such vulnerable circumstances. And Anya had to admit that her greatest fear was that his feelings might change. Gavin had told her he loved her, and she believed he meant it. That alone fed her with something she had been starving for since the Earl's death. She had thought she had found it in Cedric, but even her horrible experience with him could not make her mistrust Gavin's intentions. He was so different from Cedric. So wonderfully different. But still, she told herself, she had to be careful. Her heart was fragile. It had been broken too many times.

Gavin felt undeniably frustrated when Anya fell back into her pattern of ignoring that anything existed between them beyond a nurse-patient relationship. He wanted to just come out and ask her why she was doing this, but found he was afraid of what the answers might be. Yes, he had to admit it. His greatest fear at this moment was confronting Anya's feelings.

So he played along with her game, waiting for that day when he could face her as a man and confront the truth. But resigning himself to wait didn't keep the questions from eating at him. At times the waiting seemed endless, even torturous, and he prayed inwardly for opportunities to share these moments together with something besides a distant silence. Their relationship seemed so formal, so callous at times.

Gavin's single advantage in this situation was his insistence on rubbing the balm into her hands at least twice a day. "I can do it better than you," he justified. "And I'll make certain it gets done. Besides," his tone turned sincere, "it's something I can do for you, even if I can't get out of this bed."

Anya hardly dared look at him while he performed the ritual. She enjoyed it so thoroughly that she feared her expression would betray just how wonderful his attention was. But there were moments when she couldn't resist watching his face, as long as she was careful to look away before he caught her at it.

Gavin was well aware of the game she was playing, but it wasn't until she had darted her eyes away for what seemed the hundredth time in a matter of days that he fully comprehended what it meant. Once he understood it, he watched her carefully to verify it. Gradually it settled into him with certainty. Anya was bluffing. He didn't know why, but he knew that she was. Somehow he knew that Anya loved him every bit as much as he loved her. He felt proud of himself for figuring it out, then set his mind to call that bluff. Just as soon as he could face her as a man, whole and strong, Gavin intended to make a stand.

Chapter Eight
the glass slipper

"You do like me, don't you, Anya." Gavin said it as if he'd stated it for the first time.

She looked up in surprise from the book she was reading. "I thought we agreed to talk about that when all of this is behind us."

"We did. But do we have to pretend in the meantime that these feelings don't exist?"

"I don't know what you're talking about." She pretended to read, but he knew she wasn't.

"You're bluffing again."

"I'm what?" she asked, appalled.

"You're bluffing, Anya. You stay conveniently just past arm's length of me, and you avoid my eyes as if they would turn you to stone. But you're not fooling me." He smiled in response to her mouth hanging open. "I just thought you should know that."

Anya searched quickly for a retort. "And why should I do more? Just because you claim to love me gives me no guarantee of not having my heart trampled on, then tossed aside like a worn-out toy." Anya saw the hurt in his eyes. He'd given her no reason to mistrust him, but she figured he might as well know how she felt. "How do I know you're not just another arrogant scoundrel out for a good time?" Gavin's eyes turned hard. She looked away, immediately regretting her words.

"I think you've spent too many years at Brierley, my dear." There was a definite edge to his voice. "You seem to have acquired some of that MacBrier venom." He sighed loudly. "I may be a scoundrel, and perhaps a touch arrogant, but I do not consider your heart a toy, nor am I out for a good time, as you so quaintly put it. Don't sit there and try to tell me what I'm thinking, when you have no idea what you're talking about."

That did it! Anya slammed the book closed and came to her feet. "Who are you to be talking? You're the one who just sat there and told me all about how I feel. Don't think you can pull me away from ten years of hell and change my life with some gentle words and a few kisses. I won't stand for it!"

Gavin was stunned. He reminded himself of what she had been through. She was right—to some degree, at least. "I'm sorry," he admitted, if only to help her trust him. "You must forgive my boredom. I should not be so . . . forward."

Anya turned away, feeling foolish for getting so upset. "I'm sorry I called you a scoundrel," she said.

"At least it was honest."

Anya turned to face him, angry all over again. "Are you implying that I am not being honest otherwise?"

"Like I said, I think you're bluffing. You really like me. You're just afraid to admit it." His eyes delved into hers, challenging her to honesty.

Anya looked away, forcing herself to face it. He was right. "So, what do you want me to say?" she asked, still not looking at him.

"You don't have to say anything. Just stop pretending." She looked at him, and he saw the fear showing through. "What are you afraid of, Anya? Do I frighten you?"

"No!" she snapped.

"Then what is it?" He remained calm.

The answer went through Anya's mind over and over. All she had to do was say it. *Just say it,* she thought. She sat back down and turned her gaze toward the window. The silence was painful. *Just say it,* she told herself again.

"There is only one person who ever loved me," she began. "I mean . . . really loved me. Others pretended to, but eventually the truth always came out. It was only James MacBrier who ever really cared about me, my feelings, my dreams." She sighed and looked at her hands, folded lifelessly in her lap. "But he left me. Not of his own accord, I know. But still, he left me."

She looked at Gavin, and her eyes drove home the point. "You cannot expect me to give you all my feelings at the drop of a hat." She stood and lifted her chin. The gesture alone made Gavin tingle with pride just to know her. "You," she pointed a finger at him, "must earn the right to love me."

The words sounded terribly arrogant to Anya, and she fled the room before he could mock them. They had come with such effort that she couldn't have borne it.

Long after she had left the room, Gavin couldn't erase the image. A woman so noble, so proud, so beautiful, demanding respect but willing to give it. That was the Anya Ross he'd been searching for— the one lost in the realities of daily living. The one that only surfaced often enough to give her a taste of her own potential.

Gavin shook his head, but still the image lingered. "I will," he whispered to himself. "I will earn the right to love you, if it takes the rest of my life."

Once Anya regained her senses, she felt relief. Voicing her thoughts to Gavin had set them free. Those feelings that had painfully churned in her for years were in the open now, where they seemed less frightening.

She returned to the bedroom moments later, and Gavin looked up in surprise. He'd never seen her appear so quickly following any encounter. He felt his heart pound as her eyes delved into him, returning his challenge with such force that he was unable to move, unable to speak.

"Yes," she said, her eyes smiling, "I do like you."

She turned to leave, and Gavin found his voice. "Then why don't you kiss me?"

Anya turned in astonishment, but couldn't help laughing. "You never give up."

"Never!" he chuckled, but his eyes were intent. "Although I give you my word as a gentleman that I would never take any more than a kiss."

Anya thought about kissing him, knowing it would be wonderful. But the tension of the moment was already too much to bear.

"Well?" he added when she seemed frozen where she stood. She only smiled and left the room, not returning until she brought his dinner.

While Gavin ate, Anya completed all of her tasks for the day, then she returned to take his tray before getting ready for bed. She found the tray moved aside, and Gavin sleeping. She watched him for several moments, marveling at what she felt. Then, with little thought, she bent to touch her lips to his. She felt compelled to linger close to him, absorbing the details of his face. His eyes came slowly open, and for a moment Anya wanted to back away, embarrassed by her attention. But he smiled so warmly that she could hardly resist kissing him again. She drew back and touched her nose to his, then tousled his hair the way she had seen Robbie do it.

"Go back to sleep," she whispered, kissed him once more, then doused the lamp and took away the tray.

Gavin's recovery was slow, and his restlessness became more evident each day. Anya finally decided he could manage getting out of bed, if only to ease his mood. While he pulled on his breeches, she retrieved the cane she had purchased and hid it behind her back.

Gavin sat on the edge of the bed and wondered how he was going to even attempt walking with this leg that had briefly become the tunnel for a moving bullet. He wondered if Anya could read his mind when she presented a beautiful cane.

"Where did you get that?" he chuckled.

"I bought it with some of that money you insisted I spend. I thought you would get some good out of it."

"How very thoughtful of you." Gavin smiled and took the cane to admire it. With the cane in his left hand, and his right arm over Anya's shoulders, he came gingerly to his feet. She laughed triumphantly as she helped him walk carefully into the kitchen.

"Does it hurt?" she asked.

"Yes," he chuckled, "but I feel stronger than I expected to."

"Just don't get carried away," she cautioned.

With that he stopped and looked down at her, so conveniently tucked beneath his arm. For the first time since she had found him in the stable, he almost felt like a real man. He couldn't resist the urge to bend and kiss her, but Anya's response made him weak in the knees. Before he knew he was losing his balance, they both ended up in a heap on the floor, laughing so hard that getting back up was impossible.

"I think I'll just stay here until I completely recover," he finally said. "I don't see any hope of getting back to the bed."

"Come along," she laughed, getting to her feet and pulling at him with all the strength she could muster. With the help of his cane and her support he made it to the bed, where he sat abruptly and urged her next to him long enough to kiss her. She was just beginning to get lost in it when Gavin laughed and collapsed back onto the bed, overcome with exhaustion. As she scurried away, he smirked and said, "Saved again, eh?"

"But your word as a gentleman has nothing to do with your strength, does it?" she questioned pointedly.

"No, it doesn't," he said soberly. "But when I get my strength back," his eyes filled with determination, "I will make you a gentleman's wife."

Anya's eyes widened. He had spoken of love and promises, but never of marriage. The thought left her elated. Her timidity urged her to turn and leave, but she forced herself not to. It had been proven that such methods were useless with Gavin. "For now, just worry about getting your strength back," she stated.

"I'll do that," he said firmly. Her kiss gave him marvelous incentive.

Anya felt one of those silent cries of joy leap through her.

"Anya!" Gavin called to the kitchen where she was preparing breakfast. "I'm busy."

"I don't care. Come here."

Anya appeared in the doorway, wiping her hands on an apron. "What?" she insisted when he just stared at her.

"I love you, Anya," he said. Her eyes widened and he added, "Just didn't want you to forget."

Anya couldn't hold back a smile as she went back to the kitchen, calling over her shoulder, "You're not chopping wood yet."

Once Gavin's recovery reached a certain stage, the blood seemed to surge through his veins and he made remarkable progress. He began to dress and come to the kitchen for meals, though he moved slowly and depended heavily on the cane.

Anya had to adjust to this new stage. She was rarely alone as he wandered the house freely, and it began to feel more like Gavin's home as his presence filled more than the bedroom. They now shared their meals, and Gavin insisted on doing things to help while he sat at the table. With his assistance and increasing independence, Anya found more time on her hands and began reading to pass it. But she could hardly sit for long without Gavin sneaking up behind her, startling her so badly that it took immense effort to slow her heart. She would yell and throw things at him while he laughed intolerably and cautioned her against hurting a wounded man.

Gavin couldn't deny how good it felt to be able to get around on his own and begin to care for himself. But he was surprised to find that his increasing strength only gave him the desire to ease back and take it slow. He didn't want to recover too quickly. He liked being dependent on Anya, and had to admit that there was a measure of doubt in facing their day of reckoning. The only problem in holding back was his restlessness. He had read everything under his roof at least once. Even the books Anya picked up on her trips to town didn't take long to get through. There was little within the walls of this house to occupy a man. He found his idle mind contemplating far more deeply than it normally would—about his past and where it had brought him, and how all of it seemed to magically mesh with what Anya had suffered.

On a particularly grey day, heavy with rolling clouds and frequent bursts of rain, Gavin found the urge to do something he did very rarely. While Anya was busy in the kitchen, he rummaged through bureau drawers in search of a key that he'd left there. If only he could remember which drawer. He pulled one open to immediately see that it was filled with Anya's belongings. That was fine. He closed it. But his eye had caught something out of the ordinary amidst the neatly folded, lacy white contents. He looked toward the door to make certain she wasn't close by, then he opened the drawer again and folded back a nightgown to reveal the partially exposed little doll. It was old and ragged, as if it had been worn out with love. Gavin wondered why she would still have such a thing when she had so little else. He turned it over in his hands, feeling something poignant about a grown woman with nothing but an old doll to cry out her pain to.

Looking closer, Gavin noticed the doll had a tiny gold chain around its neck, with a little medallion on which something was engraved. The words had been worn with time, but Gavin held it close and squinted to read: *To my little Anya. Love, Uncle James.*

Gavin helplessly held the little doll, wondering what it might have been like for him and Anya if James MacBrier were still alive. He forced himself to get hold of his senses enough to put the doll back before he was caught with it. Then he proceeded with his original purpose, finding the key near the back of a drawer beneath a pile of mended and neatly folded stockings.

As he opened the wardrobe with purpose and went carefully to his knees, Gavin felt an intangible connection between the doll he'd just found and the box locked beneath this panel. In the corner he found Anya's scullery uniforms, left where she'd stashed them. "I should burn them," he muttered aloud, but he only pushed them aside for now.

His fingers searched for the tiny lock. He turned the key in it, and the bottom of the wardrobe slid open. With reverence he pulled out the ornately carved wooden box and sat down on the floor. His palms turned sweaty as he opened the lid, feeling all over again as he had the night the Earl had given him this. He dug his fingers down into the mass of jewelry, marveling freshly that the Earl had given him so much.

"What are you doing?" Anya asked.

He started, feeling like a child with his hand caught in the candy jar. "And you yell at *me* for sneaking up on *you.*"

Anya laughed, then her eyes moved to the box in his lap and he saw her curiosity. He could think of no reason not to show her. But he'd never shown this to anyone. "This is what the Earl gave me before he died," he stated simply.

Anya knelt beside him, and her eyes widened as she beheld the full extent of it. "There must be a fortune in there!"

"Fortune?" He gave an ironic laugh. "These are not just jewels; they are antiques, heirlooms. I had some of them appraised, and their worth is staggering, but I could never sell them. I sold a few pieces that were newer, not so valuable, and used that along with the money he gave me to make some good investments that have done well." He rummaged through the jewels nostalgically. "These will stay as they are."

Anya was speechless as she gazed into the open box. She couldn't believe the Earl had given so much to anybody. She wondered what Margaret and Malvina and Cedric would think if they knew what Gavin possessed—what they could have had. And she admired Gavin for his wisdom concerning them.

"I'll never understand it," Gavin said, interrupting her thoughts. "I look at this and still can't believe he gave it all to me. I heard him tell my mother he would give me Brierley if it was in his power. It seems he almost did."

"He must have cared a great deal for you," Anya said.

"He hardly knew me," Gavin admitted. "I have pondered over it for many years, and I believe what he gave me was more a tribute to my mother. And perhaps giving it to me prevented someone else from having it. I believe vengeance was part of his motive."

Anya smiled at his perception. "I believe you might be right." Her eye caught a piece of tartan showing from beneath the jewels, and she reached out to take it, fingering it carefully. "MacBrier Tartan," she said softly. She knew it well. Her mind flooded with a clear memory of James MacBrier, clad in kilt and plaid.

Reverently Anya put the tartan back into the box, and Gavin closed the lid. Their eyes met with the bond that Brierley had given them, and Gavin couldn't suppress the urge to kiss her. Anya felt strength in it. She both feared and anticipated what might lie ahead for them.

"I came in to tell you that dinner is ready," she said when the kiss was done.

Gavin smiled. "I'll be right in."

Anya left him to return the box to its hiding place, then he closed the wardrobe and hobbled into the kitchen.

The following morning, Anya found Gavin standing before the mirror to shave himself. He smiled triumphantly when he found her watching him, and Anya smiled back in an effort to hide the twinge of fear. She knew he could have done this himself long before now, but his doing it now seemed to make a statement.

Anya had observed each day as Gavin gradually did more for himself, but this step made her realize that their day of reckoning was not far off. It wouldn't be long now, and he wouldn't need her at all. Or would he? She couldn't deny the look of love in his eyes, and it did no good to try to subdue her own feelings. It was too late. Her heart was on the table, and she could only hope he would treat it gently.

As Anya watched Gavin gain strength and color, her feelings did the same. She never wanted to be apart from him, and it gave her a sense of hope and peace beyond compare to see that the love in his eyes had only increased.

Gavin had wrestled within himself for days about this turning point in his life. In a sense, he wanted to prolong this stage of their lives forever; but a very big part of him ached to go beyond this, to make Anya a part of his life in every aspect. He feared crossing the bridge, but longed for what lay beyond it. And a day came when he had to admit that it couldn't be put off any longer.

Gavin awoke to hear Anya busy in the kitchen. He quickly dressed, then went to the wardrobe to dig out his boots. It hurt his thigh to pull on the left one, and he wondered if the wounds would ever leave him in peace. He left the cane leaning as it was against the wall, and quietly went to the door without Anya noticing.

With breakfast laid out on the table, Anya called to Gavin that it was ready. She continued busily for several moments before she realized there had been no response. A quick search of the house revealed it was empty. Only then did she hear a rhythmic echo coming from outside.

A hint of autumn clung to the breeze that greeted her when she stepped through the door, feeling tears threaten. The past weeks flew through her mind. How long had she been here? Four weeks? Five? She wasn't certain. She recalled that first day here with Gavin unconscious, and then he'd been weak for so long. And now, here he was—strong and sturdy, his legs braced apart to support him as he swung the axe in forceful thrusts, the wood cracking and splitting at his command.

Gavin sensed her presence and looked up to see her. He stopped and leaned against the axe, hoping she hadn't noticed how the little display had done him in. He hoped that would improve with time.

Anya took a deep breath and moved toward him. She knew what significance rested on this moment. "Feeling better, I see," she said. He threw the axe into a log and left it. She watched as he pulled off his gloves and wiped the sweat from his brow. She couldn't help noticing how fine he looked, maintaining his strong stance, his lean legs accentuated by narrow breeches and high boots.

"Much better, thank you," he smiled.

"I think you've been holding out on me."

"Whatever gave you that idea?" he smirked. Anya shrugged her shoulders and he admitted, "I didn't want this day to come too soon."

"Why not?"

"I didn't want you to leave."

Anya looked down briefly, sensing his implication. He was saying he hadn't been dependent on her for some time now. She knew that her own feelings had done nothing but grow. Stoically she looked up at him and their eyes met with mutual intensity, each hanging on a hope that this would not be the end, but the beginning. Neither spoke, but a unified understanding fell over them. Gavin held out a hand. Anya hesitated only a moment before she took it. And then she was in his arms.

Gavin felt triumph in his ability to hold her the way a man should hold a woman. Anya felt thrilled at the strength in his arms as he nearly crushed her against him. Their embrace only lessened when a kiss replaced it, sealing an unspoken promise that Anya would not leave, and Gavin would not allow her to.

Arm in arm they walked back to the house, neither paying any heed to Gavin's persisting limp. They shared breakfast in silence until he asked, "Will I always walk this way?"

"The limp, you mean?" He nodded. "It will likely get much better with time, but I wouldn't dare tell you it will go away completely."

"At least I can walk," he smiled, then laughed. "At least I'm alive."

When the meal was finished, Gavin urged Anya to the parlor and into a chair. He sat across the room and casually picked up one of her slippers off a nearby table.

"What on earth are you doing with that?" she laughed.

"When I find the maiden who fits this slipper, I will ask her to be my wife."

"Don't be ridiculous!" she chuckled timidly.

"I'm quite serious," he stated. His eyes told her he was.

"I've got to clean the kitchen," she insisted and left the room. Gavin smiled to himself and placed the slipper back on the table, as if it were an expensive porcelain statuette.

Anya awoke early and surveyed the room as it filled with dawn's light. She watched Gavin sleeping soundly on the other side of the room, and her heart swelled with fresh love. She was amazed at how well he had kept his gentleman's word. Knowing that he wanted her, but was willing to wait until it was proper, left Anya feeling all the more loved, more appreciated, more secure than she ever had in her life. Her thoughts moved over the events that had brought her here, and she felt truly grateful. Everything she could ever want or hope for was here with Gavin.

A brief wave of nausea caught her, but she passed it off and quickly took up her thoughts once more. When it came again, she felt certain she was coming down with something. She was at least grateful that she hadn't gotten ill when Gavin had needed her.

Impulsively she got up earlier than usual and greeted Gavin with breakfast in bed, her nausea gone and forgotten. "Just like old times," she said, setting the tray on his lap.

He bent forward to kiss her. "Not quite like old times."

Anya turned back toward the kitchen and he stopped her, setting the tray briefly aside. "Come here and sit down." She did as he asked, and he took her hand into his. "Forgive the lack of pomp and ceremony," he began, looking directly at her, "but I can't wait another moment." Anya's heart fluttered. "Marry me, Anya. Soon."

Anya attempted to catch her breath. "Don't you think we should give it more time?"

"Always so practical," he smiled, touching her hair. "If you want some time, fine, but I don't need it. I know these feelings will never change. Why wait? I want you to be mine. I want to be yours—forever."

Anya was silent for a long moment, not from needing time to contemplate it as much as needing to gain control of her emotion. "Of course I'll marry you," she finally said, and Gavin laughed.

"How about next week?" he asked, holding her tightly.

"So soon?" she breathed.

"How about tomorrow?"

"Next week would be fine," she laughed, and embraced him in a feeble attempt to express how very happy she was.

With Gavin up and around, he insisted that from now on Anya should sleep in the bed, and he would take her place on the floor. At first she protested strongly, saying that it was his home. Besides, with his wounds healing, he needed the comfort of his own bed. But he was adamant, and Anya couldn't deny the comfort of the bed, especially when she became unusually tired soon after lunch. He found her lying down late in the afternoon and wondered if something was wrong, but the nap rejuvenated her through the evening.

Anya went to bed earlier than normal, and awoke again feeling uneasy. While Gavin slept she consciously tried to gain control of the increasing nausea, but instead she rushed into the other room, where dry heaves pitched her empty stomach into her throat.

When she finally gained control, Gavin was holding her shoulders. The look in her eyes betrayed her embarrassment, but Gavin smiled. "Nothing could be worse than all you did for me when I was bedridden. Are you all right?" he added, helping her to the bed.

"I don't know what came over me. I fear I'm getting ill."

Gavin's brow creased with concern as he tucked her in. "I shall take very good care of you."

Anya gave him a weak smile, turned over, and went back to sleep. She woke feeling unusually damp from sweat, but not at all feverish. While she lay looking at the ceiling, the reality struck her like a knife in the throat.

"Please, God . . . no!" she whispered aloud. Quickly her mind filed through all of the facts. Every detail of her encounter with Cedric flashed through her mind in heated spurts, and she cursed him from the depths of her soul. And he'd had the nerve to tell her that she couldn't possibly get pregnant from one encounter. What a fool she'd been! She had completely dismissed the possibility and let herself fall into this relationship, and now . . . What on earth would she do now?

Anya stopped and told herself that maybe it wasn't true. Perhaps she was just ill. Then she realized that she'd been with Gavin for weeks and she'd had no cycle. She'd been so preoccupied that she hadn't even noticed.

"Heaven help me!" she whispered under her breath.

"What was that?" Gavin asked from the doorframe where he leaned, watching her.

"Nothing." She tried to smile while her heart wrenched into her throat just to look at him. How could she tell him? How could she possibly expect him to love her now?

"You look as white as a ghost," he said with concern, moving closer.

"I'm just . . . not feeling well."

"Perhaps I should ride into town and get the doctor."

"No . . . no, don't do that. I'm certain it will pass." Anya chided herself inwardly. She was lying to him. He'd find out sooner or later. Why didn't she just tell him and get it over with? The words echoed through her mind: *I'm going to have Cedric MacBrier's baby.* Looking into Gavin's face, she couldn't bring herself to say it. How could she possibly put her voice to words that would immediately destroy all they had shared?

"I think I'll try to sleep some more," was all she said, wanting to be alone. Gavin gave her a concerned smile and left the room. Anya turned her face into the pillow and wanted to scream. This was a nightmare! Painful tears welled up, but she did her best to muffle them, wanting to cry all of this pain out and be free of it.

Gavin heard Anya's muffled whimpering and wondered if it was heaves again. He found her crying, but she emphatically insisted that she just didn't feel well. To Gavin it didn't make sense. Through the next several days, he watched her go through the daily rituals: dry heaves in the morning, occasional vomiting in the afternoon, sleeping almost constantly when she wasn't too sick to do so, and turning more pale by the day. But it wasn't just a physical thing; the life was gone from her eyes. She insisted that he not get a doctor, threatening with all sorts of ridiculous things, but he was nearly ready to ignore her threats and do it anyway.

Anya knew she wasn't doing a very good job of handling this, and she felt certain Gavin knew this wasn't what she was pretending it to be—whatever that was. She only prayed he was naive enough in such matters that he wouldn't figure it out.

After days of contemplation, Anya decided that all she could do now was go back to Brierley. She could not—would not—expect Gavin to marry her now. It was not fair to him, and she would not impose this burden upon his good nature. It broke her heart to think of leaving him, and she well knew how badly they would treat her at Brierley. But she couldn't possibly expect to find employment elsewhere in this condition. In her present state of mind, she could see no other way. Realizing that she had to get back on her feet if she was going to survive this at all, Anya forced herself to get out of bed.

Gavin came in from the stable to find her scrubbing the floor. "What on earth are you doing?" he insisted. "I thought you were ill."

"I'm feeling better," she said, but her voice was heavy with despair.

Anya continued to work despite his protests, telling herself she had better get used to it. Sooner or later, she would have to go back to Brierley.

Gavin found Anya lying on her side, gazing at the wall as if it were about to swallow her up. She had been going through her days insisting that she was better, working her heart out, cleaning things that were already clean. But the heaves and vomiting continued, and that hollow look in her eyes deepened continually. He hadn't dared bring up the postponed wedding, unconsciously fearing what her response might be.

"Anya," he said. She hardly did more than blink to acknowledge him. "I'm going to get a doctor." As he expected, that got her attention.

"No, please don't." She sat up, and her pallor increased.

"If you are so certain that you don't need one, perhaps you could let me know what's going on so I could have a little peace of mind."

"It will pass," was all she said, then she was off to do some ridiculous chore that didn't need doing.

Anya heard Gavin leave the house and slam the door. It was not unusual for him to spend a great deal of time outside, but when she heard the horse galloping away, her heart dropped a little.

"What difference does it make?" she said aloud and went about her work, inwardly knowing that she had to go soon, but wanting to put it off as long as possible.

Gavin returned feeling hope and determination. Whatever she was trying to prove, he was not going to let her get away with it.

"Anya," he said. She glanced up, startled, from where she sat in the parlor. He went down on one knee in front of her and took her hand in his. "Listen to me very carefully. I want to tell you something extremely important. When two people come together in life, what happened before that time no longer matters." He paused to let the words be absorbed. "I love you, Anya, and I want you to know that there is nothing—*nothing,*" he enunciated carefully, "that you and I can't overcome together."

She looked briefly hopeful, but the shadows in her eyes outweighed it quickly. "Anya," he went on, "I'm asking you again to marry me, and I'm promising to take you—all of you—into my heart and my home and care for you without question. Do you understand?"

Anya listened quietly to his speech, but echoes from her past blocked out the words between the lines. She could only see the unfairness of this pregnancy to him. How could she tell a man who was expecting to marry an innocent woman that she was to have another man's baby? She just couldn't do it. She told herself she had to face the reality. This baby tied her to Brierley forever. She just had to go back, and it was time he knew. Stoically she drew back her shoulders and looked him in the eye. Then she couldn't bring herself to say it, and only ended up sighing.

"Why won't you talk to me?" he asked. "What has happened to you?"

Her insipid tone cut Gavin to the core. "It doesn't matter."

"It matters to me!" She winced at his anger, and he softened his voice. "Anya, you must tell me what's wrong. You must trust me." He lifted her chin, but she closed her eyes and he realized she had hardly looked at him for days. "Anya," he persisted, "if we are going to marry, we have to be able to talk. I have to know what's wrong so I can help you."

"That's just it," she said abruptly. "I can't marry you."

Gavin felt himself go cold. He couldn't find words to respond. The silence was finally broken by a helpless rambling. "Did I do something wrong, Anya? Is it . . . something I said? Did I . . ."

"Stop it! It has nothing to do with you."

"You're telling me that you're going to leave me, and then you tell me it has nothing to do with me? Come on, Anya. Let's get all of this into the open once and for all."

Anya drew a deep breath. "All right. I'm going back to Brierley."

He gave a humorless chuckle. "You can't be serious."

"I have no choice."

"Aren't I a choice?"

"Not anymore."

He stood and drove his fist into his palm, then in desperation he went to his knees again and took her shoulders firmly in his grasp. "Look me in the eye, Anya, and tell me you don't love me."

"I do love you. That's why I have to . . . go."

"Now that makes sense!" he said with bitter sarcasm.

"Just let it go, Gavin. It's for the best."

"Why don't you let *me* decide what's best for me? Tell me the truth and let *me* decide."

Anya looked at him, and he saw the fear. What on earth was she afraid of? "Out with it, woman! If you really want to go back to that hell on earth, fine, but I have a right to know why, and I'm not letting you go until I do. So out with it—now! After all we have shared, I at least deserve a reason."

"You men are all alike," she muttered. "Arrogant, demanding scoundrels who think you can do anything you please with a woman and . . ." Anya knew she was lying again. The emotion churning inside mixed with the plea in his eyes, and every effort to fight back the tears was in vain. They came slowly at first while she continued telling him how awful he was, then the words became lost in uncontrollable sobbing.

Gavin was beginning to see what he had suspected all along. All of this was just an attempt to cover a lot of fear and pain. "It's all right," he whispered, pulling her head to his shoulder. "Go ahead and cry." He could almost feel her heart breaking in his hands, while he couldn't understand why she wouldn't confide in him. She took his shirt into her fists while her sobbing turned to anguish, and Gavin felt tears fall over his own face. His heart was breaking, too. And he felt helpless. So blasted helpless!

Anya held to Gavin and let herself cry until she sank wearily against him, then he carried her to bed. She cried herself into exhaustion and awoke in the darkness, aware of Gavin sleeping in his bed on the floor. She could only pray that he would forgive her while she found the nerve to lock her breaking heart away and climb out of bed.

Quietly she took her scullery uniforms from the bottom of the wardrobe. She dressed in one and put the other with her rag doll and her hairbrush. She couldn't resist taking some of her new underclothes, but she resigned herself to leave the rest, knowing she would have little use for such fine things. She took some bread and cheese from the kitchen and bundled everything together inside one of her aprons.

With her cloak about her shoulders, she carefully crept back into the bedroom, where she gazed down at Gavin and cried silent tears. She couldn't see him in the darkness, but his image in her mind was clear, and she ingrained it carefully into her memory.

"I love you, Gavin," she whispered, then quietly left the house. She thought briefly about Gavin's mother and felt a sudden rush of empathy. Hadn't she been a servant at Brierley who gave birth to an illegitimate child? Anya could only hope that this child would somehow be able to grow beyond such a life, as Gavin had.

The journey was long on foot and she arrived just before dawn, where she crept into an unused stall in the stable and slept. She would at least wait until she felt physically rejuvenated before facing Brierley again.

Chapter Nine
Victims of Brierley

Gavin felt the absence before he was completely awake. The house held a deathly silence. There were no smells of breakfast cooking, no sounds to indicate she was bathing in the next room.

"Anya!" he cried before he was even out of bed. His heart fell to the pit of his stomach. Only silence echoed back at him, like a sadistic taunt. He went to the door and found it unlocked. Again he cried her name from the depths of his soul, but only the rustling of the trees answered.

He leaned against the doorframe as tears burned into his eyes. But the tears only fed his anger, and he reached for the closest tangible object he could find. The hurled vase shattered into a thousand pieces against the wall, and the water inside drizzled over the wallpaper as if it wept. The roses she had gathered just yesterday fell in a tattered heap upon the floor.

"How dare you!" he shouted to the empty morning. "How dare you leave me!" Then, with no thought or hesitation, Gavin lumbered back to the bedroom in a desperate search for evidence, feeling a grain of hope that he was wrong. Maybe she had gone into town. Maybe she'd gone for a walk. But everything was there. Seven dresses hung neatly in the wardrobe, her combs were scattered over the dresser, the hand balm lay untouched. He reached into the bottom of the wardrobe and felt sick. He should have burned those uniforms while he'd had the chance.

Gavin's thoughts shifted and he threw himself into a shirt and jacket, impatient with the time it took to pull on his boots. Never had he saddled a horse so quickly, and what normally was an hour's ride took half that as he pressed the stallion mercilessly.

A coldness glazed over his heart as Brierley came into view in the morning light. The beauty of the house was mocked by the vile secrets it harbored. Gavin galloped around the house, right through the stable doors. Robbie turned wide, innocent eyes upon him as he reared the stallion back to stop.

"Well, I'll be, lad. What a s'prise!"

"I seriously doubt it!" Gavin retorted, dismounting abruptly. "Where is she?"

"I dinna ken what ye're talkin' aboot!"

"I know she came back here! And I know she wouldn't do anything without coming to the stable first." He took Robbie hard by the shoulders. "Where is she?"

"Have ye gone mad, lad?"

Gavin softened and backed away. "Maybe I have."

"I think he's looking for me," Anya said quietly, and they both turned in surprise.

"Well, I'll be!" Robbie muttered.

"You didn't even have the decency to tell me good-bye," Gavin stated, his hurt and anger overriding all other emotions.

"Good-bye, Gavin," she said tonelessly.

"And you really expect me to turn around and leave you *here*?" he asked, astonished.

"Yes, I do."

"You're a fool, Anya. You're throwing your life away."

"I'd have tae agree wi' that," Robbie interjected.

"Oh, hush!" Anya insisted, and he did.

"Get your things," Gavin stated. "We're going back."

"Will you hold me prisoner?" she asked.

"Brierley is the prison, Anya."

"But you will force me to go back? What is the difference?"

"The difference is this!" He pulled the uniform she wore into his hands.

"You think you can buy me a few pretty dresses and life will be sublime? Well, it's not that easy!"

"And you think the issue here is a few pretty dresses?"

Anya looked away tersely. Gavin couldn't believe what she was saying. He knew she was lying—to herself as much as to him. But what could he do? He was every bit as helpless as he had been when his bloodless body was bound to a bed.

"Fine!" He nearly threw her out of his grasp, knowing she was right. He could not force her to go back, any more than he could force her to love him. "Be a martyr. Stay here and rot!" He took her chin into a painful grip and pointed a finger. "But you can't say I didn't try. Don't you ever, once, in your wretched, miserable life, even dare to think to yourself that I didn't try." He dropped his hand and added coldly, "You dare speak to me about trampling upon hearts, about loving and tossing aside."

Everything inside of Anya wanted to run into his arms, beg his forgiveness. But a wave of nausea reminded her of reality and she only turned away, unable to face him any longer.

"Watch out for her, Robbie," Gavin said as he mounted. "Nobody else will."

Once Gavin had passed the border of Brierley, he slowed his stallion to a walk, hating the miles passing between him and Anya. He wondered if he would ever get over this. He had gotten over his mother's death with time, but he felt certain he would never be free of the pain he felt now. Perhaps it would ease in years to come. But it would never go away. He would far prefer that Anya had died than to have her outwardly spurn him. But he couldn't bring himself to blame her for this. She was a victim. They were both victims. The bond that had drawn them together had now torn them apart. Brierley had come between them.

Gavin was surprised to realize he was almost home, but impulsively he broke into a gallop and passed it by. Unable to face the emptiness of the house, he rode into town, not certain where he was going until he found himself there.

He was embarrassed by his disheveled appearance as he went through the door of the hat shop, pretending to look over the wares on display until a woman in her late thirties, delicately beautiful for her age, sauntered from the back room.

"Gavin!" she squealed when he turned toward her.

"Hello, Peg," he replied, his gaze taking in the lavish dress and heavily rouged cheeks.

Peg wrapped her arms around him and kissed his cheeks before she took in his appearance. "Ye look terrible!"

"I feel terrible."

"Come on back," she urged, taking his arm to lead him past the curtain that divided the shop from her living quarters. "I'm certain there is somethin' I can do tae make ye feel better." She put her arm around him as they walked, then she glanced down and nearly shrieked, "Bless me, lad. Ye're limpin'. What have ye done tae yersel'?"

"It's a long story." Gavin sat numbly in a chair, and she pulled off his boots without permission.

"I had about given ye up for dead since ye ran off tae go back tae that dreadful place you was raised. What was it called?"

"Brierley," he answered dryly.

"How did that go, anyway?" she asked, rubbing his shoulders and neck.

"Not so good," he answered.

"Tell me what ye need," she insisted.

"Let's talk," he said.

"All right. Talk. I'm all ears."

"What was that all aboot, lass?" Robbie insisted when Gavin had gone.

"He asked me to marry him," she said, turning to gather her things out of the straw.

"Then what in th' name o' heaven are ye doin' here? That Gavin is th' best lad I've ever known in all m' days. Ye're a fool, lass."

"It's too late," she said quietly.

"Nonsense. I'll tak ye back now, an' —"

"It's too late!" she insisted, taking a deep breath and heading toward the side door of the house.

"Anya!" Mrs. MacGregor gasped when she entered the kitchen. "We thought ye'd run away for good."

"No," she tried to smile, "I just had a . . . friend who needed my help."

"But it's settled now?"

"Yes. Yes, it's settled now."

"Are ye hungry, lass?" Anya nodded, and Mrs. MacGregor quickly set some breakfast before her. "Ye don't look at all well. Perhaps ye should get yersel' some rest before they set ye back to work, an' . . ."

Like an immediate answer to a bad omen, Una came into the room. Her eyes fell on Anya, and a tainted smile touched Una's lips so completely that Anya feared her face might crack. A sick dread settled into her, making her wonder why she hadn't just told Gavin the truth and begged him for help. But such thoughts were pointless. It would have been too humiliating. But would it have been worse than this? The reality of just seeing this woman who had caused her such pain put a different perspective on the circumstances already.

"Well, if it isn't Miss High and Mighty!" Una sneered. "I thought we'd seen the last of you. Lady Margaret will be pleased to know that you missed us enough to come back."

"I daresay she will," Anya mumbled.

"Be quick with that breakfast and get to work, lass! Your replacement could use some time off." She gave a wicked little laugh and took something off a shelf. "And you'd best be making up for lost time. I'll be checking your work, and if it doesn't measure up, you'll be on the street."

Una turned on her heel and left, but her oppression remained heavy, even in her absence.

"Perhaps ye'd have done well tae stay with that friend o' yers, lass," Mrs. MacGregor said quietly.

"I couldn't," Anya insisted and rose abruptly from the table. She gathered her things and left the kitchen to face the long flight of stairs to her little room.

Her heart sank further as she opened the door to find that nothing had changed. Her replacement was likely not sentenced to live in such a room. Anya tried to get rid of some of the dust, but it seemed futile. Idly she put her few things away, choked back an onset of tears, and went to face her work.

The toil was worse than it ever had been. She often felt light-headed and weak, but knew there wasn't time to rest. And each foul smell sent her stomach lurching. Anya's thoughts kept straying to Gavin. Despite all effort to block him out of her mind, his final words kept storming through her like a knife twisting in her heart.

You can't say I didn't try. . . . You dare speak to me of trampling upon hearts. . . . Stay here and rot! Stay here and rot! It echoed through her mind until she thought she would die inside. *Stay here and rot!*

When the work was finally finished, Anya ate as if she'd been starved for days, then she wearily made her way up the stairs and collapsed onto her bed. She tried to keep from crying, but the tears would not be deterred, and she wept until sleep finally released her from the pain.

It was nice to see Effie at breakfast. At least there was one bright spot in this, Anya told herself.

"Effie," she took the girl's hand, "it's Anya."

"Anya likes to play games," Effie stated, as if she'd never been gone. Then she began rambling about her breakfast and her schedule for the day, planned with a number of other servants. Anya was dismayed, though she shouldn't have been surprised, to realize that Effie's life had gone on much the same without her. She wanted to spend some time with Effie, but time was something she didn't have right now. It took every minute she had just to complete her tasks and survive.

Anya tuned an ear to the conversation at the table, surprised to find that it centered on Malvina's forthcoming marriage. The date had been set, and big plans were being made.

"Who is she marrying?" Anya asked, feeling pity for the poor man, whoever he was.

"A Mr. Clayton," Ellen answered. "He's old enough tae be her father." Everyone laughed. "Which is pretty old!"

"But who else would have her?" a livery boy asked, and the laughter resumed.

Anya's thoughts went to Gavin. She should have been married by now. She wondered what would have happened if they had married before she had discovered her pregnancy. And even if she hadn't ended up pregnant, wouldn't he have realized she wasn't innocent? She'd been a fool to ever think it could all be erased and forgotten so easily. Sooner or later, it would have come between them. She pushed the thoughts away and finished her breakfast.

Anya was both pleased and disappointed to discover that Cedric was gone for a few days. She wanted to tell him about the baby and have it over with, as much as she wanted to put it off forever.

"He'll be back th' day after t'morrow," Mrs. MacGregor informed her when she'd found an opportunity to ask without being overheard.

While she worked, Anya tried to imagine how Cedric would react. She felt certain he would be displeased, but still she felt he should know. She certainly didn't expect or even want him to do anything about it. She just wanted him to know.

Each day seemed longer than the last as Anya's body felt more tired, more sore, and her hands became more dry and aching. She scolded herself for not bringing the hand balm, but it would have run out sooner or later. There was no point putting off the inevitable.

As she scrubbed the floor, Anya paused in her work to look at her hands and felt tears welling up. She recalled Gavin saying that a woman's hands told the story of her life. How right he was, as if their condition was a direct translation of what was hidden in her heart. She might as well face and accept it. Her life would be spent with chapped, aching hands.

Coming to her feet, Anya caught her reflection in the ornately carved mirror on the wall. She hated what she saw and quickly turned away. She wondered what it would be like when her pregnancy became known. And what would life be like for this baby? Oh, she couldn't bear such thoughts! She only kept working and tried to keep her mind on the present, however miserable it was.

As Anya swept around the fireplace in Lady Margaret's room, she felt grateful that since her return she hadn't had to face the Lady of Brierley personally. She rubbed the ache in her lower back, then turned to realize she wasn't alone.

"Cedric!" she gasped.

He chuckled and folded his arms across his chest. "You can't imagine how pleased I was to hear that you'd returned in my absence."

"I'll bet you were," she sneered.

"And what fool thing made you come back here? I heard rumors that you'd run off with a man." He smirked. "Didn't want you, eh?"

Anya swallowed the hurt and lifted her chin. "What man would have me after what you've done to me?"

"Are you still upset about that?" He eyed her lewdly. Anya wondered if being here would sentence her to more of his advances. Did it matter?

"It's difficult to get over something when its results are still with me."

Cedric's left brow went up in question, then a wicked, vindictive smile spread over his face. "Anya, are you trying to tell me that . . ."

"Yes, you snake, I'm going to have your baby!"

The reality seemed to melt Cedric's amusement away. Anya saw his eyes fill with something that made her afraid. She attempted to ease away, but the back of his hand flew across her face. As she cried out from the sting, stars swam before her eyes. She reached out to steady herself against the wall, but Cedric twisted her arm cruelly.

"And you think you can come back here and make your demands on me?" he growled through clenched teeth.

"I don't want anything from you!" she insisted, but he didn't seem to hear.

"If you cause any trouble for me, lass, you'll regret ever being born. I will make life hell for you!"

"I told you!" she shouted. "I don't want anything. I wouldn't take your handouts if you paid me to, and I certainly wouldn't want you to marry me. That *would* be hell!"

"You uppity little . . ."

Anya winced as his arm rose to strike her again, but the door swung open and he quickly backed away.

"Cedric." Lady Margaret spoke to her son while her eyes fell on Anya with a deep-rooted glint. "Stop harassing the maids and find something useful to do. You could start by acting like an earl, for a change."

Anya sensed the anger spurred in Cedric by his mother's words, but she was grateful when he left with something else to fume about.

"Did he hurt you?" Margaret asked, and Anya was so surprised by the inquiry that she couldn't answer. What Anya had interpreted as a grain of concern was quickly gone, and Margaret added tersely, "Get back to work."

Once Anya was alone, the tears welled up. Did pregnancy make all women cry this much, or was she really so miserable? At least she didn't have to dread telling Cedric any longer, but she feared what the future would bring.

Gavin stood over his mother's grave and wept. He wept for the senselessness of her life, banished to a stone tower like some damsel in distress, never to be rescued. He wept for the tragedy of her death. And he wept for the sixteen-year-old boy she had left behind. Gavin wept for the years he had tried to come to peace with all of this. And he wept for the impaling fear of nearly losing his life in an effort to do just that. He wept for James MacBrier, a prisoner in the realm he should have ruled, murdered in his own bed. But above all else, Gavin wept for Anya.

Through several sleepless nights, he had sifted through all the hurt and the anger until he finally came to the raw truth. Brierley had destroyed Anya just as it was destroying him, just as it had destroyed his mother. He knelt and brushed a loving hand over the stone marker on his mother's grave. He'd ordered it special and put it there himself a few years after her death to replace the wooden cross left at the time of her simple burial. But still, it seemed so out of place in the surrounding forest. Even in death, Jinny Baird didn't fit in.

When the trees blocked out the little remaining sun and it became difficult to see the stone, Gavin wiped his face with his shirt sleeve and wandered toward the stable. He pulled the hood of a cloak up over his head and tried not to think about the bullets he'd taken here not so many weeks ago. Stepping into the dimly lit stable, Gavin was relieved to find no one but Robbie there. The old man looked up at him, disoriented, until Gavin pushed back the hood. There was no mistaking the disdain that rose in Robbie's eyes when he recognized Gavin.

"Happy to see me, eh?" Gavin said with deep sarcasm. Robbie focused his attention on currying a mare. Gavin attempted to cover his uneasiness as he added, "So, you've become subjected to the dreaded Brierley curse as well. One of its symptoms is an abject hatred toward me and everything I represent."

"Don't be puttin' words in m' mooth, lad," Robbie uttered curtly. "If ye must know, Ah'm awful glad tae see ye here. It will save me th' trouble o' havin' tae come an' find ye an' slap ye aroond a little."

Gavin tried to swallow his anger. But he was sick to death of being misunderstood and treated like some kind of leper. "And tell me, old man, what great Brierley gossip have you been listening to that makes you want to slap me around a little?"

"Gossip's got nothin' tae do with it, lad." Robbie set aside his work and put his hands firmly on his hips. "There's a lass in there," he motioned absently toward the direction of the house, "sufferin' an' hurtin', an' there's no sense tae it."

"She's the one who walked out on me, Robbie. It wasn't I who—"

"But ye're th' only un who cin do somethin' aboot it, an' by heaven an' earth an' all I hold dear, Ah'm gonna see that ye do it. Ye got no idea what's goin' on in that poor lassie's heart, lad. It doesna matter what's hurtin' her, ye gotta find a way tae put it right. She saved yer life, and ye owe her that. She shouldna be here. Whatever else ye work out doesna matter, but ye got tae get th' lass away from that witch."

"Well," Gavin let out a deep breath, "at least we're seeing eye to eye on that. You can stop looking at me like you're going to beat the devil out of me. I may be a little slow, but I'm not completely stupid. I came here with every intention of taking her with me. If I have to bind her and gag her and haul her bodily away, she will never serve in this house again. I swear that to you by heaven and earth and all I hold dear."

"Well, now," Robbie's face broke into a pleasant grin, "that's more like m' lad."

"The problem is . . . well, I'm not so sure she'll want to go with me, and . . . if I cause a scene . . ." Gavin cleared his throat. "Let's just say I'd like to walk away from here of my own accord this time." His voice nearly cracked with an earnest plea. "Tell me where to find her, Robbie. I can't just go in there and—"

"I canna tell ye where tae find her right now. She could be just aboot anywhere. But I cin tell ye where tae find her when th' work is finished."

Robbie gave him careful instructions, then Gavin waited quietly in the stable until it was completely dark.

"Are you going to forgive me, then, old man?" Gavin asked in a light tone that was more typical of their lifelong relationship.

"Ye tak th' lass away from here an' find a way tae make her happy, an' I couldna love ye more."

Gavin laughed and slapped Robbie's shoulder. "You touch my heart." Then he added more seriously, "I will certainly do my best. Whether she wants me or not, Robbie, I will be certain she's cared for."

For the first time since Jinny Baird died, Robbie put his arms around Gavin with a firm embrace. "Ye're a good lad," he said quietly. "Always were. God go with ye, now."

Gavin nodded and headed stealthily toward the side door of Brierley. Just inside the door, he could hear distant voices from what he realized was the kitchen. Following Robbie's instructions, he headed up the back stairs, stopping cautiously at each landing to be certain all was clear. He continued going up, realizing he'd lost count of the flights he'd ascended. Robbie did say it was at the very top. After what his body had been through in the past several weeks, it shouldn't have been a surprise to find his legs aching from exhaustion and his breathing labored. While he stopped to rest for a minute, he tried to imagine his sweet Anya making this climb every night after working a long day, her hands cracked and bleeding. And he also knew, from her behavior before she'd left, that she was likely not feeling well at all. The tears that burned into his eyes were a recently familiar companion, but he blinked them back and continued quietly up the stairs. He reminded himself that he was here to take her away from all of this, and with any luck she would not make it too difficult for him.

When the stairs finally ended, there was only one door available. Cautiously he pushed it open and saw the shadow of a lamp. Groping in the darkness, he finally managed to light it, then he turned to survey his surroundings. The tears came again, this time refusing to be pushed back. The room was tiny and damp, with only the most minimal accommodations. He thought of all the finery the MacBriers flaunted at the ball he had briefly attended, and tried to comprehend how they could sentence James MacBrier's great-niece to live here with the lowest of everything. He picked up the little ragged doll and couldn't hold back a groan of anguish on her behalf. The anger and hurt rose into his throat like bile. But he swallowed it and reminded himself that it would soon be over. Whether she wanted to marry him or not, he would see that she lived the life that James MacBrier would have intended her to live. Unlike Jinny Baird, this damsel in distress would be rescued—whether she liked it or not.

As the day finally came to a merciful close, Anya lumbered up the stairs, feeling as if her five days here had been months. She was so tired, just so very tired. With each exhausted step she took, the thoughts that had been mulling around in her mind through the day suddenly seemed to take hold with a vague kind of aspiration. Since her return to Brierley, she'd kept a prayer in her heart that she would be able to endure the future with some measure of peace, that she would be able to give her baby a good life, something beyond the horrors of this place. But only now did a thought take hold in her mind with such clarity that she stopped on the stairs for a full minute to absorb it. She could not wait or expect to be rescued from Brierley. Being rescued was a state of mind. She *had* been rescued. She had been blessed with the opportunity to leave here, and she knew Gavin would help her, no matter the circumstances. But she had succumbed to the inner voices of the past that had lured her to believe she had no choice but to remain here forever and be a victim. But she *did* have a choice. She could choose to walk away from here and never look back. And she would find a way to make it. She would! She wasn't certain how exactly, but feeling a glimmer of hope appear against an otherwise black sky, she pressed on toward her room, wanting only to sleep. Tomorrow she would work out a way to leave here once and for all.

At last she reached the little room, where she entered and locked the door before reaching to light the lamp. It wasn't where she had left it and she panicked, wondering what might have happened to it. Groping in the dark, her hands searched every possible place it could be. Had someone been here? Would they take that from her, too? The room was so dark she could barely make out the shadow of her bed, but she only wanted to be in it, and nearly stumbled as she tried to reach it.

Each night she tried to fight back the tears, but still they came. In spite of the inkling of hope she felt, Anya cried into her pillow until the strike of a match illuminated the room. She gasped as she turned and sat up, holding the pillow against her, certain she would find Cedric waiting here to have his way with her.

"Gavin!" she blurted out, then held her breath while he casually lit the lamp, adjusted the wick, and set it back where it belonged. She expected him to be angry, and waited for the outburst. But she was so glad to see him she didn't care.

Gavin watched Anya in the lamplight until the tension was thick. Then he glanced around the tiny room with a sadness in his eyes that only deepened as he stepped toward her and knelt next to the bed. Anya's heart quickened, and she hardly dared move. Gavin brushed his fingertips over her brow and looked contemplatively at the mixture of sweat and dirt he'd pulled away. His eyes moved over the worn uniform, then he pressed the back of his hand against the bruise Cedric had left on her face. His eyes delved into hers with a pleading question. Anya turned away. Gavin took her chin firmly, and she saw compassion flee behind the hurt.

"You would take this," he said close to her face, in little more than a whisper. "*This,*" he added, low in his throat, putting his hands up for emphasis, "over what I have given you . . . what I have promised you?" His voice lowered further. "What kind of man does that make me, to be worth less than this?"

Anya looked into his eyes, wanting to make him understand, but not knowing how. "Gavin, I . . ."

"Shhh." He pressed his fingers over her lips, then reached into a bag he'd apparently left near the bed. With no words spoken, he brought forth the jar of balm, opened it, and began his well-learned ritual of rubbing it into every crack and crevice of her work-worn hands. Anya felt tears falling silently over her face.

Without looking up, Gavin sensed them. "It's all right to cry, Anya. Go ahead and cry."

When he had finished with her hands, Anya watched through brimming eyes as he pulled the scarf from her head and reached for her hairbrush. With patience he gently pulled it through her matted tresses, following each stroke of the brush by smoothing it with his other hand.

Anya cried silent tears while Gavin performed his self-appointed tasks, then he turned to look at her. "Come back with me, Anya," he pleaded, carefully wiping her tears away. Her reverie was shattered by reality. She was determined to leave here, and she knew she needed his help, but the reality of facing her reasons for leaving him in the first place seemed unbearable.

Gavin felt tangible fear as she recoiled from him and pulled the pillow into her arms. "Fine," he said, attempting a light tone, "if you won't come back, I'll stay here. I'll sleep on the floor and take care of you each night when your work is done."

"Don't be ridiculous!"

"Don't be a fool!" he retorted. Anya heard the anger she'd been expecting and turned away. "Before you left," he said, "I told you that I deserved a reason. You never gave me one. So I'm asking again: Why are you here?"

"Brierley is my home, and . . ." She hesitated, attempting to add her more recent realizations.

"This is no home!" he hissed in a low voice. "Now, look me in the eye, Anya, and give me a reason. I'm not leaving here without you until you do. And yes, I will carry you away from here a prisoner if I must." Only silence answered. Gavin took her shoulders and forced her to face him. "Don't you trust me?"

"Yes, of course, but I . . ."

"But what!?" he insisted, wondering why five days of this hadn't made her see reason. "I love you! You love me! We can work this out." He swallowed hard and added what he felt was an important point. "Even if you don't want to marry me, Anya, I will help you. If you trust me, you can at least give me a reason." Gavin saw the fear in her eyes growing, and he forced himself to calm down and speak gently. "Do you want to be at Brierley?"

Anya shook her head, too overcome with emotion to be able to say that he was the answer to her prayers.

"Then why?"

She knew he was right. He deserved a reason. He deserved to know the truth. Even if they didn't marry, he could still help her. Her deepest hope was that he could at least find a way for her child to grow up without being subjected to the horrors she was facing.

Gathering courage, Anya pressed a hand over her belly, which was just beginning to swell. "Look at me," she sobbed.

"I am," he answered, gazing at her face.

"I'm a mess." She turned away, embarrassed.

"You're beautiful. I was a mess not so long ago."

"At least you didn't cry like a baby."

"Not when you were looking."

Anya attempted to look him in the eye, knowing he was still waiting for the reason. She turned to stare at the floor and decided to have it out and over with. "I'm pregnant, Gavin."

Anya heard him sigh and was afraid to look at him. She didn't want to see the shock and disgust in his face.

"I know," he whispered, and she felt his arms come around her.

Anya's head shot up, searching for sincerity. It was true. He had already known. "But how could you . . . ?"

"When you refused to see a doctor, I talked with a woman in Strathnell who knows a great deal about medicine. When I told her the symptoms, she said it was obvious."

Anya bent her head forward, feeling so much shame. "If you knew all this time, why have you tormented me this way?"

"I wanted you to trust me enough to tell me. I wanted you to believe me when I told you I loved you, and we could overcome anything. Now listen and listen good, woman, because this is important. I never knew my father. He ran off when he found out my mother was pregnant. But James MacBrier loved my mother, and he cared what happened to me. He gave me all I have. Now, do you honestly believe that I would allow the woman I love to come back here to have this baby?"

"Perhaps this baby belongs at Brierley," she said, if only to test him further. She didn't want any room for doubt.

"This baby belongs with you, and you belong with me."

"But this is no ordinary baby." She looked directly at him. "This baby is the Earl's illegitimate child." As she said it, Anya realized that Gavin was the same, though he didn't know it.

"Cedric MacBrier," Gavin whispered in disgust, then he corrected the thought long enough to ask, "Did you care for him?"

"I thought I did, but it was all a farce. He was toying with me. He used me, and then he forced me to—"

"Enough." He touched his fingers to her lips, and she was relieved to not have to say it. It was easy now for Gavin to put together the pieces. Knowing the full extent of Anya's fears gave him confidence. "Anya, when did it happen? How long before we first met that day in the tower?"

"Only the night before," she stated, shuddering at the memory.

"There," he said triumphantly. "As far as anyone else knows, you and I eloped the night we left here."

"Eloped?" she said breathlessly. Then her expression faltered.

"What's wrong?"

"I told Cedric . . . about the baby."

"Is that when he gave you this?" Gavin touched the bruise on her face. "Or was this Una's doing?"

"It was Cedric," she admitted. "He told me I would never get away with causing trouble for him. He didn't believe me when I told him I didn't want anything from him, and I certainly didn't want him to marry me." She paused and sighed. "He told me he'd make life hell for me."

"I think he's already done that."

Gavin touched her chin with his hand and kissed her gently. "It doesn't matter anymore, Anya. I'm going to take you away from here. I'm going to marry you, and I'm going to raise this child as my own."

Anya could hardly believe what he was saying. "Are you certain?" she asked, her voice cracking with emotion.

"Certain?" he laughed. "Anya, my sweet Anya." He touched her face, her hair. "I have never been more certain about anything in my whole life."

Anya put her hands to her face, laughing and crying at the same time. She threw her head back and looked skyward, muttering a sincere, "Thank you, God." Her prayers had truly been answered.

Gavin pulled her into his arms. Anya held to him in desperation, burying her face against his throat while her tears turned from pain to joy. Pulling back briefly, she touched his face in wonder that any man could be so good. Surely he had to be James MacBrier's son. And Cedric must have gotten a little too much of his mother in him.

"I love you, Gavin," was all she could think to say. He smiled and kissed her warmly. His eyes turned serious and he kissed her again.

Again and again. Anya felt his breath turn raspy and her heart pounded. Gavin took her face into his hands as if to hold her there forever.

"Don't you ever leave me again," he whispered. "I need you, Anya. I will never let you leave me again."

Anya pushed her fingers through his hair, marveling at the feelings he wrought in her. It was so unlike anything she had ever known, or ever hoped to know. "Gavin," she cried, wishing she could find words to express all she felt.

Gavin paused to look at her face, then he kissed her like he never had, wanting to somehow draw her within him for safekeeping. He felt Anya start in his arms before he heard the footsteps on the stairs. That wretched fear returned to her eyes as she backed away.

"Who is it?" he whispered.

"I don't know. No one ever comes up here."

Gavin moved quietly behind the door, and she gasped to see him pull a pistol from beneath his cloak and point it toward the ceiling.

"What are you doing?" she whispered frantically.

"Do you honestly think I would attempt to rescue you from this place unarmed after what happened to me last time?" He put his finger to his lips, and she understood that she should pretend he wasn't there.

Anya's heart beat painfully as the doorknob rattled. She was grateful the door was locked as the struggling ceased, then a light rap sounded on the wood.

Anya glanced in question to Gavin, and he nodded. "Who's there?" she called.

"Stop being so proper and open the door," Cedric demanded, and Gavin thanked God that he was here. To see the fear in Anya's eyes and know its source nearly tore his heart out.

"Go away, Cedric. I'm tired. I want to be alone."

"I just want to talk."

"Then talk. You can do that through the door."

"Anya," he laughed, "just open the door."

"No. Go away."

Silence prevailed for a long moment, then Anya felt her heart drop to hear a key turning in the lock. She met Gavin's eyes, so grateful he was here, shuddering to think what might have happened if he wasn't. Gavin gave her a confident nod, giving her the assurance to face Cedric stoically. There was no reason to be afraid. The door creaked open, and Cedric sauntered into the little room like a drunk peacock.

"How dare you come in here like this!" Anya hissed, and Gavin felt proud of her.

"I just came to tell you I was sorry." He smiled like the devil while his eyes betrayed that he was lying.

"You could have done that without a key to the door."

He reached up to touch the bruise he'd given her, and she recoiled. "Come now, Anya. I'm not such a bad guy. You still like me a little, don't you?"

"I hate you!" she spat.

Cedric laughed and lunged toward her. Anya tried to slap him, but he caught her wrist and held it painfully. Gavin couldn't believe his eyes, but he hesitated a moment, wanting the perfect excuse to kill him.

"Please, Cedric! Please don't." She was beginning to wonder where Gavin had gone when she felt Cedric's grip release and looked up to see the gun placed firmly against the side of his throat.

"You heard the lady," Gavin said dryly. Cedric moved back while Gavin kept the gun as it was.

"Well," Cedric managed a dry laugh, "if it isn't the misbegotten Brierley brat. We thought you were dead. But I fear you're mistaken. She is no lady."

Gavin's free hand catapulted into Cedric's face, and he reeled back onto the floor. Before he had a chance to recover, Gavin placed his boot firmly on Cedric's chest and pointed the gun at his head. "No," he stated, "you are mistaken, my lord." He spat the title like venom. "You are no gentleman."

Cedric looked extremely less confident as he muttered, "You wouldn't shoot an unarmed man, would you?"

"No," he said, "but then, I wouldn't rape a woman—any woman. Now, justice is a different matter, don't you think? An eye for an eye?" He cocked the gun and aimed carefully.

"No!" Cedric cried. "Please, don't!"

Gavin retracted the gun and leered. "I just wanted to hear you say it, you filthy coward. How does it feel to be on the other end?"

Cedric chuckled tensely and raised himself on his elbows before Gavin kicked him in the jaw, leaving him unconscious on the floor.

"Let's get out of here," Gavin said, leaving the gun pointed at Cedric as a precaution. He pulled her cloak from the hook on the wall and threw it at her. "Put that on, and get anything worth taking."

Anya took Gavin's bag and threw in her hairbrush and her little doll, then she decided that about covered it. Gavin found the key in Cedric's pocket and took up the other from the little table.

"Let's go," he said distastefully, ushering Anya out of the room. He locked the door from the outside and threw the keys on the floor. "I wonder how long it will take anyone to miss him." He took Anya's hand, and together they fled down the stairs.

It seemed forever before they reached the door, and the night air struck Anya like a balm upon her soul. She followed Gavin around the house to the forest tower, where his horse was tethered in the trees. With ease he lifted her into the saddle, glanced around warily, then mounted behind her and heeled the horse into a gallop.

Chapter Ten
Woman with a Past

Freedom washed over Anya as the wind rushed against her. Real freedom. The chains were broken with Brierley, and her whole life lay before her. Life with Gavin. He moved the reins to one hand and put his other arm around her waist in a warm, possessive embrace. Anya responded by reaching behind to push her hand into his hair.

They made good time, but Anya felt weary long before the house came into view. Gavin dismounted then turned for Anya, and she nearly fell against him. Looking up at him, she attempted to steady herself, but Gavin lifted her into his arms before she had the chance. She nestled against his shoulder until she felt the bed beneath her. She smiled at Gavin as he pulled the slippers from her feet and tucked her beneath the bedcovers.

Anya's next awareness was the sun in her eyes and the smell of something that made her stomach growl with hunger. She sat up abruptly as the emptiness lurched into her throat. Hand over mouth, she ran to the other room and leaned over the basin with dry, painful heaves. She felt Gavin's hands on her shoulders when it was done.

"Good morning," he chuckled. Anya turned in his arms, and he pressed her face to his shoulder. "Are you all right?" he asked.

She nodded. "It's just so embarrassing."

He chuckled again and lifted her chin. "I'm just getting even." Anya smiled and touched his face. She couldn't believe she was really here with him. "Do you think you could eat now?"

"I'm starving."

Gavin urged her to the kitchen and helped her into a chair.

"Thank you," was all she could think to say before he set a plate in front of her, along with a cup of warm chocolate.

"I don't cook as well as you," he admitted, "but I think it's edible."

"It smells wonderful." She proceeded to eat, relishing the filling of her stomach.

Gavin went into the bathing room, and she realized he must have already eaten. He returned to lean over the table with a grin. "I was thinking perhaps you could use a hot bath." Anya only stared in silence. "I thought so. It will be ready when you are." He nearly left the room, then turned back to say in a discuss-the-weather tone, "And I was thinking we could get married tomorrow."

"Gavin, I . . . ."

"Are you feeling up to it? I mean . . . you aren't too terribly ill, are you?"

Tears of inexpressible gratitude smoldered in Anya's eyes, but she couldn't speak.

"Oh," he quipped, "you aren't going to cry again."

"I'm sorry. It's just that I . . . well, I must confess that I'd been praying for a way to get through this without having to stay at Brierley. I realized just last night . . . before you came, that it was up to *me* to make those changes. I realized that I had to rescue myself; that it was a state of mind, and I had to change something within myself. I was ready to come crawling back here and beg for your help, even if you didn't want to marry me. I was prepared to fight for the right to live in peace and give this baby a good life. But here we are . . . and you've made it all so very easy. It's evident that my prayers have been answered, and . . . No," she added as an afterthought, "more than that. I believe I've been blessed with a miracle."

"Only because you are a good woman who deserves such blessings," he said, and her emotion deepened.

Anya laughed through her tears. "Oh, Gavin, I love you."

He chuckled. "I love you, too, Anya."

Gavin disappeared into the bathing room, and she could hear him pouring heated water into the tub. She distinctly caught the scent of lavender. Anya busied herself by straightening the kitchen and cleaning the dishes until he announced her bath was ready. With clean underclothes retrieved from the bureau, Anya closed the door and quickly undressed, longing to feel the soothing warmth enfold her body. It wasn't until she had relaxed in the tub that she noticed the new toiletries sitting on the shelf nearby. There was lavender soap and bath salts, a bottle of rose oil, and scented shampoo. Anya couldn't believe it. Yesterday she had been the lowest servant. Today she was a queen.

When her bath was finished, Anya peered through the door and saw no sign of Gavin. She hurried into the bedroom, catching her breath to see a new dress of pale blue spread over the freshly made bed. Carefully she put it on, loving the feel and smell of the new fabric, then she went to the bureau. While she'd been bathing, Gavin had left a pearl-handled hairbrush and hand mirror. Anya hardly dared pick them up. They must have cost him a small fortune. As she turned the mirror over to see her reflection, emotion quivered through her. Surely this was a different woman than the one she'd seen in an equally beautiful mirror at Brierley just yesterday.

She gasped to see Gavin in the reflection. "Did I frighten you?" he chuckled close behind her ear.

"I've told you not to sneak up on me like that!"

"You told me to let you stay at Brierley. Do you expect me to do everything you say?"

She ignored his question and fingered the mirror and brush. "Oh, Gavin. They're beautiful."

"So are you."

"And the dress," she turned to face him, "and the bath things. It's all so wonderful. Why are you being so good to me after I . . ."

"Shhh," he touched her lips with his fingers. "I can't take all the credit. I paid for the things, but they weren't my idea." Anya's brow furrowed in question. "I have a friend," he hesitated slightly, "a lady friend. I went to see her after you left, and we talked. She told me if I wanted to get you back, I had better take note of some things ladies enjoy that men never think of, or something to that effect."

Anya smiled. "I should like to meet this friend of yours."

"I fear you will get that chance."

"Fear?"

"She's . . . different. I hope you won't think badly of me for . . ."

He stopped and cleared his throat. "Anyway, she's bringing something by later that you'll need for tomorrow."

"I shall look forward to it," Anya smiled. Then she added with strength, "We are truly even now."

"What do you mean?"

"You have told me that I saved your life. Now you have saved mine." He lifted his brows dubiously. "I mean it, Gavin. I believe I would have died there. Perhaps not in body, but I would have died."

Gavin put his arms around her with a firm embrace. He bent to kiss her, but had barely begun when a knock sounded at the front door. Gavin glanced at the clock. "If that's Peg, she's early." He quickly went to answer the door while Anya brushed through her hair, keeping her ear perked toward the parlor.

Gavin pulled open the door to see Peg's face barely showing above an armload of packages. "Don't just stand there, fool!" she insisted. "Take some o' this stuff an' get out o' m' way."

Gavin took everything except the large dress box she held on the bottom. He followed her into the parlor, where the packages were deposited on the sofa. Peg began to ramble as she opened each in turn to examine their contents. "I can't wait tae meet this lass o' yours, Gavin, my love. When are ye goin' tae go an' rescue her from that awful place? What was it called? Oh, yes. Brierley!" Her voice lowered dramatically. "Do ye think she'll come back with ye? She'd be a fool not to." She stopped her chatter long enough to kiss him and pinch his cheek. "Heaven knows I've been tryin' tae sink m' teeth intae ye ever since th' day ye set those baby brown eyes upon me."

"You're teasing me again, Peg. You shouldn't say a—"

"Bless me!" she interrupted. "What a handsome lad ye were, sauntering intae th' pub like ye'd just stepped off a deserted island. Ye didna answer m' question, Gavin." She fluffed out a stiff petticoat and held it against her contemplatively. "When are ye going tae get her?"

"You haven't stopped long enough to let me tell you."

She laughed boisterously. "Ye know me." She spread the petticoat over the back of a chair. "But surely this lass must be somethin'. I dinna think I've seen any man go tae such trouble for any woman. Should I put these things in th' wardrobe? What I wouldna give tae hae a man—any man—go tae half that much trouble for me. When did ye say you were goin' tae get her? Tonight? But you said you were gettin' married t'morrow, didna ye? How are ye goin' t—"

"Peg!" Gavin laughed, taking her by the shoulders to stop her. Then he whispered with a smirk, "She's already here."

"Oh, my!" Peg gasped and put a hand over her mouth. "Do ye think she heard all that? Oh, I always manage tae embarrass m'self. I think it's better when ye talk and I listen. Ye always said I was a good listener when I need tae be. Why dinna ye tell me tae shut up, Gavin, and . . ." Peg stopped mid-sentence when Gavin's gaze moved to the doorway of the kitchen, his eyes full of adoration.

"Oh, my," Peg whispered. Her eyes absorbed Anya, who filled the room with an undeniable presence. "She's very pretty, Gavin," Peg remarked as if they were still alone. "I'm not certain what kind o' lass I expected ye tae marry, but I would say she suits ye well enough. Of course I always wanted ye tae marry me, but I'm too old for ye, and I'm not yer type at all, am I."

Anya glanced at Gavin, feeling embarrassed and uncertain. She turned back to Peg expectantly.

"I hope she knows I'm teasin'," Peg said at last. "I never say anything I mean, do I?"

"You said she was pretty," Gavin chuckled, reaching out for Anya's hand and urging her into the room. "Anya, I would like you to meet a very dear friend of mine, Peg MacTodd."

"It is a pleasure." Anya offered a hand that Peg took as if it might break. "Gavin tells me it was your idea to shower me with lavish gifts."

"Ah," she pushed her hand humbly through the air, "I just told him what ladies like. I hope I didna go wrong."

"It seems you have impeccable taste," Anya smiled freely. Gavin wondered if Anya had any idea what her acceptance meant to Peg.

"Ah," Peg repeated with the same gesture, and Gavin chuckled.

He broke the silence. "Why don't I put these things away and—"

"I'll help ye," Peg offered, and together they scooped everything up before Anya had a chance to assist.

Anya was left alone in the parlor, sensing they didn't want her to follow. Already she liked Peg, but it was obvious that she and Gavin had known each other for a long time. Their familiarity left her feeling vulnerable, when she knew there was no reason for it. She could hear them talking and laughing in the bedroom but couldn't discern what they were saying. So she just sat and waited, hoping she would get a chance to acquaint herself with Peg enough to understand their relationship.

They returned to the parlor, where Gavin sat close to Anya and took her hand while Peg remained on her feet, hovering tensely near the doorway. Anya felt a wave of empathy, realizing it was now Peg who felt like the outsider. She thought quickly of a way to remedy the tension, wanting to make Peg feel at home.

"Haven't you got anything to do?" Anya asked Gavin, looking directly at him. His eyes widened at her demanding tone. "Peg and I were going to share a cup of tea before she manages to run off, and don't think for a minute we can enjoy a womanly chat with you sitting around like an unmade bed."

Gavin smiled. Anya likely had more in common with Peg than either of them expected. "I can take a hint." He pretended to be insulted, but inwardly he appreciated Anya's insight.

He left the room while Anya commented to Peg, "Is that what most men consider a hint?"

Peg chuckled quietly, and Anya wondered what it would take to get her started with the kind of chatter she had overheard earlier. "Why don't we go into the kitchen, and I'll make some tea?" They heard the door close as Gavin left the house. Peg followed Anya silently into the other room and sat at the dining table while Anya lit the stove.

"Have you known Gavin long?" Anya asked, hating the silence, wondering what Peg was feeling. Envy? Anya glanced toward her. No, sad would be more accurate.

"Known him?" She laughed, and the tension seemed broken to a degree. "Why, it must be nearly nine years, I would guess."

Anya lifted her brows, knowing Gavin had been gone from Brierley little more than that.

"Now there is no point me pretending with ye, is there, dearie? I suspect ye overheard me talkin' with him. I dinna ken how ye couldna have." Anya looked down timidly to confirm Peg's suspicion. "I dinna want ye thinkin' badly of me, or . . ."

"Oh, I would never—," Anya attempted to correct her.

"Hush now," Peg said, putting her hands up to stop Anya. "The truth of it is that Gavin Baird is th' most honorable, decent man I have ever met in m' life. And I have known a lot o' men. Th' truth about me is that m' life hasna been honorable at all."

Anya betrayed surprise in her expression, wanting to convey that Peg had no obligation to spill her secrets.

"Ye might as well know," she continued, as if she'd read Anya's mind. "Everyone else does."

"But, Peg, you needn't—"

"Ah, hush. It'll make me feel better. I suspect Gavin would tell ye sooner or later anyway. Not that he's a gossip, but . . . well, he just would. I know it."

Anya poured out the tea and sat across the table from Peg, who took a careful sip and hurried on with her story, using elaborate hand gestures and wild expressions. "Gavin was hardly more than seventeen when he came intae th' pub where I worked afternoons, and I must confess, though I'm ashamed tae admit it now, I set my eyes on him as a good time and some extra income." Anya's eyes narrowed, not fully understanding the implication. "That's right, dearie, I worked nights sellin' myself tae th' highest bidder or th' smoothest talker."

Anya's eyes widened in disbelief, but Peg went on as if it were nothing. "Of course that's all behind me now, but at th' time, I saw that handsome lad stride in an' was quick tae offer him a drink. My shift was nearly done at th' pub, and we started talkin'. One minute I was tryin' to talk him intae a good time, and the next minute he had me cryin' on his shoulder, tellin' him how miserable an' awful m' life was."

Anya smiled to herself, recalling similar scenes with Gavin and herself. "I believe he has a gift that way."

"Aye, he does," Peg agreed. "But you and I can feel privileged, m'dearie. Gavin doesna spread his gifts around. But back tae th' story. I was just gettin' tae th' good part." Anya nodded eagerly. "There I was, a decade older than this lad, and he took me to an inn, and . . ." Anya was holding her breath. "He bought me a fine dinner, then told me tae go home an' get some sleep. He met me th' next day at th' pub, gave me more money than I had ever seen in m' life, an' told me tae buy myself a ticket oot o' th' gutter. He left tae go abroad some-where that very day, an' told me he'd be back tae check on me."

Peg leaned back in her chair with a triumphant finish. "I took that money and bought m'self a hat shop. Oh, I love hats." She pointed to the one on her head, overly burdened with feathers and flowers. "It makes me a good enough living tae get by, and I enjoy it. O' course I never married. I've had lots o' men wantin' tae show me a good time, and I've stuck to a few for a while—one at a time, mind ye," she clarified with a wink. "But they always move on, lookin' for someone fresh and young, who doesna have a past."

Anya felt empathy sweep through her. "Doesn't everyone have a past?"

"Not like mine," she laughed, but Anya sensed that it hurt some-where inside. "But Gavin, he never cared about that. Every time he'd come back home, we'd talk, an' laugh, an' paint th' town, but he never once said or did anythin' dishonorable. That lad is a jewel, dearie. Consider yersel' lucky."

"Oh, I do," she smiled, tingling just to think of him. "It will take a lifetime to repay all he has done for me."

"Ah," she lifted a wise finger, "but he's not that kind o' man. Just ye be there for him, and ye will feel no debt. Aye," she nodded, "ye are lucky. And I'm lucky, too," Peg said with sincerity, a pleasant gleam shining in her eyes. "He has become m' best friend, and he tells me I'm his. Of course he'll have a wife now, but I hope tae be yer friend as well."

"It would be an honor," Anya stated firmly.

Peg seemed relieved as much as she was pleased. "That would be fine," she affirmed. "I was hopin' ye wouldna hold any o' that against me. But I figured it would be better tae be honest with ye and have ye hate me, than tae hide all o' that just tae get ye tae like me. And as long as we're talkin' about Gavin, ye might as well know that he asked me tae marry him. Oh, it must o' been years ago."

"He did?" Anya laughed, surprised but somehow pleased.

"At first I thought he was jokin'. He does that, ye know. O' course I laughed, then I realized he was serious. I know he was just doin' it for my sake. I mean we care about each other and all o' that, but not th' way two people should. And that's what I told him. O' course, a year later I got him to admit it. Can you believe it? He was goin' tae marry me just tae make me happy. And he would have, too. But I told him I was too old for him, and not at all his type. Which o' course is true. I told him he had tae wait until he fell in love. He had tae find a sweet, pretty little thing that made his heart stop just tae think o' her, and from th' way his heart bled after ye left here last week, I know he's found th' love of a lifetime!" She gave a dramatic wave of her arms.

"He was in such distress," Peg continued, "and came tae me for advice. He says I know what a woman thinks and feels. Says he couldna figure it out. O' course he told me everything." Her eyes filled with compassion. "I hope ye dinna mind that."

Anya shook her head, relieved to know that Peg was aware of her situation, and she didn't have to be the one to tell her.

"I told Gavin he couldna live with a free conscience if he hadna done everythin' in his power tae get ye back. And if he wanted tae get ye back, he had to show ye tangible evidence that he cared. Words can mean a lot to a lass, mind ye, but it's nice tae have somethin' ye can hold an' touch tae remind ye that a man cares." Peg nodded with surety and Anya smiled.

"And do ye know what he asked me?" Peg leaned over the table and narrowed her eyes. "That lad had th' nerve tae say, 'Do ye think she wants me tae come after her?'" Anya recalled the outward way she had rejected him and could well understand his asking that, though Peg seemed appalled. "But do ye know what I told him? I guess I set him straight. I told him right out! Just because a woman leaves th' room and closes a door doesna mean she doesna want ye tae follow her and open it. Now isna that th' truth of it, dearie?"

Anya felt warmth consume her. Peg apparently knew human nature well. Anya had fled from here in desperation, certain she had no choice, while all the time she had wanted deep in her heart for Gavin to come after her and keep her from facing her trials alone.

"I owe you much, Peg," Anya said, reaching her hand across the table. Peg squeezed it eagerly. "I'm so glad you came today."

"Aye, so am I, m'dearie."

"Will you be there for the wedding?" Anya asked hopefully.

"You should know I wouldna miss it. Gavin did invite me. Do ye suppose he's found somethin' tae occupy himself with, or perhaps he's afraid tae come back in?"

Anya laughed, and Peg finished off her tea rather quickly. "Should we go and find him?"

As she and Peg walked into the yard, Anya realized she'd never had a friend before. How does one reach the age of twenty-one without ever having a friend? Of course there were Effie and Mrs. MacGregor, and Robbie had always been kind to her. But that was different. Anya hoped she would see a lot of Peg in the future, and felt grateful to Gavin for this, along with everything else.

They found Gavin half asleep under a tree. Peg nudged him in the ribs with her shoe to rouse him.

"Wretched woman," he mumbled, coming to his feet. "I always wanted a big sister, but not one as ornery as you," he teased, his eyes full of mischief.

Anya laughed, and Gavin sensed that everything was right between them. At least there didn't appear to be any tension.

They walked Peg to her gig, left in front of the house. Anya hung back as Gavin helped Peg step into it.

"I envy her," Peg said quietly. She touched his face, then glanced to Anya and pulled her hand away.

"You had your chance," Gavin smiled, then kissed her cheek.

"Silly lad!" she quipped and snapped the reins. Gavin stood looking down the road for several moments after she had gone, then he turned to Anya, who stood near the door.

"Is everything all right?" he asked, walking toward her with his hands deep in his pockets.

"I feel a little nauseous, if you must know."

"I mean besides that."

"You mean with Peg."

"Yes, that's what I mean."

"I think she's wonderful."

Gavin sighed with relief. "I hoped you would. I couldn't imagine you not being able to see what I could see, but I . . . well, did she tell you that—"

"I think she told me everything," Anya grinned.

"Yeah," he looked down sheepishly, "she can tend to do that."

Anya watched Gavin closely a moment and realized he was nervous. It was something she'd never seen in him before. "Is anything wrong?" she asked, then turned quickly to go inside. "Forgive me, I have to eat something. Hold that question."

"Gladly," Gavin muttered under his breath as he followed her in, grateful for some time to think this through. He sat at the table while Anya gathered an odd assortment of food and spread it out, all the while nibbling on a dry biscuit that Gavin thought looked terribly unappetizing.

"So," Gavin finally gathered his nerve, "what did Peg tell you?"

"Everything," she stated nonchalantly.

"Clarify that, please," he said, the tenseness still evident in his voice.

"She was a prostitute. You met her in a pub. You helped change her life. You've become the best of friends over the years." Anya sat down and began loading a plate. "And you asked her to marry you."

Gavin gave a relieved chuckle. "That about covers it."

"Didn't you want me to know?" she asked.

"On the contrary, I wanted to make certain you did."

"Why is that?"

"Because you are going to be my wife, and sooner or later it will come back to your ears that your husband has been seen in public over the past nine years with a prostitute. Peg is very dear to me. I love her like a sister, but most people could never understand or believe that. Her past haunts her, and I have tried over the years to make it clear that it makes no difference to me." He took Anya's hand while she chewed vigorously, as if she hadn't eaten for days. "And I thank you for accepting her. She'll never let you down."

"I like her," she said, the words barely intelligible with her mouth full. Gavin leaned back in his chair, sighing with relief. "Besides," she swallowed, "who am I to talk?"

Gavin didn't like the way she said that. But she continued to eat as if it were nothing, so he decided to ignore it. He smiled to watch her eat as if she were dying of starvation. "It's all right, darling," he chuckled, "there will always be plenty. You needn't eat it all right now."

"But I'm hungry," she insisted.

"Didn't they feed you enough at Brierley?" he asked.

"Yes," she stated, "but I rarely had time to eat it."

Gavin felt a recently familiar pain on her behalf, but he smiled it away. "Well, you can eat all day if you wish. I want you and that baby strong, my love."

"You'd better eat, too," she said, coming to her feet and brushing the crumbs from her hands. She bent over to kiss him and pressed her forehead to his. "You're going to need your strength to carry me over the threshold."

"So I am," he laughed, loving it when this side of her showed through.

"I think I'll lie down." She touched her stomach. "It seems to settle better if I do."

"Good idea." He lifted his brows mischievously. "You're going to need your strength, as well . . . after I carry you over the threshold."

Anya smiled timidly and went into the bedroom, seeing no evidence of the packages he and Peg had brought in earlier. She wanted to search them out but decided she shouldn't. Her head barely hit the pillow before she fell asleep, as the past week suddenly caught up with her. Knowing all was well, it was easier to rest.

Anya slept the afternoon away and Gavin let her be, knowing she likely needed it after what she'd been through the past several days. Dusk settled in while he sat in the parlor with a book. He was thinking more about tomorrow than reading when he heard her cry out in fear. He was at her side in a moment, sitting on the edge of the bed, holding her against him.

"Gavin!" she cried in anguished relief, pulling his shirt into her fists, pressing her face against his chest. "Don't send me back. Please don't send me back."

"Never," he whispered soothingly, brushing his lips over her brow. "I will never let you go, my darling." He waited for her to calm down, then lifted her chin until their eyes met. "Do you want to tell me what you were dreaming?"

Anya swallowed and sniffed. "You were holding me . . . kissing me. It was so wonderful, and then . . . then . . ." She pressed her head to his shoulder. "It wasn't you at all. It was Cedric, and he was hurting me, and . . ."

"Shhh," he whispered to quiet her. "It was only a dream," he soothed. "You are mine now. It doesn't matter." He held her until the room was dark and she seemed to be herself again. "Are you hungry?" he asked.

"I'm afraid I am."

"Wait here, and I'll get you something."

"No, that's all right. I need to get up anyway."

Anya spoke very little as they shared a meal and readied for bed the same as they had many times before.

"Gavin," Anya said quietly after he had built a fire and settled into his bed on the floor. "Forgive me for being so bold, but I . . . I can't stop thinking about . . ."

"About what?" he asked, leaning up on one elbow to look toward her through the firelight.

"Gavin . . . I . . . well, what happened between Cedric and me will be with us for the rest of our lives. Can you so easily forget who fathered this child?"

"Yes," he insisted, "I can."

Anya turned her face toward the ceiling. "I'm not certain *I* can."

"Anya," his voice softened, "I've told you how I feel about raising another man's child. I will be a father to this child, and no one will ever know differently." She made no response, and he guessed with a degree of certainty, "It's not just the baby, is it."

Anya shook her head and sighed. "I used to daydream," she mused, "that I might be rescued from Brierley and marry for love. I had nothing to bring to a marriage, but I knew I could give the man I loved the one thing they could not take from me." She sighed, and he knew what she meant. "But then they took that, too. I wanted to die, Gavin. I just wanted to die." Her eyes saddened. "I suppose that's why I left you. The tangible evidence of what had happened to me seemed to block the path to every happiness. It's difficult for me to understand how you can accept it, when it tears me apart inside just to think about it."

Gavin lay back on his pillow and sighed, wishing he knew how to explain it without hurting her feelings. "Anya," he said carefully, "you were a victim."

"Victim or not, you are still not marrying an innocent woman."

"So?" he chuckled, sitting up to look at her in astonishment.

"I thought every man wanted to marry an innocent woman."

"Brierley gossip again?"

"Isn't it true?" she asked.

"That question is relative." She looked at him pointedly, expecting a clarification. "I would think that any man who is a man at all would marry a woman he loves, and if he loves her, whatever she was before he met her makes no difference."

"But I'm still not . . ."

"Anya," he spoke softly, "have you ever given yourself to a man, freely, of your own will and choice?"

"No," she stated with confidence.

"Then you are an innocent woman."

Her eyes filled with mist, and Gavin figured he'd gotten his point across. But just to make certain, he added, "Give me one night—one night, Anya, with you as my wife, and you will forget that Cedric MacBrier ever touched you. Once I become your husband, that baby will be as much mine as it is yours. And you, Anya, you will be all mine—forever."

Anya felt a tingle of anticipation from his promise.

"Besides," he settled himself into his bed again, "look at Peg. When I asked her to marry me, I was well aware of the past she had lived. But it didn't matter."

"You're a good man, Gavin, and I love you for it."

"I love you, too, soon-to-be Mrs. Baird. And you're a good woman. The best, in truth."

Anya sighed contentedly and drifted to sleep with the promise of tomorrow wrapped securely around her.

Chapter Eleven
The Touch of a Hand

Anya awoke to find Gavin rubbing balm into her hands. She sighed and nuzzled against the bed, relishing the luxury as she contemplated what today would bring.

"You are so good to me," she cooed.

"I'm just trying to get even," he chuckled.

Gavin waited for the usual morning nausea to hit. When Anya clapped a hand over her mouth, he quickly provided a basin. Nothing ever came up in the morning, but he knew she wouldn't be caught taking any chances. "It'll save you a trip," he smirked, then turned away until her heaves settled.

"Thank you," she said, leaning back against the pillow. "That morning run can be exhausting."

"I've got your breakfast ready. You'd best hurry, or we'll be late."

"Late?"

"For the wedding, of course."

"Of course," she answered, her heart quickening as she grasped the reality.

While Anya ate, she could hear Gavin fussing with something in the bedroom, and once she was finished, she went to investigate. She froze in the doorway while Gavin spread a white satin dress over the freshly made bed. He looked up to see her there and simply said, "Peg picked it out. She was afraid you wouldn't like it. The tailor already had your size, of course. But then you must have figured that out, because you wore a new dress yesterday that . . ." He stopped and shook his head with a chuckle. "I must be nervous or something. I'm beginning to sound like Peg."

"Do you still want to go through with it?" Anya asked, only half teasing.

"With all my heart and soul," he replied, and she smiled. "You'd best hurry," he added and left her alone.

Reverently Anya touched the gown, hardly daring to believe that it was intended for her. Knowing she mustn't tarry, she put on the stiff petticoat and slipped the gown over her arms. It fell in satiny billows around her body, but reaching back to fasten it, she found it nearly impossible. She knew now why servant girls never had dresses that fastened down the back. Instead, she went to the bureau to brush through her hair and found hair combs inlaid with pearls. Anya tingled as she reached out to touch each one, then she set to work brushing through her tangled hair. She was pulling the combs into the sides to hold it back when she felt Gavin closing the buttons on her dress.

"You have the lightest step of anyone I know," she laughed softly.

"I like sneaking up on you," he whispered.

"I've noticed."

Before he was finished, Anya turned with an irresistible urge to kiss him. But she briefly forgot about it as her eyes beheld him. He wore an old-fashioned shirt the color of cream, with sleeves that bloused below his shoulders until they cuffed at the wrist. His waistcoat was deep grey, with crisscross laces closing the front. A blue-grey plaid was fastened at his left shoulder with an elaborate brooch, leaving it to hang over his back, where it almost brushed the floor. A kilt of the same tartan hung in pleats to his knee, with a tasseled sporran in the front. His stockings were wool, the color of his shirt, and his brogues were of polished leather. Anya's appraisal ended with his face, where a contented smile teased his lips, and his brown eyes danced with anticipation.

"Were you going to say something?" he asked.

Anya reached up to touch his face. "You are so handsome!"

Gavin chuckled to brush off the compliment. "We'd best hurry."

She went on her tiptoes to kiss him. "Thank you, Gavin, for everything. I hardly know what to say."

"Then don't say anything . . . except 'I do.' You must say that." He kissed her quickly, then turned her to finish the buttons, whispering behind her ear, "You are so beautiful."

"The gown is lovely," she said in response. "I've never had anything so fine in my life."

"Peg will be pleased," he said. "Are you ready?"

"Almost," she replied, needing shoes and stockings. "Give me five minutes."

"As you wish." He bowed gallantly and left the room.

Anya found new silk stockings in the bureau drawer and marveled at their softness as she put them on. She felt frustrated when her rough hands snagged the beautiful silk, but there was little to be done about that. In the bottom of the wardrobe she searched for her best slippers, but could only find one.

"Missing something?" Gavin said, leaning in the doorway with his hands behind his back.

"I can't find my other shoe." She continued to search until Gavin reached a hand down to help her to her feet. He held out the missing shoe and gave a complacent grin as he eased her to the chair, lifted her gown, and slipped it onto her foot.

"A perfect fit," he announced.

"Of course it is. It's my shoe."

"And so was Cinderella's." He squeezed her hand. "She just lost it temporarily." He looked up at her and felt a sense of fulfillment to see the joy in her eyes. "And they lived happily ever after," he added.

"But this is only the beginning, isn't it?"

"Yes, indeed. Shall we go?" he asked, offering his arm. Anya placed her hand over it and walked with him to the door. She didn't have time to wonder how they were going to travel dressed this way before she saw the elegant trap waiting in front of the house, hitched to two fine bays. She looked up at him in question as he locked the door.

"A married man ought to have one, don't you think?"

"Peg's idea?"

"Actually, I came up with this one on my own, I'm proud to admit."

Gavin helped her into the trap and sat beside her, stirring the horses to an easy trot. As they rounded the bend and the strath spread out before them, Anya could hear the distant trill of bagpipes. She glanced to Gavin in question, and he smiled. "I think they're waiting for us."

"They?" She lifted her brows.

"I invited the whole village. They love weddings."

She laughed. "But they don't even know me."

"They hardly know me." He stirred the horses a little faster. "But Strathnell is a village rich with tradition. Their seclusion has given them customs unique to the rest of Scotland, and the people are proud of them. When I returned from University once, I arrived in the midst of a wedding celebration. It was incredible. And I decided right then that when I did marry, I wanted it to be just like that." He chuckled. "You'll find that these people love an excuse—any excuse—to put the work aside and have a celebration. So, I gave them an excuse." He kissed her cheek. "I hope you don't mind."

"I don't mind," she said, but he saw a glimmer of doubt in her eyes.

"What?"

"Won't they eventually figure out that I was . . . pregnant first?"

He smiled. "I told them I'd taken sore advantage of you, and it was about time I made it right."

"You *what?*"

"Well, it's true!" he insisted, but Anya couldn't recall him ever taking advantage of her in any respect.

"What did you do, walk into the market square and announce it from a street corner?"

"Something like that," he smirked. "Actually, I bought a round of drinks in the pub and announced I was getting married. I told them they were all invited, and the rest was easy. If you think women are gossips, you should see what happens when you say something at the pub. The whole village will know before sundown. Men love to talk—especially when they've got some ale at hand." Anya laughed to see the amusement in his eyes.

The sound of bagpipes drew closer as they neared the market square. She could see a trio of players standing together in the center as Gavin drove the trap to the edge.

"Right on time," Gavin announced as they drew to a halt and the bells in the distant church tower began to ring. Before the chime had ended, a throng of bagpipes replaced it, playing a shrill melody of little music that echoed over the strath in time with a distant drum cadence.

"Now," he said quietly, "you should know that dancing is a big part of a wedding to these people." She looked briefly alarmed, but he quickly reassured her. "Don't worry, it's easy to pick up. But the important thing is you." He pointed a finger. "If you feel ill, or become too tired, just say the word, and we'll get what you need in no time. Understand?" Anya nodded. "Take it easy, now." He squeezed her hand.

Gavin helped Anya down from the trap, and from nowhere, two men clad in the tartan of their clan approached and took the horses, while two women wearing tartan mantles and overskirts took Anya by the hands and led her away. She glanced to Gavin in question, but he nodded with reassurance and she went along willingly. She was taken to the opposite side of the square, where she was urged to sit on a stone bench surrounded by heather, and a crown of heather was placed on her head.

"Such a pretty bride," one woman said with a sharp trill of the r's.

"Aye, that she is," the other agreed as they sat quietly beside her to watch and listen as clans came from every direction into the market square. Their music mingled to a deafening roar that pierced Anya's soul with tradition. She was mesmerized by the brightly colored tartans worn by men and women alike. The people formed a great circle around the square, broken only by the benches where she and Gavin sat on opposite sides. Already she could see what Gavin had meant by their traditional celebrating, and yet it had hardly begun.

Anya caught Gavin's eye across the square and felt butterflies rush through her. All at once the drum cadence changed rhythm and the music came to an abrupt halt. The contrast of silence in the air left an unexplainable anticipation that made Anya's heart quicken.

The silence was broken by a minister coming from the crowd into the center of the square, where he lifted his hands with an invoking gesture. Anya was urged to her feet by the ladies on either side of her, and she noted that Gavin was standing also. A drum cadence began as the bride and groom were ushered to the center of the square. With a great deal of pomp, their right hands were put into the minister's. He smiled and joined their hands, leaving them to face each other.

Anya felt the warmth in Gavin's touch that matched the adoration in his eyes. She felt so happy in this moment that she feared the joy would explode and burst the seams of her gown. The minister gave his memorized preamble concerning matrimony, then he turned to Gavin, and without use of any book or notes, he looked him in the eye and asked, "Do ye, Gavin James Baird, take this woman tae be yer wedded wife, tae have and tae hold, for richer or for poorer, in sickness and in health, as long as ye both shall live?"

"I do," Gavin said with strength and a squeeze of his hand.

The minister turned to Anya. "And do ye, Anya Elizabeth Ross, take this man tae be your wedded husband, tae have and tae hold, for richer or for poorer, in sickness and in health, as long as ye both shall live?"

"I do," she answered from the depths of her soul.

"The ring?" the minister questioned.

While Gavin continued to hold Anya's right hand, he placed a finely etched gold band on her left. Anya felt warmth radiate from the ring as it slid into place.

"Kiss her, lad," the minister said. "Ye are married now." Gavin smiled and didn't hesitate. Before the kiss had ended, a cheer went up from the crowd. They laughed amidst the kiss, then Gavin put his arms around her and kissed her again.

The crowd quieted as a slow, smooth drum cadence began. A single bagpipe joined in with big music, poignant and slow, as a matron with her tartan mantle pulled over her head took several stems of heather from a basket on her arm and laid them in a line over the ground. Gavin lifted Anya into his arms and carried her over the heather. He set her down, kissed her again, then took the heather crown from her head and threw it into the crowd to be caught, according to tradition, by the next bride of Strathnell.

While the bagpipe continued to play, Gavin pushed his right arm around the front of Anya's waist and placed her arm around him in the same manner. They circled slowly around each other, then Gavin changed arms to turn the other direction and Anya easily followed his lead. When that was done, Gavin took a step back and went to one knee before her in a gesture of admiration. After bowing his head to her hand, he came to his feet. The music stopped, and Anya assumed the ritual was done.

"Now just stand there and look pretty," Gavin whispered, hardly moving his lips. He stepped back, and a single bagpipe began a Highland

Fling. Anya smiled as Gavin performed it for her according to tradition. It seemed his wounds had healed well. She recalled learning this dance as a child under her great-uncle's tutelage, and each year during the second weekend of August, when the servants were given a day off to celebrate the declaration of Scottish independence, she had been able to participate in the Highland Fling and other such festive dances.

Anya read the question in Gavin's eyes. She nodded firmly to indicate that she knew the dance, and he reached out to take her hands. Together they went around three times, doing the simple steps in vibrant time with the multitude of bagpipes. They turned away from each other and Gavin took the matron's hands as Anya took the minister's, then they went through the steps again. This continued until the square was filled. The entire village of Strathnell, minus the children and the players, danced the Scottish reel until the music gained such momentum that they turned more to laughing than dancing. Anya finally became exhausted and moved to the little bench surrounded by heather.

Gavin sat close beside Anya, relieved that she'd finally given up. He was worn out, and his left leg had had about all it could take. "Are you all right?" he asked, putting his arm around her shoulders.

"I'm wonderful!" she smiled, and he kissed her quickly. "I'm also exhausted."

They watched as the reel finally fell to pieces, and the players took a rest. Food and ale were set out and passed freely, while many of the villagers came to offer congratulations to the happy couple.

"Do you want something to eat?" Gavin inquired of Anya when they finally had a quiet moment.

"Not yet. Where is Peg?"

"I saw her a while ago," Gavin reported. "She was on the arm of Mr. Morgan. I think he's the one she mentioned to me last week; a butcher whose wife died a year ago."

"Does she like him?"

"Very much, I think."

Their attention turned back to the square as preparations were made for the sword dance, then it was skillfully performed over and over by various participants. During this entertainment Peg slipped over and sat close to Anya, squeezing her hand.

"My, but ye make a lovely bride. Doesna she make a lovely bride, Gavin?" she asked him.

"Aye," he grinned, setting aside his educated speech in the spirit of the celebration. "She's the most bonny bride on th' face o' this earth."

"Can I kiss th' groom?" Peg asked.

"But of course!" Anya gave her consent eagerly.

Peg stood before Gavin, took his face in her hands and kissed him on the lips with a loud smooch. "Now, dinna ye ever kiss another woman again besides yer bonny wife as long as ye live!"

Gavin grinned. "Do you think I would want to?"

Anya was caught off guard by a wave of nausea, and Peg took notice of her expression. "Are ye all right, lass?" Gavin turned in alarm.

"Perhaps I should eat something," she said. Gavin was on his feet to get it for her without hesitation.

Anya felt a little better with something in her stomach, but an uneasiness lingered that made her hesitant to eat too much. She was beginning to feel terribly tired, and she feared that all things combined would make her stomach worse. The results could be very embarrassing.

When the sword dance was finished, the fling began all over again. Anya wanted to stay until every last soul had left this beautiful square where she had married, but finally she had to listen to her body and give in to its demands. She turned hesitantly to Gavin. "I fear we must go. I'm not feeling well at all."

Gavin only smiled and squeezed her hand. Anya felt almost guilty, but he immediately went to have their trap brought around. A short while later the trap was driven directly in front of them, now decorated with heather and tartan bows. The driver stepped down and bowed gallantly as he handed the reins to Gavin. Anya was helped inside, and they started forward. A cheer went up from the guests, and those who were in the midst of dancing the fling began to follow the trap out of the square as they continued to dance. A crowd slowly gathered, and a parade of dancers and players escorted them to the edge of town, where they all waved and blew kisses and called out wishes of congratulations.

"Are you all right?" Gavin asked, leaning close to Anya as he stirred the bays into a gentle trot.

"I'll be fine." She attempted a smile, but it was difficult not to feel disappointed that their celebration had been cut short by her condition. In an effort to focus her attention somewhere besides her churning stomach and swimming head, Anya marveled over this day. "It was the most beautiful wedding, Gavin." She squeezed his hand. "Thank you."

"It was my pleasure, Mrs. Baird," he replied, and she smiled. But Gavin could tell she didn't feel well at all.

"Are you certain you're all right?" he asked, keeping a wary eye on her as the horses pulled them home at a steady pace.

"Same old thing. I suppose I just overdid it." She smiled in an attempt to convince him, but he saw through it.

"I must admit, I overdid it a bit myself." She smiled at this but still looked uneasy. Gavin took her hand and brought it to his lips, then hurried the horses along, knowing by her increasing pallor that she needed to get home as quickly as possible. He pulled the trap to a halt in front of the house and helped Anya down, feeling his concern deepen. "I think it's more than overdoing it," he said, noting the unsteady way she moved toward the door.

Gavin carried her across the threshold and straight to the bedroom, where he set her on the edge of the bed, bending to unbutton her gown. "Are you hungry?" he asked.

"I don't believe so. Just . . . lightheaded, and . . . uneasy, I suppose."

"I want you to lie down and rest. I'm going back to get the doctor."

"Oh, Gavin, I—"

"Don't you dare protest." He pointed a finger at her. "You've gone far too long as it is. We'll both have a lot more peace of mind if we know everything is all right. I only wish I had thought of it yesterday."

He pulled the dress from her arms and lifted her legs onto the bed to pull it beneath her. "I'm so sorry, Gavin," she said, trying not to get emotional. He hung the dress in the wardrobe, then turned to remove her shoes and tuck her in.

"Now, what have you got to be apologizing for?"

"This is not how our wedding day should have been." She bit her lip. "If I weren't pregnant, we—"

"Stop it!" he demanded gently and kissed her brow. "We will make up for it. We're married now, and that's all that matters. There will be plenty of days and years ahead for celebrating."

Anya tried to smile, but she felt too sick, not to mention terribly disappointed at how she'd ruined their day.

"I'll hurry," he said. "You stay put." She nodded and closed her eyes.

Anya's next awareness was Gavin's kiss, and she opened her eyes to find the room lit by a lamp. Had she slept so long?

"The doctor is here," he whispered. "I had to wait for him to finish with someone else. His horse is lame. I'm sorry we were so long, but he wants to see you now."

"All right." She sat up and forced her eyes open while Gavin ushered Dr. Forbes into the room, then left them alone.

Gavin felt impatient and tense as his concern for Anya burgeoned beyond reason in his mind. The doctor reappeared sooner than he had expected, and Gavin looked at him expectantly.

"Your wife is just fine, Mr. Baird. Fatigue and lightheadedness are common with pregnancy. She just needs to take it easy."

"And the stomach disorders?" Gavin asked. He had been told that it was all part of pregnancy, but he needed reassurance.

"Nothing more than an inconvenience, which should pass before she is halfway along. And as I told you earlier, physical intimacy is perfectly normal during pregnancy. You have no reason to be concerned, as long as she's feeling up to it."

"Thank you, Doctor." Gavin couldn't hide the depth of relief in his voice to know that she was all right and everything could go on normally, if only to ease Anya's concerns about the effect this child would have on their lives.

"Give me a moment and I'll take you home," Gavin added, moving toward the bedroom.

Gavin knocked lightly and heard Anya call for him to enter. He found her standing near the bureau, fingering the pearl combs she'd worn earlier in the day.

"Is everything all right?" he asked gently.

"The doctor says everything is fine."

"Yes, he told me. So, what's wrong?" he persisted, sensing the tension in her voice.

"I only wish that . . . this baby was yours."

"It is," he stated with no hesitation, and Anya's eyes softened with love. "Get some rest." He kissed her quickly and touched her face with adoration. "I'll take the doctor home and be right back." Anya nodded and he turned to leave, stopping at the door to add, "I love you, Mrs. Baird."

Anya swallowed her emotion and smiled. "And I love you."

Once he had gone, Anya sat down on the bed and cried. Despite all of Gavin's goodness, Cedric's cruelty still haunted her. This was not how it should have been! Gavin would scold her for having such thoughts, but she couldn't help it. She only hoped that she could somehow make it up to him.

Realizing she still felt tired, Anya wondered if those days of working at Brierley were finally catching up to her. She quickly got something to eat, then got ready for bed and crawled between the sheets. "Some wedding night," she muttered aloud.

Gavin returned to find Anya sleeping. He stood by the bed to watch her in the moonlit room, feeling no regrets. She was his wife now, and the rest would work itself out in time. Everything he wanted was his. There was nothing to hold them back now.

With the house settled for the night, Gavin undressed and eased between the sheets, thinking only how good it felt to know that she was his now. That alone was enough to make life worth living.

He found sleep hard to come by as he imagined his future, his only regret being that James MacBrier was not still living. Gavin hadn't thought of it quite like this before, but now he felt certain that the fifth Earl of Brierley would have been pleased by this union. There was plenty of evidence that he had cared for both Gavin and Anya. It was too bad he hadn't been able to attend their wedding.

Gavin's mind wandered to that day—that single day—he had encountered James MacBrier, and he found those words echoing through his mind . . . that line of poetry his mother had told him to recite in order to get the Earl's help. It pounded so loudly in his mind that he felt forced to say it aloud. "Love can be found with the touch of a hand."

Anya's breathing didn't change rhythm, but the words seemed to fly to the ceiling and float back down in a blanket of warmth. Gavin found Anya's hand beneath the sheet and brought it to his lips, fingering the gold band she now wore that bound her to him. He touched the rough skin to his face and found it was improving, however slowly, then he kissed it again and placed it against his chest. He loved Anya's hands. And despite what she might think, it was a beautiful wedding night.

Gavin was still awake when he felt Anya stirring. A little gasp told him she was awake and uncertain.

"Gavin?" she whispered.

"I'm here," he answered, catching the shadows of her face and hair.

"How long have you been home?"

"Hours."

"I can't believe I slept so long. I'm sorry, I . . ." He silenced her with a kiss. It was quick and meek, but it changed everything. She was his now. He was hers. And nothing would ever take that away from them.

Anya felt the hidden meaning behind Gavin's kiss, and her breathing sharpened in time with his. His sigh washed over her face. He kissed her again, just as quickly. And again.

"Anya!" he whispered. His arm went possessively around her waist. He kissed her still again, meekly at first, then a subtle urgency seeped into it.

Relief enveloped Anya. If she had heard any more references to her health or this baby, she would have screamed. For now, she just wanted to forget those things. This was her wedding night, and Gavin's affection sent all else fleeing. He had told her his love could make her forget that Cedric had ever touched her. And already she had. Already, Gavin's affection, combined with his complete love and acceptance, had forced memories of Cedric far into oblivion, along with all else that had marred her life. Her parents' neglect, the Earl's death, the years of servitude—all of it fled in the face of Gavin's power.

Later, while Anya slept in his arms, Gavin continued to marvel at how completely she had blessed his life. Here, with her, he found the answer to a formless question that had hung over him since the first time he had been looked in the face and had his illicit origin questioned. He knew now what he had been seeking all these years: belonging. He belonged with Anya, and she with him. They were bound together in a way that time and the taunts of the past could not dispel. Yes, he thought with certainty, attempting to ease her closer, this was where he belonged.

Chapter Twelve
MACBRIER'S CHILD

Anya stretched herself awake, feeling a sense of contentment long before she was conscious. She finally opened her eyes to find Gavin leaning up on his elbow, watching her.

"Good morning, Mrs. Baird," he said as if he'd announced royalty.

"Good morning," she smiled, then her expression faltered.

"Feeling sick?" he asked, as if it were nothing.

She nodded regretfully and he pointed to the bedside table. "Dr. Forbes told me if you eat something before you even get up, it might ease the problem." Anya reached for the dish of shortbread, certain it couldn't hurt. "If it doesn't help," Gavin added, "there's a basin on the floor." Anya glanced down and tried to smile, but Gavin saw the dismay in her eyes. "What's the matter?"

"Romantic, isn't it," she grumbled with her mouth full.

"I think so," he grinned, and she made a noise of disgust that made him chuckle.

"What if I get crumbs in the bed?" she asked.

"We'll brush them out."

Anya finished her snack while Gavin continued to watch her. She might have felt unnerved under his gaze, except that she had gotten used to it long ago.

"I think that did help," she announced, brushing the crumbs from her lap onto the floor.

"Good."

"Now perhaps I should get dressed, and . . ." Gavin took her hand to kiss it, then worked his way up her arm.

"And what?" he asked matter-of-factly, moving his lips over her shoulder to her throat.

"I need to cook breakfast, and there is laundry to be done, and . . ."

"Not today, you're not," he said, and kissed her.

Given the choice, Anya decided against traveling for a honeymoon, though she was more disappointed about it than he.

"Home or abroad," he told her, "it's still a honeymoon."

Gavin was anxious to take her to all of the beautiful places he'd seen, especially on the continent. But they agreed that another season in their life would be more practical.

After weeks of living under the same roof, it was no problem to settle into married life. Autumn passed with long walks on the moors, shopping sprees in Strathnell, and just being together, whether in peace or in passion.

A mutual contentment deepened between them, and in time Anya not only came to accept the existence of her baby, but she actually began to anticipate its birth. Gavin spoke often of the child, speculating over its gender, planning its life and all they would do together. And he never failed to mention that it would have brothers and sisters.

"And with any luck they will all look like their mother," he insisted one afternoon as they returned from town. The original purpose of their journey had been to purchase grain for the horses, but they had spent hours at the tailor's ordering new clothes for Anya, as little would fit around her anymore.

"What a shame that would be," she retorted, "when their father is so dreadfully handsome."

Gavin laughed as he drew the trap to a halt in front of the house. He helped Anya down, and she reached into her pocket for the key as he returned to the trap to drive it to the stable.

As soon as Anya opened the door, she had a feeling that something was different. But she checked the house thoroughly and felt certain she was imagining things. Gavin soon came in with the packages and threw them on the bed.

"Guess what I forgot?" he said in a tone of self-punishment.

"The grain for the horses," they said in unison. Then Anya added in sarcasm, "That's pretty smart, Gavin. Wasn't that why we went into town in the first place? Are we all out?"

"Yes," he glanced at the clock, "but I can go back and be home by dark."

"If you must," she sighed, "but please hurry."

"How could I not hurry home to you?" He kissed her warmly.

"I'll have dinner waiting."

An uneasiness fell over Anya almost as soon as Gavin had gone. She couldn't recall ever feeling this nervous since she'd left Brierley. It wasn't yet dusk, but she lit a lamp and carried it carefully from room to room, just to make certain all was in order, leaving the house lit as she did so.

Her first glance into the parlor told her nothing was out of the ordinary. Then she caught a shadowy movement in the far corner, near the draperies. With her heart pounding, she lifted the lamp slightly, ready to turn and run. The shadow came to life, stepping boldly into the center of the room. Anya backed toward the door, then the light caught Cedric's face and she dropped the lamp to the floor, grateful as she turned to run that it had gone out rather than igniting the spill.

Cedric caught her around the waist before she made it to the kitchen. Anya cried out and turned to strike him, but he caught her other arm and laughed like the devil.

"What are you doing here?" she snarled. "How did you find me?"

"It wasn't easy, but I can assure you it will be worth it."

"How dare you come here and—"

"Don't get uppity, lassie. I just came for a social call."

"Anyone with a thread of decency would come to the front door and knock," she retorted, struggling to free herself from his painful grip, hating the memories and pain evoked by his mere presence. "You have no right to treat me this way. If Gavin finds you here, he will kill you."

"Or the other way around," Cedric laughed. "Wouldn't that be fun? But I suspect he'll not be returning for at least half an hour. That should give us time."

She finally broke one hand free and raked her nails across his face, cursing him with all the hatred she felt. Anger seethed in Cedric's eyes, and Anya felt her blissful life with Gavin slipping helplessly away.

Gavin had barely started into the strath when a voice cried from somewhere inside his mind: *Go back!* He argued with it, thinking he needed the grain. Of course there was hay, but the horses were used to their grain, and . . . There it was again. *Go back!*

Without hesitation, he turned and headed home as quickly as possible. He entered the yard quietly and jumped down from the trap. Gavin couldn't believe his ears as he approached the house and heard Anya shouting. He hesitated only long enough to hear Cedric MacBrier reply, and a seething hatred boiled through his veins.

Stealthily he went around the house to the front door, paused in the parlor to retrieve his loaded pistol from a drawer, then quietly moved into the kitchen. He felt bile rise into his throat as he saw Cedric pinning Anya against the wall with his body. He wondered how far it would have gone if he hadn't come when he did.

"You filthy wench!" Cedric snarled, holding her hands against her sides. Anya kicked and screamed in protest. "How dare you—"

Gavin pressed the gun between Cedric's shoulder blades and stopped him in mid-sentence. Cedric took a step back from Anya and she slumped to floor, holding her hands over her face. Gavin felt his gut wrench to see her fear, but he fought to handle this calmly. "We've got to stop meeting like this," he quipped.

Cedric covered his anxiety quickly, lifting his arms and sighing, as if this were all very amusing. "Come now. I was only having a little fun."

"Fun? You break into my home and take liberties with my wife, and expect me to think twice about killing you because you claim it was all in fun?" Gavin cocked the pistol, and Cedric drew a sharp breath. "I should have killed you the last time I had the chance. How dare you show your cowardly face here! Now get out of my house, and if I ever see you within five miles of here again, I will hunt you down and kill you just for sport."

"*Your* house?" Cedric chuckled and turned, apparently relieved as Gavin admitted he would let him go. But Gavin left the gun pointed directly at Cedric. "Whose house is it? I couldn't help noticing the MacBrier crest carved above the door. Isn't that quaint! Who gave it to you, Baird? Your father? Or did you steal it when you killed him?"

Gavin forced himself to remain in control. "I never knew my father. It was your father who gave me this house. And you can think what you like, but I've never killed a man . . . ," he corrected his aim, "yet."

"Before you get trigger-happy . . ." Cedric put his hands to his hips. Gavin motioned upward with the gun, and Cedric put them back in the air. ". . . perhaps I should tell you my real reason for coming."

"Assaulting my wife was only a trivial pastime, as long as you were in the neighborhood?"

"I don't know if I would put it so brashly as to say that—"

"State your business and go!" Gavin shouted.

"I came to claim what is mine," Cedric stated as if he were quite pleased with himself.

"I don't know what you're talking about." Gavin formulated a quick plan in his mind. He would give the house to Cedric. He would even give him the key to the safe, just to be free of him forever. Then he would take Anya away from here, and they would begin a life elsewhere. Nothing was worth this. Not even James MacBrier's last wishes.

"I came for my baby," Cedric clarified. Anya covered her mouth, but a whimper of fear escaped. Gavin felt his heart drop like a dead weight, but his expression remained cold. He was not about to let Cedric see anything but complete confidence.

"I don't know what you're talking about," Gavin repeated.

"Anya is carrying my baby." Cedric's tone betrayed a childish pride, and Gavin wanted to beat him to a pulp.

"Anya is my wife. Anything that is a part of her is a part of me."

"That's a clever way to put it, Baird. But it's still my baby."

"Over my dead body."

"That could be arranged," Cedric chuckled.

"I wouldn't talk like that with a gun pointed at your head, if I were you."

"But you're not me."

"I thank God every night for that."

"Do you? I had always imagined that you would give a lot to have what I've got."

"I wouldn't give a shilling to have what you've got. And you will never—ever—set a finger again on what I've got. Now let me clarify something. Anya lied to you. She was angry with me when she went back to Brierley. She lied to you to hurt me. It worked. The truth is that I stole Anya away from Brierley months ago. That baby is mine."

"Are you sure?" Cedric asked, seeming interested in Gavin's theory but not ready to believe it.

"Absolutely!"

"You're bluffing, Baird. Though you do it well, I must admit. But I know you're bluffing, because your little wench of a wife is the most pathetically honest person I have ever known. She wouldn't have lied to me any more than she would to her own mother. And she hates me too much to ever admit that such a thing was true without knowing it."

"Get out!" Gavin seethed. "Before I . . ."

"Before you what?" Cedric laughed. "I don't think you have the guts to kill me, Baird. I wonder if you even have what it takes to keep such a fiery little wench satisfied."

That did it! Gavin moved the gun to his left hand and sent his fist into Cedric's jaw. Anya cried out as Cedric reeled backward, shook his head slightly, and came back to his feet with a broad sweep of his arm that knocked the gun from Gavin's hand and across the floor. Gavin cursed under his breath and Cedric laughed.

Gavin blocked Cedric's first punch, but the next landed in his stomach, and he doubled over in pain. He couldn't quite believe that Cedric MacBrier had that much strength. He thought of Anya subjected to his will, and the pain intensified.

Anya scrambled for the gun but Cedric kicked it out of her hand, then turned and hit Gavin in the face. Anya cried out his name, feeling as helpless as if there were a knife at her throat.

Gavin regained his equilibrium while Cedric took a moment to gloat. "One of these days," he pointed a finger toward Anya, whose eyes shot fire, "you'll realize who the real man is."

Gavin briefly pretended to be hurt worse than he was, then he lunged for Cedric with a fist to the jaw, followed instantly by a fist in the gut and a knee to the groin. Cedric went to his knees, groaning from the pain, while Gavin kicked him in the jaw and sent him reeling backward against the table. Cedric slid to the floor and Gavin was on him like a rabid wolf, wanting only to beat him to a bloody pulp. He hit him over and over, while all of his bitterness toward Brierley surged through his veins, adding fuel to the fire burning on Anya's behalf.

"Gavin!" she cried somewhere on the edge of his anger. "Stop! You'll kill him!" Her hand on his shoulder brought him back to reason. He hesitated but came to his feet, wiping the blood from his mouth with his sleeve.

"Can you believe it?" he spoke to Cedric in heated spurts as he fought to regain his breath. "After all you've done to her, she just saved your pathetic life."

Cedric moaned while Gavin pulled Anya close to him. Once assured that she was all right, he threw water in Cedric's face and pulled him to his feet by the shirt collar. His face was so covered with blood that Anya could hardly recognize him. Hatred shot from Cedric's eyes as Gavin brought his face close enough to hear his whispered threats. "Now you listen to me, MacBrier. I will leave you in peace, and you will leave me in peace. My house, my baby, and my wife are strictly off limits to you, you filthy snake!" Gavin shook Cedric, and he winced from the pain. "If you ever—*ever*—come anywhere near any of them, you will regret having ever lived. I've let you go twice now, when I could have killed you. The next time you cross me, MacBrier, you will not live to tell your mother about it."

"Don't bet on it," Cedric retorted, the words barely discernible through his swollen lips. But Gavin saw the defeat in his eyes and knew that he'd won—at least for the moment.

It took little effort to escort Cedric out of the house and onto his horse, left tethered discreetly in the trees. Cedric seemed barely stable in the saddle, but Gavin headed the horse toward Brierley and slapped it into a gallop. Then he nearly ran back to the house, where he found Anya sitting on the floor in tears.

"It's all right," he whispered. "He's gone."

"Oh," she cried, touching his face, "look what he's done to you." His wounds distracted her from her own pain as she tended to them, and Gavin was reminded of the day she had found him bleeding in the stable at Brierley.

Before she had a chance to think too hard about what had happened, Gavin made certain she ate some supper, trying to keep the conversation light. Then he tucked her into bed, leaving her only long enough to feed the horses. He locked the house up tightly and prayed she would get over this, then he climbed into bed beside her, grateful to find her sleeping peacefully.

The next morning, Anya behaved as if nothing had happened. Gavin's attempt to discuss their encounter with Cedric was lightly brushed aside. She claimed it didn't bother her, but Gavin feared she had only locked it somewhere deep inside.

Anya awoke to see snow falling in heavy flakes, then she realized, as she got out of bed and dressed, that she didn't feel ill at all. In fact, she felt quite good. Perhaps that stage of her pregnancy had finally passed. She felt even better the next day, except for a low ache in her back that came and went. Gavin was pleased to see her up and about more than she had been in weeks, but still he encouraged her not to overdo it.

Late in the afternoon, Gavin came in with an armload of wood and found her rolling out biscuits on the table. He set the wood down and shed his coat and gloves, then leaned against the door to watch her as she rubbed her nose with the back of her hand and left a smudge of flour there. He chuckled, and she glanced toward him in question.

"Nothing," he said, not wanting her to remove it. He had the urge to kiss it away. Anya turned her attention back to her work until his arms came around her from behind, and she felt the urgency in his embrace.

"Not now," she chuckled. "Can't you see I'm busy?"

"It can wait," he whispered, pulling her up into his arms. She laughed and wiped her floury hands all over his shirt before he got her to the bed.

"Wretched woman!" he laughed.

An hour later, Anya was finishing the biscuits while Gavin leaned back in a chair and watched her. "They will be dry and tough," she teased. "And it will be all your fault."

"I'll take the blame," he conceded, and she could only smile.

She was slapping biscuits onto a baking sheet when the ache in her back felt suddenly more tangible. Dr. Forbes had spoken of growing pains and aches that could never be explained, so she passed it off and put the biscuits in the oven, then turned to clean up the mess.

Gavin noticed her stop and grip the edge of the table. He leaned forward and reached for her hand. "Are you all right?"

"I'm sure it's nothing," she assured him and went on with her work, but Gavin was more alert. Only moments later a cramp wrenched inside her and Anya cried out, pressing her hand low on her belly.

"What?" Gavin rushed to her side. "What is it?"

"I don't know, I . . ."

"Should I get the doctor?"

"No . . . I mean, not yet. I . . . I don't want you to leave."

The cramp lessened, and she stood up straight. "It's gone now. Perhaps I just need some relief."

Gavin knew what she meant and waited while she went in the other room, returning a few minutes later looking unusually pale. She met his eyes briefly as she untied her apron and threw it over a chair, then headed for the bedroom.

"What's wrong?" he asked, following close behind.

"I think I'll lie down."

"What's wrong?" he repeated. It wasn't like her to so easily give up on her self-appointed duties about the house.

Anya lay on her side and gazed toward the window, stating with no inflection, "I'm bleeding . . . just a little, though," she added with a smile that couldn't hide the concern in her eyes. "Perhaps if I stay down it will stop."

"I hope so," he said, wishing he knew half as much about this as she did. He wanted to ask a dozen questions, but it was evident she didn't want to talk right now.

"Could you check the biscuits?" she said absently. "I don't want them to burn."

"Of course," he answered and returned to the kitchen.

Anya lay quietly while her heart beat in painful thrusts. She hadn't even wanted this baby. Now she was losing it, and it was breaking her heart. How could she tell Gavin? She likely wouldn't have to. Sooner or later it would just happen, and as closely as he attended to her, he couldn't be ignorant for long. Soon he would know that she'd lied to him. She was bleeding much more than a little, and the cramps were too hard and regular to mean anything else.

Anya tried to think sensibly. She had seen miscarriages before. It was not a pretty sight, but it was a natural process. No, she didn't want the doctor here, mostly because she didn't want Gavin to leave long enough to get him. If it happened while he was gone, she would have no one at all. She wasn't worried about the physical pain as much as she dreaded feeling the loss of this life that had become a part of her.

Gavin reappeared and sat beside the bed, leaning his forearms on his thighs and intertwining his fingers.

"How are the biscuits?" she asked, attempting a smile.

"Dry and tough," he stated. "But I take the blame. How are you?"

"Not good," she said, realizing there was no point in soothing him now. The pain was a good indication that this wasn't far off.

"And should I also take the blame for that?"

"Whatever do you mean?"

"This didn't start until I carted you off to the bedroom and—"

"Gavin, please don't. No one is to blame." She grimaced and clenched her fists. Gavin moved to her side, feeling a complete loss of words. He wanted to ask but didn't dare. He was relieved when she took it out of his hands. "I need your help. You mustn't leave now. It won't be long."

"You're losing the baby, aren't you." She met his eyes and gave a slight nod. Gavin swallowed hard as her answer struck pain. "What do you want me to do?"

"First, get some clean towels. A lot of them . . . to protect the bed. Put some water on to boil, and get some clean rags . . . and a basin."

Anya leaned against the headboard while Gavin saw to his tasks.

"Now what?" he asked tensely when there seemed nothing more to do.

"We wait."

Gavin hesitated, but had to ask. "Tell me what to expect. Does it hurt much?"

Anya took his hand. "It hurts," she admitted. "When it's over," she added, "then you can get the doctor." Her voice cracked in an effort to choke back the emotion. She blinked and swallowed hard, and it appeared to be gone. "He can examine it to make certain everything came out all right, and he might even be able to tell us why it happened."

Gavin had a good idea why it was happening, and he felt sick inside each time she grimaced and squeezed his hand in response to the pain.

"I love you, Gavin," she said in the midst of it all.

"I love you," he repeated, wondering if she, too, was blaming him for this.

"I think it's coming," she said moments later, and it was over much faster than Gavin had expected. He was also surprised to find that it looked much more like a baby than he had imagined. It was incredible. So tiny, yet so much human detail. He felt a definite sadness at its loss.

"It's a girl," he said to Anya, whose eyes were closed.

"Take it away," she whispered. "I don't want to see it."

Gavin did as she asked and cleaned up the mess as much as possible before he went for the doctor. He returned to find Anya sitting up in bed with a book.

"The doctor is here," he announced quietly, and she set the book aside as Gavin ushered him into the room. "He's already seen the baby." Gavin closed the door and left them alone, hating the silence surrounding him as he drummed his fingers on the kitchen table. He came abruptly to his feet when the doctor finally opened the bedroom door, then closed it behind him.

"Your wife is just fine," he reported. "Have her rest and eat well, and she should be up and about quite soon."

"Can you tell me why it happened?" Gavin asked, fearing the answer.

"As I explained to your wife, that baby has been dead for several days at least. It's hard to say why, but something must not have been right with it. Often this kind of thing is a blessing in disguise. Your wife can get pregnant again as soon as she feels up to it, and I would dare to say that little girl will come back to you one day."

Gavin felt unexplainable relief as he settled with the doctor, then returned to find Anya reading. He sat carefully on the edge of the bed, not liking the indifference in her expression. "Are you all right?" he asked.

"I'm fine," she stated, as if it were the most fascinating story she had ever read.

Gavin took the book and laid it aside. "Let me try that again. Are you all right?"

This time she turned her eyes downward. "Of course I'm all right. Why shouldn't I be? I should be relieved to be free of Cedric MacBrier's baby."

"Anya," he brushed a stray lock of hair from her face, "it was your baby, too. It was a part of you."

His words voiced the pain she was trying to hide, and she took hold of his shoulders, pulling her face to his chest. "My baby," she cried. "I've lost my little girl."

"There will be more," he soothed.

"But I . . ."

"I know," he whispered gently when she faltered. He wanted to tell her it would be all right. They would get past this. But right now the words wouldn't penetrate the pain. So he just held her.

Chapter Thirteen
Crooks and Nannies

Winter settled over Scotland with a bitter coldness. Gavin became a distant observer in his new marriage, as Anya seemed lost and alone in grief over the loss of her child. He had attempted endlessly to console her, and speculated often about their future children. He'd suggested they go away for a few weeks on an overdue honeymoon. Anya politely rejected his every effort with the simple excuse that she would feel better with time.

But time was passing, and nothing seemed to change. Gavin tried to understand her grief, certain that a man couldn't possibly comprehend losing an unborn child. But still he sensed something unnatural about her emotions, something he wasn't seeing. It seemed that all he could do was guess her thoughts from a distance, and stay on his side of the bed.

Dr. Forbes had assured them that Anya was in good health, but he had mentioned to Gavin something about women going through changes that could make their emotions more sensitive. That didn't tell Gavin anything; it only made him more confused.

He talked to Peg about it, but she told him what he'd already figured out. "How could a brute like ye ever know what such a thing feels like in a woman's heart? Just leave her be, an' it'll pass with time."

"How much time?" he asked pointedly.

"Impatient as always."

"I've never been impatient a day in my life," he retorted.

"Huh," Peg snorted. Gavin furrowed his brow, and she giggled. "I was just teasin' ye! Give th' lass some time. She loves ye. She'll come 'round."

"But I sense there is something more," Gavin said, pressing his brow into his hands. "What I wouldn't give to read that woman's mind!"

"If a man could read a woman's mind, th' world would come tae an end," she laughed. "What fun would we have if we always knew what our friends and sweethearts were thinkin', eh?"

Gavin narrowed his eyes, irritated by her joviality when he was under such duress. "Consider it a challenge," she added, pinching his cheek. "If ye can beat Cedric MacBrier into a mess, surely ye can fight him out o' that corner o' her heart."

Gavin gasped in disgust. "Her heart?" He chuckled humorlessly. "She despises him!"

Peg pushed her finger against Gavin's chest. "That is exactly what I mean. Ye're like th' old bull tryin' tae fight his way through th' fence while th' grass beneath yer feet is just fine."

"Could you translate that, please?"

"Ye're lookin' for some complicated answer to a complicated problem. Ye're not findin' what ye're lookin' for, b'cause it's so simple."

"For example?" he persisted, still not grasping the implication.

"Men!" She shook her head. "She lost th' baby. It hurt. Why did it hurt? B'cause she wanted th' baby. She loved th' baby. It was part o' her. Now she's not gettin' over it. Why? Th' baby was Cedric MacBrier's. She hated him. There's th' facts, lad. Ye figure it out."

"It's too contradictory." He pushed his hands through his hair in frustration.

"Congratulations!" she quipped. "Ye win the prize!"

"Peg!" he shouted. "Stop playing games with me, and—"

"That's just it, oatmeal brain! It's too contradictory. I would bet a hat that if ye turn around and go back home, ye'll find nothin' more than a woman with a confused heart."

Gavin's eyes widened. He silently absorbed it all for a long moment, then he grinned and came to his feet, kissing Peg on the cheek. "You're a genius, Peg."

"Good thing somebody is." She shook her head and watched him leave. "Men!" she added when he was gone.

Gavin found Anya sitting in the bedroom rocker, her eyes fixed on nothing. He prayed that Peg was right.

Anya glanced toward Gavin as he entered the room. She wondered why he was always there, so concerned, so attentive. She didn't deserve a husband as good as him, when she gave so little in return. She had to find a way to be free of this burden she carried and get on with her life. If only she could make Gavin understand. But how could she? She didn't understand it herself. It simply didn't make sense to feel such grief over losing something that had been conceived in an act so callous and hateful.

Every time she closed her eyes, Anya could see Cedric's taunting eyes, instilling a fear that tore at her insides like a knife. A vivid memory still haunted her of those moments when Cedric had held the advantage over Gavin as they'd fought right here in her home. She wondered what might have happened if Gavin hadn't defeated him. Would Cedric have killed Gavin? And what would he have done to her and the baby?

How could Anya begin to tell Gavin these fears without sounding like a fool? And why hadn't these things bothered her before she'd lost the baby? Or had they? Perhaps the miscarriage had brought to light the reality of life's vulnerability. Whatever it was, Anya felt afraid for reasons she couldn't decipher, and somehow guilty for feelings she didn't understand.

But here was Gavin, always by her side with words of comfort, his eyes filled with love and acceptance. And she couldn't even bring herself to tell him what she felt. Just the thought of voicing her fears made them seem too real, too tangible. But the only grain of hope within her was the thought of facing all of this and having it over with.

"Anya." He knelt beside her, sitting against his boots. "Can we talk?" She nodded, aching to have him understand, but not knowing where to start.

Gavin saw the hope in her eyes and felt confident he was doing the right thing. He took her hand into his and gave a loving squeeze. Anya watched him expectantly, but the few words he'd planned to say were caught somewhere in his throat. He finally asked, "Are you feeling all right?" He felt a need to clarify. "Physically, I mean."

"Yes," she smiled meekly, "of course."

He decided to get to the point. "But not otherwise."

Anya looked away quickly, but Gavin caught her chin. "I know that for some reason, you're having trouble telling me what's wrong. But we need to talk. Am I right so far?" Anya nodded almost eagerly. Gavin wondered if he could get somewhere by the process of elimination. "Can I just ask you some questions, and you can tell me yes or no?"

"All right," she agreed.

"Are you upset with me . . . for any reason at all?"

"No, of course not." She touched his face tenderly, and Gavin felt hope. Perhaps Peg was right. This wasn't as insurmountable as he'd begun to think.

"Are you still feeling bad about losing the baby?" he asked carefully.

"It was a difficult thing," she answered, but her tone suggested that this wasn't the root of the problem.

"Does it have to do with Cedric?" Anya felt herself react and hated it. Why couldn't she just tell him?

Gavin's heart began to pound as he saw that hollow look glaze over her eyes. He knew it was there to hide the pain and fear. Her hand turned sweaty in his, and he could hear her breath quicken. But he told himself they had passed these kinds of barriers before, and they would do it again. He just felt so frustrated and impatient. Peg had been right again. He *was* impatient. Why did she always have to be so right?

"Anya," he persisted, hating the fear in her eyes. He reminded himself that her anxiety was not directed at him. "Why do you react that way when I mention Cedric MacBrier?" She hesitated. "Why?" he repeated.

Anya flew to her feet. "Why shouldn't I?" she shouted. "The man has forced himself upon me, left me to bear his baby in shame, broken into my home, and tried to kill my husband."

"Forget about it!" To Gavin it seemed so easy, but Anya felt infuriated.

"You don't understand!"

"Then make me understand, woman."

"I can't forget about it!"

"Why not?"

"I just can't!"

"And that's it?" he asked, getting no response but a turn of her back. Gavin took her by the shoulders and turned her to face him. "What do I have to do to get that worm out of our lives?"

Anya melted into a pool of fear and hurt as Gavin's question struck the core of the problem. "I don't know," she sobbed. The anguish pushed into her throat while he held her, nearly suspended in the air like a rag doll, her toes barely touching the ground.

Gavin's helpless frustration whirled all the hurt and anger together with the love and the pain and the echoing taunts of the past. As Anya fell apart in her tears, he carried her to the bed and held her, encouraging her to unleash all that had been bottled up inside of her since Cedric MacBrier had tainted her life. He kissed her brow and traced a finger over her lips. When her tears finally settled, he knew his best chance at finding the source of her pain was now.

"Anya," he whispered, "I want you to tell me what's bothering you." He held his breath, waiting for a response. She only pulled him closer, and he felt hope. "Tell me your fears and I'll throw them away," he soothed. "Tell me your pain and I'll bury it."

"I almost believe you could," she replied. Gavin tightened his embrace, and suddenly her words came easily. "What will he do to me next?"

"Cedric?" He felt her nod. "Is that what has been bothering you?"

"That's part of it."

Gavin leaned up on his elbow to look at her. "I want to know all of it."

"I don't know. I'm just so . . . confused."

Peg was right again, blast her! "Because you loved the baby and hated Cedric?" he asked, and her eyes widened to affirm it. "Is there anything wrong with that?"

"I suppose not," she conceded. "But I . . . I need to find a way to be free of this. I cannot spend the rest of my life fearing him and what he might do to me." She turned pleading eyes upon him. "Will you help me, Gavin?"

Gavin wanted to cry, but his masculine nature made him laugh instead. "Help you? Oh, Anya—my sweet Anya. I would go to the ends of this earth to help you."

Anya said no more. For now, she had what she needed. Her fears were vented, her reasons in the open. She knew Gavin was there for her, and once again he had helped her across her own barrier to facing the truth. Now she just needed time to sort out her thoughts and find the best way to confront it.

It soon became evident to Anya that the problem was not solved. Some glorious steps had been made in finding the source of it and relieving the tension, but she knew this had to be faced. With careful thought and prayer she came to a decision, planning it out carefully in her mind before she sought the courage to approach Gavin. She knew he would hate the idea.

"I have come to a decision," she said just after breakfast. He knew what she meant and simply nodded to indicate that she should continue. "I ask that you hear me out before you jump to any conclusions." He nodded again and she took a deep breath. "I want to go back to Brierley."

Gavin nearly choked on his coffee. "You *what?*"

"You said you would hear me out!" She pointed a finger at him.

Gavin raised his hands in surrender, but she could see the fire in his eyes.

"I have to see Cedric," she stated softly. "I have to face him and—"

"Have you lost your mind?" he shouted, coming to his feet and placing his palms flat on the table.

"No!" She stood to face him. "I have not! I must show him that I am not what I used to be. When I prove to him that I am not afraid of him, I will prove it to myself. And I want him to know the baby is gone. I want him to know there is nothing left to bind us together in any way."

Gavin sat down. He didn't want to admit it, but she was right. And he had to admire her courage. But still, he didn't like it. "So," he said with sarcasm, unable to hide the trace of bitterness, "did you plan to just traipse through the front door and announce yourself, or did you want to sneak in by the dead of night?"

"I am asking for your help, and I don't need that kind of an attitude. This is important to me, Gavin. Now, do you love me or not?"

"This has got nothing to do with—"

"Yes, it does!" She hit her fist against the table and the dishes rattled.

Gavin looked down and sighed. Pride swallowed, he lifted his eyes to face her. "What do you want me to do?"

Anya sat down, sighing with relief. "You must come with me, of course, although I have to face him alone."

"And I ask you again, just how did you plan to go about this? I'm not certain showing my face there in daylight would be conducive to my well-being."

"I thought about that."

"I had a feeling you did."

"I doubt they would dare try to do anything to you again, but perhaps I could leave you in Robbie's care while I go to the wedding."

"Wedding?" He lifted his brows.

"Malvina's wedding. Didn't I tell you? It was all they talked about when I . . . went back." The memory of those days caught her briefly off guard, but she quickly returned to her purpose. "I will congratulate Malvina, have a moment alone with Cedric, and we will leave . . . with freedom and peace."

"But there's more to it than that," he stated. "Isn't there?"

Anya glanced down at her nervous hands, then she looked him straight in the eye. "I want them to know that they didn't succeed." Gavin furrowed his brow in question. "I want them to see what I have become . . . what you have made me," she corrected.

Gavin smiled. "A man can't make gold out of iron."

Anya warmed to the compliment and took his hand. "I love you, Gavin Baird."

"And I you." He shook his head and chuckled, then he rose and threw his napkin to the table. "Very well, if we're going to do this, we might as well make it good. When is this wedding?"

"In four days."

"Four days?" He shook his head again. "Then you'd better get dressed."

"Where are we going?"

"Shoppin', m'dearie. We are goin' shoppin'." His expression turned to disbelief. "Malvina is really getting married?" Anya nodded. "I wonder what poor man is sentencing himself to life with her."

"You're cruel," Anya insisted, but she couldn't help laughing.

"I'm honest," he stated. "Perhaps an ugly face wouldn't be so bad if she had a degree of sweetness. But all things considered, I certainly wouldn't want to get up every morning to look at her." He grinned and eyed Anya with obvious desire. "Now, on the other hand, with a wife like you . . ."

His silent appraisal said more than the words he didn't finish. Anya absorbed the warmth from his eyes, and peace settled into her.

With careful instructions from Gavin, Peg escorted Anya to the tailor's shop and assisted in choosing an appropriate gown to be made for Anya's return to Brierley. The only problem for Peg was choosing a color. Anya chose black. It seemed appropriate, if not amusing.

With the gown promised the day after tomorrow, they returned to meet Gavin at the hat shop. He wasn't there yet, so Peg took time to fit Anya with an appropriate little piece. "Tasteful and elegant," Peg called it.

"But I'll need you to help me put it on," Anya insisted, knowing she could never set it right.

"My services will be included in th' price."

Gavin walked through the door, smiled his approval at the hat, and Peg announced, "That hat will cost you five pounds."

"Five pounds?" He laughed at the ridiculous amount.

"The price includes m' services."

Peg actually refused any payment for the hat, but she appeared on their doorstep just past breakfast on the morning of Malvina's wedding. Anya opened the door, and Peg went through to the bedroom without so much as a hello. "Hey, laddie!" she called to Gavin. "Get this kilt an' plaid out o' here and find yersel' another place tae put 'em on. I've work tae do."

"What storm ushered you in?" Gavin insisted, showing himself in the doorway. Peg stuck her tongue out at him, then proceeded to brush through Anya's hair in long, even strokes. Gavin watched for a moment, until Peg turned and threatened to throw the hairbrush at him.

"I'm going!" He quickly gathered his things from the wardrobe and bureau, then took up the plaids laid over the bed, hurrying from the room before Peg got serious with that hairbrush.

Anya felt a bubbling excitement as Peg dressed her hair in a fashionable coiffure. Peg helped her into the black gown, trimmed with cream lace at the cuffs, collar, and in rows around the hem. Peg adjusted the dress and fastened it up the back, then carefully set the hat into place.

"That should do it," Peg announced, stepping back with triumph.

"Oh, Peg," Anya surveyed her reflection with pleasure, "if I were a great lady, I should need you with me each day to help me dress."

"What a pleasure that would be! But ye are a great lady," Peg insisted. "Otherwise, Gavin wouldna have married ye."

"I guess you would know," Anya laughed. "After all, he did propose to you."

"Aye, that he did!" Peg laughed as a light rap sounded against the bedroom door.

"Have you got the lady ready yet?" Gavin called. "We'll be late."

"I don't want to be on time," Anya called back. "I don't want to see Malvina get married. I just want to interrupt the party."

"Aye, that she will!" Peg chuckled.

"May I come in?" Gavin asked impatiently.

"If you must," Peg answered.

Gavin opened the door, and Anya turned slowly to face him. She soaked in his appearance with adoration, certain he was the most handsome man alive. He wore the same kilt and plaid he'd been married in, and the memory alone filled Anya with warmth and pride.

"How handsome you look!" Anya murmured, oblivious to the dazed adoration in Gavin's eyes.

"Aye, that he does!" Peg agreed.

Gavin didn't hear them. He was trying to imagine Anya as she had looked the first time he'd laid eyes on her as a scullery maid.

Surely it wasn't the same woman. "You are so beautiful," he finally managed to say, thinking he sounded trite. But there were no words to describe the delicate combination of grace, dignity, and beauty standing before him. It was as if she'd been born to it. But then, she had MacBrier blood.

"Why dinna th' two o' ye stop gapin' at each other and get out o' here while there's still daylight."

"What would we do without you, Peg?" Gavin grinned, offering his arm to Anya.

"Ye'd be standin' here gapin' all day, that's what."

Gavin drove the trap in silence toward Brierley. A mixture of emotions hung over them. The day was bright and cold, but Anya felt comfortable beneath the furs spread over their laps.

"Are you nervous?" Gavin finally asked as they neared the estate.

"I'd be lying if I said I wasn't," she admitted.

Gavin squeezed her hand. "Whatever happens, they'll never forget you." He looked at her adoringly. "I know I never could."

"But you're biased," she laughed.

"Yes," he said proudly, "I am."

Gavin slowed the trap as they began to pass the tenant farms. He'd hardly noticed them on his previous journeys to and from Brierley, due to darkness, emotion, or being half dead. But he recalled well how they had appeared as he'd left Brierley more than ten years ago. What he had remembered as a series of quaint little houses, surrounded by thriving farms and healthy children, now stared back at him in a silent cry for help. The houses and fences were neglected badly. A barely detectable stench of poverty hung in the air, while tired, sallow eyes glanced their way. He thought of the magnificence of Brierley House, and the lavish social he had attended last summer. Was that how Cedric MacBrier handled his estate, stealing from the poor to support his mother's amusements? The MacBriers were all a bunch of crooks!

Gavin stirred the horses to a steady gallop, grateful that Anya was apparently too caught up in her meeting with Cedric to have noticed the dilapidated farms. He attempted to put the scene out of his head, but it hovered there like a threatening storm, while a voice from inside seemed to speak to him: *You could change it, Gavin.*

He told himself such a thing was ridiculous, and turned the trap down the lane. The four great towers of Brierley House rose before them like a monument to something neither of them cared to define.

"I remember how it looked the first time I saw it," Anya said. "It has changed."

"I was twelve years old before I ever saw it from a distance," Gavin mused in a melancholy tone. "I was astounded to realize how big it was."

"It's a shame—something so beautiful holding such hate, such deceit."

"Yes," Gavin agreed, turning the trap toward the stable rather than entering the main gate, "it is a shame."

"Well, I'll be," Robbie declared when Gavin stepped in to find him at work. "I didna expect tae see ye here t'day."

Gavin glanced around to see many servants in varied livery, passing the time as they waited for the wedding festivities to end. "Hello, Robbie." They shook forearms heartily.

"I must say ye're lookin' fine, lad. But what brings ye out here, all gussied up that way?"

"I brought my wife for a visit." Gavin turned slightly, and Robbie's eyes moved to Anya as she stepped out from behind him.

Anya couldn't recall Robbie ever remaining silent when there was nothing to stop him from talking. Until now.

"Hello, Robbie," she smiled.

"Well, I'll be!" he finally managed, removing his hat and sweeping a hand over his brow. "If I didna hear th' voice, I wouldna have believed it." He turned to Gavin with a grin. "What have ye done tae her, lad?"

"Don't look at me," Gavin chuckled. "Like I told Anya, a man can't make gold out of iron."

"Well, I'll be," was his only response, and Gavin chuckled again. "But we must get ye inside. Mrs. MacGregor would have me hide, she would, if I didna bring ye in tae see her at once." He ushered them out of the stable, and Anya walked a few paces ahead. "Did ye say ye came tae visit, then? I canna say as I blame ye. It would serve 'em right to see her, eh, lad?"

"She just wants a word with . . . the Earl. I doubt it will take long."

"Aye, lad," Robbie chuckled. "I dinna think she would have much tae say tae the likes o' him, eh?"

"There's a thing or two I'd like to tell him," Gavin murmured under his breath.

"What was that, lad?"

"Nothing." Gavin slapped his shoulder playfully, and the older man grinned.

"It's good tae see ye, lad—and the lassie there, too. 'Twould seem that ye worked out yer diff'rences."

"Aye," Gavin admitted, watching Anya walk just ahead of him, "we did at that."

Anya paused at the side door and motioned to Robbie. "You go in first." She turned to Gavin as Robbie opened the door. "I'm nervous."

"Do you want me to stay with you?"

"Whatever you think is best."

"We'll see," he winked, and followed her inside.

Robbie had apparently gotten the news out fast as Mrs. MacGregor bustled from the kitchen with her hands pressed to her face, a few kitchen maids at her heels.

"Bless m' soul!" she squealed. "The heavens must o' smiled upon us t'day. I dinna believe m' eyes!" Mrs. MacGregor took both Anya's hands and held them out to her sides as she surveyed her. Anya smiled to see her beaming with pleasure and pride. "But it is you!"

"Yes," Anya replied, "it is." The girls huddled around Anya, fussing over her gown and prattling about this and that while Gavin leaned against the wall, watching from a distance, feeling a sense of wonder on Anya's behalf. He noted the other girls' uniforms, some similar to the ones Anya had worn, but hers had been more ragged, more worn. He took special notice of their hands. Work-worn perhaps, but not ailing. He felt the pain surface and shoved it back under, knowing now was not the time to be feeling contempt against this place or those who ruled it.

Gavin felt Mrs. MacGregor's eyes fall upon him. "So, ye found yersel' a fine husband, did ye." She spoke to Anya but kept her focus on him. "I had heard rumors, but I didna know fer sure." Mrs. MacGregor brought Anya's hands close to her face, then she directed an expression of gratitude and warmth toward Gavin, who could only smile.

Anya moved to Gavin's side. "This is my husband, Gavin Baird."

Gavin knew by Mrs. MacGregor's eyes that she recognized the name, but she simply held out a gracious hand. "It's a pleasure indeed, lad."

"The pleasure is all mine," he replied, bending to kiss her hand. Mrs. MacGregor feigned a swoon, and the girls giggled. She held tightly to Gavin's hand and urged them into the kitchen, insisting they must eat.

"I s'spect they were a wee bit overzealous in plannin' Miss Malvina's weddin' feast. The food prepared for all those who didna care tae see her wed will get thrown out tae th' swine."

A front hall maid wearing dress uniform sat at the big table, nibbling on the fare that had just been brought in from the main dining room. Other maids bustled in and out of the kitchen, apparently still clearing the wedding dinner.

"Now ye just sit here, Mr. Baird." Mrs. MacGregor urged him to a chair and Robbie sat on the other side of him, not hesitating to dig in. "Dinna mind Ellen here," Mrs. MacGregor said, indicating the maid at the table. "She wouldna bite ye."

Ellen gave a little laugh that sounded like a baby pig. "Surely ye r'member wee Anya," Mrs. MacGregor said to Ellen, who nodded politely toward Anya, doing a poor job of concealing her envy. "This is Mr. Baird, Ellen. He is Anya's husband now."

Gavin nodded, then he realized Anya was still standing. Mrs. MacGregor apparently took notice in the same moment. "Are ye no' goin' to eat, lass?"

"I think I'll go and give Malvina my regards first." Her eyes turned to Gavin. "Then perhaps my stomach will settle."

Gavin came to his feet. "Do you want me to come?"

Anya wanted him there, but something inside told her it would be better if she did this alone.

"No, I'll be fine, thank you." Gavin kissed her quickly. Anya felt Ellen's eyes on them.

"Ye just sit right down here, lad," Mrs. MacGregor urged him back to his chair, "and I'll see that ye get a proper meal."

"Where might I find the . . . ," Anya began to inquire of Mrs. MacGregor, but Ellen interrupted.

"I'm finished here. If ye want tae come with me, I'll announce ye proper." She smiled warmly, as if the envy had settled into something hopeful on her part.

Anya wondered if Ellen, as well as the other girls, would hope to be rescued from this life by a man such as Gavin. Anya had surely wished for such a thing herself. How privileged she felt! She smiled at him as she followed Ellen out. He blew her a kiss and muttered a quick "Good luck."

Anya attempted to calm her pounding heart as the long hallways passed behind her. Ellen's conversation helped a little. "It must be excitin' tae come back here this way. After they treated ye s' bad an' all."

"In truth, I'm rather nervous."

"Ah, they bark louder than they bite," Ellen laughed again like a piglet. "It is true, then, what they say about ye?"

"And what is that?" Anya's curiosity briefly overshadowed her nerves.

"That ye was the fifth Earl's great-niece."

"Yes," Anya said sadly, "it is true."

"Here we are," Ellen announced, pausing before huge double doors. "Good luck to ye."

"Thank you, Ellen," Anya said. She took a deep breath as Ellen pushed open the doors, bobbed a curtsy, and gave her announcement.

"It's Madame Anya Baird, come tae pay her respects, my lady."

Ellen moved aside and backed out of the room, closing the doors behind her. Anya found herself facing a small group of people, many of whom she wasn't acquainted with, but their faces looked familiar from her ball-peeping days. A quick glance told her that Lady Margaret was there, gaping in silence, while everyone else continued to mingle, paying her little heed. Una hovered near the edge of the room like an ever-present sentry. Anya avoided her hard gaze and rubbed the scars on her hands.

Malvina was the center of attention, hanging like an icicle on her new husband's arm. The elegant wedding gown, overdone with frills, did little to hide her homeliness. Anya recalled Gavin's description of Malvina, and her nerves eased slightly. Malvina's husband appeared old enough to be her father, as she had recalled hearing. Personally,

Anya found him revolting. If Malvina had married for money, she would surely earn it. They likely deserved each other.

Anya didn't get a chance to see if Cedric was in the room before Lady Margaret approached her. Anya felt the urge to curtsy but quickly curbed it and stood to face her, chin lifted, shoulders back.

"Auntie Margaret," Anya smiled, belying all she felt inside. Margaret's eyes flared with an angry surprise. Anya hadn't called her that since the Earl's death. Margaret glanced toward Una, who nodded, as if they had some secret way of communicating.

"What on earth are you doing here?" Margaret demanded as her attention turned back to Anya. "How dare you come in here, like some long-lost . . ." She faltered briefly.

"Relative?" Anya provided. "I simply came to pay my respects to Malvina. She does make a lovely bride, doesn't she," Anya lied. "And I had wished to have a word with Cedric. Is he here?" Anya moved past Margaret, took up a glass of champagne from a tray being held by a stone-like butler, and moved toward Malvina and her husband. It was the husband she approached first, using a technique she had learned well from watching Malvina attempt to catch a man all these years.

"I haven't had the pleasure, sir," she said, holding up a hand for him to kiss. He looked flattered, then his eyes raked over her and he licked his lips. She was glad she wasn't pregnant, or she would have become nauseous. Malvina's eyes were as wide as saucers, and her expression left little doubt as to her envious thoughts.

"Conway Clayton," he informed her, as if announcing royalty. "And your name? I don't believe I've seen you here before."

"No, I used to live at Brierley. But I married recently, and thought today would be a perfectly lovely time to come back and visit. I did so wish to congratulate Malvina on her good fortune." Anya eyed her directly. She then informed Mr. Clayton, "Her stepfather was my great-uncle, you see."

"Ah, then you are of MacBrier blood," he smiled, and Malvina turned a near-visible green. That was one thing she did not possess in the slightest.

"Yes, but well, I must be running along. I've left my husband waiting for me, and I—"

"Oh, is he?" Malvina interrupted with malice cleverly disguised in her tone. "And I had thought you'd made him up."

Anya paused to absorb this. It was true; Malvina didn't believe she was really married. She was certain she had caught Anya in a bluff, and was determined to call her on it. Anya was so pleased she could hardly bear it. "You haven't met him?" she asked, perfectly inane.

"No, I haven't. Where have you been hiding him, my dear?"

"I fear he isn't the social type," Anya said, hoping she sounded tense enough to make Malvina believe she was lying.

"But you say he's here waiting for you?"

"Uh . . . yes, he is, but . . ."

"Forsythe!" Malvina called to the butler. "Would you call in Ellen for me, please."

"Aye, mum," he muttered, and turned toward the hall with his tray of champagne glasses. Ellen appeared a moment later. Anya attempted to look nervous, while she actually felt quite smug.

"Ellen, could you please go and get Mrs. Baird's husband at once. I should like to meet him."

"Aye, mum," she said without hesitation and turned away.

"I'll wait for him over here," Anya suggested, but Malvina stopped her, as if she didn't want to give Anya a chance to cover herself for a moment. It crossed her mind that Cedric obviously hadn't informed his half-sister of their marriage.

Anya sipped champagne while they waited. Mr. Clayton kept his eyes more on Anya than his wife, but Malvina was gloating too much to notice. When the wait had seemed too long, Malvina's cat-that-swallowed-the-canary look intensified.

"Perhaps I should just go and . . ." Anya began. Then the door came open, and Ellen stepped in. Anya caught her breath as Gavin appeared beside her. Ellen pointed toward them; he nodded, then caught her eye.

"Ah, there he is now," Anya said, and Malvina's eyes moved toward the door. Anya put her focus on Malvina as Gavin approached them. The astonishment in her expression, the way her mouth fell visibly open, and the surprised envy in her eyes gave Anya a lifetime's worth of revenge. She wanted to come right out and say *My husband is better than yours!* Then she scolded herself for her own childishness, certain she wasn't being very nice about this.

Anya was ready to introduce Gavin as he came beside her, but he took her hand in greeting, oblivious to Malvina's gaze. He kissed her cheek, then kissed her hand, his eyes falling on her with an adoration that Malvina couldn't have missed. "Did you need me, my love?" he asked gently.

"No," she smiled, "but Malvina informed me she hadn't had the opportunity of meeting you. She insisted."

Gavin set his eyes on Malvina, certain that she recalled seeing him at a particular ball last summer. She was every bit as homely as he remembered. He took her hand to kiss it, but didn't quite touch it with his lips, which he hoped she interpreted as an insult.

"Miss MacBrier . . . ," he began, enunciating enough to mock her, while his expression betrayed no trace of it. "Ah, but I am mistaken. You are married now, of course."

"Mrs. Clayton," Anya corrected, putting her hand over his arm.

"Mrs. Clayton, then." Gavin bowed slightly. "It is a pleasure. My wife has told me so much about you."

Malvina didn't seem pleased by this. "But haven't we met before, sir?" she asked, attempting to smile prettily, perhaps wanting the attention from him that her husband had given Anya.

Gavin made it clear that her efforts were wasted. "I don't recall it," he said lightly, intending that to be an insult as well.

"Perhaps we should let the happy couple mingle with their guests," Anya said to Gavin.

"Yes, of course."

"Congratulations to you, my dear," Anya said, her voice dripping with a false sweetness that she had also learned from Malvina.

Malvina gave a terse smile, and Anya moved away on Gavin's arm, letting him take a sip from her champagne glass. She felt Malvina's eyes on them, and wondered if Gavin did as well when he bent to kiss her quickly on the lips, then glanced around as if he'd hoped nobody noticed.

"I love you, Gavin," she said.

"And I love you." He chuckled. "You appear to be enjoying yourself."

"I am, actually."

"Good. Perhaps I should stay close to you for protection, since you don't appear to be needing mine." He glanced toward Una, who was keeping a close eye on them, and Anya saw the bitterness in his gaze.

"Perhaps we should go," she said in concern.

"Have you spoken with Cedric yet?" he asked.

"No, but . . ." She stopped, feeling his presence before she even saw him.

Gavin was quick to say, "Speaking of the devil."

"Well, well," Cedric chuckled arrogantly, ignoring Gavin. Anya turned to face him, certain his nose was more crooked than it used to be. His eyes raked over her, and she was pleased to see his surprise. She wanted it to be evident that she had changed. She was not his plaything anymore.

"You're just the man I want to see," Anya said immediately.

Cedric lifted his brows in surprise, and Gavin took a step back. He was leaving this battle to Anya.

Chapter Fourteen
The Earl's Daughter

Anya had to fight the hurt and anger, but she did her best to show Cedric a face of indifference, certain it would be the one thing to keep him at bay. If she didn't care, neither would he.

"I'll only be a moment, darling," she said to Gavin, handing him her champagne. He nodded and took a sip, watching as Anya moved discreetly to an unoccupied sofa where no one was lingering near enough to overhear.

Anya sat down and Cedric followed, crossing his legs carelessly. "Now, what do you need, love? Money? A man?" He glanced toward Gavin, who lifted his champagne glass in a mocking gesture.

"Don't be ridiculous!" Anya insisted. "I simply wanted to tell you that the baby I had told you was yours is . . . gone."

"Gone?"

"I miscarried some weeks ago. So you see, there is nothing left to bind me to you, or to Brierley. I just wanted you to know that."

Anya knew there was a great deal more she could have said, but she felt that the hardness in her eyes, the indifference in her manner would tell him more plainly than words that she was finished with him, that she would not tolerate any more of his abuse. With that she stood. Cedric did the same, but apparently had nothing to say.

"Good day," she said tersely. Cedric nodded, appearing somehow disappointed, and she walked away.

"Is everything all right?" Gavin asked as she put her hand into his.

"Everything is fine." She smiled up at him, and he knew she meant it.

"Shall we eat?" Anya moved toward the door. "I'm starving."

"One moment, please." Gavin stopped her. "As long as we're at it, I think I'll have a word with the charming Miss Una."

Anya didn't have a chance to question or protest before he glided across the room, his plaid nearly flying out behind him.

Gavin stopped before Una and looked down at her, attempting to pierce her through with his eyes the way she had always done to him in the years he'd spent at Brierley. "It's such a pleasure to see you," he said with obvious sarcasm. "It was always so good of you, the way you kept such an eye on me and my mother. I want you to know that I will *never* forget all you did for us." He nodded and turned away, taking Anya's hand and leaving the room before any more bitterness had a chance to seep in. A quick smile toward Lady Margaret put the finishing touch on their little escapade.

With the door closed between them and the MacBriers, Anya met Gavin's eyes and they both laughed. He hugged her tight and pulled her off the floor. Triumphantly, they headed back toward the kitchen, arm in arm.

Mrs. MacGregor fed them until they could hardly move, then they sat about visiting with the servants as they came and went, most of them sharing a familiar word with Anya and taking time to meet her husband.

Anya wished she could begin to tell Gavin how good this day had made her feel. It seemed a silly thing, but she felt that leaving Brierley behind would be easier now because she had faced it with courage and triumphed.

They were finally preparing to leave when Anya gasped, appalled at herself for overlooking the obvious. "Where is Effie?" she asked Mrs. MacGregor. "She's usually here at some time during the day. I must see her before I go."

"She would be up in her room, poor lass," Mrs. MacGregor said.

"What happened?" Anya asked in a tone that let Gavin know this Effie was important to her.

"Slipped and fell down th' stairs, though not one of us saw it happen, an' Effie might tell ye diff'rent."

Anya's eyes narrowed in concern, but she dared not inquire further. "I must see her," she told Gavin. "Will you wait?"

"Of course. I'll be in the stable with Robbie." He turned to Mrs. MacGregor and took her hand to kiss it in farewell. "It has been a most enjoyable day, Mrs. MacGregor. I thank you humbly for your hospitality." She blushed like a little girl. "And I thank you for teaching my wife some of those wonderful dishes you concoct."

Anya hurried up the back stairs to Effie's room, pulling her skirt up high in order to go more quickly. She knocked at the door, and a strange voice called for her to come in. Anya entered to find Effie sitting up in bed with a sketch pad. A nurse sat nearby until she stood to greet Anya.

"I am an old friend of Effie's," she explained. "Could I see her for a moment?"

"Of course." The nurse curtsied and slipped into the hall, though Anya was certain she hovered nearby.

"Effie," Anya sat and took her hand, "it's me, Anya."

"Anya likes to play games," Effie said with no expression. Anya took notice of the bruises on her face and touched them tenderly. "Mrs. MacGregor told me you fell down the stairs. Did you fall down the stairs?"

"Nanny say Effie fall down the stairs." Her expression turned pouty, but she continued to draw. "I can draw a very good picture."

"Did Effie fall down the stairs, or is that what Nanny says?"

"Nanny say if Effie talk too much, Effie fall down the stairs again. I can draw a very good picture."

"I see," Anya said tersely.

The nurse quietly entered the room and Anya squeezed Effie's hand. "I shall come back one day," she promised, "and we will play games."

"Anya likes to play games."

Anya asked the nurse a few questions, then hurried downstairs. She found Gavin chatting with Robbie about the horses. As soon as he saw her, Anya knew she'd not done well in hiding her concern.

"What's wrong?" Gavin asked.

Rather than answer the question, Anya posed one to Robbie. "Could you tell me what you know of Effie's accident?"

"Accident?" he laughed. "If ye ask me, 'twren't no accident." This confirmed Anya's suspicion, but Robbie went on. "Nanny clems that Effie fell down th' front stairs. Ye know as well as Ah do, lass, that Miss Effie doesna' use the front stairs."

"Nanny?" Gavin questioned.

"Una," Anya clarified quietly, and Gavin's brow furrowed.

Robbie continued, "Now Effie'll tell ye that someone hurt her. That's all. It's like she's 'fraid to tell. Ye know what I mean, lass?"

"Yes," Anya frowned, "I know exactly what you mean."

"Is there anything we can do?" Gavin asked.

Anya shook her head. "Perhaps we should go."

"The trap is waiting." Gavin motioned toward the door, then he turned to Robbie and shook his hand. "It was good to see you, old friend. Come and visit sometime." Gavin pulled on his gloves.

"I'll do that, lad. 'Twas a fine thing tae see ye doin' s' well—and tae see what ye've done with th' lass." His eyes turned warmly on Anya. "It's a wonderful thing."

"Good-bye, Robbie," she said, kissing his cheek. Gavin escorted her to the trap and helped her in.

Dusk was falling as they set out. Anya nuzzled beneath the furs, leaning her head wearily on Gavin's shoulder. He shifted the reins to his left hand and put his arm around her.

"Thank you, Gavin," she said quietly.

"For what?"

"For letting me have this day. I know it will make a difference." She laughed. "It already has."

"Good." He pulled her close and kissed her brow. Anya settled against him and fell asleep, but he felt wary and tense until Brierley was far behind them.

They made it home safely and found everything in order. While Gavin helped Anya out of the dress Peg had helped her into, he decided to just come out and ask. "Who is this Effie that you are concerned about?"

Anya turned to him in surprise. "Surely you must know."

"Know what?" He was obviously baffled.

"But then," she chuckled, "I suppose Effie rarely ventured into the forest to be spied upon."

"That explains it."

"Effie is the daughter of James MacBrier and his first wife, Ishbelle."

Gavin's eyes widened. "I didn't know he had a daughter."

"Her existence was not known to many people. Ishbelle died giving birth to Effie. She has a condition that has kept her secluded from the world."

"Do you think she's in danger?" he asked.

"I wouldn't think so. She's well looked after. The servants all love her and take good care of her. The nurse watching over her was hired by Mrs. MacGregor. If Una knows the others are suspecting foul play, perhaps she'll mind her business."

Gavin wanted to ask more, but the dress fell in a heap on the floor and Anya turned toward him. "There is only one appropriate way to end such a day as this, my lord."

"And what is that, my lady?" he asked, feigning innocence.

Anya kissed him. "Use your imagination." She kissed him again and felt certain he had figured it out.

Gavin awoke on a clear morning to find that Anya wasn't feeling well. She claimed it was nothing, but he had heard her up in the night and wondered if she was all right. She stayed close to the bed for much of the day, seeming embarrassed when he made mention of it. He couldn't help entertaining the thought that she might be pregnant.

Later in the day, after she'd gotten up and about more, he found clean white rags, freshly rinsed and hanging over the edge of the tub to dry, just as they had been in the days following her miscarriage. He now understood her ailment, but couldn't help being disappointed.

Anya was dismayed to find that she wasn't pregnant, but she quickly looked to the future, knowing it would happen soon enough. She was amazed to realize how much better she felt, being free of the burdens Brierley had left upon her. Though she couldn't be absolutely certain that Cedric wouldn't cross their path again, she felt confident that it could be faced and dealt with. The important thing was that she felt no fear, and the hurt dissipated further with each passing day.

Life gradually fell into a deep contentment for Anya. She continually marveled at Gavin's goodness. But her past had taught her to never, even for a moment, take such bliss for granted. The sun never set on a day with Gavin when she didn't make certain he knew that she loved him and appreciated all he did for her.

Spring touched the Scottish countryside with heavy rains that watercolored the straths and glens into a deep green and the moors to a brilliant purple. For Anya, the shift in seasons brought to mind how her life had been a year before, and the changes left her stunned.

But Gavin felt something wrench inside when spring made him realize that months had come and gone, and still Anya had not conceived. At first he didn't want to think about it, but when still another month came and went, he forced himself to face what it meant. The problem wasn't with Anya; she had conceived Cedric MacBrier's baby after one encounter. And the problem certainly wasn't a lack of trying. Perhaps that was it—was it possible to try too much? Or maybe the problem was him. If that was the case, he had to admit it would not be an easy thing to face.

He tried not to think about it, and as yet, he and Anya had never talked about it. But it began to stir in Gavin's mind like a festering wound. He did well at hiding it, but he could hardly close his eyes without seeing an imagined argument between himself and Cedric MacBrier. The conversation always ended with Cedric pointing an accusing finger at him, his eyes full of arrogance and vengeance, saying smugly, *"You're not man enough to give her what she wants!"*

"Is something troubling you?" Anya touched his shoulder and he started.

"No," he lied, then wondered if this was how Anya had felt after she'd lost the baby and found her mind absorbed with formless fears.

"You seemed so far away," she persisted.

"Just thinking. Really, I'm fine."

He was grateful for the knock at the side door that distracted her interest. Anya went to answer it but he stopped her, wondering who on earth would be calling so early in the morning. "I'll get it," he offered.

Gavin swung the door open. "Robbie!" he exclaimed, noting that he looked less jovial than normal.

"Good mornin', lad."

Gavin motioned him inside, then he realized Robbie wasn't alone. Standing just behind him was a woman with the face of a child and eyes that seemed lost in another time, darting around without looking at anything at all. "Come in, please. What can we do for you?"

Robbie took the girl's arm and ushered her through the door. "Might I speak with yer wife, lad?"

"I'm here." Anya appeared in the doorway, her eyes filling with pleasant surprise. "Effie!" She flew across the kitchen to take the girl in her arms. "Effie," Anya spoke softly, holding Effie's face close to hers, "it is Anya. You are at Anya's house."

"Anya likes to play games," Effie said without looking at her.

Anya laughed. "That's right, Anya likes to play games." Then her gaze caught the bruise below Effie's eye. Gingerly she touched it, turning her face to the light. It was apparent this was not the result of any kind of fall. "Who did this to her?" she demanded of Robbie. "You will never convince me this was from falling down the stairs!"

"We can only guess, lass."

"And what would your guess be?" Anya insisted.

"Rumor among the servin' folks is that Nanny's been houndin' the poor dear for some reason or t'other."

"Did Nanny hurt you?" Anya asked Effie in a gentle voice.

"Nanny say Effie bad girl."

"Ooh . . . that woman!" Anya pulled Effie to her shoulder in a comforting gesture while her eyes turned to Gavin in concern.

Gavin observed the scene, feeling ignorant for the most part. Anya had told him that Effie was the Earl's daughter, and he'd heard her mention a "condition." He had assumed it was a health problem. The entire situation was foreign to anything Gavin had ever encountered.

"I dinna know how long it's been goin' on," Robbie said gravely, "but that woman has such a hand over that place, we decided th' best thing for Effie was tae get her out o' there."

"We?" Gavin questioned.

"The servin' folks," he answered.

Anya clarified. "Effie has never been accepted by Lady Margaret and her children, so the servants have always taken care of her. We all did our best to look out for her, but . . ." She trailed off in a tone of concern.

"I didna know what else tae do," Robbie seemed to apologize. "I didna know where else tae bring her, but we all feared what might happen tae th' lass if she was left there."

Anya turned to Gavin, knowing it was up to him whether or not Effie could stay.

"Of course she can stay here!" Gavin said emphatically. Anya smiled warmly at him, and Robbie sighed with relief.

"Do you want to stay with Anya?" she asked Effie.

Effie nodded. "Effie stay with Anya."

"I'll get her bag." Robbie moved toward the door while Anya urged Effie to sit at the table.

"Would you like to draw a picture?"

"I can draw a very good picture," Effie announced. Anya quickly supplied her with pencil and paper.

Robbie returned with a bag that he handed to Anya. "'Twas Mrs. MacGregor gathered her things, but she couldna get away with much, us takin' off in th' night an' all."

"I understand," Anya replied. "Don't worry. We'll get her what she needs." Gavin nodded in agreement, then his eyes turned back to Effie. He was intrigued.

"I must be on m' way," Robbie insisted.

"Won't you have some breakfast with us?" Anya offered.

"Thank ye, lass, but I must see tae m' duties. There'll be the devil to pay when th' Lady finds Effie gone. I canna say how glad I am that ye can take her. I hope I did th' right thing."

"Of course you did the right thing," Gavin assured him. Robbie tipped his hat and left, then Anya turned to find Gavin watching Effie sketch the view out the kitchen window, though she hardly seemed to look that way more than a second at a time.

"She's a marvelous artist," he said quietly.

"A genius, in truth," Anya replied.

"Effie is a good artist," Effie said absently, and Gavin chuckled.

"That's right, dear. You are." Anya patted her shoulder, then eased Gavin toward the parlor. "We'll be in here. You just sit and draw."

"I hope you don't mind," Anya said as he sat beside her.

"It might be crowded," Gavin said, "but we will manage just fine." He felt somehow privileged to have Effie under his roof. "She is the Earl's daughter," he said to verify it, and Anya nodded. "Is that why Una is so cruel to her?" he asked intently.

"Effie's mother, Ishbelle, died giving birth to Effie, and with her condition, Una, who had attended the birth, felt certain that Effie was some kind of evil spirit. Of course, no one else ever believed that. The servants all followed the Earl's example, treating her like any other child, and we all came to love her. She's never really had any one person to care for her. We all did a little here and there. Someone was always with her. She's really quite charming, and except on rare occasions, very well-behaved."

"Perhaps you should tell me more of her . . . condition, so I'll know what to expect."

"Very little is understood about it, but from what I've heard, together with observing her all these years, I believe that it's . . . well, how can I explain it? It's as if part of her mind has shut down. She has little or no comprehension of certain things, and yet the rest of her mind seems to have overcompensated for the loss. She's a genius at drawing, and she has a memory so clear that it's almost eerie. She's gentle and lovable, and likes affection. She has learned to be adaptable because of all the different people who have cared for her. She will like anyone who is kind to her."

"What about these . . . rare occasions, when she is not so gentle and charming?"

"It's as if something triggers a memory that was frightening for her, or perhaps something she just doesn't understand. If she gets frightened, she does a number of things. She can scream, hit her head against the nearest wall or piece of furniture, or she will rock herself and murmur odd phrases over and over."

"How do you handle it?"

"Physical comfort helps. She likes to be hugged, and you simply tell her everything is all right, or distract her with things that make her happy. It can take some patience, but she usually comes around quickly."

"I hope I can learn all of this," he admitted. "I want to—"

"Anya!" Effie called loudly. "Picture done."

Anya went directly to the kitchen, telling Gavin who was close behind, "She almost always does exactly what she's told. I told her to stay here, and unless she had a very good reason, she would stay until I returned."

"I can draw a very good picture." Effie held it up.

"It's beautiful, Effie. Should we hang it up?"

"Hang it on the wall by the tapestry."

"We don't have a tapestry here, Effie, but we can hang it here in the kitchen near the table, where we can see it every time we eat."

"Hang it in the kitchen. We can see it when we eat."

Anya motioned Gavin closer and urged him to take Effie's hand. "Effie, this is Gavin. He is my husband. He is my friend. He wants to be your friend, too. Would you like to be Gavin's friend?"

"Gavin should have stayed in the tower where he was put," she stated, lowering her voice as if to mimic someone else's words.

Gavin's eyes widened, and Anya laughed. "Effie repeats what she hears," she explained.

"I wouldn't have to guess who said that," he remarked with a frown.

Effie looked at the watch hanging on her neck chain. "Time for breakfast."

"Are you hungry, Effie?"

"Effie hungry. Time for breakfast."

"What would you like for breakfast?"

"Effie likes bannocks and porridge."

"All right," Anya laughed and hugged her. "You turn this over and draw another picture while I make you some bannocks and porridge."

"Effie likes bannocks and porridge."

"You tell Gavin if you need something," she added, since he apparently intended to stay close by.

"Gavin should have stayed in the tower where he was put," Effie repeated.

Gavin chuckled and shook his head. "Perhaps I should have." He set teasing eyes on Anya.

"Not without me."

Through the course of the day, Gavin hardly took his eyes off Effie. He was intrigued by her "condition," as Anya had called it, and he was trying to comprehend the reality that she was James MacBrier's daughter. It somehow made him feel closer to this man he had always admired.

Anya spent time showing Effie carefully through the house to acquaint her with the surroundings, explaining what she could use as she pleased, and what she shouldn't touch. In the evening Anya made a bed on the sofa that Effie seemed to like, then she looked over the shelves to find Effie a book.

"She always reads at bedtime," Anya explained to Gavin, but he was surprised when she pulled out a book of Shakespearean plays.

"Do you want to read Shakespeare?" Anya asked Effie, giving her the book.

"Effie likes Shakespeare," she announced, opening the book and beginning to read immediately.

Anya ushered Gavin out of the room. He peeked in an hour later to find that Effie had gotten into bed and fallen asleep.

Over the following days, Gavin discovered that Effie was quiet and polite, and for the most part could take care of herself. She kept quietly occupied with reading and drawing and observing her world. In a word, she was so simply endearing that Gavin couldn't help feeling an affection for her, and he enjoyed what little he did to help care for her. His preoccupation with Effie kept him from dwelling on his inability to give his wife a baby, and within a few weeks he realized that he never wanted Effie to leave them.

He wondered why no one had inquired after Effie here. Cedric knew where they were, and logically, if Effie had disappeared, Anya's home would be an obvious place to look. Then it occurred to him that perhaps no one cared whether Effie was gone or not. How sad, he thought, that those people were too caught up in their treacherous ways to appreciate what a special girl she was.

As the weather grew warmer, Gavin made a point to take Anya and Effie out as often as possible. They picnicked on the moors, went for long walks with no destination in mind, and made frequent excursions into town, where they would treat Effie to a taste of the outside world. A stop at the hat shop was mandatory, and Effie quickly found Peg amusing. It wasn't easy to get Effie to laugh, but Peg could always do it, for reasons none of them understood. Gavin knew the entire situation was the subject of talk and speculation to the people of Strathnell, but he didn't care. He found it a joy to provide Effie with a new wardrobe, and anything else that caught her fancy.

Gradually, the parlor became more Effie's room than a place to receive guests. "No one comes to see us except Robbie and Peg," Gavin declared, "and they don't care. If anyone else did come, we'd show them to the kitchen and feed them. There, that's settled."

Anya felt unexplainably grateful to Gavin for all he'd done for Effie. And she felt her contentment deepen as Effie became more a part of their lives. It was only the regular coming of her monthly cycle that gave her any dismay at all. She began to wonder if her miscarriage had damaged something, and she would never be able to conceive again. She didn't dare voice her fears to Gavin, and only hoped he hadn't noticed the passing of time as she had.

It was common for Anya and Gavin to set out toward the moors with a picnic hamper and a blanket. Effie would follow close behind, mumbling about all she saw.

"You know," Anya commented on a sunny day while Gavin spread out the blanket and plopped himself upon it, "I believe Effie is happier here."

"Why shouldn't she be?" he asked, putting his hands behind his head to gaze up at the sky. "Life is wonderful—and I have the Earl to thank. Look at all he's given me, and for what?"

"I don't think he realized you would end up with Effie and me."

"Well, I wish he could see us now, here on the moors. A hamper full of your cooking and a blanket are all we need."

He reached up to kiss Anya, but it was interrupted by a whimsical comment from Effie. "Papa say the moors in summer are like a pretty purple blanket. Papa likes the moors."

Gavin moved close to Effie and knelt beside her. He knew the capabilities of her memory, but it had never occurred to him that she had actually known her father very well.

"Do you remember Papa?" he asked. She nodded. "Your papa was the Earl of Brierley, Effie."

"Papa was the Earl. Papa say he love Brierley. Brierley part of him. Papa love Brierley." Gavin glanced at Anya. The tenderness in her eyes was apparent.

"Do you miss Brierley, Effie?" he asked carefully.

"Brierley bad place." She shuddered visibly.

"But your papa loved Brierley."

"Ishbelle died. Papa say Brierley died when Ishbelle died."

Gavin felt emotion gather in his throat, and he didn't dare speak for fear of betraying it. At this moment it all became very clear. James MacBrier had likely once been as happy as Gavin was right now. Then his wife had died giving birth, and he was left with a child that many said was cursed. He was manipulated into marrying Lady Margaret, found affection for a servant girl who disappeared for sixteen years, then was murdered in his own bed.

That voice came into his head again, seeming to declare, *You could change it, Gavin.* But he knew he couldn't. He had given Anya and Effie refuge here, had loved them and given all he could. What else could he possibly do?

"Effie," Anya set a hand on her arm. Her voice startled Gavin back to the present. "Would you like to stay with us always? Would you like to stay with Gavin and Anya?"

"Anya likes to play games. Gavin likes picnics."

"Do you like picnics?" Anya asked.

"Effie likes picnics." She looked at the timepiece suspended from a chain around her neck. "Time to eat the picnic."

Gavin chuckled and kissed Effie's cheek, but his mind stayed with James MacBrier far into the night as Effie's words echoed in his mind. *Brierley died when Ishbelle died.*

How sad, he concluded. The poor condition of the tenant farms, the treachery and hate within the walls of Brierley—all was put into perspective by this poignant statement. How sad. Then he forced it out of his mind and went to sleep.

Chapter Fifteen
Judgments

Gavin came in from the yard to wash the dirt from his hands while Anya rolled pastry dough over the table. "I'm going into town," he announced, drying his hands.

"Good, I'll come with you."

"Why?" he questioned, tossing the towel aside.

"Is there a reason I shouldn't?" she asked, wondering if he didn't want her to accompany him.

"No," he smiled, "I just thought you were busy, and I have an appointment with the barber."

"I'm nearly finished," she insisted. "By the time you change your clothes, I'll be ready. Effie wants to buy some new books."

Gavin shrugged and went into the bedroom to change. A few minutes later, he found Anya and Effie waiting in the trap he'd left harnessed in the yard. He noticed Anya nibbling on a dry biscuit and looked at her speculatively. She answered with an expression of innocence, dashing his brief hope that there might be a reason for it.

Anya fought hard not to smile as Gavin turned his attention to the horses. She had felt the urge to tell him a few days ago that her cycle was late, but not wanting to get his hopes up, she had decided to wait until she was certain. Just this morning she had risen with an undeniable twinge of nausea. Anya had little doubt that she was pregnant.

The thought filled her with excitement. But more important was a sense of fulfillment. At last she would be able to have a child—Gavin's child. She made up her mind to tell him tonight after dinner. She wanted the moment to be perfect.

Lost in her musings, Anya was surprised to see that they'd arrived in town. Gavin pulled the trap up in front of the bookshop and tied off the reins. He jumped down to help Anya and Effie out of the trap, then he ushered them inside where Mrs. Kirk, a widow of many years, greeted them with a familiar smile. With the rate that Effie read books, this was becoming a frequent stop.

"Have ye already read all ye bought last week, lass?" She directed her question to Anya. Mrs. Kirk, like many people, attempted to ignore Effie. For that reason, Anya didn't particularly like her. But in a town the size of Strathnell, they were lucky to have a bookshop at all.

"Effie has read them all," she retorted while Gavin looked over the newest arrivals to see if something appealed to him. Nothing caught his eye except one that Effie might like, and he handed it to her as he turned to Anya. "I should go. I'll meet you at Peg's when I'm finished."

Anya nodded, and he kissed her quickly. Mrs. Kirk gave a loud sniff of disapproval the moment he was gone. Anya looked up in surprise. "Is something wrong?"

The question seemed to give Mrs. Kirk permission to speak her mind. "I dinna know why ye let him get away with that, lass."

"I have no idea what you're talking about."

"Dinna be a fool, Mrs. Baird. Why do ye let him come an' go in such a way, with that . . . *woman?*"

"Peg MacTodd is kind and understanding, and a very dear friend of ours."

"Ah," Mrs. Kirk lifted a finger, "but I wonder what kind o' friend she is t'another woman's husband when th'other woman isna' around."

"Don't be absurd!" Anya chuckled tersely.

"I dinna want tae see ye blinded this way," Mrs. Kirk continued as if she were doing Anya the greatest favor. "Ye should know, lass, he was frequentin' that woman long b'fore ye came around."

Anya felt angry but remained calm. "You make it sound as if she is nothing but a cheap commodity."

"That about sums it up!" She pursed her lips triumphantly.

Anya took the books Effie had gathered and handed them tersely to Mrs. Kirk to add up the prices. "I shall not stand here and listen to you insult my husband and my dearest friend. If you wish to think the worst, so be it, but kindly keep your thoughts to yourself."

"As ye wish," Mrs. Kirk sniffed again, "but if I were in yer shoes, lass, I dinna ken if I would only wish tae think th' best. That Gavin Baird hasna hesitated tae make himself seen with that woman for years. Do ye think all o' that mischief come to an end just b'cause th' man is married?"

The words Anya had a desire to throw back would likely have given her a reputation equal to Peg's. She bit her tongue to hold them in, but made certain Mrs. Kirk caught the disgust in her eyes. Silence accompanied their transaction, and Anya sighed with relief to leave the shop with Effie possessively carrying her new books.

"Would you like some shortbread?" Anya asked in a light tone, attempting to push Mrs. Kirk's nonsense out of her head. Gavin had warned her long ago that such a thing might happen, but it irked her nonetheless.

"Effie likes shortbread," she announced.

Anya and Effie sat together to share their snack on the bench at the edge of the square where Anya had sat during her wedding festivities. Her thoughts filled with memories of that day, one of the best in her life, and Mrs. Kirk's accusations held little significance. Anya knew Gavin loved her.

When Effie was finished, Anya handed her the package of books. "Let's go meet Gavin at Peg's now. He'll be waiting for us."

"Peg is funny," Effie declared, following Anya toward the hat shop.

Gavin was in and out of the barber's quickly, but he was dismayed to find the hat shop locked up tight with a "closed" sign in the window. He didn't recall ever finding Peg's shop closed in the afternoon, unless she was with him or Anya. He felt concerned and wondered if she was ill, or if something unusual had come up that had taken her away. He smiled to himself, thinking perhaps she was with her friend the butcher. They had been seeing each other a lot lately, from what Peg had told him.

Just to make certain, Gavin walked down the alley to the rear entrance. It was locked as well, but he knocked loudly and waited for a response. When none came he tried again, and distinctly heard her call, "Go away!"

Gavin was relieved to know she was all right, but this wasn't at all like Peg. He wondered what was wrong. Reaching above the doorframe, he found the key where she always left it. He unlocked the door and returned the key, then stepped inside and closed it behind him.

"Peg!" he called. "What are you hiding from?"

"I thought I told ye tae go away!"

He glanced quickly into the parlor and kitchen to find them empty, but coming to the door of the bedroom, he noted a lump in the bed, attempting to burrow further beneath the covers.

"You didn't know it was me," he chuckled.

"Who else would come tae th' back door? Now go away!"

"You don't really want me to go away," he said smugly. "Just because a woman locks her door and tells you to go away, that doesn't mean she expects you to do it."

"Who told you that?" She peered over the covers, but remained hidden from the nose down.

"You did . . . after a fashion."

"Go away." She pulled the covers over her head again.

"You don't look ill. And you certainly don't sound ill."

"Go away!" she shouted.

"Give me a good reason to, and I will."

"Because I dinna want ye here, that's why."

"Not good enough. Now, why don't you tell me what you're hiding from?"

"The whole world," she retorted.

"Including me?"

"Especially you!"

"Why?" he chuckled.

"B'cause yer always s' cheerful and positive. And yer th' only man in the world that likes me. I dinna want anybody tae like me. Now go away."

Gavin heard the words between the lines and understood. He had a pretty good idea what had happened, and his heart ached for her. "Peg," he began gently, "did Mr. Morgan—"

"Yes!" She sat up, and he realized that she must have slept in the dress she was still wearing. "Dinna ye dare say it! I dinna want tae hear it."

"Well, someone's got to say it! You can't just hide here and ignore the world."

"I can if I want!"

"Peg," he scolded gently, and she broke into tears. He moved to the edge of the bed and sat down, taking her hand into his. "Do you want to tell me about it?"

"There isna need," she sniffled, and her tears streaked the rouge left from the night before. "It's th' same old story with me. Peg is there for a good time, but when it comes tae settlin' down, she's not that kind o' woman."

"Why don't you tell me what happened . . . more specifically."

"People started talkin'," she sniffed again, "and he said he wouldna tarnish his reputation by seein' me any further. It would ruin his chances for ever findin' a . . . wife."

Gavin bowed his head, feeling the hurt and frustration on her behalf. "What is wrong with me, Gavin? Why canna they ever forget what I used tae be?"

"There's nothing wrong with you, Peg. The problem seems to lie with everybody else. Unfortunately, it takes a degree of acceptance to survive in this world. It's too bad you can't go someplace else and make a fresh start, where no one knows about your past."

"I canna do that." She wiped her nose on the bed sheet. "I have nowhere tae go, and . . ." Her eyes turned soberly upon Gavin. "I want ye tae tell me, Gavin. What is it about me that makes people hate me so?"

"I don't think people hate you. They actually quite like you. They just don't want to be the subject of gossip."

"Why dinna ye care about th' gossip?"

"Because I know it's not true."

"Now, I mean it, Gavin. I want tae change. Ye come in here all th' time askin' about women and th' way they think an' feel. I want ye tae tell me how a man thinks. I'm not gettin' any younger, lad. Ye must tell me what I can do tae make a man see me different."

"I like you the way you are."

"But ye're already married!"

"You had your chance," he smirked, attempting to lighten the mood.

"An' I shoulda taken it." She managed a feeble smile. "Ah," she pushed her hand through the air, "I was just teasin'."

"I know."

"Now, tell me, Gavin. I mean it. My feelin's couldna get hurt any worse."

"As I see it, the problem is the way you feel about yourself." She looked dubious. "You cling too much to your past, and make people too aware of it. You need to make them forget. You need to change so drastically that they will see the changes."

"I dinna understand."

"I know and you know that you haven't done anything scandalous for years. Inside you have changed, but on the outside you haven't." Her eyes showed a glimmer of understanding. "You need to throw out those flashy dresses and get something new, something nice and prudish." He smiled. "But not too prudish. And what do you need this for?" He rubbed the remnants of rouge from her cheeks with his thumbs. "You're a beautiful woman, Peg. Let your pretty face speak for itself."

"Do ye think it would make a difference?"

"It couldn't hurt," he smiled. "If you can't leave here, at least you can show these people you're willing to change. It might even catch the butcher's eye."

"I dinna want him!" she insisted, and Gavin chuckled. Peg gave a soft laugh, then her eyes filled with tears again. "Or maybe I do."

Gavin urged her to his shoulder and let her cry, stroking the back of her head as he would a hurt child. At moments like this, he wanted to find every self-righteous gossip in Strathnell and force them to see these tears. But he doubted it would make a difference.

Anya was surprised to find the hat shop closed. She just stood for several moments, wondering what to do. The trap was here, but where was Gavin?

Knowing there was a back door that went into Peg's rooms, Anya searched out the most logical way to get there, and headed down the alley with Effie close behind. She found the door unlocked and timidly pushed it open. She was about to call out for Peg, but she could distinctly hear Gavin's voice and figured it was all right to come in. She was surprised to find the parlor and kitchen empty, then she peered into the bedroom, and Mrs. Kirk's words came to her like a knife in the back.

There sat Gavin on the edge of the bed, his arms around Peg, holding her close. He touched her face in a loving gesture, then kissed her cheek. Peg's eyes moved to the doorway, and Anya read the guilt and fear in her expression.

"Anya!" she said, pulling away from Gavin's embrace. Gavin turned, startled. But Anya was too absorbed in her fear to note his expression of innocence.

"Hello, darling." He came to his feet and stepped toward her, but Anya moved back, not daring to meet his eyes.

"We're finished now. Can we go home?" she said shortly.

"Yes, of course, but—"

"We'll be waiting in the trap," she informed him, and hurried Effie back outside.

"Will you be all right?" Gavin asked Peg.

"I'll be fine," she stated, "but I'm not certain ye will."

"What do you mean by that?" he chuckled.

"'Twould seem yer wife is upset about somethin'," she said flatly.

"I'm sure it's nothing serious." He bent to kiss her cheek. "Now, you think about what I said, and next time I see you, I want you out there selling hats, do you hear?"

Peg nodded gratefully, but already she was fearing the results of what Anya had just seen. She wondered how she would feel to be Gavin's wife and find him here like this with a woman who carried a reputation. If Anya was anything like Peg, he would have the devil to pay.

Gavin hurried to the trap and seated himself between Anya and Effie. They were nearly to the edge of town before Gavin realized that something was definitely not right. "Did anything happen in town to . . . upset you?" he asked carefully.

"Whatever gave you that idea?" she answered tersely.

"You're a little . . . quiet."

Anya gave no response. She was full of a seething anger that she knew was only there to blanket the fear. Was it possible that she had trusted Gavin too easily? Everything she believed about his relationship with Peg had come from either his lips or Peg's. Had they contrived this story to appease her, fully intending to carry on a relationship behind her back? She didn't know what to think—or what to believe. She only knew that it hurt. Just the image of seeing her there in his arms made her want to die inside. She had loved and trusted them both, and for what?

Gavin took full notice of the mood surrounding him and felt the evidence deepen. He looked at Anya, and she pointedly avoided his gaze. He wondered what Peg had caught onto that he hadn't.

"Peg was rather upset," he said, attempting light conversation that might ease the tension. "It seems her butcher friend has spurned her because people are talking."

"I shouldn't wonder!" Anya said with a little too much vehemence.

"Anya, is something bothering you?"

"And what is it to you, Gavin Baird?"

Effie piped in with an excellent mimicking of Mrs. Kirk. "That Gavin Baird hasna hesitated tae make himself seen with that woman for years."

Gavin turned to look at her in surprise. Then he turned to Anya, whose eyes were full of fire, as if to echo Effie's words.

"Who said that?" he insisted.

"It doesn't matter who said it. You know I don't listen to idle talk."

"Then what are you upset about?" He pulled the trap up in front of the house and jumped down.

"I don't need to listen to gossip." She pulled away from his touch as soon as he'd helped her down. "I've got eyes."

Gavin was baffled as he turned to help Effie down while Anya unlocked the door. Effie scurried into the house, obviously sensing the unrest in the air. Anya went to follow, but Gavin grabbed her arm. "Don't turn your back on me without explaining yourself."

"I think you're the one who owes *me* an explanation."

Gavin began to grasp what she was implying. He was so appalled that he couldn't find the strength to stop her when she jerked away and strode into the house, slamming the door hard enough to make him wince.

Gavin took care of the horses, then went into the house with a determination to get this taken care of—here and now. He found Anya in the rocker, pushing it back and forth so vigorously that he feared it might tip over. "All right, Anya. Out with it."

Anya didn't want to say anything at all. She wanted him to see the obvious and admit to it. But then what would she do? How could they possibly overcome something that had been in his life for a decade?

"Come on, Anya. I'm not going to let it sit and fester. If you have any decency, you'll let me in on the secret. I will not stand here feeling guilty for something without knowing exactly what I'm being accused of."

Anya knew he was right. Letting it sit would only make it worse. She turned angry eyes upon him and stopped rocking. "You want it straight out?" He nodded, and she came to her feet. "Fine! How dare you . . . *How dare you!*" His expression of innocence made her all the more angry. "All this time you allow me to inanely stand by and accept this . . . *friendship* you share with Peg, while it's nothing more than a ruse."

"Anya!" He couldn't believe his ears. "You can't possibly believe what people say about—"

"I told you! It has nothing to do with gossip! I saw you . . . the way you . . . ," emotion cracked her voice, ". . . held her, and . . ."

"Anya," his voice softened, "you must understand that I . . ." He tried to touch her shoulder, but she recoiled and glared at him.

"Oh, I understand completely. And I won't stand for it any longer."

The anger caught Gavin. He wanted to just take her by the shoulders and shake some sense into her. "I don't know what it is you won't stand for," he retorted, "but I won't stand for being accused of something I would never do. I have never been anything but completely honest with you, Anya, and you have no right to jump to the worst possible conclusions without even giving me a chance to explain."

"All right," she put her hands to her hips, "explain."

"When I found the shop closed, I went around to see if she was all right. She was upset. We talked. She cried on my shoulder. Now, what is wrong with that?"

His explanation made sense, but she couldn't let this go so easily. She needed to know beyond a shadow of a doubt that he had been honest with her. If not, they had nothing.

"Do you know," she asked, "what they are saying about you . . . about me?" She didn't give him a chance to reply. "They say I let you get away with it. I'm a fool because it goes on right under my nose and I can't see it. Is that right? It's there but I can't see it?" He attempted to answer, but she didn't let him. "It seems apparent to everyone but me that your relationship with Peg is not innocent at all."

"And didn't I tell you what might happen . . . before I married you?" he shouted. "Didn't I tell you people would say that?"

"Yes, you did. It's a perfect alibi, isn't it? Make me believe that it's just gossip, so I don't see the obvious."

"You're talking nonsense, and you know it!"

"Do I?"

"Have you bothered to ask me? Do you trust me enough to even do that?"

"So I'll ask." She pierced him with her eyes. "Have you been sleeping with her, Gavin?"

"No!" he shouted. "I never have!"

"And you expect me to believe that you can share such an intimate relationship for ten years, and not once go to bed with her?"

"Yes, I expect you to believe it, because it's true."

"How can I believe it, when I know what kind of life she's lived? Can I so easily discredit that woman's reputation?"

Anya's words bit deeply, and Gavin felt his defenses shoot up like a brick wall. In view of his unquestioning acceptance of Anya's past, he wondered how she could be so intolerant. Without thinking, he retorted with spite in his voice, "You ought to talk."

Gavin immediately regretted the words as it became evident that he had been sorely misinterpreted. He felt sick inside to see the anger melt away to reveal a pain deeply etched in her eyes. His words had torn freshly healed wounds open to bleed all over again. "Oh, Anya," his voice softened with remorse, "you misunderstood. I'm so sorry, I . . ." He reached out to touch her and she backed away, biting her lip and fidgeting nervously with her hands.

Anya couldn't hear the apology. Only the accusing words rang through her head, cutting her to the core. It was no longer mistrust alone that hurt. It was the way he'd just torn her down from the pedestal he had kept her on since the day they'd met. Did he see her that way—a woman with a past that marred her, making her less than she should be?

"Forgive me, Anya," he muttered helplessly. He took her arm but she pulled it away.

"Don't!" she insisted, pressing a hand to her mouth to hold back the cry hovering in her throat. A whimper escaped, but the worst of it remained buried. "Don't touch me or I'll . . . I'll . . ." She looked hopelessly around the room, searching for some escape that wasn't there. "I don't know what I'll do, but I . . ."

Gavin felt a familiar fear as he recalled her unreasonable flight to Brierley. He wasn't about to let that happen again. "Whatever you do, don't think about running back to Brierley," he said with a threatening edge. "That won't solve any of this."

Anya found enough anger to suppress the hurt. "I wouldn't in a million years. If there's one thing I have learned, nothing is worse than being at Brierley. Not even living with an unfaithful husband."

"Oh, well," he was only partly sarcastic, "at least that's a degree of progress."

As they both remained silent for more than a few seconds, a sound rose distinctly from the other room. Effie was crying.

"Now look what you've done!" Anya threw an accusing glare at Gavin as she rushed past him to find Effie huddled on her bed, rocking back and forth, afraid and upset from the evidence of contention between the people she had come to love and depend on.

Gavin watched in silence as Anya sat beside Effie to rock with her, whispering soothing words. He couldn't believe what had just passed between them. He felt as if their lives were shattered. And why? He had always been honest with her. He could see no reason why she shouldn't trust him. Admittedly, it hurt to have her think he would do such a thing. Didn't she know how much he loved her, how she was the center of his life?

Anya was almost relieved that Effie had given her an escape from the nightmarish episode. Her mind swirled through everything good she and Gavin had shared that seemed to be crumbling beneath the present moment. His heated words kept storming through her mind, threatening to burst into painful tears. But tears would show her vulnerability, and she was certain he'd seen far too many of them during their time together.

Effie was soon calmed and Anya left her to read, mostly wanting to be free from Gavin's gaze as he hovered in the doorway.

"Next time you must shout at me," she whispered hotly as she passed him, "do it quietly!"

Gavin wanted to respond, but everything he could think to say sounded so trite, so useless. Hadn't he already made things worse by trying to outdo her heated words?

Anya went to the kitchen to clean up the mess she'd left earlier and prepare dinner. She worked with extra vigor, hoping to release some of this emotion, but it only seemed to intensify. She was relieved when Gavin went outside. It gave her room to breathe more easily, and she let the silent tears flow as she worked. She wouldn't be surprised if he ran to Peg to cry on her shoulder. She felt certain Peg could make him feel better. The thought made her churn inside. Anya had known a great deal of pain in her life, but she didn't recall anything hurting the way this did. Either her memories were distorted, or Gavin meant more to her than anything ever had. She feared it was the latter.

Gavin wandered aimlessly around the yard, fighting the urge to go back into town to seek Peg's advice. He knew that was the worst possible thing he could do right now. Besides, it would break Peg's heart to know what was happening. And this problem was between him and Anya.

But he felt so helpless. He recalled his mother telling him that if he ever had a disagreement with someone he cared for, he had to look inside himself and see what he was doing wrong before he ever tried to put the blame elsewhere. In desperation he tried to analyze what he might have done to bring this on. But the hurt and anger blurred his vision, and all he could see was his faithfulness and honesty to Anya. The rest had him baffled.

Dinner passed in awkward silence. Anya felt tired and wanted to just go to bed, hoping that morning would somehow magically erase all of this. She was relieved when Gavin offered to finish cleaning up, but if he thought for one minute that such a feeble effort would make a difference, he was quite mistaken.

Seething with contempt, Anya prepared a bed for herself on the floor and made certain she was settled into it long before Gavin finished in the kitchen. But she intended to stay awake, hoping deep within that he would force her to talk about it, and they could come to some kind of resolution. She wondered if such a thing was even possible. If he promised to stop seeing Peg, could she forgive him and put it in the past? She had told herself earlier that if they didn't have trust, they had nothing. But she knew that wasn't true. A life without trust would not be easy, but she had known worse things. She loved Gavin, and he had taken good care of her. He had helped her put the nightmares of Brierley behind her. He had made her whole again. Good heavens, she reminded herself, she was going to have his baby! In that moment the thought was poignant. Would this child give them enough to hold their lives together?

Anya scolded herself. She was thinking nonsense! They loved each other. Love could hold anything together. Were her emotions blowing this out of proportion? Perhaps he *was* being honest. She felt a glimmer of hope, but recalling his heated words quickly stifled it. He'd come right out and said enough to make her wonder if the things he'd said about her past with Cedric had been honest. Did it bother him more than he let on? But even if it did, wouldn't that prove all the more that he loved her?

Anya's thoughts exhausted her, and she realized she had been asleep when Gavin came into the bedroom and woke her up. "What do you think you're doing?" he insisted, throwing the blanket off her.

"I was sleeping," she said wearily.

"Not down there, you're not." He went down on one knee to scoop her into his arms. He came to his feet despite her protests, and carried her to the bed.

"Put me down!" She pressed her hands against his chest and tried to kick him, but he paid little heed.

"I'll put you down," he dropped her onto the bed, "right where you belong." Anya was about to insist she would not sleep in the same bed with him when he said softly, "I'll sleep on the floor."

Anya was almost disappointed. She had wanted him to crawl into bed beside her and force her to see reason. She wanted him to beg her forgiveness and promise to love only her. But she knew it would not be solved so easily. It would take a miracle to erase the marks made against them in one day. Anya lay awake far into the night, praying for that miracle.

Gavin finally gave up on sleep just past dawn. He rose quietly and dressed, pausing to watch Anya sleep. Gently he touched her face and hair, taking care not to wake her, wanting only to be rid of all that stood between them. She stirred slightly and he retracted his touch, waiting to leave the room until she had settled again into a sound sleep.

He was watching his cup of coffee turn cold when a light rap came at the front door. A quick glance on his way past the bedroom told him Anya was still sound asleep, as was Effie in her bed on the sofa.

Anya awoke at the sound of the door opening, but she lay still, listening to discover who it might be.

Gavin unlocked the door and pulled it open, not so much surprised to see Peg as to see her clean, pale face and the simple yellow dress she wore, with a tartan mantle around her shoulders. "You look nice," he said. But his pleasure at seeing her was quickly doused by the reality of circumstances in his life. "What are you doing here?" he added tensely.

Peg didn't have to wonder over his attitude. Lack of sleep was evident in his face, and his eyes were infused with emotion.

"I came tae have a word with ye," she said, pushing her way into the hall. Gavin closed the door and Peg leaned against it. "Where is Anya?"

"Asleep."

"Are ye certain?"

"Absolutely," Gavin said, not caring whether she was or not. He almost hoped she overheard them. He had nothing to hide.

Anya fumed inside to know that Peg was there. But even with their obvious attempt to keep their voices low, she could hear every word. She was almost grateful for this opportunity. Perhaps this was the answer to her prayers. Perhaps it would give her the evidence she needed to settle this once and for all.

"I was afraid she wouldna want me here," Peg said. Anya thought that at least she was perceptive.

"Why not?" Gavin questioned, wondering as always how Peg knew so much.

"Why not?" she repeated, appalled. "Sometimes I could swear there's nothin' but oatmeal between a man's ears. If I was Anya an' walked in on what she saw yesterday, I wouldna be any too pleased."

"But there was nothing to see. We weren't doing anything wrong."

"Wrong is relative, m'dearie."

"I don't understand."

"Ye never do until I spell it out in black an' white."

Gavin pressed one hand against the door and leaned toward her. "Then you'd better start spelling. Not understanding one woman is bad enough, but two is more than any man could handle."

"I take it my assumptions were right, then?" she asked. "Anya is angry with ye."

"Quite."

"An' I dinna blame her."

Anya's heart softened a little, but the problem was far from solved.

"That is what I came tae tell ye," Peg continued. "It is wrong for ye t'expect things tae go on th' same between us now that ye're married. Any decent woman wouldna put up with it!"

Anya felt her heart pound. It was true! She squeezed her eyes shut to block it out, listening attentively for the evidence to deepen.

"But there's nothing to put up with," Gavin insisted. "We have never done what we are being accused of!"

"I know it, and ye know it, but as long as ye and I are spendin' time alone—any time at all—there'll be talk. When it was just th' two o' us, it didna matter, but ye have a wife now, an' she deserves tae have a husband that isna bein' talked about. It doesna matter that we've done nothin' wrong, Gavin. Ye're a married man now, an' it's wrong tae be alone with me at all."

"But I've hardly been alone with you for ten minutes at a time since I married Anya."

"It's still alone!" She sighed and calmed her voice. "I would hope we can still be friends, but that is up tae Anya. I will see ye no more unless she is with ye. She is a part of ye now, and that is all there be to it."

Gavin stepped back, stuffed his hands into his pockets, and blew out a long breath. What could he say? It was apparent that he had missed something. Peg was right—as always. He wanted to have his cake and eat it, too. But the priorities had to be shifted. Anya was his wife. Making a rule to see Peg only in Anya's presence would not be difficult. Unless Anya continued to mistrust them and found herself unable to accept Peg after what had happened. The thought of losing Peg in his life was not easy, but for Anya he would give up the world.

"Now," Peg went on after she figured he'd had time to absorb her memorized speech, "I want ye tae listen good. If ye have anything besides oatmeal in that handsome head o' yers, ye'll tell her th' truth."

"I have."

"Not about that! Wash out yer ears an' listen tae me. The truth of it is that she has a good right tae be angry. Ye were in th' wrong, lad, and ye'd best tell her an' have it out, or I'll have yer hide." She nodded firmly and took the doorknob. "I'm leavin' now. If ye're smart, ye'll not let that woman be awake five minutes b'fore ye make yer heart known tae her."

"Thank you, Peg," Gavin said with sincerity.

She smiled and turned to leave, pausing briefly to add, "An' I should thank ye, Gavin, for what ye said tae me yesterday." She glanced down at her dress. "I know ye were right, an' maybe I'll have a chance yet."

"I'd bet my life on it," he said warmly. "Thank you again."

Peg nodded and closed the door behind her. Gavin leaned his head back against the door and took a deep breath. He knew what he had to do. He only prayed Anya would hear him out.

Anya heard his footsteps coming toward the bedroom, and she quickly attempted to wipe away the tears of relief. But Gavin caught her dabbing at her eyes with the corner of the sheet. She looked up at him timidly, wondering what to say. Where could she possibly begin?

"You're still upset," he said, misinterpreting the tears.

Anya shook her head. "I heard everything, and I . . . oh, no!" She clamped a hand over her mouth, threw back the bedcovers, and ran to the other room. Gavin's heart jumped.

Anya felt Gavin's hands on her shoulders before the painful dry heaves finally stopped. Timidly she turned toward him, seeing the hope close beneath the concern. "Are you all right?" he asked, wiping the trace of sweat from her brow.

"I'm fine," she said, then moved into the kitchen, "but I need something to eat."

"Anya," he followed at her heels, not knowing which issue to pursue first, but an apology seemed a good place to start. "You must forgive me, Anya." She looked up at him, but her vision blurred with mist. "It was wrong of me to carry on as I was. I mean that. You are the most precious thing in the world to me, and I would give up everything just to have you. You must believe that I have never betrayed you—and I never will." He took her hand. "I love you, Anya. I love you."

"Oh, Gavin." She pressed her face to his chest and held his shoulders, overcome with astounding relief to feel his arms go around her, crushing her against him. She pulled back to look at him. "I'm sorry I behaved so badly. You were right. You have done nothing to cause mistrust, but I—"

"And there is another matter," he interrupted. "What I said yesterday." Her brow furrowed. She knew what he meant. "You misunderstood. I was speaking of trust and acceptance. It had nothing to do with what's happened in the past. You have to know that."

Anya sighed with indescribable relief. "I do, Gavin. You have given me so much, done so much for me. It was wrong of me to . . ."

"Shhh," he pressed a finger to her lips, "enough said." He smiled. "Now, I have to know. Are you . . ."

He didn't have a chance to finish before she pushed her arms around his waist in a forceful hug. "Of course I am," she said.

Gavin felt the need to clarify. "You're going to have a baby?" he asked meekly.

Anya pressed his hand to her belly. "Yes," she whispered. "Your baby."

Gavin laughed and held her close.

"I am so relieved," Anya admitted now that the waiting was over. "I was afraid something was wrong with me, and—"

"With you?" he laughed. "I thought something was wrong with *me.*"

She grinned up at him like a child. "It would seem that everything is all right with both of us."

"Yes," his eyes sobered and his words held tender meaning, "everything is all right. It couldn't possibly be better." If nothing else, their turbulent ordeal had taught him freshly to appreciate what they shared.

Anya's expression went sour, and she reluctantly turned away to find something to eat. Mumbling noises coming from the parlor told them Effie was awake. Gavin sat at the table to ponder the richness of life.

"We must go into town after breakfast," Anya said while nibbling on one of those atrocious-looking dry biscuits.

"Do you need something?" he asked.

"No," she replied, "but we need to tell Peg the good news."

Gavin smiled.

Chapter Sixteen
The Mark

Peg heard the little bell tinkle over the shop door and quickly dried her hands. She came through the curtain to see Gavin trying a hat on Anya that looked ridiculous. But the warmth was back in their eyes, and Peg sighed with relief.

"Ye got no taste at all, Mr. Baird."

"I beg your pardon," he laughed, then silence took hold unexpectedly. Peg looked at Gavin, then at Anya, then back to Gavin.

Anya broke the silence by taking note of Peg's reformed appearance. "You look lovely, Peg."

"Do ye think so?" She looked down at her dress with a dubious wrinkle of her nose. "I suppose it'll take some gettin' used tae. I'm havin' more clothes made. Yellow isna m' favorite color, but it was all they had that was done."

Peg turned her eyes back to her visitors and got to the point. "I take it everythin' is all right," she said tensely, "or I s'spect ye wouldna have come tae see me," Peg went on. "Or did ye just come tae buy an ugly hat for yer wife and wish me off?"

"You don't make ugly hats," Gavin insisted.

"Well, that one looks terrible on her!"

Anya laughed and pulled it off. She stepped toward Peg and reached out a hand. "I came to apologize, Peg."

"Whatever for?"

"I should have never mistrusted you, and I'm sorry." Peg looked embarrassed, and Anya figured enough had been said. "And Gavin has something to tell you."

"Eh?" She looked at him with a smirk. "Did ye come tae

apologize too, lad?"

"Don't expect too much in one day."

"Well then, what is it? Dinna keep me waitin'!"

"Actually," he said, "Effie wants to tell you."

Peg turned to Effie, who was toying with some silk flowers that adorned an outlandish sunbonnet. "Do ye have somethin' tae tell Peg, love?" she asked, putting her arm around Effie's shoulders. Effie gave a quick laugh, as she always did when Peg spoke to her.

"Tell Peg the good news," Gavin said.

"Good news," Effie nodded. "Tell Peg good news."

"And what is the good news?" Gavin asked Effie, grinning like a little boy.

"Good news. Anya will have a baby. Good news."

"Bless me!" Peg turned to Gavin, who nodded to confirm it, then Anya did the same. "That is good news." She turned to Effie. "Do ye like babies, lass?"

She ignored the question and turned her attention back to the hat.

"I think she likes th' hat," Peg informed them.

"Do you like the hat, Effie?" Gavin asked her.

"Effie likes the flowers."

"Do you want the hat?" Gavin asked.

"I'd say it's about time ye bought her one," Peg inserted. "An' if I charge ye enough fer it, it'll pay for m' new dresses."

Gavin put the hat on Effie, and she seemed pleased. He pulled some notes out of his pocket, counted out several, and slapped them into Peg's outstretched hand. "You're a thief, Peg." He grinned as he added, "Keep the change."

"Got tae stay in business," she smirked, stuffing the money up her sleeve without counting it.

"Well, I've got business to see to," Gavin said. "Are you coming with me?" he asked Anya.

"No," she announced brightly, "I think Effie and I will talk Peg into some tea and shortbread. She should be willing after what she just made off that ridiculous hat."

"Aye, the lass is right." Peg took Effie's arm and led her past the curtain to the little parlor. Anya kissed Gavin then turned to follow, but he caught her arm to stop her. With fervor he pulled her into his arms and gave her a kiss that curled her toes. Anya pulled back breathlessly. Gavin looked quite proud of himself. "Let people talk about *that*," he smirked, and left the shop.

Anya was nibbling on her third portion of shortbread when she noticed it. Peg had Effie thoroughly entertained as she talked about her childhood, telling stories of helping her father poach game in the dead of night. It didn't seem to matter what Peg was talking about, Effie always laughed. It was as if something about Peg's voice or manner was funny to Effie, and the novelty hadn't worn off with time.

That was it, Anya thought, watching Effie closely. She'd never noticed the resemblance before, because it was only apparent when she laughed. But now that she'd caught it, Anya couldn't deny that it was true. When Effie laughed, she looked like Gavin.

"Good heavens!" Anya murmured aloud.

"Did ye say somethin'?" Peg asked.

Anya shook her head and motioned for them to go on. She wanted to just sit here and watch Effie show that expression. It was fascinating. Gavin was always so full of smiles and laughter that the expression was common for him. Yes, it was the same.

She had long since stopped speculating over the origin of Gavin's birthmark. He had insisted he was not the Earl's son. She felt certain that somehow he was, but had chosen to let it go. It certainly wouldn't change anything. But now there was new evidence, and Anya couldn't help being obsessed by it.

When Gavin returned to get them, Anya watched closely as he sat near Effie and laughed as they observed Peg entertaining her. Anya felt goose flesh rush over her. He and Effie shared the same blood. She didn't know how, but they did. And what would Gavin think if he knew?

The question hung in Anya's mind for several days as she tried to imagine what effect it might have on Gavin to know that James

MacBrier was his father. Was it better left unsaid? Perhaps his igno-rance was the best thing for him. He had come to accept his life as it was, after all. He was happy.

Anya tried to put it out of her mind, but found it impossible. One night as she crawled into bed, she impulsively decided to approach it and see what happened. "Gavin," she said quietly through the darkness. He rolled over to put his arm around her against the pillows. "Can I ask you something that might sound bizarre?"

"Of course," he mumbled, his face buried against her hair.

"I've wondered about it since that first day I was here, but I felt certain it didn't matter, and was perhaps better left unsaid. But now with Effie here, I just can't get it out of my mind."

"Go on," he said, lifting his head as his curiosity was piqued.

"I simply have to ask again: are you certain you aren't the Earl's son?"

"I'm positive," he said almost tersely. This was not what he'd expected her to say.

"But perhaps they lied to you to save you from—"

"Anya," he sat up and ignited the lamp so she could see his face, "they didn't have to lie to me. I overheard them talking. They didn't know I was there. The Earl never slept with my mother. It's as simple as that."

Anya shook her head, feeling confused. "It just doesn't make sense."

"What doesn't make sense?" he asked intently.

Anya glanced at him warily, regretting that she had brought this up. "Nothing," she smiled. "I'm sure I must be mistaken."

She turned to extinguish the lamp, but he stopped her. "Mistaken about what?" he asked severely. "Obviously this is bothering you. Out with it."

Anya cleared her throat and resigned herself to telling him what little she knew, partly relieved by his insistence. "It just seems that under the circumstances, you would be his son."

"I think you spent too many years listening to Brierley gossip." He sounded perturbed.

"It has nothing to do with gossip," she insisted.

"Then what *circumstances* are you referring to?"

Anya wondered how she could convince him there was a missing link somewhere. "Come here," she said, slipping out of bed and taking up the lamp. "I want to show you something."

Gavin followed her silently into the parlor, where Effie slept peacefully on the sofa. "Look at her," she said quietly. "Look at the color of her hair, the shape of her face, and . . . something intangible. I think she looks like you."

"I think your imagination is running away with you."

"It's not!" she insisted, grateful that Effie was a sound sleeper. An idea so obvious occurred to Anya that she wondered why she hadn't thought of it before. "Gavin," she looked directly at him. "Do you agree that Effie is the Earl's daughter?"

"Of course she is."

"If Effie's mother died at her birth, then only the Earl's blood in her could be the same as anyone younger than her."

"I don't understand what you're saying, but I get the general idea."

"And you know that Effie is three years older than you."

"Yes, I know."

"Then look at this."

Anya gave the lamp to Gavin and carefully untied the top ribbon of Effie's nightgown. With ease she slid it over her shoulder. Effie hardly changed the rhythm of her breathing, but Gavin sucked in a sharp breath. He wanted to move closer and examine it better, but there was no need. It was nearly an exact replica of the birthmark he bore on his own shoulder, in almost the same place.

"James MacBrier once showed me the same mark on his own shoulder, Gavin. He told me it had been inherited for generations."

Gavin said nothing. He didn't even blink. Anya tied the gown and kissed Effie's brow. She took the lamp in one hand and Gavin's arm in the other, urging him back to the bed, where he sat numbly and gazed at the floor.

"It doesn't make sense," he finally whispered.

"Isn't that what I said?"

"But how? I heard them talking . . . then I asked the Earl myself, and . . . he told me the whole story. I know he wasn't lying to me. He told me that he wished his own son had . . ." He pushed his hands through his hair. "It doesn't make sense."

Anya was at a loss for words, but she felt it best that he be left to contemplate it. She urged him into bed and extinguished the lamp. Silence remained, but Anya knew that he was awake far into the night.

Gavin couldn't believe it. In his head he tried to recall every detail of his brief encounters with the Earl, then he went over everything his mother had ever said that might give a clue. But it just didn't make sense. When no answers came he began the pattern again, certain he had missed something, some clue that things were not as they seemed.

"Anya!" he heard himself say before the thought even took root.

"What? What is it?" She was immediately close to him, looking down into his face through the darkness.

"I'm not sure, but I . . . I just recalled that . . . oh, good heavens, I . . ." He sat up abruptly. "I'm certain now that . . ."

"Wait, slow down." She brushed her fingers over his brow. "Think it through and tell me one thing at a time."

"My mother sent me to find the Earl. I brought him to her. It was the first time they had seen each other in sixteen years. They talked, then he talked with me, then he left, promising he would return the following morning. He came instead in the middle of the night. When he woke me, I remember him looking at the mark, and . . . it was as if he'd seen a ghost. Now I understand. He was shocked to see it. I'm certain of it. But how can a man father a child and not know it? Wouldn't he have known if he had been intimate with my mother?"

"But he must have been. Perhaps because you've just thought for so long that he wasn't, it's difficult to believe otherwise. Is it possible that they had known you might be listening? Or could they have made a vow when it happened that they would forever claim otherwise in order to protect you?"

Anya didn't want to bring this up, but she knew it was a possibility. "Perhaps he didn't remember." Gavin looked puzzled. "I mean, maybe he was . . . drunk." Gavin was surprised. "They say he drank heavily in the years following his marriage to Lady Margaret. He overcame that for the most part after I came to Brierley."

"I guess I'd heard something to that effect," Gavin said. "I suppose anything is possible." He drew in a deep sigh. "The astounding thing is that . . . well, it seems that James MacBrier is my father after all."

"How does that make you feel?" she asked gently.

"It's difficult to put into words," he murmured. "I mean . . . I have to admit that I always wanted a man like the Earl to be my father. It was a childhood fantasy for me. But then . . . when I learned the situation between him and my mother, I . . . well, at first I was disappointed, but as the years have gone by, I've felt a deep respect for both of them. It wasn't pleasant to think that my father was a jerk who took unfair advantage of my mother, treated her very badly, then abandoned her. But at least I knew my mother was a woman with values and integrity, in spite of what people said about her. And I've felt the same way about the Earl. His marriage to Margaret was unhappy, and he cared very much for my mother, but they never did anything inappropriate." His voice faltered. "Or so I had believed."

Gavin sighed deeply and pushed his hands through his hair. "I have to admit now that . . . well, there is a part of me that's disappointed in them . . . both of them. But how can I regret the fact that I exist? And how can I not be pleased to find out that James MacBrier is my father? He was a good man, but . . ." He groaned from the sudden confusion. "Why would they construct such a lie? It just doesn't make sense. I don't understand."

"Should I not have told you?"

"On the contrary," he said firmly. "I'm very glad you did. It's just going to take some getting used to, that's all. It doesn't make me any less illegitimate. But in spite of it all, I have to admit that I'm glad to know he's my father."

Anya squeezed his hand and smiled. And she was pleased to see him smile back.

Little more was mentioned about the discovery of Gavin's paternity, but Anya sensed a change in him. There was an air of belonging about him that had not been evident before. But there was also a new restlessness in him that seemed to be growing. It was as if the unanswered questions were eating at him, preoccupying him more each day.

Anya didn't let it concern her, knowing that it was likely an adjustment and he simply needed time to feel at home with the discovery. She felt ill much of the time with her pregnancy, and found that just doing what she needed was a challenge. So she left him alone with his thoughts, making certain he knew she was there for him if he needed her.

One night, Anya was just drifting off when she became aware that Gavin's sleep had turned restless. She listened quietly, wondering if he was dreaming. Suddenly he sat up abruptly, crying out in near anguish. She took his shoulders in her hands, and he grabbed hold of her with desperation. "What is it?" she asked, but he only groaned in response. His breathing remained sharp, and he pressed his face to her shoulder. "Tell me, Gavin." She pressed her lips to his sweaty brow. "Tell me what you were dreaming."

"A voice," he muttered, "nothing more than a voice. As if Brierley itself were calling me, pleading with me."

"Pleading to do what?" she asked.

"I don't know."

"Was that all?"

"No!" he answered, holding her tightly. "I could see the Earl in his bed, and that knife . . . that knife came down again and again. And then . . . then . . ." He pulled back to look at Anya through the darkness. "Then it was me, Anya. The knife came down on me!" He swung around and came to his feet. She could see his silhouette against the window. His stance was strong, but his head was bowed into his hands. "He was my father, Anya!" He turned and came back to her, taking her shoulders firmly. "He was my father, and someone in that house murdered him in his own bed!" His grip tightened, his voice lowering to a quiet intensity. "And I didn't even get a chance to know him. He was my father, Anya, and I didn't even know him!"

"I know," she soothed, pushing his hair back from his brow. "I know."

"And now this voice keeps calling me. Sometimes I hear it out of nowhere. It comes from inside me, telling me that I could do something about it. As if he were calling to me from the grave, pleading with me to avenge his death, to reverse all of the pain and suffering at Brierley. But I can't!" He hit his fists on the bed. "What could I possibly do? It is not within my power to change any of it, Anya. They have believed I was his illegitimate son for years, and they try to kill me if I even attempt to carry out his wishes."

"It's all right, Gavin," Anya attempted to soothe him. "You must calm down and remember that nothing has changed. Nothing has changed except your knowledge. The circumstances remain as they have for more than a decade. You're right; you can't do anything about it. An illegitimate child is like no child at all when it comes to such things. You must let it go." Anya wondered if her words were having any effect whatsoever. She could feel his tenseness hanging in the room like a threatening storm. "Perhaps I should never have told you," she stated.

"You would withhold the knowledge of such things from me?"

"No," she admitted, "I couldn't, but I feared what that knowledge might do to you." She paused and kissed him quickly. "You must remember, Gavin . . . nothing has changed."

Gavin pulled her close to him and sighed, wondering how he could make her understand. Everything had changed. *Everything!*

Gavin did his best to heed Anya's advice, mostly because there were no other options. As far as he could see, there was nothing he could possibly do. With great effort he steered his thoughts toward all that brought him happiness. He began buying things for the baby, and spoke with a carpenter about adding rooms to the house. He spent every waking moment surrounded by the goodness of life, then cursed this inward voice for making him feel that something was missing.

Why couldn't he be content just knowing he bore the mark of James MacBrier? He contemplated the Earl's words. The safe held a treasure that only he could appreciate, and it should only be opened in his presence. But he did say it should be opened. Of course; he had attempted that once before. Did Lady MacBrier want whatever was in it all to herself? Hadn't the Earl mentioned that as well? He said that others would kill to possess the ring Gavin now wore. And Gavin had the scars to prove it. Each day he turned more earnestly to prayer over the matter, but found he was only more confused. Something wasn't right, and he knew it.

The bright spot in all of this was Effie. He was thrilled to know he had a sister, and he came to love her in a way she could never understand. And through it all, Anya was always there. He knew her pregnancy made her feel less than good much of the time, but her inner strength was continually present, giving him an endless supply of love and sustenance. He looked forward to the birth of their child, and they spoke of it often. Life was good. But still that voice refused to cease its taunting.

Anya was thrilled to see Gavin's love for Effie growing, but she was concerned about the increasing restlessness in him. He continued to treat her like a queen, and not once did his moods make her feel unloved or unappreciated. But his restlessness made her afraid. She found herself praying more and more on his behalf concerning the matter, while she was unaware that the answer to her prayers had been in their midst long before the prayers were uttered.

Anya heard Gavin come in from outside, and he called to her. "Anya, I need your help."

"What is it?" She came quickly from the bedroom, catching an edge of urgency in his voice.

He chuckled and pointed to his back, where his shirt was torn and a small amount of blood was soaking through. "It's not worth trying to explain how I lost my balance. I'm not certain I know. But I fell back against the wall in the stable, right against the pitchfork. Trust me to set it against the wall in the wrong direction."

"I'll bet you don't do it again," Anya told him while she eased the shirt over his shoulders. "Don't move. I'll be right back."

Anya threw the shirt in the tub to be soaked and mended, then she gathered some bandages and disinfectant. "Just like old times," she commented. She smiled to see him looking sheepish.

"At least I'm conscious," he chuckled. "Clumsy perhaps, but conscious."

He winced from the disinfectant, then Anya covered the wound to keep it clean. She was just finishing when Effie came into the room. "Effie made a picture of the moors for . . ."

Gavin glanced toward Effie as she stopped in mid-sentence. It wasn't like Effie to let her thoughts be easily distracted. Seeing her gaze fixed upon his birthmark, he nudged Anya, who turned toward Effie just as she put her hands to her head and gave a high-pitched shriek. Gavin held his breath, wondering why Effie felt such fear, and why he seemed to feel it, too. Anya had told him that Effie did such things, but seeing it left him feeling extremely unsettled.

"Effie! What is it?" Anya quickly wrapped her arms around Effie, who was trying to back into the corner while she continued to scream in short spurts. Anya urged her to her knees, where she cradled Effie and rocked her in an effort to soothe her. "Effie, calm down." Anya smoothed her hair and face and continued to rock with her. Gradually the screaming softened into shuddering intakes of breath.

"Is there anything I can do?" Gavin finally managed to ask, nearly frozen where he stood. His knuckles had turned white from gripping the back of a chair.

"Put a shirt on," Anya said without changing the rhythm with which she rocked Effie. Gavin slipped into the bedroom for a shirt, then returned to sit on the edge of the chair, wringing his hands together tensely.

"Effie," Anya said so softly that Gavin could barely hear her, "tell Anya what frightened you." Effie made no response, but Anya repeated the question carefully. Effie glanced quickly toward Gavin, then back to the wall, and Anya decided to get specific. "Were you frightened by Gavin's birthmark?"

"Bad mark," Effie muttered. "Bad mark. Bad mark."

"No, Effie. It's a good mark. It's like yours." Anya touched her shoulder. "It's a good mark."

"Effie has bad mark. Baby has bad mark. Baby has bad mark like Effie. Bad baby."

Anya glanced at Gavin with wide eyes. His heart began pounding.

"What baby? Tell me about the baby."

"Bad baby come in the night. Baby has bad mark."

"Who said the baby was bad, Effie?"

"Nanny say bad baby. Baby has mark like Effie. Effie bad girl. Nanny say Effie . . . evil."

"Superstitious old bag," Gavin muttered under his breath.

"Effie is not evil," Anya insisted. "Effie is a very good girl. The mark is a good mark." She paused and waited for a response, but Effie just rocked back and forth. "Tell Anya about the baby."

"Bad baby."

"Where was the baby born?"

"Baby born in Mama's room."

"But her mother is dead," Gavin quickly said, wanting desperately to understand this.

"She means Lady Margaret," Anya clarified.

"Lady Margaret. Yes, Lady Margaret had baby. Bad baby. Baby has a mark."

"She must mean Cedric," Gavin said. "Maybe she is afraid of Cedric."

"Perhaps, but . . ." Anya was going to say that she couldn't recall Cedric having such a mark, but the memory caught her off guard. Effie spoke again before she could rethink the statement.

"Cedric good baby," Effie said. "Cedric have no mark. Cedric good baby."

"Did Nanny tell you that?" Anya asked, feeling angry on Effie's behalf to see how misguided she had been.

"Nanny say Cedric good baby. No mark."

"What else did Nanny say?" Anya persisted, realizing she was only more confused than ever. She wondered if any other children had been born to the Earl without their knowledge.

"Nanny say not to tell, or . . ." Effie started to rock and scream again. Gavin came to his feet and began pacing, feeling utterly help-less. Anya continued to rock and soothe her until she calmed down again.

"Anya and Gavin won't let Nanny ever get near you again. I promise you, Effie. Nanny will not hurt you. Can you tell me what Nanny said?"

"Nanny say not to tell, or . . ." She began to get upset again, but Anya persisted with her reassurances and Effie tried once more. "Nanny say not to tell, or . . . or she would kill Effie."

"Good heavens!" Gavin nearly shouted.

"Hush!" Anya said with an abrupt gesture toward him.

"Did Nanny tell you a secret?"

"Nanny tell Effie a secret."

"Why did Nanny tell you?"

"Effie watched Nanny. Nanny yell at Effie. Effie watched Nanny and Nanny yell at Effie. Nanny say Effie shouldn't spy."

"Did you see what Nanny did?"

"Effie see what Nanny did."

"And Nanny threatened to hurt you if you told the secret."

"Nanny say she kill Effie."

Anya turned to Gavin again and drew in a deep sigh, then her attention went back to Effie, who appeared to be calming down somewhat.

"What did Nanny do? Did she do something to the baby?"

"Bad baby. Baby has a mark."

Anya felt herself turn cold, wondering if Una would be so low as to destroy a child because of her superstitions. "Did she do something to the baby with the mark?"

Effie murmured something that grated through her lips with so much effort that they couldn't understand her. "Anya couldn't hear you," she said, bending her ear close to Effie's mouth. "Tell me again."

Anya heard it that time, but she had to make her repeat it. She couldn't believe it! But a combination of warmth and goose flesh rushed over her, as if to confirm its truth.

"Are you sure?" Anya asked. Effie nodded with certainty.

Gavin was holding his breath when Anya turned to him with tears streaming over her face.

"What did she say?" he demanded in a soft voice.

Anya couldn't bring herself to repeat it. She turned again to Effie. "Can you tell Gavin what you said?" Effie nodded. "Please say it so Gavin can hear you." Gavin squatted down beside them and leaned close to Effie. Anya covered her mouth with her hand in an effort to suppress her emotion. Together they distinctly heard it. "Nanny switch babies."

Gavin felt the color drain from his face. Unwillingly he sat down hard on the floor, while Effie's confidence gained momentum and she murmured it over and over, as if she felt relief in being free of it. "Nanny switch babies. Nanny switch babies."

The echo rang through Gavin's ears until he felt certain his head would burst. Everything made sense now; abhorrent, unspeakable sense. It took great effort to come to his feet and go outside. He was grateful that Anya couldn't see the tears that fell over his face once he was alone.

Anya persisted with Effie to get more of the facts, and it gradually became evident exactly what had happened. Anya had great faith in Effie's accurate memory, and she felt certain it was all true. It just made such perfect sense.

Anya didn't leave Effie alone until she was tucked into bed and sound asleep, then with haste she went out to find Gavin. She felt panicked. He had been gone for hours. Despite the glow of a nearly full moon, Anya couldn't see him anywhere. She wandered the yard and stable, and finally began calling his name over and over as dread made her heart thud painfully. The horses were there so he couldn't be too far away, but she feared what he was feeling.

"Gavin!" she called for what seemed the hundredth time.

"I'm here," he said right behind her, and she nearly screamed.

"Where have you been?" she asked breathlessly, pushing her arms around him.

"Just wandering," he whispered, pulling her so fiercely against him that it hurt.

"Are you all right?" she asked, touching his face gently.

"No," Gavin answered, grateful the darkness hid any sign of the time he'd spent in anguished tears.

"Do you want to talk about it?"

"No, but I suppose we should."

Anya sought quickly for the right words to begin. "So, it makes sense now. You are the Earl's son."

He chuckled tensely and turned away. "Yes, imagine that. I am the rightful blood heir to Brierley." His voice rose angrily. "And I spent my whole life banished to a tower, being called illegitimate, watching my mother . . . Ooh! She wasn't even my real mother!"

Anya bit her lip, trying not to let her emotion make this harder for him.

"Curse that woman! How dare she play with people's lives that way? The superstitious old fool ought to be drawn and quartered."

"Gavin! Please, calm down."

"Don't tell me to calm down!" he shouted. She never recalled seeing him so upset. "I just found out that my whole life has been a farce, because some old woman had a warped obsession about playing games with babies! Damn her!" he shouted to the sky with fists clenched.

"Gavin, please." She touched his shoulder with one hand and his face with the other. "Please. You've told me many times that you wouldn't want Brierley. Surely you–"

"This has nothing to do with Brierley!" He looked her in the eye and continued to shout, though he was so close she could feel his breath. "I don't want Brierley! I wanted to be raised with a father, to know who I was. I wanted purpose to my life. I wanted to be raised with the truth!" He gritted his teeth and clenched his fists.

"Well, you wouldn't have gotten that being raised by Margaret MacBrier." Gavin looked to her in question. "Do you think you would have grown to be an honest, respectable man being raised under that roof? I wonder! Do you think you are totally a result of your blood, or the loving guidance that nurtured you from day to day? Compare your life—now—to Cedric MacBrier's, and tell me which you would rather be living."

Gavin shook his head and turned away. It was just too much to take.

Anya heard him sigh, then he wrapped his arms over his head and groaned as if the pain was unbearable. She touched his shoulder, but his groan deepened and he fell to his knees.

"I thank God Jinny didn't live to see this day," he said with heated breath. "It would have broken her."

"I don't believe it!" Anya insisted, kneeling beside him. "She would not have traded you for any other son. And I, Gavin, I love you for the man you are now. A result of circumstances that molded you with humility. The struggle to survive made you a good man, Gavin. I'm not saying you wouldn't have been otherwise, but you have much to be grateful for. You can't change the past. You must use the answers from your past to mold your future into what you wish it to be. And whatever that is, I will be beside you—always."

Gavin felt Anya's words giving him the comfort he needed to sustain him. He took hold of her as if she were the only link in his life to something real and right and tangible. "Anya." His voice cracked and he nearly fell against her, feeling much like Effie as she held him close to her, running her soothing fingers over his face and hair, whispering reassurances and words of love.

"Oh, Anya," he cried, "I love you. I love you with my whole heart."

When Gavin's emotion quieted, he lay back in the grass and silently watched the moonlit sky while Anya lay against his shoulder. After a long while in silent contemplation, he said quietly, "I believe he knew, Anya."

"Who?"

"My father . . . the Earl. He knew. When he saw the birthmark, he must have realized I was his son. If he knew there had been no intimacies with my mother, then he must have known that foul play was involved somewhere. I wonder if there is any connection to that knowledge and his death within hours. Well, there has to be. And yet, all he gave me was already in his hands before he saw the mark. He was willing to treat me as his son without that knowledge."

"I suppose we will never know for sure."

"I suppose not." Gavin sighed and pushed his hand through his hair. "What I wouldn't give to look him in the face now and be able to call him Father."

Anya turned to kiss away his futile longings, until he suggested they return to check on Effie. Gavin sat near his sister, lost in thought as she slept. The coming of dawn left him surprised that the hours had passed so quickly. When Effie awoke and saw him, he felt momentarily concerned that she might fear him after yesterday's episode.

"Can Gavin have a hug?" he asked, and she complied without hesitation. "I love you, Effie," he cried. She started to rock with him against her, as if she sensed he needed comfort, and this was her way of giving it. After a long while in Effie's arms, he found that it had worked. For some reason, he felt better.

Chapter Seventeen
Return to Brierley

After breakfast, Gavin finally went to bed and slept. Anya spent the time quietly contemplating the reality. Knowing Gavin well, it was not difficult for her to guess where all of this would lead.

She was sitting beside him when he awoke to find the light of afternoon filling the room. He stretched and rubbed his eyes, then leaned back against the headboard. Anya watched him closely and realized she was afraid. The change in him was evident, and she feared what decisions he would make in light of their discovery. Just last night she had promised she would stay beside him, no matter what he chose to do. Now she wondered if she could.

"How are you feeling?" she asked.

"Rested, at least," he answered.

"Are you hungry? You missed lunch."

"How long until dinner?"

"An hour or two."

"I'll wait." He sat on the edge of the bed to pull on his boots, then he stood and bent over to kiss her. "I think I'll go for a little walk, if you don't mind."

Anya nodded, knowing he needed time alone. But she hated the uncertainty. Wanting to be busy, she began preparing dinner, but her mind was in a turmoil. A wave of nausea caught her off guard. The sickness had become less frequent in her fourth month, but she hadn't eaten well today, and her carelessness had taken its toll.

When dinner was ready, Gavin was nowhere to be seen. Anya knew she couldn't wait any longer to eat, so she called for Effie and they ate without him. His absence at the table began to make her nerves raw. She finished her meal and was about to get up and go find him when the door flew open.

"Sorry I'm late," he said, but rather than washing up to eat, he hurried into the bedroom with no explanation. Anya threw her napkin to the table and followed, peering through the partially open door while he opened the bottom of the wardrobe and pulled the carved box from its resting place. He dumped the contents out on the bed and let them lie there. It was the torn piece of tartan he pulled into his hand. He examined it closely, then clenched a fist around it as if it were more precious than the priceless array of jewels left scattered over the bed.

Anya felt a tangible fear at the determination etched into his brow, the purpose in his eyes. She wanted to fall on her knees and beg him not to do it. But she knew there was no point. She was well aware of his feelings, and there was no good pretending that he would rest until his quest was complete. She could hardly begrudge that when she had made such a fuss about going to Brierley to be free of her own burdens. But this was so much bigger, so much more real. And that reality was frightening.

She watched Gavin closely, his mind absorbed by the finely woven wool in his hand, his eyes distant and full of fire. She wanted to feign ignorance and simply tell him to come to dinner. But just as when she'd faced her fears with Cedric, she had to deal with this now. It would only fester if she didn't.

"Gavin," she said and he looked up, startled. Their eyes met with expectancy. "You're going back, aren't you."

The answer was on Gavin's lips, but the look in her eyes made him hesitate to say it. He didn't need to say it; Anya already knew. She turned and left the room. Gavin wondered what to do. Peg's advice came back to him. *Just because a woman leaves . . .*

"Anya!" He went to the kitchen just in time to see the side door close. "Anya!" He followed her outside and saw her running toward the moors. A setting sun turned the fields to a brilliant pink. She seemed to fly across them, her hair billowing behind her, reflecting the hues of light. Gavin ran to catch up with her, wondering where she was getting her strength. His long legs finally gained advantage, and he wrapped his arms around her waist to stop her. "What are you running from?" he demanded, forcing her to face him.

"I just want to be alone."

"Fine, but don't run out on me before I have a chance to even answer a question."

"I don't want to know the answer."

"Then why did you ask it?"

"Because it's my life, too! You are my husband, so don't stand there and think you can run off to conquer the world and it won't affect me."

"I never thought it wouldn't, and I had every intention of telling you that—"

"That you're going back to Brierley? I already know that!"

Gavin hesitated, but answered with strength. "I have to, Anya. Don't you see?"

"Yes," she said bitterly, "I see."

"I don't understand why you're so upset. Didn't we do the very same thing when you had to go back and face your fears?"

"It was not the very same thing!"

"And why not?"

"Don't you see what is happening here?"

"Apparently not!"

"Well then, I'll tell you!"

"I wish you would."

"I am a servant girl, Gavin." He opened his mouth to protest, but she didn't give him time. "And yesterday I was married to the illegitimate son of a servant girl. Today I am . . ." She choked back a sob, drew in a deep breath, and shouted at him, "Today I am married to the Earl of Brierley!"

The title hung as a preamble to silence. Anya turned away to wipe at her tears. Gavin searched deeply for the right words. "Anya," he said gently, "when you wanted to go back to Brierley, to talk with Cedric, you asked that I hear you out. I am asking the same of you now." He took her silence as approval, and decided it was now or never. "Anya, I have every right in the world to take Brierley for my own—every nook and cranny of it." She turned bitter eyes upon him, and he finished quickly. "But I don't want it. You should know that. There are three reasons I am going back. The first is to undo all that has been done. I want my mother to know who I am, and I want to see that justice is done for the wrong that has altered so many lives. The second reason is to see that something is done to help the tenants of Brierley. As long as it is in my power, they will not suffer any longer. And the third is to carry out my father's last wishes. I will open that safe and do what I see fit with its contents, and then I will tear that house apart stone by stone until I find out who killed my father, and why." He sighed. "I believe it's what my mother would want me to do. And yes, no matter what I know now, Jinny Baird will always be my mother. She gave everything for me, and I will always love her and remember her as my mother. Deep in my heart, I believe that she knows the truth now, somehow . . . somewhere. And I believe she would want me to do this."

He clenched the tartan into his fist and held it near her face. "You're right, Anya. I am the Earl of Brierley, and by all I hold sacred, I will honor what I was born to be."

Anya couldn't help but admire his courage, his strength, his honor. And there was a part of her, the child who had loved the Earl so deeply, that wanted to see Gavin's quest come to fruition. But the fear was still stronger. "And where does that leave me?"

Gavin grasped her shoulders, pulling her face close to his. "Right by my side, every step of the way."

Anya freed herself from his grasp. "You can't expect me to do that! I used to scrub floors in that place." A bitterness rose in her voice. "I cleaned chamber pots, swept ashes, scrubbed pots and pans. You cannot expect me to go back there to—"

"But you already have," he stated calmly. "They've all seen what you've become. A title doesn't change that. It's not the title I'm after. I'm certain Cedric doesn't want to give it up, and frankly I don't want to fight him for it. If he wants it, he can have it. But I will see that some changes are made, once and for all." He took her hand. "Anya, I need you with me through this. Please don't turn your back on me now. You told me last night that you would be beside me—always."

"I'm not certain I can do it."

"You can!" he insisted. "You have more MacBrier blood in you than Cedric, Malvina, Margaret, and Una put together." She looked up in surprise. "Isn't that true?"

"I suppose it is."

"You are my wife, Anya. Nothing, not even something as big as this, could ever change the way I feel about you."

"And if I asked you not to do it?"

Gavin swallowed hard. "If that is what it would take to prove my love for you, I would not go. I would only hope and pray that you'd try to understand why this is so important to me."

Anya sighed, knowing such a thing would not be fair. "Can you promise me, Gavin, that no matter what happens, what exists now between you and me will never change?"

"It will only get better," he said with strength.

"I'll hold you to it." She pointed a finger at him.

"I promise!" He put his hand over his heart, and Anya couldn't help smiling. Gavin bent forward to kiss her, pulling her into his arms before it was finished. He eased her closer while Anya pressed a kiss to his cheek. He hadn't shaved since yesterday morning, and the coarseness of his face stung Anya's lips. She urged them to his, and the sting was soothed by the warmth of his mouth.

"Perhaps we should get back," he smirked. "I'm starved."

"And you haven't eaten your dinner yet, either," she quipped.

They walked back home over the darkening moors to find Effie quietly reading in her room. "She's such a good girl," Anya commented as she heated Gavin's dinner. "It doesn't matter where I am or what I'm doing, she always does what she knows she should. Do you suppose our children will be so well behaved?" Anya set his plate before him, and he took up a fork.

"No," he laughed. "Not if they're anything like me. My mother used to curse at me when I'd . . ." He stopped, and the fork fell against his plate.

"What is it?" Anya asked. "Does it taste bad, or—"

"Every time I stop to think about it, I realize she wasn't my real mother, and I . . . just want to . . . Ooh!" He hit the table and came to his feet. "It's like a knife, right here!" He hit his chest with his fist, then set his palms down on the table, bowing his head with a sigh. "When I think of what she gave to raise me, and I wasn't even her son."

"Hypocrite!" she muttered, and he looked up in shock.

"What?"

"You, who gave me speech after speech about how you were going to raise Cedric's child as your own, and it didn't matter who the blood father was. You told me you would be a father to that child every bit as much as if it were your own. Now don't stand there and tell me that Jinny Baird was not your mother."

"And Margaret MacBrier?" he asked severely.

"She gave birth to you. That is all."

"That is *all?* Is it such a small thing?"

"No," Anya admitted, touching her belly where their child grew, "it is no small thing."

"Then there is a bond between us—between Lady Margaret and me?"

"That would depend partially on her feelings . . . and yours. Twenty-seven years is a long time."

"Yes," he sat down, "it is." But he wasn't certain what to do about it.

In a Scottish town, no matter its size, one could always find a weaver. And Strathnell was no exception. The finely woven tartan was an important part of the people's lives, and Strathnell's weaver was considered one of the best. Mr. Ervin was the fifth descendant in his line to learn the trade, and he was in the process of teaching the skill to his two sons. Gavin found Mr. Ervin hard at work over his loom when he entered the shop with Anya by his side and Effie close behind.

"What can I do for ye?" he asked, continuing to work as if it were no more difficult than breathing.

"I need to have a tartan made," Gavin informed him, bringing forth the sample. Mr. Ervin stopped his work and stood before Gavin to take the piece of wool into his hands, absorbing it with his fingers as if they had eyes of their own.

"It's a fine one," he said firmly. "Do ye want it just like this one?" he asked.

"As close as you can get it."

"Ye wouldna be able tae tell th' diff'rence," he said proudly. Anya squeezed Gavin's hand, feeling a rush of goose flesh. "When do ye need it, lad?"

"Just as soon as possible, though I don't want to rush you."

"I can have it by th' first o' th' week," he speculated.

Anya felt her heart pound. Would all of this happen so soon? But she had to admit that having gotten used to the idea, she couldn't help but feel the anticipation. Or perhaps she just wanted to have it over with.

"An' would ye have m' missus sew it intae plaid an' kilt?"

"Yes," Gavin replied, "that would be fine."

Mr. Ervin looked to Gavin, then Anya, seeming to catch the pride in their eyes. "It's a special tartan, eh?"

"It was my father's," Gavin said. Anya felt warmth from the words.

"Aye," Mr. Ervin smiled. "Come back on Monday, an' if it meets yer approval, we'll have ye measured and set tae sewin'."

"That should be fine. Do you need anything in advance?"

"Nah," he insisted, "ye can pay me when ye're satisfied with th' work."

"Thank you, Mr. Ervin," Gavin said, and ushered the ladies from the shop. He held Effie's hand while Anya took his other arm.

"I'm scared, Anya," he admitted.

"So am I."

"I keep thinking we should have some kind of a plan, but I don't know where to begin."

"I've been thinking the same, and . . ." She hesitated to voice it, but Gavin saw the twinkle in her eye.

"You've got an idea. I can see it."

"Well, it's just a thought, but I couldn't help wondering how I would feel to learn that my baby had been replaced with another just after its birth. Now, if I had raised a son who was kind and good, I might not feel much regret, but . . . ," she paused elaborately, "if I had raised a son like Cedric, I might find it a great relief."

"I don't understand."

"Lady Margaret has never gotten along with Cedric. Mrs. MacGregor once told me that they've been bitter toward each other since he was old enough to talk. Lady Margaret can be a hard woman, but I wonder if there isn't something in her that could be softened. I've seen hints of it now and then. She might be relieved to learn who her son really is."

Gavin absorbed what she was saying and felt a definite warmth. "Perhaps that is something to go on. It certainly gives us a place to start."

"You know," she added, "it just occurred to me that perhaps we shouldn't take Effie with us. Wouldn't it be better for her sake?"

"I think you're right," he agreed. "Perhaps it's time we let Peg in on all of this. I think she could help us in that respect."

"You know what all of this means," Anya said with a gentle smirk. He lifted his brows in question. "If Effie is your half-sister by your father, that makes Malvina your half-sister by your mother."

"Ugh!" Gavin groaned, then he laughed. "I suppose there's a cloud to every silver lining. Isn't that what they say?"

"I think you've got that backwards."

Peg was leaning over the counter, doodling on a newspaper when they entered the shop. "Hello," she said brightly. "I was wonderin' when ye'd get in tae see me. It's been a while."

"There's a good reason for that," Anya said soberly. "Which is why we came. We need to talk to you."

"Is it so important?" she asked, noting Gavin's grave expression as well.

"It is," Gavin stated.

Peg immediately locked the door and turned the sign over in the window. "Let's talk." She threw her hands in the air and urged them to the parlor.

"You sit here and read," Gavin told Effie, motioning to the book she carried. Peg sat expectantly on the edge of her seat while Gavin squeezed Anya's hand and their eyes met with mutual reassurance.

"We haven't told anyone . . . yet," Gavin began. "It seems more astounding all the time. I can still hardly believe it."

"I dinna understand," Peg said impatiently.

Gavin turned to Anya, uncertain where to begin. She gave a nod of encouragement. "Well," he chuckled tensely, "do you remember when I told you . . . it must have been years ago . . . how I was raised—at Brierley?"

"I r'member," Peg acknowledged.

"And last year, I told you my reasons for going back to Brierley." Peg nodded. "Well, it was Anya who figured out that something didn't make sense . . . about who I was. I was certain I was not the Earl's son, because I had heard him talking to my mother and—"

"I know all that." Peg gave an impatient gesture with her hands, wanting to hear the meat of the story.

"But Anya had reason to believe that I was the Earl's son."

"But how could that be, when . . . ," Peg began to ask.

"That's what I wondered," Anya inserted. "But you see, it was Gavin's birthmark that . . ."

Peg's eyes narrowed in question. Her ignorance was obvious. Anya had no doubt that she and Gavin had never been intimate. "Birthmark?" She uttered the word as if it were magic.

"Well, show it to her," Anya said to Gavin.

"What?" he retorted, surprised and hesitant.

"Surely there's nothing scandalous in seeing a man's shoulder. You might as well get used to it. I'm certain you'll need to bare it again if you're going to prove any of this."

Gavin sighed and unbuttoned his waistcoat, then his shirt, just enough to pull it aside. Peg's eyes went wide with wonder, and Gavin quickly covered it again.

"And this mark," Peg said to Anya, "has somethin' tae do with th' Earl?"

"It's rather obvious really," Anya continued. "Effie has a nearly identical birthmark in the same place." Peg gasped. "And we have no doubt that she is the Earl's daughter. Her mother, Ishbelle, died long before Gavin was born."

"Brierley died when Ishbelle died," Effie said, then continued reading.

Effie's words struck a poignant note in Gavin, but he tried to concentrate on the present.

"Then someone musta lied tae ye, lad," Peg said with vehemence. "The Earl musta known yer mother better than they let on."

"That's what I thought, too," Gavin said, then he took a deep breath, "but it's much more complicated than that."

He turned to Anya, unable to say it, and he realized he had to be more prepared before they returned to Brierley.

Anya took over again, and he was relieved. "You know, of course, how accurate Effie's memory is," she said.

"Aye, that I do."

"It was Effie who told us, when she saw Gavin's birthmark, that . . . well . . ." She glanced at Gavin, who began rubbing a nervous thumb over his cheekbone. Just thinking about it made him boil inside. "Apparently Gavin was not illegitimate at all. He and Cedric MacBrier were born within hours of each other, and the woman who delivered the babies thought the mark was evil because of Effie's condition. We assume she didn't want a child like Effie to be the Earl, so she . . . switched the babies."

Peg caught her breath so sharply that Anya feared she would stop breathing. She finally let out an airy, "Bless me!"

"That's about how I felt." Gavin's voice was tainted with anger.

Peg looked at Gavin and squinted, as if she was seeing him for the first time all over again. "Then ye're . . . ye're . . . Bless me! He's an earl!"

"Not that I particularly want to be." Peg looked surprised. He quickly added, "But I am going to do something about all the rotten things going on in that place."

"That's th' spirit!" Peg pushed an enthusiastic fist through the air. "Bless me!" She turned to Anya. "He's an earl, an' all these years I thought he was just th' most handsome man in Scotland."

"He's that, too," Anya agreed.

"Oh, good heavens!" Gavin said with disgust.

"So yer goin' back then?" Peg asked, her eyes full of excitement. "Ooh! What I wouldna give tae see th' looks on those people's faces when . . . Ooh!" She laughed, and Gavin couldn't help smiling.

"I'm looking forward to that myself," he admitted.

"But we need your help," Anya said.

"It would be an honor." Peg raised her chin as if she'd just been knighted.

"We don't want to take Effie with us, for obvious reasons, and we wondered if you would look after her for a day or two."

"What? Me and Effie? Oh, won't we have a good time! Do ye hear that, Effie? Ye get tae stay with Auntie Peg."

"Peg is funny," Effie said, and continued to read.

"I'm certain she would do fine with you, as long as we prepare her for it, and I'll discuss with you anything that might happen."

"Ah," she pushed her hand through the air, "'twould be no trouble. Effie's a good girl. Just when do ye plan tae make this grand switch of the Earl?"

"I'm not going to switch. I like my life. He can have his. I just want to see justice done. That's it."

Peg gave him a dubious sidelong glance.

"We're planning tentatively on the end of next week," Anya provided.

"And do I get tae help ye dress . . . m' lady?" she added lavishly.

"Oh, you must."

"And you might as well go today and pick out something to wear, so it will be ready. Go with her, Peg. I'll take Effie to get some short-bread."

"Effie likes shortbread," she announced with enough enthusiasm to set her book aside.

A thought occurred to Peg. "Then Effie is yer sister?"

"That she is," Gavin admitted proudly.

"Effie Gavin's sister," Effie muttered.

"Well, bless me! If this isna cozy, an' all."

"Hurry along, ladies." He stood and took Effie's hand. "We've got too much to do to be sitting around gossiping."

"I'll get m' hat." Peg dashed into the bedroom.

"Are you all right?" Anya went on her tiptoes to whisper in Gavin's ear.

He nodded. "But I'll be glad when it's over."

She kissed him quickly. "We'll meet you back here."

Peg had Anya out the door in an instant, then Gavin put his arm around Effie and kissed her brow. "Let's get you some shortbread, little sister."

"Effie not little sister," she protested. "Effie born July, 1779. Gavin born May, 1782. Gavin little brother."

"You may be older, but I'm bigger. That makes you my little sister."

"Effie not little sister," she repeated.

"All right, all right," he chuckled. No matter how many times they discussed this, she couldn't grasp the concept. But to Gavin, she would always be his little sister.

The room was barely becoming light with dawn when Anya felt Gavin nudge her gently. "I'm going out for a while," he whispered.

"Where?" she asked, sitting up abruptly. His countenance made it evident that he was troubled.

Gavin sighed and sat on the edge of the bed, making it evident that the answer to her question was not simple. "I woke up a while ago with this overwhelming feeling that . . . well . . ." He sighed again. "I've been praying very hard, Anya . . . that we would be able to get through this safely, that we would have all the information we need to come through this successfully. And now I have this incredible feeling that we *don't* have all the information we need. And I just feel like I need to talk to Robbie."

"Robbie? Why?"

"To be honest, I don't know. But I have to believe there's a reason. He's been at Brierley a long time. Maybe he knows something that will give us some insight. Or maybe he just knows of someone who might. All I know is that I need to talk to him before I go any further."

Anya bit her lip, resisting the urge to protest this impulsive visit. She couldn't discredit his feelings, but neither could she help feeling apprehensive at the thought of him going back to Brierley. She reminded herself that they would both be going back very soon. But this felt different somehow.

"Be careful," she said, and he kissed her.

"I will," he said. "And I'll be back before you know it."

Anya snuggled back into bed and listened to his horse galloping away. She uttered a silent prayer on his behalf and told herself not to worry just before she drifted back to sleep. The next thing she knew, he was sitting again on the edge of the bed. She wondered if she had dreamt the previous episode, then she glanced at the clock and realized nearly three hours had passed. She was amazed at how tired pregnancy could make her. He took her hand and kissed it as she forced herself to her senses, anxious to know what had transpired.

"Well?" she demanded when he said nothing.

"Well," he repeated, "I can't say that I came away with some great wealth of information that will make a world of difference. But I do think I found out something that gives me a little insight."

"So, tell me!" she insisted.

"Did you know that Robbie worked at Brierley long before the Earl married Ishbelle?"

"No," she said.

"In fact, Robbie's own wife died the same year Ishbelle did."

"And I didn't even know he'd been married."

"He told me," Gavin continued, "that he didn't know much, but he'd heard rumors that when Margaret and Una had come to Brierley, before Ishbelle was due to have Effie, Margaret was basically penniless. It was something to do with an indiscretion that had earned her father's disdain, and he'd withdrawn her dowery. Her brief marriage to Malvina's father apparently left her no better off financially after his death. The interesting thing about that rumor, according to Robbie, is that he'd heard nothing about it until after the Earl's death. But he said that from the first day Una and Margaret arrived, it was evident that Una seemed to be holding some kind of threat over Margaret. He told me that Margaret's mother died when she was a young child, and Una has cared for her since her birth. I believe I already knew that. In his opinion, Lady Margaret has a good heart deep down inside. He believes the problem is more with Una than Margaret."

"That's good news, isn't it?"

"Yes, unless Una has finally managed to squelch what good there might have been. If Margaret was indeed penniless, and Una was dependent upon Margaret for her survival, being a personal servant, that puts some light on her desire to get hold of Brierley and maintain control of it. However sick Una's methods were, I suppose I can at least understand what she was after. Putting together what we know, it's not difficult to imagine how Margaret could feel controlled by Una. If Una is the only caretaker Margaret has ever known, it could be difficult for Margaret to see the world beyond Una. But it seems there's something more. I tend to agree with Robbie's theory that Una is holding some threat over Margaret."

"If the threat is still there, perhaps Margaret will continue to cling to Una, no matter how horrible we can prove her to be."

"Maybe," Gavin said. "Or maybe the habit of being controlled is just too strong to break, even if the threat no longer exists."

"Or maybe," Anya said with hope in her voice, "we'll be blessed with a miracle, and you will be the lifeline that can save Margaret from this horrible, evil woman who has done so much damage."

Gavin took Anya into his arms and sighed heavily. "That is my deepest hope, Anya. A part of me believes that's true, even from what little I know. But there's another part of me that doesn't dare believe it's possible. We just have to keep praying and hope for the best."

Anya agreed with him, trying hard to focus on the possibilities for a favorable outcome. But she wondered if it was possible to have enough faith to counteract such evil. Not always, perhaps. But maybe, just maybe, they would be blessed with a miracle.

Anya felt the excitement churning inside her as she cleaned up the kitchen after dinner, then she went into the parlor to talk to Effie.

"Are you nearly ready for bed, Effie?"

"Effie needs to read."

"Now tell Anya, where is Effie going after breakfast?"

"Effie going to Peg's house. Effie gets to stay with Peg. Peg is funny."

"And you do what Peg tells you. She'll take good care of you until Gavin and Anya come back. Can you remember that? Gavin and Anya are going to come back."

"Gavin and Anya come back. Effie stay at Peg's house."

"That's right." Anya felt certain Effie would feel no apprehension about these brief changes. "You read now, Effie, and I'll see you at breakfast."

"Effie read now. Time to read."

Anya turned to see Gavin in the doorway. She took his hand, and they went together into the bedroom.

"Do you think she'll be all right?" he asked.

"I'm not worried . . . not about Effie, at least."

"Well, I'm glad you're worried about something." He sat on the edge of the bed to pull off his boots. "Because I'm scared to death. If I could even begin to guess how they will react, I would feel a little better."

"We've planned it out as carefully as we can," Anya said. "We just have to take it one step at a time and hope for the best. That's all we can do."

"Thank you, Anya," he whispered close to her ear. "You've been so good through all of this. Your support makes all the difference."

"You have supported me through much," she replied humbly.

Gavin declared that he'd never be able to sleep, but his breathing fell into a peaceful rhythm long before Anya could even relax. "Good night, my lord," she whispered. Only a soft snore responded, and with it she finally drifted off.

Anya was startled awake by an insistent banging, and realized it was morning. She glanced at the clock and reached for her wrapper. "Good heavens, we've overslept!" She nudged Gavin and he groaned. "Did you hear me? We've overslept. Peg is here. Get up and get dressed."

He sat up in bed as she rushed to answer the door. The reality of this day struck him, and a knot twisted inside his stomach.

"What on earth are ye doin' in bed at this hour?" Peg insisted, hurrying past Anya into the kitchen.

"It's barely eight o'clock." Gavin appeared in the doorway, buttoning his shirt.

"There isna time tae waste," she insisted, and began bustling around as if she owned the place.

At half past nine, Peg stood back to admire them, dressed to perfection from head to toe. The forest green of Anya's gown coincided with the predominant color in the tartan, which was mingled with gold and red. Anya wore a MacBrier heirloom necklace and earrings that had come from Gavin's box. The brooch that held Gavin's plaid in place against his shoulder was of equal value.

"Bless me!" Peg said with approval. Gavin kissed Anya's hand, and then her lips. They exchanged an admiring glance, feeling well prepared for what lay ahead.

A hired carriage arrived from Strathnell only three minutes behind schedule. Effie was sent off with Peg in her gig, and moments later Gavin helped Anya into the carriage's plush interior. He sat across from her and the carriage and four rolled forward, sending an uneasy quiver lurching through them both. But an undeniable excitement tempered the anxiety enough to make it bearable, though silence hovered for most of the journey.

"Gavin," Anya said carefully when the Brierley farms began passing by the windows, "whatever happens this day, I want you to know that I love you. I always will."

"You make it sound as if I'm going to die or something," he chuckled, but Anya's uneasiness increased as he said it.

"You won't, will you?" she said too soberly.

"We may not be received with open arms, but I seriously doubt that our lives are in danger."

"I'm sure you're right," she agreed, but the thought was left hanging around her like a bad presage. How could she not think of Gavin's brush with death when he'd attempted much less than this?

In an effort to distract herself, Anya decided to bring up a thought that had been hovering in the back of her mind. "I remembered something . . . ," she said quietly, and Gavin turned from the window. "Something that never made sense to me, but perhaps now it does."

"I'm listening," he urged when she hesitated, a nostalgic look in her eyes.

"When the Earl showed me the mark on his shoulder, he said something, more to himself, about . . . well, he said he believed Brierley would fall in the coming years, for reasons he didn't understand." Gavin's eyes narrowed as he attempted to perceive her implication. "If he was referring to the birthmark, I believe it truly disturbed him that Cedric had not inherited it. James MacBrier was not a superstitious man, Gavin, but I wonder if he instinctively knew something was wrong."

"Perhaps he did," Gavin said quietly, moving his gaze back to the window.

Several minutes later he reached for Anya's hand, saying quietly, "We have escorted each other through much pain, my love. I am grateful to have you with me now."

Anya didn't respond for fear of betraying her emotion. If she started to cry now, she would never be able to hold up once they arrived.

The drive leading to Brierley House disappeared behind the thundering wheels of the carriage. It slowed to move beneath the huge entry gate, and Anya's heart beat in time with the horse's hooves as they echoed on the cobblestones and the carriage drew to a halt.

"Gavin, I'm frightened," she said, feeling the carriage rock as the driver jumped down.

"So am I." He tried to laugh, then he pointed a finger at her. "But you must remember, no matter what we are feeling, we will appear calm and in control."

"I remember," she nodded firmly, and the door came open.

"Here we go," Gavin said breathlessly. He kissed her quickly and resigned himself to face this and get it over with. "All right, God," he murmured aloud, "You know what we're up against. I'm leaving it in Your hands."

"Amen!" Anya added fervently.

Chapter Eighteen
The Ally

Gavin stepped down from the carriage and quickly glanced over the house from this point of view. Heavy grey clouds rolled overhead; he hoped they weren't a bad omen. He turned and offered his hand to Anya, and she stood beside him. A squeeze of her hand gave him added courage as the carriage rolled off toward the stable.

Gavin calmly presented his card to an unfamiliar maid at the door, and he merely smiled when she shot him a dubious glance.

"Please inform Lady MacBrier that I come with word concerning Miss Effie."

"Yes, my lord." She curtsied and scurried away while another maid showed them to the front drawing room and offered them refreshment.

Once they were alone, Anya quietly confessed, "My stomach is in knots, Gavin."

"So is mine," he admitted, "but they'll never know it."

"I'm glad you'll be doing all the talking, because my tongue will surely be frozen. At least I'm not nauseated anymore. Wouldn't that be lovely."

He smiled tensely and bent to kiss her. The kiss apparently had a relaxing effect, so he kissed her again. In the midst of it, the door flew open with a blustery, "What is the meaning of this?"

Outlined in the doorway was Margaret MacBrier, the ever-present Una at her side. Gavin smiled to himself. This was exactly what he'd hoped for. He felt an unsettling emotion to see Margaret now and realize she was his mother. But he pushed that thought away for the moment.

"If it isn't the legendary Lady MacBrier." Gavin picked up his glass of brandy and took a casual sip. "Do sit down."

"I repeat," Margaret said, moving into the room and closing the doors behind her, "what is the meaning of this? How dare you come here and present yourself as the Earl of Brierley?" Her eyes shifted to Anya, who stood a step behind and to the right of her husband, doing her best to look dignified and calm. Her gaze came to rest on the necklace Anya wore. Did Margaret recognize it as a Brierley heirloom?

"If you will calm down, my lady, I will explain myself. I came with the purpose of getting your attention. It would seem I have done that." He smiled placidly and set his snifter aside.

"Very well. You have my attention." She hesitated, and a glimmer of concern filled her eyes. "The maid told me you came with news of Effie. Do you know where she is?"

"Yes. She is being well cared for, but under the circumstances, I think it best she stay where she is." His eyes moved pointedly to Una as he added, "She is safer there."

"If you had no intention of bringing her back, then why are you here?"

"I told you," he said coolly, "I came to get your attention."

"By making false claims?"

"Claims, yes. False—no." Gavin sat down and stretched out his legs, crossing them at the ankles. Anya remained standing close by. "I might as well get to the point. I've never been one to beat around the bush." He paused for effect. "I thought you might be interested to know that I really am the Earl's son. I know," he proceeded before she could comment, "you always thought I was." His eyes fell again on Una. "But I didn't. You see, I had evidence—solid evidence—that the Earl and my mother were never intimate." He smiled carelessly at Lady Margaret. "Now that puts a whole new light on things, doesn't it?"

Gavin lifted a speculative finger. "I puzzled over this for quite some time, and I thought you might be interested in hearing my conclusions."

"Not particularly, but I have a feeling you'll tell me anyway."

"I thought I would. You see, my lady, I have reason to believe that I am the legitimate son of James MacBrier."

Anya watched Una closely and caught the first hint of uneasiness she had ever seen in the woman.

"How preposterous!" Margaret nearly shrieked. "I was married to the Earl when you were born. Now, that discredits your claim, does it not?"

"But you must take into consideration, as I said before, that my mother was never intimate with the Earl. In truth," his voice turned sad, "she was not my mother at all."

"You're making no sense!" Margaret was becoming obviously agitated. Anya noted Una fidgeting with her hands. Beyond that she appeared to be in control, but her eyes betrayed otherwise.

"On the contrary," he said, "I have proof that I am not only the Earl's son, but yours as well."

"You're mad!" she cried, but Gavin noted Una's confidence beginning to wane. He could nearly feel Una's mind struggling to come up with an appropriate rebuttal. He came abruptly to his feet and took Lady MacBrier by the shoulders, knowing he couldn't give her time to be affected by Una's efforts to undermine him.

"Look at me," he whispered gently enough that he caught her attention. "I could tell you to notice how I resemble the Earl, or I could show you the birthmark that brands me as his, but you would only call me illegitimate. The truth of the matter is that your husband was faithful to you, my lady. You've been lied to and used."

Margaret seemed mesmerized for the moment, so Gavin persisted. "Now, I'm asking you to trust your instincts, my lady. All I ask is that you pose a question to your nanny as to what she did to your son the night he was born."

Anya held her breath. She let it out in relief to see that Gavin's speech had been convincing enough for Lady MacBrier to turn her eyes on Una with a questioning gaze.

"Don't listen to him, my lady. He's talking nonsense." But Una's nervousness alone told Margaret that something in what Gavin was saying had merit. Never in all her years had Margaret seen Una with the slightest lack of confidence. She had always been like a stone.

"What did you do to my baby?" Margaret asked directly as bizarre memories of that night came haunting her again, just as they had all these years. Una took a step backwards. All of the little doubts

Margaret had brushed off concerning Una over the years suddenly rushed forward. She ached for something tangible to make Una less than perfect. She was tired of being manipulated into everything she did and then hating herself for it afterward. With fervency she repeated the question. "What did you do to my baby!?"

"I told you. He's talking nonsense."

"Am I?" Gavin broke back in. "Let me ask you this, my lady." Margaret's attention turned back to him. Gavin felt touched to see something hopeful in her eyes. "Surely you know the reliability of Effie's memory. What would you think if she said that . . . Nanny had switched the babies?"

"What?" Margaret caught her breath sharply. She turned sickly pale, and for a moment Gavin feared she might faint. But she held her stance and turned a hard glare on Una, who had taken on the expression of a cornered animal.

"Isn't it true," Gavin continued, "that Jinny Baird's son was born only hours after yours? The truth is that I was born first. Una saw the birthmark and assumed it was evil, as if that mark itself had caused Effie's condition. She gave Jinny Baird herbs to bring on labor early, and kept you drugged until it was done. In the middle of the night she switched the babies, then made you believe I was the Earl's illegitimate son to justify my resemblance to him."

Margaret listened in shock as Gavin told his story. She sat weakly, but her voice was commanding as she spoke to Una. "What have you got to say for yourself?"

Una drew back her shoulders and attempted to appear calm. "Who are you going to believe? After all I have been through with you, you would turn on me? He's got everything to gain by coming here with his tall tales. You must know he is lying. I've been with you since before you—"

"Yes, I know," Margaret said bitterly. "You've been with me since before I was born. You remind me daily, as if that made everything all right. I've seen your dishonesty, your thirst for power, the way you treat those beneath you. Do you think I've been blind to it all these years?"

"And if not for me, you would have lost Brierley." Una's eyes moved to Gavin. "You may yet." She turned back to Margaret, talking herself deeper into the pit she had been digging for years. "If not for me, you'd have been penniless on the streets, undone by your own indiscretions."

"And you'd have been penniless right along with me," Margaret said. "And that *is* where all this began, now isn't it? But more and more, I think I would have preferred being lowered to petty labor than to have lived beneath your intimidation all these years."

"That's easy for you to say, when you've never known poverty," Una snarled. "It is I who have kept you in power here. It was only your good sense in listening to me that got the Earl to marry you in the first place. Where would you be without me?"

"I loved my husband!" Margaret spat. "It was your manipulating that came between us, and now . . . now I come to find out that you . . ." Emotion made her voice tremble. She turned to Gavin as if for support. He attempted to give it with his eyes, and strength seemed to infuse her as she came to her feet and turned on Una like a lioness defending her cubs. "How dare you?" she hissed. "I remembered . . . I remembered my baby. He was strong and big, with dark hair . . . and the mark on his shoulder, so much like my husband's. And then you . . . ," she nearly choked on the words, "you gave me a tiny, blond child . . . weak and frail, and tried to tell me that I had dreamed it. To the devil with you!"

"I couldn't have said it better myself," Gavin muttered, feeling immense relief to see that Margaret—his mother—was on his side. Surely the worst was over.

"What proof do you have in any of this?" Una attempted to defend herself. "It's all a web of lies, likely spurred on by that little tramp who came here trying to take it all away!" She pointed an accusing finger at Anya, who eased closer to Gavin.

Anya wondered what she had ever done to make Una believe such a preposterous thing. Was that the reason she had been tormented all these years? Had her MacBrier blood been a threat?

"She wants proof," Margaret said to Gavin, as if it were nothing.

"And you?" Gavin asked. "Are you willing to accept this so easily, without proof?"

"I have learned to trust my instincts."

Gavin smiled. "I have no proof, except this." He unlaced his waistcoat and unbuttoned his shirt just far enough to pull them aside and reveal the birthmark. "Though I know beyond a shadow of a doubt that Jinny Baird and James MacBrier were never intimate." Margaret's eyes filled with emotion, Una's with horror. She must have been certain her secret was safely hidden long ago.

"I knew the moment I saw that mark," Una said from low in her throat, her malevolent eyes penetrating Gavin's, "that I could not let Brierley be ruled by someone cursed with evil. I had worked hard to see that Margaret had Brierley. I could not let her lose it because of the curse."

Una's confession left the room taut with silence. The reality of what Una had done to Gavin's life filled him with a burning fury. He stepped toward the old woman and looked down into her eyes. "What kind of human being would play with people's lives the way you do? Do you have any idea what kind of pain you have inflicted?" Gavin took hold of Anya's hands and held them close to Una's face. She looked down at the scars with no expression. "What kind of person would do this to a child?" He let Anya go and she stepped back, hating the memories stirred by his words. "If I had my wish, old woman, you would spend eternity suffering the torment you have spent your life inflicting on others." His voice lowered. "May you rot in hell."

Una apparently had nothing more to say in her own defense. The truth was known.

"I never want to see your face again," Margaret said to Una without looking at her, "and God willing, I will live long enough to undo all you have manipulated me into doing these many years." She pointed to the door. "Get out!"

Una did so immediately, but silence hung over the room long after her footsteps had died away down the hall. Margaret finally turned to look at Gavin. Her eyes softened and her hands trembled. Anya's emotion got the better of her as she observed this poignant reunion. She was deeply grateful to realize she had misjudged Margaret all these years, and even more grateful to have the truth in the open.

"Your name is Gavin," Margaret said, and her voice cracked. Gavin nodded. "Gavin MacBrier," she corrected with pride. Gavin swallowed hard at the sound of it. Anya squeezed his hand knowingly.

"My baby," was all Margaret could say before the emotion burst forth. Gavin opened his arms, and she hesitated only slightly before coming toward him. He took her hand, then wrapped his arm around her, urging her to his shoulder, where she cried like a child. Gavin met Anya's eyes as he held her, and an unspoken understanding passed between them.

When Margaret finally gained control, she pulled back, looking embarrassed as she dabbed her face with a handkerchief. Her attention turned to Anya. She smiled and touched Anya's face as if to pull away all of the hurt. "I pray you will forgive me, my dear." She took Anya's hand and looked contemplatively at the scars. "I had no idea."

"It's in the past," Anya assured her, and the three shared a tight embrace. Margaret took them each by the hand and led them to a sofa, where she sat between them.

"I know there is nothing I can say to undo the past," Margaret said, "but I need to tell you that I've learned more recently, through a great deal of prayer and soul-searching, that Una is not entirely to blame for what has taken place here. I allowed her to use and manipulate me. Of course, I always managed to rationalize her behavior away. But in my heart I think I knew she had an evil disposition; she was always so superstitious, giving credibility to ridiculous notions and wives' tales. I tried to just pass her ideas off as nonsense, but I spent most of my life feeling stifled and powerless. She took the place of my mother from as far back as I remember, but she was never warm and loving, only harsh and intimidating. And when I was sixteen or so, I got involved with . . ." Margaret hesitated as emotion caught her voice. "I fell in love with a young man that my father forbade me to see. When I was out late with him one evening, my father assumed the worst and withdrew my dowry and allowance. When this young man was sent away, thanks to my father's bribery, I was left alone. My hopes that he would come back and marry me were dashed when word came that he'd been killed. Beyond that, I had nothing to offer in marriage, and Una seemed certain that the only way to be sure we wouldn't be left in poverty was to manipulate our way into wealth. I didn't agree with it, but my heart was broken and nothing else seemed to matter. I married Malvina's father out of desperation. He was so much older than I was, and when he died, it quickly became evident that his claim of wealth had been false. Following Ishbelle's death, I grew to care very much for James, but Una was certain if he knew the truth about my past, he'd have nothing to do with me. It wasn't until after James was killed that I realized I'd never really done anything wrong, in spite of how my father had seen it. And I somehow know that James would have understood. But it was too late." She sniffled and dabbed at her eyes with a handkerchief. "And it seemed that by then I had little to care about, and therefore, little reason to stand up to her. I let myself go on, living in a kind of fog, allowing her to control everything around me. But still, I never dreamed that she could be capable of such evil. And I blame myself for allowing it to get so out of hand."

"Everything's all right now," Anya said in a comforting voice.

"Yes," Gavin took Margaret's hand again, "it's all in the past. We need to make a fresh start."

Margaret smiled sadly and nodded. Before letting Gavin's hand go, she noticed the ring there and smiled. "You'll be wanting what is rightfully yours."

"I have what is rightfully mine," Gavin said gently. "The Earl gave me more than sufficient for my needs before he died. I would like to follow his wish and open the safe. We will decide what to do with the contents between us—whatever they may be."

"But surely you intend to stay." Her brow furrowed.

"I don't want Brierley," he said.

"You what?" She chuckled as if she'd been insulted.

"Cedric has been raised to it," Gavin argued.

Margaret came abruptly to her feet. "Cedric has done nothing in his entire life to deserve Brierley. He would gamble it away if I let him. Please," she looked into his eyes, "you must consider what your father would have wanted for you. Don't make a decision so abruptly. All of this is happening so fast, but I . . ." She gave a soft laugh. "You can't imagine what a relief it is to know he is not my son. He has been a heartache to me since the day he was . . . born." Her eyes betrayed how bewildering all of this was.

"Please," she sat down again and took his hand, "you must not turn your back on me. Brierley is yours, and you must have it."

Gavin felt fear envelop him, while a sense of peace sprang to life somewhere inside. He looked to Anya. So much depended on her. Her feelings, her desires, were the most important thing.

While Margaret's plea hovered over them, Anya felt Gavin's questioning eyes on her. When all of this had come into the open, Anya had felt certain she could not come here as the Earl's wife and fill that position. All of the horrible things she had lived through beneath this roof came back to her, and for a moment she wanted to just run. But seeing Una defeated gave her hope that the evil could be expelled from Brierley. While the question in Gavin's eyes deepened, Anya realized she was confused. But she knew he would do nothing brash. She also knew that he was her husband, and she had vowed to support him, for richer or for poorer. With confidence she nodded firmly, giving her unspoken support in whatever he might endeavor.

Gavin's immediate reaction to Anya's firm response was a deepening fear. He marveled at her goodness, knowing the inner fears she had concerning the matter. But he could almost wish she had insisted that he not do it. He would then have been able to refuse to even attempt this, and the blame would not have been his. Still, he felt a measure of relief. And as he briefly contemplated this, the peace within him became more tangible.

He turned to Margaret and spoke firmly. "This is not an easy thing you're asking me to do. Twenty-seven years is a long time. I can't just march in here and take over Cedric's position."

"His position?" Margaret gave a sarcastic little laugh. "He uses the title to get what he wants. I'm the one who rules this place. But I'm not going to do it any more." She nodded. "You are."

Gavin met her eyes, wishing he knew what to say, how to handle this. He felt the thoughts between them mutually change as they each tried to grasp the reality.

"Oh," Margaret touched his face and mist filled her eyes, "you look so much like him." Her fingers moved to his hair. "So handsome—and those eyes." She touched the tartan over his shoulder, and he saw her emotion deepen.

For Gavin, it was difficult to displace Jinny Baird as his mother. She had raised him. She had given all she had for his benefit, and her sacrifices had not gone unnoticed. But there was something in

Margaret MacBrier's eyes that touched him deeply. She had given of herself to give him life. Surely that was a great thing.

"Oh, my." She laughed at herself and looked down, seeming embarrassed again. Anya found it endearing in a woman who had always shown such a cruel exterior. "I must not get so carried away. Surely we have important things to discuss. Perhaps the two of you would like to freshen up. You've traveled and must be hungry as well."

Margaret came to her feet and they followed. She made no effort to hide how her eyes went to Anya's swollen belly, as if she'd just now noticed it. "You're expecting?" she said with pleasure. She turned to Gavin. "Does this mean I'm going to . . ." She laughed giddily. "Of course it does! I'm going to be a grandmother."

Gavin put his arm around Anya and pulled her close, while Margaret moved toward the door, exclaiming, "This is all so wonderful, I can hardly believe it. It's just too good to be true."

"I couldn't have said it better myself," Anya said softly, and Gavin laughed.

"Jean," Margaret called, opening the drawing room door, "our guests will be dining with us. Inform Mrs. MacGregor. Oh, and when you get a moment . . ." She lowered her voice, but Anya could tell she was giving instructions concerning Una, something about providing transportation to Glasgow. Her voice became more audible as she completed her instructions to the maid, "Oh, and send Ellen to take our guests upstairs where they can freshen up. Did you get all that?"

"Aye, mum." The maid curtsied and scurried away.

"Come along," Margaret motioned to Gavin and Anya.

"Excuse me," Gavin said as they came into the hallway, "but I must ask. Where is Cedric now?"

"Lucky for us, he's gone away until tomorrow. If I can talk you into staying tonight, that will give us time to work out a few necessary details, and you can have some time to think this through."

"That is what I had hoped," Gavin admitted. He hadn't expected all of this to be so easy. Perhaps his prayers had been heard. Then he thought of facing Cedric, and hoped that God was still watching over them.

"Ah, here is Ellen," Margaret announced, then gave instructions. "Show them to the red room. They will be spending the night.

Inform their man to have their things sent up, and make arrangements for him as well." Ellen bobbed a curtsy while Anya caught the wonder in her eyes. Had gossip spread so quickly? Of course it had. Anya knew this household well. How strange it felt to be here like this! It was as if the world had turned upside down, and she and Gavin had ended up on top.

Ellen took them to an elaborate guest room with decor of deep red and an adjacent sitting room. "It's incredible," Gavin said, looking around in wonder.

"I used to clean in this room," Anya mused.

Gavin swept compassionate eyes over her. "I'm sorry. Are you all right?"

"Yes," she admitted. "I'm feeling quite good about it, actually."

Gavin sat on the edge of the bed and fell back onto it, resting his head in his hands. "I only hope that something can be worked out with Cedric." He leaned up on his elbows. "Nothing is worth having to live with him against us," he added gravely. "Nothing!"

Anya was relieved to hear him say it. She feared Cedric's return, and it eased her anxiety to know that Gavin was not determined to take Brierley at all costs. Such a thing would be so pointless, and she was grateful to know that Gavin shared her feelings.

They freshened up and hurried to the dining room, where Margaret was waiting for them. As soon as they were seated, she said to Anya, "You must tell me news of Effie."

Anya told Margaret all she knew of the reasons behind Effie's flight, and between her and Gavin they informed her of how well Effie had done in the time since.

"You can't imagine how relieved I am to know she's all right," Margaret confessed. "Robbie told me she was being cared for, but I've worried so."

"But Cedric must have known where she was," Anya stated. "He knows where Gavin and I live, and we assumed that we were an obvious possibility."

"Cedric claimed to know nothing," Margaret said with disgust, "but he never cared for Effie a whit. I shouldn't wonder that he lied to me. Of course, I never spent the time with Effie that I should have. I could blame that on Una," she said distastefully, "but there is no one to blame but myself. In truth, it has been Effie's absence that has made me stop and think about the circumstances here, and your coming was just what I needed to confirm my doubts." Gavin smiled at Margaret, then Anya. "I only wish Effie had come with you," she added.

"Under the circumstances," Anya explained, "we thought it best to leave her. We weren't certain what to expect."

"But you must send for her," Margaret insisted. Anya looked to Gavin in question.

"I don't see why we couldn't," he said. "Peg would be delighted to come, I think."

"Wonderful," Margaret said and nibbled on her haggis. "We'll send your driver for them as soon as we're finished here. Do you think they can come tomorrow morning? I was thinking it would be appropriate to have the family together to open the safe."

"Will Malvina be here?" Anya asked, and Margaret looked surprised.

"No, but . . . well, she is not a MacBrier then, is she."

"How is she doing?" Anya added to ease the seeming harshness of her last statement.

"Well enough, I suppose. I don't see her as often as I would like, but it would seem marriage is not what she expected it to be. And I shouldn't wonder. I told her it was better not to marry at all than to marry someone she hardly cared for. But that is no concern of ours, now is it."

"And Cedric?" Gavin asked. "Did you want him to be present?"

"Not if I can help it," she said, apparently disgusted by the thought. "He's not got a bit of MacBrier anything in him, after all."

"His mother was a wonderful person," Gavin felt compelled to say.

Margaret looked surprised, then a shadow fell over her face and she turned her eyes downward. "Did she raise you well, Gavin?" she asked without looking at him.

"Yes," he said proudly, "she did."

"Better than I could have, I daresay," she said matter-of-factly. "Mothering is not my best quality. That is evident in the results."

"One cannot make gold out of iron," Anya inserted gently.

Margaret lifted her eyes in wonder, then turned to Gavin. "And what do you suppose I would have made out of you?"

"Is a man what he is born to be, or what he is raised to be?" When there was no response, he added, "It poses some food for thought, if nothing else." He raised his glass to Margaret in a gesture of admiration. "You gave me life, and for that, there is no repaying." Anya saw a warm peace settle into Margaret's expression. Gavin drank and raised his glass to Anya. "And to my wife, who gave me life again."

He took a sip, then said to Margaret, "Did you know that Anya saved my life?" Margaret shook her head, showing curious eyes. "After I had been shot, she found me in the stable and . . ."

Gavin stopped when a blatant horror filled Margaret's expression. She stood abruptly and turned away, putting a hand over her mouth.

"What is it?" Gavin stood but remained where he was.

Margaret only shook her head. Anya knew well when a woman was fighting with emotion, and she went quickly to Margaret's side. She placed a soothing hand around her shoulders and saw the tears burning into her eyes.

"What is it?" Anya softly repeated Gavin's inquiry.

"I gave him life," she said at last, "and then I sent someone to destroy it." Anya threw a glance of understanding toward Gavin. He moved to come toward them, but she shook her head, indicating that he should stay put.

"It doesn't matter anymore, my lady," Anya said gently, though she was unable to deny that the irony caused her some consternation. She had seen what Gavin went through as a result of this.

"Oh, but it does. Una was so pleased when our man informed us that he was dead. But I felt sick inside. It ate at me for so long, and it was such a relief when Cedric told me that he had seen him alive." Margaret turned abruptly and blurted, "I'm so sorry, Gavin. If I had known . . ."

"It's all right." He enunciated carefully, "The wounds are healed."

Margaret nodded and gave a feeble smile. They returned to their meal while Gavin apologized. "I didn't mean anything by bringing it up. I was only going to tell you how Anya saved my life. And I might add that when I became conscious and found her with me, I realized that I was grateful I had been shot. Otherwise, I wonder if I would ever have found Anya . . . or ever learned the truth."

Gavin went on to tell the story of how they'd come to love each other, and Margaret's mood soon lightened. When the meal was nearly finished and there was a lull in the conversation, Gavin took the opportunity to make his desires known. "You should know, my lady," he began, "whether or not I choose to remain at Brierley, there are some things that I intend to deal with."

"Yes?" she smiled, apparently liking his authority.

"I will see that the tenants of Brierley are well cared for. I intend to supervise the repair of houses and grounds, and adjust rent and benefits to see that these people's needs are met. As long as I have MacBrier blood in me, I will not let such things go unkempt any further."

"You're a good man, Gavin." Margaret's voice filled with admiration.

Gavin ignored her compliment and persisted. "And I would like to know if anything has ever been done concerning my father's death." Margaret looked surprised. "Do you know who killed him?"

Margaret shook her head, betraying emotion in her expression. "There was the usual inquisition, but nothing was found. It could have been anyone."

"I intend to find out who killed him, and why," Gavin said with vehemence. "He was killed within hours after he discovered that I existed, and he was aware of my birthmark." Margaret's eyes widened. "I believe there is a connection."

"You don't think that Una . . ." Margaret couldn't bring herself to say it.

"I don't know, but I intend to find out."

"Perhaps we shouldn't send her away until we know."

"Either way, I will find out who killed my father. After all he gave to me, it is the least I can do."

"And what was that?" Margaret questioned.

"He gave me the home we live in," he said proudly, "and . . ." Gavin was going to tell her about the jewels, certain she had a right to know, but Ellen came into the dining room, looking upset.

"What is it, Ellen?" Margaret demanded.

"It's Miss Una, mum," she barely said before she visibly fell apart.

"What is it, Ellen?" Anya rushed to her side. "What has happened?"

"It's an awful sight," she managed to blurt out between sharp breaths. "Her room is . . ."

"Can you take me there?" Gavin asked when she trailed off.

"I canna go back up there," she insisted.

"I'll take you," Anya offered, and they left Ellen in Margaret's care.

"What on earth do you suppose she's done?" Anya lifted her skirts high and hurried up the stairs with Gavin close behind.

"I shudder to think."

Anya paused at the door to Una's room, feeling an unexplainable dread. The door was left slightly ajar, and Gavin stealthily pushed it open.

"You wait here," he insisted.

As soon as Anya couldn't see him any longer, she began to wonder if he was in danger. They had gotten very little information from Ellen. Anya's heart began to pound, telling her she should go in after him, but she'd barely taken a step toward the door when he came out and closed it tightly behind him.

"What?" she insisted.

Gavin sighed. "She cut her own throat."

"She's dead?" Anya couldn't believe it.

"Quite. I don't wonder that Ellen is upset. I daresay she'll have nightmares for weeks." He started back toward the stairs. "I may have them myself."

Margaret took the news with no response. She simply sent orders with a maid to inform the police, and to have someone called in to take care of the body and clean up the mess. Then she changed the subject. Anya suspected there was some kind of emotion she wasn't showing. Anya herself felt a sense of tragedy. She had hated Una as much as anyone, but had never thought her life would end this way. She wondered what Gavin felt. He of all people had good reason to hate her. In truth, Anya had to admit, it was difficult to feel sorrow.

"I was thinking," Margaret said, putting one hand over Gavin's arm and the other on Anya's, "there is something I want you to see." She ushered them through a series of hallways, up some stairs, and down another long hall. Anya knew where they were going before they arrived, and she watched Gavin closely as they entered the upstairs front hall, where the family gallery was located. He glanced around quickly and soon found the portrait of his father.

Anya hung back with Margaret as Gavin stepped forward reverently to get a better look. Anya sensed his emotion. She knew he was futilely longing to have known his father, and it was tragic that he never would.

"I knew him so briefly," Gavin said. "One day," he muttered in frustration. "I had known him one day when he was killed."

"You are so much like him," Margaret said from behind, and he turned in surprise. "Don't you think so, Anya?"

"Yes," she agreed warmly, "he is."

Gavin turned back to gaze at his father's image, wishing it was something more than a mixture of oils and canvas. He was grateful to know this was here. His meetings with the Earl had been so brief that at times he could hardly remember what he'd looked like.

Moving to his right, Gavin found a portrait of his mother, though she looked much younger. He turned toward her and smiled. "Very nice."

"I could look pretty enough in my younger days," she admitted.

"You still do," Gavin said while studying the portrait, "especially when you're not trying to look cruel."

"What are you implying?" Margaret asked uneasily.

Gavin turned and gave a slight bow. "I am implying nothing. I will come right out and tell you that you are more beautiful today than I have ever seen you . . ." Gavin felt the urge to say it, and figured it couldn't hurt. ". . . Mother."

Margaret's eyes brimmed with emotion. She glanced helplessly toward Anya, who smiled and took her hand. "Don't fret. He's always doing things like that."

"Like what?" Margaret asked.

"Saying and doing things that are so incredibly wonderful, you could think he's too good to be true." She lowered her voice to a whisper. "Though he does snore."

"That's because he's a MacBrier," Margaret assured Anya.

"The snoring . . . or the other?"

"Both," Margaret answered, and they laughed.

"What are the two of you talking about?" Gavin called from where he examined a portrait of the Earl's first wife, Ishbelle MacBrier.

"Mind your own business," Anya called back.

"This is Effie's mother," he stated. "I can see the resemblance."

"She was very beautiful," Margaret mused. "She was my cousin, you know."

"Yes, I had heard that."

"Gavin, I've been thinking," Margaret said, changing the subject. "If it's all right with you, I would like to summon my solicitor right away, and . . ." He turned and lifted a curious brow. "I think you should have your name changed, and . . . of course that would mean putting an affidavit to your marriage records as well, but . . . well, whatever you decide to do, you should bear your proper name."

"She's right, you know," Anya added quickly.

Gavin pondered it briefly. "Rather than change the name," he speculated, "do you think we could just add it?"

"I'm certain that would be appropriate." Margaret seemed pleased. "I have some things to attend to, so I'll leave the two of you alone. I'll see you at dinner."

"We'll be there," Anya replied, and Margaret left.

Gavin took one last gaze at his father's portrait, then quickly passed over the others. They were long dead and held little interest for him, other than the fact that they were his ancestors.

"Do you want to be Mrs. MacBrier?" he asked Anya.

"I want to be your wife. The name makes no difference to me, as long as it's your name."

Gavin pulled her into his arms and kissed her. "I've been wanting to do that all day. Do you know how beautiful you look?"

"Gavin," she giggled and eased away, "not now."

"I'll take that as a promise for later," he smirked.

"If you must."

Anya took Gavin on a tour through the main part of the house. They spoke very little as words seemed unable to express the emotions rendered through this day.

They found Robbie hard at work in the stable. He'd already heard the gossip, and could hardly stop talking about what an incredible thing it was. Gavin took it all in stride, but the ironies continued to fuel the unrest inside of him.

Returning to the house, they looked in on Mrs. MacGregor. They stood behind her for several moments while she remained unaware that anyone was there. Gavin broke the silence with a jovial, "So, what's for dinner?"

Mrs. MacGregor dropped her spoon into the pot and turned with a start. "Bless m' soul!" she gasped. "I was wonderin' if th' two o' ye would show up back here. Can ye imagine what I thought tae hear th' word that's goin' 'round here t'day. Is it true?"

"It's true," Anya beamed, putting her arm around Gavin's waist.

"I dinna believe it," Mrs. MacGregor laughed. "M' little Anya has gone an' married th' Earl without even knowin' it. An' look at ye." She pointed to Anya's belly. "Yer gonna have a wee bairn. Now, isna that th' nicest thing of all?"

"Aye," Gavin said, "it is."

"I've been showing Gavin the house," Anya informed her.

"An' do ye think ye might stay?" she asked him.

"I don't know yet," he replied. "It depends on . . . a lot of things."

"Well, do what ye must," she said, attempting to fish her spoon out of the pot of soup with a long-handled fork, "but we all are hopin' ye'll find a way tae do it."

"We?" he questioned.

"Th' servin' folks."

Anya saw something turn heavy in Gavin's eyes at the reality of all that weighed on his decision.

"We must be off," Anya said, "but we'll see you soon."

"Ye do that now." She waved as they left the room. It occurred to Anya that nothing had been said about Una's death. Did anyone care at all? Anya rubbed the scars in her hands and realized that she certainly didn't.

"You're worried," Anya said, noting Gavin's silence.

"I don't know if I can do it, Anya. There are so many people who would be affected by my decision. But I think Cedric would kill me before he would hand it over. And it's just not worth it."

"No," she agreed, "it's not."

Nothing more was said about it through the remainder of the afternoon. They changed into less formal clothes, then Anya took the opportunity to rest. Gavin lay on the bed beside her, lost in thought. Anya let him be, knowing he needed this time to himself.

They found Margaret especially happy through dinner. Anya watched her closely and found it hard to believe this was the same woman she had feared and hated all these years. But knowing Una, it was not difficult to imagine the manipulative tactics she had used to control Margaret so completely.

The jovial mood of the meal was doused when the dining room door flew open and Cedric MacBrier sauntered in. Margaret came to her feet, as if her newly found joy had just shattered over the floor like a piece of carelessly dropped porcelain. "What are you doing here?" she demanded. "You weren't due back until tomorrow."

He ignored her and turned hard eyes on Gavin, who remained seated. "Well, what have we here?" he smirked and leaned his hands onto the table. Anya felt bile rise in her throat from his mere presence. "A cute little maid told me that some cur was here, pretending to be me. And I come to find out he's brought a tramp with him." His eyes raked over Anya, and she had to fight to remain calm.

Gavin wanted to jump out of his chair and kill him with his bare hands, but he reminded himself to remain civil. He had a hunch Cedric was just trying to rile him, and he was determined not to give him the satisfaction—though it was difficult when Cedric came around the table and took hold of Anya's chin. "I've missed you," he said lasciviously. "My life was never quite the same without you in it."

"You're drunk!" Margaret insisted in the same moment that Anya slapped Cedric's face as hard as she could. Gavin was proud of her.

Anya's hand stung terribly, but the pain rushed to her arm as Cedric grabbed it and pulled her out of her chair.

"Enough of your chivalry," Gavin said with disgust as he came to his feet and returned the gesture on Cedric's arm.

Cedric's grip loosened immediately, and he turned his attention to Gavin. "And what gives you the guts to come here and announce yourself as the Earl of Brierley?"

"Something you don't have," Gavin said calmly, belying the emotions churning within.

"And what is that?"

"MacBrier blood."

Cedric laughed and turned to his mother as if to share the joke. Her cold, hard eyes were apparently a surprise to him. He stopped laughing but retained a smile, until she said with no regret, "It's true, Cedric. You and Gavin were switched as babies. He is the Earl's son . . . my son."

"Where on earth did you come up with a story like that?" he demanded of Gavin, as if it were comical.

"It's true, Cedric," Margaret stated, showing no emotion toward him whatsoever. "Nanny did it. She admitted to it. Gavin has his father's birthmark."

"Really?" Cedric quipped.

"Show him, Gavin," Margaret said with authority, "then tell him to mind his manners."

Gavin unfastened two buttons and pushed his shirt aside to reveal the mark.

"That might prove he is the Earl's son," Cedric said, his gaze fixed on the mark, envy evident in his eyes, "but it doesn't prove legitimacy."

"There is plenty else to prove his legitimacy," Margaret said, and Cedric turned visibly pale. But Gavin saw the rage in his eyes. He knew the worst was yet to come. He only prayed he would live through it.

Chapter Nineteen
The Earl of Brierley

"So," Cedric pulled out a chair and sat down hard, "you're just going to traipse in here and take it all."

Gavin returned to his seat. He could feel a scale tipping in his mind, trying to balance Cedric's capability for vengeance with all that Brierley had to offer. And as much as he hated Cedric, he had to wonder what it would feel like to be in his shoes right now. He looked to Margaret with apology in his eyes, then said with finality, "I don't want Brierley."

Cedric laughed cynically. "And you expect me to believe that?"

"*I* don't believe it!" Margaret came around the table in a flurry. Gavin remained seated. "I can't believe you would turn your back on all of this—on me."

"What Brierley has to offer does not outweigh what we would face if we stayed," Gavin said calmly.

"What about what you have to offer Brierley?" she retorted.

Gavin sighed. Why did she have to put it like that?

Cedric leaned back, directing his comment to Margaret. "He's certainly got you bewitched. I'm gone for one day, and come back to find you wrapped around this imbecile's finger. And what about Una? She's *dead!*" he shouted. "You drove her to suicide, and you don't even care!"

"You don't even know what you're talking about," Margaret shot back. "Gavin is the Earl of Brierley. It was Una who wrongfully kept him from his birthright. She was deceitful and wicked. Una took her own life, and that has nothing to do with me. If you had any sense, lad, you'd get out while the getting is good. You'll be provided for well enough. There's no need to be concerned about that."

"Oh, I see," Cedric's voice turned sarcastic, "Gavin was denied his birthright, but I come home to find out that I don't have one. But that's all right. Kick Cedric out on the street. Forget about what he was raised to."

"You haven't lived to be what you were raised to for a moment," Margaret hissed. "You lie and cheat your way around this place, using and abusing anyone who crosses your path. You neglect your duties and play your life away. How dare you speak of what you were raised to!"

"He's right," Gavin said. "I have no right to come here and take away what he has had for twenty-seven years. I will see to my business, then Anya and I will return home."

"Oh, now that's fair." Cedric came to his feet and put his hands to his hips. "You play the martyr and turn and walk away. Do you think maybe I'll get comfortable and figure you've given all of this up? Do you really think I would believe you are so noble?"

"You're judging him by your standards," Anya interjected. "He is more noble than you could ever dream of being."

Cedric laughed again. "Still spunky, eh, Anya? Tell you what, Gavin—you take Brierley, and I'll take Anya." His eyes fell on her like a vulture. "I've never known a woman quite like her."

Anya felt tangibly ill at his implication. She was relieved to feel Gavin's hand come over her shoulder as he stood behind her. "Personally, I would prefer it the other way around," Gavin said coolly.

"You're bluffing!" Cedric pointed an accusing finger at Gavin, his eyes full of bitterness. "You will never make me believe that you intend to walk away from here empty-handed. No man could be such a fool."

"Go up to your room and cool off," Margaret ordered.

"Apparently," he turned bitter eyes on her, "you are not my mother, so don't act like it." He moved toward the door. "At least something good has come of this day. It's a relief to know you and I don't share the same blood."

"That feeling is mutual," Margaret retorted.

With his hand on the door, Cedric turned to stare long and hard at Gavin. "This is not over yet . . . my lord." He spoke the title with hatred and sarcasm.

The door came open and Jean appeared, gasping to find Cedric so close. She backed away and turned her attention to Margaret, bobbing a quick curtsy.

"What is it, Jean?"

"Miss Effie and her nurse have arrived."

"Her nurse?" Gavin chuckled quietly, trying to imagine Peg with such a label.

"Wonderful," Margaret said. "Bring them in here. Perhaps they've not eaten."

"Aye, mum." Jean curtsied again and moved quickly past Cedric. He glanced dubiously toward Gavin and gave a noise of disgust, then left the room.

Once free of his presence, Margaret fell weakly into a chair. "Will he never cease to torment me?" she said sadly. "If Una weren't dead, I would kill her myself for sentencing me to a life with him." She added with conviction, "If you're leaving here, I'm coming with you."

Anya touched Gavin's hand against her shoulder. "That could be arranged," he said warmly. "But in the meantime, I think we should open that safe and get out of here. Until Cedric's pride heals somewhat, I wouldn't put it past him to sentence me to my father's fate."

"You don't really think he would be so low as to . . ." Margaret couldn't bring herself to voice her fears.

"Yes, I do," Gavin said firmly.

The door came open and Peg entered timidly, dressed in grey with a mantle around her shoulders. Effie came close behind. Anya reached out her hand to greet Peg, wanting her to feel at ease. "We didn't expect you so soon."

"But we're glad you're here," Gavin added, wanting to be done with all of this and leave as soon as possible. In a word, he felt vulnerable. Here at Brierley, he and the people he loved were too easily affected by Cedric's lack of scruples.

"I didna see a reason tae wait," Peg explained.

"Effie, my dear." Margaret moved toward her, but she backed behind Peg with a fearful whimper. Margaret stopped, uncertain and concerned.

"Ye must forgive her." Peg put a reassuring arm around Effie and attempted to soothe her. "She didna want tae come."

"Her more recent experiences at Brierley were not pleasant," Anya explained. "I'm certain it will take time."

"I understand," Margaret said, unable to hide her dismay.

"Effie," Anya said gently, taking her hand, "it's Anya."

"Anya likes to play games," Effie said quietly.

"That's right. We are at Brierley." Effie winced slightly. "Gavin is here too, and everything is all right."

"Gavin likes picnics," Effie said. Margaret smiled at her son.

"Mama is here too," Anya said. "Mama missed you."

"Nanny say . . . Mama not like Effie."

Anya and Margaret shared a glance of dismay. "Nanny lied to you, Effie." Anya persisted. "Do you understand? Nanny lied to you. Anya and Gavin want you to know that Mama likes you very much. She missed you."

"Mama likes Effie," she said meekly, but added with more zeal, "Brierley bad place."

"Gavin will watch out for you while we are at Brierley."

"Nanny hurt Effie."

Anya looked to Gavin for support. He came close to Effie and put his arm around her. "Nanny is gone now, Effie," he explained. "She will never hurt Effie again. Gavin won't let anyone hurt Effie, not ever."

Effie clung to Gavin's sturdy frame, seeming to find the comfort she needed. With Effie soothed, he said to Peg, "Do you know you were announced as Effie's nurse?"

"Really?" she grinned. "That isna s' bad, is it?" she said proudly.

Anya realized introductions were in order. "Peg, this is Gavin's mother, Lady Margaret MacBrier."

Margaret beamed at the introduction, while Peg curtsied ridiculously deep. "It's a pleasure, m'lady. Perhaps it isna proper tae say, but yer son is one o' th' finest men I have ever known."

"I see nothing improper in that," Margaret replied.

"Lady Margaret," Anya continued, "this is Peg MacTodd. A very dear friend of ours."

"I'm so glad you could come," Margaret said warmly, but Anya sensed Peg's uneasiness as she seemed to comprehend the gap between her world and Lady MacBrier's.

"Are you hungry?" Margaret asked, and the tension eased somewhat.

"No, thank ye, m'lady. I packed a hamper an' we ate on th' way."

"Perhaps now would be a good time to open that safe," Gavin suggested.

"I suppose you're right," Margaret sighed, as if she'd like to put it off indefinitely.

"Where is it?" Gavin asked.

"Come along," Margaret said, leading the way into the hall. Effie clung to Gavin, and Peg stayed close to Anya.

"'Twould seem everythin' is goin' all right," Peg whispered.

"For the most part," Anya replied, hoping Cedric would stay away to lick his wounds until they left.

"I canna wait tae tell ye," Peg added quietly, though there was no concealing the excitement in her voice. "Mr. Morgan came tae see me this mornin'."

Anya paused and let the others move on ahead. "That's wonderful, Peg. Tell me."

"He wants tae start seein' me again; says he couldna stop thinkin' about me. He said I might just make a fine wife after all."

"Oh, Peg." Anya embraced her, wishing she could explain the joy she felt on Peg's behalf. Anya understood well what it was like to feel an ugly past fall away through the love and acceptance of a good man. "I'm so happy for you."

Peg beamed and dabbed tears from the corners of her eyes. "We'd best be movin' along, but I had tae tell ye."

They quickly caught up to the others, since Gavin had held back, waiting for them. Margaret led them to the library, where she took up a lamp and opened a door into a musty-smelling chamber. The light revealed a long-unused office, overrun with dust and cobwebs. Gavin felt a strange shiver go through him.

"It was your father's office," Margaret explained. "Cedric wanted to take it over, but I wouldn't let him."

She set the lamp aside, then moved to a painting that hung behind the desk and carefully took it down. Gavin's heart pounded. Anya squeezed his hand knowingly. The safe was smaller than he had expected, but childish fantasies were often blown out of proportion.

Margaret motioned toward it with a gesture of resignation. Gavin carefully took Effie's arm from around him and eased her to Anya's side, where she seemed content enough. He stepped around the desk and eased the ring from his finger. It wasn't difficult to see where it fit. He took a deep breath and set the configuration of stones into the lock. They matched perfectly. He turned the ring easily and something clicked within, but it took effort to push down on the handle while holding the ring in place.

Silence hung tensely over the room as the safe door creaked open. Gavin could see little more than shadows, and he motioned to Peg, who was closest to the lamp. She handed it to him and stepped back. He didn't know what he'd expected to see, but he was surprised to find a jeweled dagger, standing by its point, pierced through a piece of folded parchment. The only other contents of the safe were a few pages torn from a book, folded together and leaning against the side. Gavin took out the papers and turned to set down the lamp.

"What is it?" Anya asked.

"I don't know, but we're going to find out." He unfolded the pages and turned them over in his hands. "It appears to be a journal entry. It's dated the night he was killed."

"Of course." Anya recalled the pages torn from the Earl's journal.

"Please read it," Margaret said.

Gavin glanced over it, then handed it to Anya. "I'll let you read it."

Anya hesitated, but Gavin was insistent. Her hand trembled as she reached out to take it, fearing the secrets the Earl's last words might hold. She cleared her throat and began.

> *"18 August 1798. It's a hard thing to face when a man finds evidence that he has been wronged in a way that pierces the very soul. This day I have discovered that a friend, dear to me, that I had believed was gone from here sixteen years ago, has been hidden from my knowledge, beneath my own roof. She has a son, fine and strong, that she has asked I make a provision for. As of this moment, I have emptied the Brierley safe and go now to give him its contents. There is no one else beneath this roof who deserves it. Not even my own son."*

Anya looked up at Gavin to explain, "There is a break here, and then it continues.

> *"Later: The distress I felt earlier has turned to anguish. The lad to whom I gave all my treasures is my own son. Of this I am certain. If this is the case, then Jinny Baird is not his mother. Of this I am also certain. In spite of certain struggles in my life, my faithfulness to Margaret has not waned. There is only one possible explanation, and it makes me sick to see now that I have been living victim to a lie. I first wanted to blame Margaret, but I know, despite the appearances she puts forth, that her heart is soft. She would not freely let her baby go."*

Anya lifted empathetic eyes to Margaret, who was crying silent tears. Anya continued.

> *"No, the fault lies elsewhere, and I intend, this night, to see that the truth be known. Before morning, Una will know that justice is about to be done.*
> *"As a precaution, I intend to seal these words away, along with the attached document. If Gavin heeds my words, he will find the means to read what I have written, and God willing, he will achieve his birthright. I will see to it, if it's the last thing I . . . live to do."*

Anya turned to the last page, and her eyes widened.

"What is it?" Gavin questioned.

"It's a will. It says simply: *'Being of sound mind, I leave all that is mine to Gavin Baird MacBrier, to do with as he sees fit.'* It is signed and dated."

Gavin took the document gingerly. He wondered how he might have felt to read this before he'd discovered the truth on his own.

"Una killed him," Margaret cried softly. "I heard him in her room in the middle of the night. They were arguing, but I couldn't understand what they said. He was dead before morning, but I dismissed the possibility that Una would have done it. At the time, I just couldn't believe she was capable of such a thing. She was so sensitive to my grief . . . I can't believe how she . . . how she deceived me." Margaret made a futile effort to gain control of her emotions.

Anya touched Gavin's face, as he seemed lost in the Earl's final written words. "Now you know," she said gently.

"Yes," he said. "Now, I know."

"Know what?" Cedric demanded. They turned to see him leaning casually in the doorframe, his hands deep in the pockets of his breeches. Effie winced at the sound of his voice and eased toward the wall. Anya held her close, attempting to offer comfort. Peg opted to remain near Anya as well. No one answered, and Cedric added to Margaret, "What are all the tears for, my lady? You were as glad to be rid of him as I was."

"That's not true!" she insisted.

"My, but you've changed your tune these days," Cedric said with a sardonic tone.

"Yes, I have," Margaret retorted proudly. "I only wish I'd had the sense to do it sooner."

"So," Cedric turned to Gavin, "will you take the money and run?"

"The safe is empty. I've had the Brierley treasure for more than a decade. You can have Brierley, but you won't get that."

"I've told you," Cedric smirked, "I think I'll take Anya."

"I'd rather die," Anya snapped.

Cedric sauntered into the room and stood before Peg, "But then, what have we here?" He touched her chin. She jerked away, but kept her eyes fixed on him.

"Keep yer hands tae yersel', lad!"

Cedric laughed, but put his hand behind his back, while the other remained in his pocket. "I would venture to guess who this is." He said to Gavin, "You know, a man can learn a lot in a pub, and you can imagine how much I learned about you when I stopped to buy a drink in a quaint little place called Strathnell." He turned to eye Peg shamelessly. "I would bet this is the wench you kept on when the tramp you married ended up pregnant with my baby."

That did it! Gavin's fist connected with Cedric's jaw. Cedric reeled backward, but Gavin quickly had him back on his feet, holding him against the wall by his shirt collar. "This is between you and me,"

Gavin breathed hotly. "If you ever—*ever*," he slammed him against the wall, "say a disrespectful word to any one of these ladies again, I will tear you into little pieces."

Cedric laughed. "Will you now?" From nowhere, Cedric's hand came between them with a knife that he placed strategically against Gavin's throat. Anya cried out and pressed Effie's face against her shoulder to keep her from seeing. Gavin lifted his arms and stepped back.

"Don't do it, Cedric," Anya implored, "I beg you."

"You just do that," Cedric said without looking at her. "I've seen you beg before, and it was unforgettable."

Gavin's fists clenched unwillingly, but he was in no position to get heated. "Don't be a fool, Cedric," he said, trying to sound calm. "If you kill me, they'll hang you for murder, and neither of us will get Brierley."

"Better that than to stand by and see you with it."

"I told you, I don't want it."

"And you lie like every other MacBrier."

"Get out of here and take your childish threats with you," Margaret insisted. "I'll see that you're provided for, but I won't have you causing any more trouble." Cedric ignored her. With purpose he eased the knife closer. Gavin groaned, and a trace of blood trickled over his throat.

"Please, Cedric," Anya implored. She felt so helpless, so afraid.

"Wait your turn, love," he smirked. "Once I'm done with this, you'll get yours."

"So noble," Gavin stated, fighting the bile rising in his throat.

Cedric gave a gloating laugh and turned his eyes on Anya. Peg took advantage of the opportunity, lunging forward and snapping her hand against Cedric's wrist. The knife fell to the floor. Peg had told Gavin she'd learned to keep a man from having what he wanted without her permission, but he'd never seen evidence of her abilities until this moment. And now he blessed them.

Cedric threw a furious fist toward Peg, but Gavin blocked it and sent a blow into Cedric's belly. While Cedric was doubled over, Gavin kicked him back against the floor, where he moaned helplessly.

"I've changed my mind," Gavin said with fervor. "Brierley is mine, and I'm going to take it. I will not subject these people to your whims any further. You can just *rot!*"

A unified sigh of relief fell over the room. Anya continued to hold Effie, trying to soothe away her fearful whimpering. Gavin touched his neck where it bled, relieved to find it was only a nick. Assured that Cedric was temporarily out of commission, he turned back to the safe to see what was on the parchment tacked beneath the dagger. As soon as his back was turned, Cedric abandoned his bluff and bolted to his feet, knife in hand.

"Gavin!" Anya cried as Cedric lunged for Gavin's back. Gavin lurched forward as the knife came at him, slicing the muscle at the back of his shoulder. Peg and Anya held to each other with Effie between them, while Margaret looked on, sharing their horror.

Gavin turned to strike Cedric, but the knife came toward Gavin's face. He dodged to miss it, but it glanced off his cheek, drawing blood again. The wound only gave Gavin more determination. He would not die now and leave the people he cared for at Cedric's mercy. He hit Cedric's face, temporarily knocking him off balance, but the pain in Gavin's shoulder left him briefly lightheaded.

Cedric poised himself, ready to lunge forward, a determination to kill etched in his expression. Anya held her breath, her heart pounding violently. Gavin remained motionless, his eyes alert and hard.

"You should have killed me when you had the chance," Cedric laughed. "You told me once that if the chance ever came again, you would. But I don't think you've got the guts to kill me."

"If you've got the guts to kill me," Gavin challenged, a glint showing in his eyes, "then let's see you do it."

Cedric took the challenge and lunged forward. Gavin jumped strategically aside. All eyes went to Cedric as he turned back, ready to try again. He lunged toward Gavin. Anya cried out as Gavin made no effort to move. Gavin went to his knees, and for a moment Anya knew he was dead. Peg hid her eyes. Anya held her breath while her heart threatened to stop. Then she realized it was Cedric's weight that had pushed Gavin down. Gavin pulled his arm back, and she saw the bloodied dagger in his hand. He shoved Cedric away from him and watched as he rolled back onto the floor. Peg hurried Effie into the library before she realized what had happened. Cedric looked up at Gavin as he came to his feet.

"I didn't think you'd do it," Cedric rasped, holding his hands over the wound in his chest while blood gushed through his fingers.

"Looks like I fooled you," Gavin said bitterly. He threw the dagger to the floor and wiped his blood-covered hand distastefully on his breeches. A loud breath escaped Cedric's mouth, then his eyes rolled back and his breathing stopped.

Anya gazed at the body in disbelief. A sick sense of irony engulfed her as she realized it could have been Gavin. Gavin! She met his eyes and saw the unrest. He had just killed a man, and despite the circumstances, Anya could see it was not settling easily with him. She read a formless plea in his expression. With arms outstretched, she rushed toward him.

Gavin held Anya desperately. The relief and freedom began to sink in, helping to ease the anguish. Anya pulled back and touched his face where it bled. "You're hurt. And your back. We must see to it."

"At least I'm alive," he said. "Oh!" He pulled Anya close and looked up. "Thank you, God. It's so nice to be alive!"

"Where did you get the dagger?" Margaret moved closer but avoided even glancing at Cedric's body.

"It was in the safe." He reached inside and pulled out the parchment. "Stuck through this."

"What does it say?" Anya asked as he opened it, and his eyes turned sad.

"'Peace within the walls of Brierley,'" he read, his voice quavering with emotion. "'That is the treasure I implore you to seek.'"

Gavin gave an ironic chuckle and threw the parchment to the floor. It lay discarded at Cedric's feet. He glanced once more at the body, praying that Jinny Baird would forgive him for killing the son she'd given birth to. He stepped carefully around the body and put his arms around his mother, kissing her brow.

"Please tell me you're staying," she said.

Gavin held an arm out for Anya, and she came beside him. He looked into her eyes and she read the silent question. "I'm staying with you, wherever that may be," she said quietly.

"Yes, Mother," he smiled and embraced them both, "we're staying."

Just before dawn, a piercing wail broke the silence of Brierley House. Gavin ran from his room and down the hall as if fire were at his heels.

"Mother!" he called. "Mother!"

"What is it?" She met him just outside her bedroom door, pulling a dressing gown around her and knotting it securely.

"Oh, Mother," he laughed, "it's a boy!"

"That's wonderful!" She threw her arms around him, and he lifted her off the floor with a forceful embrace. "Is everything all right?" she asked.

He set her down. "The doctor says everything is perfect. Come along. You must have a look at him. He's the cutest little thing you've ever seen in your life."

Gavin took her hand and sailed down the hall like a child, nearly dragging her along. He paused at the master bedroom, made a visible effort to calm himself, then pushed open the door.

A maid busily finished getting the room in order, paying no mind to their entrance. Gavin moved timidly to the bed, where he knelt and took Anya's hand. Her eyes came open and she gave him a weak smile.

"Mother's here," he said. "How are you feeling?"

"Tired . . . and sore," she admitted.

"It will pass," Margaret said gently from behind Gavin's shoulder. Anya turned to accept the warmth of her expression.

"Have you seen him yet?" Anya asked. Margaret shook her head. Anya turned to look the other direction, where a tightly wrapped bundle lay close to her side. "I can't reach him, Gavin," she said weakly. "Will you get him?"

With little hesitation, Gavin picked the baby up. The infant appeared all the tinier in his father's big hands. Anya looked on with pride as Gavin turned the baby over to his mother. Margaret pulled the blanket back to reveal a head of dark curls and a face that stirred her to tears.

"You lied to me, Gavin," she said in a cooing tone, as if she were speaking more to the baby.

"How is that?"

"You said he was the cutest thing I had ever seen in my life. That's not true. My baby was at least this cute." She looked up at Gavin. "I saw you so briefly, but I remember it well." She looked back to the baby, urging her finger into his little fist. "How does a mother forget such a moment? He's beautiful, Anya." Margaret laid the baby in the crook of her arm. "You should be proud."

"I am." Anya met Gavin's eyes, feeling such joy to see the way he beamed. She motioned for Margaret to come closer, untying the top of the baby's gown to bare his right shoulder.

"He has his father's mark," Margaret smiled.

"He's a MacBrier," Gavin added.

They left Anya to rest through the day, while Gavin spread the news personally through the tenant farms, attempting to beat the speed of gossip. Anya finally felt rested enough in the evening to eat a big dinner, while Gavin sat near the bed, holding his son. When she was finished, Gavin put the sleeping infant into his bassinet and took her tray to set it aside. He sat carefully on the edge of the bed and brushed a stray lock of hair from Anya's brow as she leaned back against the headboard.

"My father would have been proud," Gavin said.

"No doubt," she smiled.

"Peg says that Effie will hardly stop talking about the baby. She's calling herself Aunt Effie."

Anya laughed softly. Since Peg and Mr. Morgan had married, they'd both found comfortable positions at Brierley. Peg looked after Effie and helped Anya here and there. And Mr. Morgan was turning out to be a fine overseer, working closely with Gavin on caring for this vast estate.

"The farmers brought gifts," he said. "Can you believe it? They say it's a day of celebration. The Earl has an heir."

"They like you," Anya said. "I tend to agree with them."

Gavin bent forward to kiss her. "I love you, Anya."

"And I love you . . . my lord."

He kissed her again, and she laughed.

ABOUT THE AUTHOR

Anita Stansfield has been writing for more than twenty years, and her best-selling novels have captivated and moved hundreds of thousands of readers with their deeply romantic stories and focus on important contemporary issues. Her interest in creating romantic fiction began in high school, and her work has appeared in national publications. *Towers of Brierley* is her fifteenth novel and third historical work to be published by Covenant.

Anita lives with her husband, Vince, and their five children and two cats in Alpine, Utah.